THE MAN
NEXT
DOOR

E.M. SCOTT

THE MAN NEXT DOOR

NO EXIT PRESS

First published in the UK in 2025 by No Exit Press,
an imprint of Bedford Square Publishers Ltd,
London, UK

noexit.co.uk
@noexitpress

ISBN
978-1-83501-033-4 (Paperback)
978-1-83501-032-7 (eBook)

2 4 6 8 10 9 7 5 3 1

Typeset in 11 on 14pt Minion Pro
by Avocet Typeset, Bideford, Devon, EX39 2BP
Printed and bound in Great Britain by
CPI Group (UK) Ltd, Croydon CR0 4YY

The manufacturer's authorised representative in the EU for
product safety is Easy Access System Europe, Mustamäe tee 50,
10621 Tallinn, Estonia
gpsr.requests@easproject.com

1

After twelve months, the site of the injury still felt strange.

His skull had been opened, the blood drained, the laceration healed.

Nevertheless, someone was trapped in there.

Kill me.

'God Almighty,' Thomas muttered. He was sick of the sound. He got up at first light and went to the window.

He'd arrived at the cottage in Cornwall ten days ago at midday. It was a couple of hundred years old, built in the lee of the hill and with nothing to show in the garden but a scrap of grass and a stunted tree shaped into an arc by the wind from the sea.

Two reasons had made him take a six-month lease. To paint. And to rid himself of memories. He could do the first. The second he wasn't so sure about. Yesterday, he had put his hand on the wall to steady himself, his head aching. Ghosts: the pruned roses on the outside wall of his own home, the dripping trees of the drive. The same day a stranger had died and he'd been cursed for it.

'Stop,' he muttered. 'Stop.'

Late on the day of his arrival, he'd taken a walk to the village shop, along the lane and up the narrow winding street.

The woman there had smiled at him. 'Are you the new gentleman in Sawyers Lane?' she asked. 'At the old coastguards' cottages?'

'Yes,' he'd told her. He didn't mind her interest, and didn't see it as intrusion. He hadn't come here to be isolated, but to shake off the awful memory of home.

'You look a bit familiar,' she'd commented, filling his carrier bag.

'I used to come here for years with my wife,' he said.

'Not now?'

'No, not anymore.'

She said nothing, just nodded.

He was glad that he'd made the decision to come back. The idea had come on him suddenly one day as he stared out of his own window to the burned ruins of the studio in the garden. He knew then that he couldn't stand another day of it. Sometimes he thought that he could still smell the reek of petrol. He'd looked online that same morning and seen that the Cornish cottage was a long-lease rent, and it was empty. It was a kind of sign.

There was only one thing that bothered him about coming here, and that was his neighbour.

There was something wrong with Aiden Ruskin.

Watching Ruskin now go through the field gate onto the coast path in the first hazy light of day, Thomas opened his window. He could hear the distant booming of high tide. He watched the younger man, hands in pockets and head down, moving quickly down the field towards the ocean. Every morning, exactly at six, Ruskin took a walk. Not a minute later. Not a minute sooner. He'd go along the lane and down into the field that led to the beach.

Ruskin had kept his door closed and didn't answer when Thomas knocked to introduce himself. More often than not, his curtains were closed. He lived alone but most days Thomas would hear him talking – a muted, incessant drone. There would be the sound of furniture being moved, dragged. Once or twice, breaking glass.

He wondered what possessed Ruskin.

Perhaps it was a nightmare like his own.

He had walked along the short lane at his home to tell his neighbour Christine of his Cornwall move.

'Oh,' she had said, and she did a funny little dance, one foot to the other as if she didn't know whether to hug him or not. She was elderly – hard to tell how old. Maybe seventy-five. Maybe more. They'd known each other a long time, and last year she'd been a godsend to him. She stumbled a little now, and righted herself. 'I shall miss you.'

'I'll be back in late October.'

'You will?' she said. 'You promise?'

He had smiled. 'I promise.'

'Oh,' she repeated, and he'd seen her eyes fill with tears.

'Christine…'

She'd scraped her grey hair back from her face and wiped her face. 'Don't mind me,' she'd said. 'I'm used to seeing you, that's all. Doesn't matter. You should go. You need the break.'

'I'm not going forever.'

'No.' She'd turned her back on him and filled the kettle, and made a fuss of taking cups and saucers from the cupboard, wiping the cups with a tea towel absent-mindedly. 'Will you rent out yours?' she asked, still with her back to him.

'No.'

'Oh good,' she'd whispered. 'I wouldn't want to see anyone else there.'

He thought of her now, going out to feed her chickens at first light, and letting them out from the run. Once or twice that autumn she had forgotten and he'd had to go round and do it for her, and each time she'd come out of the house flustered, apologetic. 'You're too good to me, Thomas.' In a voice that had begun to have a slight tremor to it. He blamed himself and all the pressure he had put her through. On the day he left she hadn't come out to wave goodbye. He knew she must be in the house –

her car was in the drive – but she didn't answer the door when he knocked.

As he'd driven out through Dorset and westwards towards Cornwall, he had felt the weight lifting off him. The hill at Honiton, the route through Exeter and the eventual sight of the moors at Bodmin: with every mile he felt a little better. At the top of his own road, he had glanced in the mirror and seen the thatched roof over the low hedges, and he'd wondered if he would ever go back, and immediately felt guilty that he had lied to Christine. All last year clung to that house. All the pain.

He shook his head now. He hadn't wanted to bring that with him. He'd driven a hundred miles to get away from it. He leaned on the windowsill and gazed out at the fields. Behind him, the clock struck half six. The house felt icy, he thought. He would have to light the fire this morning and get the deep cold of the past winter out of its bones.

'These old places,' the agent had said, smiling with a shrug. 'Cosy once you get the fires lit, you know? You'll be all right with that?'

'I'll be all right,' he'd replied.

'You've seen one of these, I suppose?' They had been standing in the kitchen and the man had tapped an ancient Ascot heater over the sink. 'Hot water.'

Thirty years ago, there'd been one in the kitchen at the police station. It used to drive them mad, a temperamental thing. He and the agent had exchanged a wry glance. 'I could always boil a kettle.'

'At least there's electricity.' The agent pointed at the stove. 'And an electric shower upstairs. Equally old, I'm afraid. But it works.' He smiled, handing Thomas the keys. 'We've tried to encourage the owner next door to modernise, but there's some difficulty or other. Family property.'

'Next door?'

He'd inclined his head towards the identical cottage alongside. 'Used to belong to his wife's grandmother.'

'I see.' Thomas had immediately envisaged his neighbour as some very elderly person stuck in their ways, loyal to the memory of someone long dead and now old themselves, resistant to change. 'I'll manage.'

At the door, the agent had stopped. 'If you ever want any other information…'

'I'll call.'

'You're here alone?'

Everyone, it seemed, wanted an answer to that question.

He sighed now, straightened his back and pulled on his sweater and jeans quickly. There was a tracery of frost on the inside of the window. He hadn't seen that since he was a boy in the old council house that his parents used to have. Or the windows in the police house where he'd been stationed as a young recruit. He reached out with his fingertip and watched the ice melt around his touch. He would be sixty soon, another three years. Strange how time rushed by. He could still remember the scratchy couch in Fran's first flat. It was only yesterday. Still see her expression as she wriggled out of her clothes. Her lovely face and her long dark hair. He could still remember her voice, although she'd been gone over three years, her life drifting away after the last chemo, her sardonic smile when they'd got the first diagnosis. Another life that felt like another century, with the events of last year forming a brutal divider between past and present.

It was all gone, that was what he had to get his head around. Fran, the job, his peace of mind replaced with the voice he heard at night and the knot deep inside. He rested his head on the window.

'Get better,' he whispered.

*

It was eleven o'clock that same morning when he thought he would walk up through the fields to the main road a mile away. When he came out of the house, he knocked again on his neighbour's door. There was no answer.

A man coming along the lane and walking a terrier smiled at him. 'You'll get no answer from there,' he said.

'I saw him this morning.'

The man drew level with him and looked him up and down. Thomas guessed his age as around sixty. He gave off an air that Thomas recognised: a straight-backed stalwart loneliness. It showed in his face, and Thomas immediately wondered if it showed in his own. A slight drawing-down of the mouth, a sort of disappointment. A defensiveness in the eyes. It had once been his job to notice such things. Not that he would ever tell anyone that he felt cast adrift. He guessed that this man wouldn't either.

'You're the one that's taken the lease?' the man asked.

Thomas shook his proffered hand. 'Yes. Thomas Maitland.'

'Bill Pascoe.'

They both glanced back at the cottages. 'Do you know the owner?' Thomas asked.

'Not really.'

'I see.'

'Strange sort,' Pascoe responded brusquely. Ex-Army, Thomas suddenly thought. Career soldier. He reached down and petted the man's dog. It looked up at him with the kind of shrewd expression that he knew – none of the willingness to please of some breeds. Just that flat self-assured look of an animal who has better things to do than let himself be stroked. Sure enough, it moved away from him just as Fish used to do. He smiled. 'I used to have a terrier,' he said.

'This one here's a Patterdale. Name of Pat. Not very imaginative.'

Thomas smiled. 'I don't know what breed mine was. Bit of a mixture.'

'Not got him now?'

'We had a road accident, he and I,' Thomas said. 'Last year.'

There was a silence. 'You going along the coast path?'

'I was going to The Sailmaker's, if it's still open.'

'Not a bad plan. Want company?'

Within the hour they were settled in the pub bar, each with a pint in front of him. Pascoe had kept a good pace, faster than Thomas was used to. He was out of condition and knew it, the scar on the back of his head starting to make itself felt the more he walked. Pascoe took him along a path he didn't know, up away to the east of the village through a steep and battered scrubland. As they got higher, the wide arc of the bay grew clearer. You could see the lifeboat station, a square white building with a woodland and a few houses in front of it. Beyond that neighbouring headland, the coast lost all its little bays and became wide open to the ocean.

'How long have you lived here?' Thomas asked.

'Fifteen years. Retired here. Used to be in Sussex.'

'A nice coast that way. You didn't want to stay?'

'A change.' Pascoe eyed him over the rim of his pint. 'Six months is a long lease. I'm surprised he gave it you. Could have made more out of holiday trade.'

'There was some discussion, apparently.'

'It's been unoccupied a while. The owner's Aiden Ruskin. The man who doesn't answer the door. Maybe he wanted the money from a lease now. You're the first.'

'Wife?' The estate agent had said so.

'Partner. Gone a few months now. Both cottages belonged to her grandmother. Ruskin moved into the grandmother's.' He gave a shrug, as if to say *who knows*.

'And the grandmother?'

Pascoe sat back. He pursed his lips, and picked up a pub menu from the next table. 'Getting something to eat?' he said. 'I could use a pie and chips myself.'

11

Nothing was said when the food arrived. Each man attacked their meal with grateful concentration. Thomas hadn't realised how hungry he was. The dog fixed Thomas with such an accusatory look that once he was finished, Thomas threw him a piece of crust.

'Don't do that,' Pascoe said. 'He's a greedy little bugger. Don't appease him.'

Thomas laughed. 'You were telling me about the grandmother.'

'I was not,' Pascoe retorted.

'Is it a secret?'

'Not especially. Just sad.'

'Why?'

Pascoe considered him for a while. 'You're police, I should think. Am I right?'

'Not for a long time. I took early retirement.'

'You never lose the knack, though. Much like myself. Stationed in Germany for my last lot.'

'Army?'

'Of a type.' Pascoe pulled on his coat. 'Come with me,' he said. 'I've something to show you.'

They didn't go back the same way, but along the road, turning down again into the village and towards the sea after half a mile.

As they walked, Pascoe asked him about his career. 'Inspector's a good grade,' he commented. 'Rose through the ranks?'

'Yes.'

'Like myself.'

They smiled at each other, both having combatted the fast streamers, the university graduates who knew it all, or the favoured offspring of wealthy and well-connected families.

'Worst case that you remember?' Pascoe asked.

Thomas paused.

'You don't want to say.'

'Not really.'

'Understood.' They were almost at the sea now, at the last bend in the road. The sun had gone in and the sky was swept with racing clouds. It was getting cold. Pascoe paused outside the church: an unassuming building set far back as if it were hiding underneath the hill. The graveyard was surrounded by a slate wall and the church itself was slate and stone.

'You a churchgoer?' Pascoe asked.

'Not at all.'

'Neither am I,' Pascoe told him. 'No faith now.' He looked at the ground a moment, then laid his hand on the wrought-iron gate. 'She's here.'

'I'm sorry… who?'

'The grandmother.' He had cocked his head back towards the cottages. 'Or grandmother-in-law, I should say.'

They walked along the path between the graves, and just before the church door Pascoe turned left. There was a low hedge at the back where the stones were much smaller, memorials to those parishioners who had been cremated. Pascoe stopped in front of one. A few narcissi were laid in a little posy. *Greta Brodie 1935–2023.*

Thomas was surprised. 'Someone remembers her,' he said, nodding towards the flowers. 'My neighbour?'

Pascoe shook his head. 'Not him. She had friends in the village.'

'You knew her?'

'I did. She'd been a horticulturist. She had a garden at Chelsea when she was young. She was still designing gardens for others. She did mine fifteen years ago. Did both gardens at the cottages.' He smiled. 'She swam in the sea, even the year she died. There's a seawater pool along from you, over the last field. D'you know it?'

Thomas tried to cast his mind back.

'Fills every high tide,' Pascoe prompted.

'Yes, I think so. I've never swum there, though.'

'It was her favourite place.'

Thomas glanced back towards the headland and the cottages. 'But her garden – the one I'm renting. It has nothing in it. Nor does the one next door.'

'Not now.'

'Did her granddaughter change it?'

'*He* changed it. Your neighbour, last year.'

'Not while she was alive, surely?'

'After the funeral. After the woman left him and he came down here to live.' Pascoe turned away from the stone, and Thomas joined him as they made their way back to the gate. 'He calls her his wife, but she wasn't his wife. Greta's daughter never married him. They were together, but no marriage.'

Thomas stopped and laid a hand on Pascoe's arm. 'He took out the gardens?'

'Dug up every plant. Took out everything but that stunted hawthorn. She had a path, she had vegetable terraces, flower borders. Took it all out and laid the grass in yours and tarmac in what had been hers. Bloody tragic, it was. Would have broken her heart.'

Thomas considered. He'd seen what grief could do.

'Sadness and shock do strange things to people,' he murmured.

Pascoe snorted. 'Sadness?' he said sharply. 'They hated each other. She told me so.'

Thomas shook his head. It was more than he wanted to hear. He didn't want to engage in Pascoe's evident anger or his neighbour's revenge – if that was indeed what it was. He wanted peace.

'I'm sorry,' he said.

Pascoe looked at him keenly, and sighed. 'Not your business, I know.'

'It's not that.'

Pascoe tapped his walking cane on the ground for a moment, then looked up. 'You know the funny thing about him?' he said. 'He smiles.'

'Smiles?' Thomas repeated. 'Is that bad?'

'Doesn't sound bad, does it?'

'But it is?'

'Tell me what you think once you've met him.' Pascoe sighed. 'I liked her, you see? Rare old bird. Determined, friendly. Nice person. Didn't deserve what she got.'

Thomas couldn't help it. He should have walked away then.

He should have said nothing else.

He should never have asked the question.

'What she got? How do you mean?'

'She drowned. Early one morning. And Aiden Ruskin found her.'

The next morning the metallic closing of next door's gate made him sit up in bed. He could hear rain pattering against the window and, faintly, the sound of the footsteps.

This time, he went to the uncurtained landing window at the top of the stairs. He saw Aiden Ruskin pause at the same field gate and look back at the house. He knew then that Ruskin wasn't looking for him. He was looking back to see something else, or someone else.

2

DRIVING THROUGH THE NARROW LANES INLAND, he almost missed the turning for the house. There was a piece of granite with the name – Chalfont Edge – etched into it, but half-buried in undergrowth. The drive turned to the left between a line of trees, climbing all the while, and it was so long before he saw the house that Thomas thought he must have still missed the way.

It was far back from the coast on the hillside. It must have once been lovely, but it wasn't lovely now. As he drew into the turning circle, with a mass of overgrown rhododendrons and hydrangea in its centre, he noticed a car off to one side of the Jacobean frontage. It was an old Volvo, a faded and rusted blue. Looking up at the house, Thomas figured it must be twenty years since the windows had been cleaned. Although, to be fair, it would be one hell of a job. He counted. Four floors, thirty-six windows. He shook his head, went to the door, and knocked.

Isabelle Crosby. He'd got the letter a week after his visit to the pub with Pascoe. *I'd be grateful if you'd come and see me,* it said. *I'm rather a fan of yours. Are you free for lunch on the 26th?* He'd turned it over several times in his hands. Nice thick paper. Fountain-pen handwriting. Postmark Truro. The address in the top right-hand corner of the page. An embossed stamp on the envelope – one that he couldn't make out.

He'd thought it was a company logo until he googled the name.

Lady Isabelle Crosby. Wikipedia had quite the life story. Widow of Sir Alexander Crosby, crossbench MP, latterly Lord Crosby of Chalfont, industrialist. Lady Crosby a supporter of various charities. UNICEF. The National Theatre. RSPCA. RNLI. There was a photo of her that surprised him. He would have expected some well-coiffed woman in an expensive suit and hat. She was of that age, apparently. Born in Liverpool in 1943. A twinset and pearls, perhaps. A Hermès headscarf, Queen-like, holding an opera programme.

But the blurred image was nothing like that. It had been taken years before and showed Isabelle Crosby in a crowd on the steps outside the House of Commons. *Fund Women's Refuges* said the banner she was holding.

He had put down his coffee and stared out of the window.

A fan of yours.

It was too interesting to pass up.

It took her a very long time to come to the door.

A dog got there before her. The old golden retriever came barrelling out from the side of the house, barking. Thomas smiled at the mock ferocity. Retrievers were the pushovers of the dog world. True to form, it licked the hand held out to it in a show of friendship. He ruffled its coat.

'Who are you, then?' he asked.

It took Isabelle Crosby a long time to open the door. It was heavy, probably the same age as the house, shaped in a Gothic arch to match the doorway. The tall and thin woman who shook his hand with a fierce grip was instantly recognisable despite her being probably forty years older than the Wikipedia photograph.

'Lady Crosby,' he said.

'Isabelle,' she responded, and took a step back. 'Come in, come in.'

Both he and the dog walked through, the dog rushing past them both.

'I see you've met Max,' Isabelle said. Once inside, she smiled at him. 'Do you know how many times I answer that door?' she asked. 'Never. People who know me come in the back. Please do that from now on.'

He followed her across a huge hallway, silently noting the 'from now on'.

'Max?' he asked. 'Good name.'

'After Ernst, the surrealist.' She was walking briskly forward, waving her hand to one side. 'Medieval hall,' she said. 'Library.' And to the right: 'Drawing room, study. Never use them. Too bloody cold.'

The Liverpudlian accent was loud and clear. Good that it had never got filtered down in London. He presumed they'd been in London when her husband was in the Commons and Lords. The temptation to drop the Liverpudlian twang must have been strong. Perhaps she'd been proud of it. He used to have a colleague who had come from Merseyside and once he'd started being teased about it, had made it even stronger. Proud to be from the city. Plodding on behind Isabelle Crosby's fast pace, Thomas tried to remember the man's name. Red-haired lad, always claiming he was Viking stock. Ethan? When he was only thirty, he'd been run down by a shitty little bastard, barely fifteen, in a hit and run that had left his lifeless body crumpled in the street. Thomas recalled the funeral on a sunny day in a quiet Somerset town, and the two little daughters holding their mother's hands.

They were coming to the back of the house. He had to duck to get through this door. It opened onto what must have once been a busy kitchen, a huge Victorian affair still with its cooking range, a cast-iron monument, in the chimney space.

In one corner was a more up-to-date kettle and mugs. Isabelle Crosby was busying herself. Max kept by Thomas's side, looking up at him.

'Coffee? Instant, I'm afraid.'

'Yes. Thank you. And thank you again for the invitation.'

She delivered the cup to the table, and settled herself opposite him. 'Sit, sit. You too, Max.'

They both did as they were told.

'Since there's no signal here for modern technology, and I don't own a mobile phone anyway, I'm reduced to writing letters.'

'It's an event to get one.'

He noticed the arthritis in her hands, and she caught his glance. 'Bloody dreadful, aren't they?' she remarked, spreading her fingers and looking at them. 'I used to have such nice shapely fingers. Rotten luck.'

'I've a touch of it myself.'

She leaned forward and inspected his hands. 'Hardly. Affect your painting?'

'On cold mornings.'

'It doesn't show in your work,' she said.

Ah, so that was it. When he had got the letter yesterday, he'd wondered if she'd heard of the coroner's court case and been one of those people who thought they were entitled to hear the inside story of last year. Looking at her now though, he thought it unlikely. 'I'm surprised that you know me,' he said. 'The paintings.' He paused. 'But I'm even more surprised that you knew I was living in Trewarith.'

She smiled. 'I have my sources.'

'Well… I'm flattered.'

She waved her hand as if shooing away a fly. 'I'm not flattering you,' she said. 'That would suggest that you don't deserve my interest. But you do.' She picked up a magazine next to her on the table. 'You were in here.'

He looked at the article. It had been written two or three years ago. He'd sold a canvas to a London client, a man whose friend – Tam Jefferies – turned out to own a gallery. Tam had given him his own exhibition and pulled every string to get it noticed. He got everything that Thomas had done so far and put a high price on each. Thomas had received the news of the exhibition's success in a dreamlike state, however. Fran had died a few months before.

'I went to see the paintings,' Isabelle said.

'You did? In London?'

Isabelle Crosby gave him a quizzical frown. 'I do get out, you know,' she said. 'I'm not stuck here for the duration.' She took a sip of her coffee. 'I like to keep up,' she murmured. 'I might live in the back of beyond but when Alexander bought this house I told him, "If you think it'll stop me gadding about you've another thing coming".'

Thomas laughed. 'And did you? Gad about?'

'Of course. I always liked a holiday on my own. Not lying in the sun. But archaeology. It was one of my father's preoccupations. I suppose I inherited it. I have some nice pieces in the house. I'll show you sometime.'

'You mean archaeological pieces?'

'Yes.' She pulled a slight face. 'I wouldn't do it now. You don't know exactly where they've come from.'

'An illegal trade, you mean?'

'In my father's time I suspect it was waved through. Not now.'

'And art?'

'Oh yes, always art. Ancient civilisations, that sort of thing.'

'Your husband too?'

'No. Too much the pragmatist. He liked boating, fussing about on water. Thankfully, I get terribly seasick.' She leaned towards him conspiratorially. 'And boating people. Can't stick 'em. Yacht clubs. Worst places on earth.'

He grinned. He was getting to like Isabelle Crosby.

Abruptly, she stood up. 'I'd like you to see something,' she said.

They went out of the cavernous kitchen and into a flagstone-floored back corridor that smelt of damp. 'Rising groundwater,' Isabelle said. 'You wouldn't think it, would you? Not out here.

They say there's a well under the floor here, but even a builder couldn't find it. I'm thinking of getting one of those – what d'you call it...'

'Diviners?'

'Yes.'

She opened a door onto another corridor. This was the back of the house proper and opened into a sitting room with a glorious view of the country behind the coast. Thomas commented on it.

'The owners before us were a mining family,' she said. 'Tin, you know? They would have once looked out onto the miserable evidence of their mines, two hundred years ago.' She stopped walking, and turned to him. 'There's a small minority of humanity that is quite evil. No doubt you've seen evidence of it. The article says you were a police officer.'

'I was.'

'Retired early.'

'Yes.'

She looked as if she was thinking of saying something else. Instead, she looked around the room. He suspected at that moment that she didn't need to cross-examine him about last year. She was as sharp as a tack, and probably knew it all already. 'Fine ceiling,' she was saying. 'Plasterwork. I don't much like it myself. Cherubs. As for those portraits, well! All the Georgians were chinless wonders. They came with the house, and I can't bear their supercilious glances. They all tried to look like the King, you see? Fashion. Idiotic.'

'You don't like the house.'

She shrugged. 'Alex loved it. It's all right if I could afford it. But the heating bills, the roof. Not to mention the bloody garden, always growing. I used to have a friend who came and worked at it and she hated me letting it run riot. I tend to live in the kitchen, you see? I like to spend money on things that I love. I have my special place, here.'

And she opened another door – Max dutifully padding behind them – to show him a kind of studio. It seemed to have been built onto the side of the Jacobean wing, and had a row of skylights that cast a beautiful oblique light on the room. Thomas wondered at once if she had ever applied for, let alone got, planning permission for it. He doubted it. It looked to be an extension thrown up in breeze block. But what was inside the room was what mattered.

It was full of modern art: sculpture, canvasses, and dominating the space was an installation that he had last seen in Tate Modern. He could hardly believe his eyes. He'd gone to that same exhibition and wandered around it and marvelled at its ingenuity. In the centre was an old estate car, an Austin Countryman, completely dismantled, the doors forming an elongated set of wings and the inside of the car distributed on wires – motoring manuals and maps and driving gloves and a disintegrating picnic hamper and a 1950s record player all describing an explosive arc.

'Isn't it wonderful?' she said.

He walked up to it. He liked it, the humour of it.

He'd always wondered who bought these works. These strange expeditions into unreality. Or reality. He looked back at her. 'It must have—'

'Cost a fortune, when I have a roof to mend and a boiler that died eighteen months ago?' She began laughing.

'I'm sorry.'

'Don't be.' She patted him on the shoulder. 'If I mend the roof it'll cost fifty thousand, plus whatever horrors they discover underneath it. No doubt the timbers are rotted too. And who'll get the benefit of it? Not me. I shan't be around long enough.'

'I thought museums bought this kind of thing. Or collectors.'

'Or the collectors who live in museums. I come and look at it every day,' she said quietly. 'Some people pray in church. I pray in here.'

He looked at her, raising an eyebrow. 'What do you pray for?'

'Oh, to not lose sight of what matters. To keep curious.' She dropped her eyes from his. 'And people. I pray for some people.'

To keep curious. He'd tried to cure himself of curiosity in the last ten years. It had got him into trouble dozens of times, taken him to things that he didn't want to see. That no one would want to see. Deaths, crimes. Listened to a thousand stories in an effort to get to the truth. Heard confessions and lies, the second far outweighing the first. Learned to distinguish. And always that slow, patient waiting, the digging down until you found the answer. It wasn't usually dramatic. Or even what you might have been expecting. Often at the end of a crime was an exhausted perpetrator, a shadow of what they'd intended to be. Or else just an empty approximation of a human being, the small proportion of evil that Isabelle Crosby had referred to.

'You've missed the best thing,' she told him.

He looked back at her, and it was then that he saw his own painting, *Riverside*, on the opposite wall.

'You bought it,' he whispered.

'I surely did,' she said. She was standing with her arms crossed, assessing his reaction.

'Well, thank you.'

She smiled. 'You can thank me in another way,' she said. 'Would you come here and give an exhibition? For charity?'

Driving back through the winding lanes on the way home, Thomas had shaken his head. He didn't really want to do an exhibition – he hadn't enough materials and large canvasses with him, it would mean going home for a start – but the words *for charity* had meant it was impossible to refuse.

As he had been leaving, as they shook hands again, a thought had occurred to him.

3

H<small>E HEARD THE ROAR OF HELICOPTER</small> blades before he saw them.

Halfway down the village street it passed overhead, going towards the sandy beach that was just over the headland from his cottage. There was a car park just there, and he went into it knowing that it gave a full view of the sands.

There were several cars parked despite the winter day. He got out and joined the group of people staring out at the helicopter as it landed, the downdraft spraying sand in all directions. Even the spectators in the car park shielded their eyes for a moment.

'What's happened?' he asked the nearest man.

'Swimmer had a heart attack apparently.'

'Swimming, in this weather? I'm not surprised.'

'It takes all sorts.'

He agreed. Whoever had gone in the sea had more guts than him, although he seriously doubted their sanity. He liked a swim himself, but only in summer and autumn. The sea could still hold a fair temperature until late October, if you could withstand the gasp when you first got in. But in April? Not bloody likely.

He turned back to the car, and that was when he saw Aiden Ruskin standing at the far side, looking down at the beach. He walked quickly over to him.

Curiosity killed the cat. He just couldn't leave it alone.

'Mr Ruskin?'

There was no reply. Ruskin looked as if he was about to run. He was shorter than Thomas, with pale blond hair. Thomas held out his hand. 'Thomas Maitland,' he said. 'Your next-door neighbour.'

Ruskin hesitated, then returned the gesture. Unlike Isabelle Crosby's iron grip, Ruskin's hand was warm and unusually soft.

'I've been trying to say hello,' Thomas persevered. 'Knocked once or twice.'

'I don't always hear.'

'I just wanted to say that I appreciate you letting the cottage to me.'

Ruskin shrugged.

God, this was hard work.

'I understand that it used to belong to your wife's grandmother.'

It had just been something to make conversation. To his surprise, Ruskin's face broke into a smile, and Thomas could see at once what Bill Pascoe had meant. There was something wrong in that expression. You wouldn't think that a smile could unnerve you, but there it was.

'Welcome to… whatever this is.' Ruskin waved his hand at the beach and the village and the church. He began to walk away.

Thomas noticed a slight hitch to his walk, a limp. He made off after him, snatching at a topic to prolong the conversation. 'Would you consider letting the cottage for a longer period?' he asked. 'Or selling it?'

Ruskin stopped dead. 'Selling it?'

'To me.'

'What for?'

Thomas spread his hands. 'Well, to live in.'

Ruskin looked at him closely. 'Live?' he repeated, as if this were an astonishing suggestion. 'Look, you'd better come in.'

The estate agent had been right about Ruskin's cottage being the same as his own. Nothing much seemed to have been done to it, aside from a coat of whitewash. He did have central heating though – Thomas glimpsed the Calor gas cylinder behind the shed as they went in, and the temperature was twenty degrees warmer than his own place. No Ascot heater over the sink either.

Ruskin seemed to pick up on his brief glance around.

'I know it's a bit rough and ready next door,' he said. 'Not my fault.'

'I don't mind it. My own house is old.' He took the chair that Ruskin pulled out for him. Ruskin himself didn't sit, however. He leaned against the sink, crossing his arms, looking at Thomas as if he were an interesting specimen. Thomas noticed the Rolex on his wrist before it was hidden.

'If you've got your own house, why are you here?' Ruskin asked. Nothing if not direct.

'My wife and I used to come here all the time.'

'Didn't your wife want to be here with you?'

'She died a while ago,' Thomas told him. 'I came here to paint.'

Ruskin didn't offer the normal condolences. Instead, he was looking over Thomas as if assessing him. Taking the measure of him. 'You're an artist?'

'Getting there.'

'An amateur, then?'

'Yes.'

Ruskin smiled again. 'Ah now,' he murmured. 'That's not quite right, is it?'

'I'm sorry?'

'You've sold paintings. You've got a name.'

Thomas didn't reply. He was interested to see where Ruskin was going. And surprised that he'd asked the question if he already knew the answer. 'My wife Keira owns a London gallery,' Ruskin said. 'Did you know that?'

'No, I didn't.' It was a genuine surprise. A surprise too to hear him calling Greta's granddaughter his 'wife'.

'It's not large. Actually, we both used to own it. Then Keira bought me out. I bought this cottage from her – a sort of swap, really – and we co-own yours.' He gave a little self-deprecating shrug, a kind of helpless gesture. 'I thought if I kept the cottage, she might come back. We're not actually divorced yet. I wanted to still have something she loved, in a place she loved. But I seem to be seriously deluded about that.'

There was an awkward silence. *You're deluded about a couple of things there*, Thomas thought. *Not least that you were married. According to Pascoe.* And he wondered why Ruskin wanted to tell him so much.

'Did you live in London?' Thomas asked.

'Yes. I worked for a dealer. My father, actually. An art dealer. But Keira wanted a gallery.'

'You left your job with your father to run the gallery?'

'Yes. Happy to.' He spread his hands as if to show what a sacrifice he'd made, and immediately Thomas knew that he was very far from happy, a martyr to the cause. No, it was more than unhappiness. He was resentful, thwarted. And there was something too in his expression when he mentioned his father. Something worse, akin to disgust.

'And you lived there?' Thomas asked. 'In the gallery?'

He shrugged. 'I'm an exile now.'

'From London?'

Ruskin thought for a second or two. 'From the life I used to live,' he said eventually. 'My father died a little while before Greta so there's no one at all for me back there.'

'Would I know the gallery?'

Ruskin named it. He didn't.

'It's not well known,' Ruskin acknowledged. 'So you see, to answer your original question, I wouldn't object to selling your cottage. I could do with the money. I haven't a penny. But Keira's a different story. I don't know where she is. I suggested letting it through her solicitor – it's not a great idea to keep a house unoccupied for a long time, is it? – and she eventually replied to instruct an estate agent. Communication is tortuous.'

'You don't know where she is?' Thomas repeated.

'No. She used to consult for the V&A when I met her. Not now though. I checked.' Now there was more than a touch of anger, Thomas noticed. Ruskin nodded several times, his mouth set, while Thomas sat considering a wife who ran away and covered her tracks completely.

'Okay,' Thomas replied eventually. 'I'll consider it, certainly.'

'To be here permanently?'

'I don't know.'

'A bolthole then, in summer?'

'I really don't know. It's an option.' Thomas was finding it difficult to concentrate on Ruskin's questions. He was wondering why the man didn't have a penny if his father had owned a house in London, and had died last year. Perhaps it was stuck in probate for some reason.

'Listen,' Ruskin said, 'I'm sorry I didn't come out to welcome you. I should have done.'

'It doesn't matter.'

'It would to some,' he replied.

'We all have our moments.'

Ruskin considered him for some time. 'You're lost, are you?'

'Sorry?'

'Between worlds. I know that feeling.' He paused. 'Have you had lunch?'

'Not yet.'

'Want a sandwich?'

'Only if you're making one for yourself.'

'I am.'

But Ruskin still didn't move. He dropped his eyes from Thomas and looked at the floor. 'I've never known a place that likes to gossip as much as they do here.'

'I suppose all small towns are the same.'

'Tough,' he murmured, almost under his breath. 'Stubborn.' He shuffled his feet. 'You didn't cross Greta. She was cold.'

Thomas was wanting to know where the garden had gone, the one around his cottage that Greta had seemingly loved. And he wanted to know the significance, if any, of the six o'clock walk every morning. He wanted to know that quite badly.

'She was both mother and grandmother to my wife,' Ruskin was saying. 'She brought Keira up. Father died, mother went off to Canada. Biological sciences professor. I think she's involved in a land reclamation project out there. Or water. Or waste.' He laughed a little, and shrugged. 'I never did understand it.'

There it was again. 'My wife'.

Aiden turned aside, and opened the fridge. 'Ham? Cheese?'

'Cheese is fine, thank you.'

Thomas sat considering the description he'd given of Keira's grandmother. *Cold.* It didn't tally with Bill Pascoe.

He sat watching Ruskin cut the bread and cheese, and thought, *you checked with the V&A, did you?*

'So Keira hasn't visited at all since you sold your part in the gallery?' he asked. He wanted to see that fleeting expression again. The kind of momentary resentful pout that his own mother would have called whining. There was some sort of strange plasticity about Aiden Ruskin, changing expressions, none of which looked genuine. He'd seen that before. Lies always looked the same.

Ruskin put the plate of sandwiches in front of him. He had a slow and deliberate way about him. Not relaxed, but contained.

He sat down and looked at Thomas with a sudden kindly expression. 'Careless couple of buggers, aren't we?' he murmured. 'We both seem to be missing a wife.'

It was only much later, when Thomas gave up on some preparatory drawings and sat looking out at the fields, that it happened.

Perhaps it was the early dark.

He got up quickly and went out into the kitchen. He didn't like the prickling feeling on his scalp and God knew he hated the nightmares, but this wasn't the same. He felt short of breath. He looked around himself, trying to motivate himself to think of what to cook. Fran had hated cooking. Oh, she used to do a few favourite things. Curries, stews. She did baked potatoes a lot, and salads, joking that it didn't take a genius to chop up lettuce or sling a potato into a dish and put it in the microwave. She'd asked when they first met if he minded, and he'd told her that he liked his food, and God bless the woman she'd tried to make pies and pastry and cake, all of them a disaster. It had become a standing joke. 'I'm hardly a proper wife, am I?' she'd said, laughing over some ruin or other that was supposed to be lunch. He'd hugged her. 'You're all the wife I'll ever need,' he'd told her.

Jesus, memories. They were a bastard.

Cancer too.

A heartless, remorseless bastard.

He held onto the sink, wheezing, trying to slow his breaths down, expand his lungs. He'd put the light on in a minute. The trouble with old houses. Old windows that excluded light. The same at home. Home. Smoke and fire. The thick clay-bound ground. Ground fog rolling off the fields, the sluggish stream at the bottom of the garden.

It came roaring out of nowhere, a kind of soundless roar in his head.

Kill me.

Why don't you kill me?

'Oh,' he muttered, winded as if someone had run into him. As if some enormous object had come rolling into the room he was standing in and taken all the oxygen away. He headed for the door and flung it open and stared out at the empty garden, and after a while the breath came back into his body. He clung onto the door frame. It had felt as if the ground was giving way underneath him.

A doctor at the hospital had warned that he might feel depressed after he got home – surgery and a long stay could feel like a safe institution, he'd explained – and then when you got home the true impact of the events could rush in on you. Thomas took another deep breath and willed his heart to slow down.

Apparently there was no time limit on a possible reaction. Like grief, it had its own agenda.

All he could think of – ridiculous that a stray thought should come into the gasping space – was Ruskin saying to him *ah, that's not quite right* – and what else? – *you're lost, are you?*

Thomas realised in that peculiar, anxiety-ridden moment, that Ruskin had not been searching in the dark with his questions or simply making conversation.

He knew the answers already.

4

Aiden Ruskin had met Keira quite by chance, in Paris, five years ago.

It had been a rainy Saturday morning at Clignancourt.

He had gone to collect another piece for his father.

Not a large piece at all, but it had a buyer, the sort of item you might just put in your pocket, a little bronze of the Capitoline wolf. It was Roman, something that had been tarted up in the Renaissance, adding Romulus and Remus; but they made quite an income from that sort of thing. And that morning in Paris, once the original mission was accomplished, he had also been offered, and bought, a tiny chimera: the body of a lion, a snake for a tail. You could hold it in the palm of your hand. So clean, straight from the tomb.

He was walking back through the enormous flea market, a newspaper held over his head, when he saw her standing next to one of the stalls. He recognised her from the last auction at Toynton & Mark. He had asked someone then – a dealer, a fat middle-aged man – who she was.

'Keira Brodie. Freelance,' had been the answer. 'Sharp eye, apparently. Paintings, ceramics.'

'Doesn't work for anyone?'

'Victoria and Albert, I think,' the dealer said. 'And the Tate.'

'Know anything else about her?'

The man had smiled at him, picking his teeth with a cocktail stick as he leafed through the catalogue and the distant voice of the auctioneer boomed through the lots. 'I've tried, mate,' he said. 'You won't get anywhere there. Art historian. First from Oxford. She'll make a fortune for herself, I reckon. Advising yon bloody gentry.'

They looked at her across the room.

Aiden had been struck by her soft, rounded prettiness; she was like one of the paintings on Archie's wall. Old-fashioned looking. He liked that. And he had also been struck at their physical similarity, he and her: both short, both blond, both with an almost childlike look about them. An innocent look that came in useful. It was like seeing another version of himself. Except that his resting expression was a smile. And hers, apparently, a frown.

For his own amusement about a fortnight later he had gone to the Victoria and Albert and up to the top floor, working his way down to see if he could find her. He had been there only a quarter of an hour when she had come walking past.

'Hello,' he had said. 'Is it Keira Brodie?'

It was very sweet the way she coloured up. How many women did that anymore? Mostly they would look at him scathingly, despite what he thought of as his handsome charm. But she was appealing in an almost childlike way: her body was rounded, not thin. Only a little shorter than him, with wide-set grey eyes, blond hair curling around her face. And a full mouth. Like a cherubim.

'Oh, hello.'

'You don't remember me.' He held out his hand. 'From Toynton's the other day.' She put her head on one side. He used to have a dog that did that. 'Well, why should you?' he said, smiling. 'I asked you about the Villanovan pottery.'

He hadn't, but she was too polite to say so. Much later, she would smile, shaking her head reprovingly, and tell him, 'You never spoke to me at Toynton's at all.' But not now.

He had shrugged towards the immense museum shelves behind their glass protection. 'Fascinating.'

'You've got an interest in this era?'

He'd gazed at the display thinking, *what the hell is it?* 'I'm a total novice,' he admitted. 'I'm trying to learn.'

'Are you?' For the first time, she expressed doubt. He saw it settle in her expression.

'No, really,' he said. 'I've got a card here somewhere.' And he had fished it out. *Archie Ruskin.* He gave it to her. She looked at first one side and then the other. 'My father. And my boss. You don't know him?' he asked.

'No. Should I?'

'He's got a place off Brompton Road,' he said.

'And you specialise in ceramics?'

'Paintings.'

She frowned a little. He could see that she was thinking of something much more interesting than him, that he had distracted her, and he was standing in her way. *She'll make a fortune for herself,* he thought. She didn't need him.

He looked to his side at the display. 'That's nice.'

'It's glass, not ceramic,' she pointed out. 'First century BC, Italian.'

He had started laughing. 'I'm not doing very well, am I?' he said. 'The truth is, I came here to find you.'

'Why?'

She was such hard work. You would think that no one had asked her out before. Or shown any interest in her at all. 'Do you have any time for a coffee?' he said.

She gave him back the card. Perhaps someone had warned her about dealers, perhaps even about him and Archie. In that one soft gesture, Aiden had understood so much about her. She had intuition, and she had determination. And she was chronically shy. 'I'm sorry,' she said. 'I'm quite busy today.'

They had parted, and he had watched her going down the broad and beautifully patterned stairway flanked with its stone columns, and he had thought that if he were ever to know her, he had to disarm that intuition and persuade her that she was mistaken. It came to him in a flash, just like that. That it might be possible to have power over her. And that she might open doors. Wealthy, wealthy doors.

And now he saw her in Paris.

'Bloody weather, isn't it?'

She glanced up. She had been in the process of talking to the stallholder, and was holding a small framed picture in her hands. For a second, she looked confused, and then recognition dawned. 'Archie Ruskin,' she said.

He dodged under the canopy and shook the rain from the newspaper. 'Yes,' he said. 'But I never told you *my* name. Aiden Ruskin.'

She shook his hand.

'What have you got there?' he asked.

'Something I like.'

It was a grubby little image in an overworked frame that was coming to pieces. 'You should always buy what you like,' he told her. 'Regardless of value.'

'Yes,' she murmured. 'Thank you.' He noticed just two faint spots of colour on either cheek. She kept her gaze downcast.

'Shall I buy it for you?'

She stared suddenly at him. 'Why would you do that?'

'As a present.'

'No, no,' she murmured, looking away. She stepped back from him. She had a conversation in French with the owner of the picture; there was a lot of shrugging, and finally a handshake. He admired her for knowing the language. He had never learned it himself. All the while, the pouring rain dripped down the canopy in front of him. He watched as the painting was wrapped up. She put it in her bag. It was only about eight inches by ten, even with the frame.

When she turned round again, he was standing in her way. 'May I buy you the coffee that you refused me in London?' he asked.

They walked for a while, and found that they had gone the wrong way: they were at the Cimetière de Saint-Ouen, next to the railway line.

Because he'd been leading, ushering her across roads in his best gallant fashion, he had to stand there like an idiot and apologise.

'I don't know how I did this,' he said. 'You're a distraction.'

They retraced their steps. All the while she kept her head down, only glancing up at him occasionally. He had a perception that she had known that they were going the wrong way, but had been waiting to see what a fool he could make of himself. To cover his irritation, he talked himself hoarse. About London, auctions, galleries. About himself. The clients he knew. Every amusing incident that he could think of. Sometimes she showed a flicker of interest. But mostly she seemed as if she had got caught by her own politeness and was trying to think of a way to escape him.

At last they found their way to the Boulevard Montmartre. They went inside a café and sat by the window, and she put her bag on the floor and her umbrella next to her. The rain had held off while they had walked.

'Do you often come to Paris?' he asked.

'From time to time,' she told him. She reached down and checked the parcel in the bag. 'Do you?'

'About eight or nine times a year.'

The coffee was delivered. They looked out at the traffic. 'I don't much like cities usually,' she said. 'Paris is different.'

'But you work in London.'

'Not always. Only three days a week.'

'What do you do the rest of the time?'

'I see customers. Research for them.'

'Provenance.'

'That kind of thing. I do some work for others.' And she named two private galleries, places of holy intimacy guarded by locks. You had to be a card-carrying oligarch to get into them. He felt like saying, *you must be shit hot at what you do.* But instead he murmured, 'Interesting.'

'Yes, it is.' She stirred her coffee.

'If you don't like cities, where do you come from, originally?'

There was at last a spark of real pleasure in her face. 'Cornwall.'

'Ah, surfer girl? I know Cornwall.' He didn't. But he knew one or two people who had places there. And he'd been with Archie to St Ives.

She leaned forward, elbows on table. 'Do you know Trewarith?'

'Trewarith...' He pretended to think.

'A little bay. Two bays next to each other, actually. One rock and one sand. I was brought up there.'

They talked about their childhoods. They discovered that they were both only children.

'How old were you when you went to boarding school?' she asked.

'Five.' It didn't matter that it was a lie.

She gasped, and shook her head. 'To be sent away so young. How horrible.'

When they walked back out, the sky was clearing. 'Where are you staying?' he asked.

'I'm not,' she told him. 'I'm getting the Eurostar back tonight.' She looked embarrassed, as if she didn't know how to say goodbye. 'You're here a day or two?'

'Yes, just a small place. Not very alluring. The curtain rail fell off the wall this morning and hit me on the head.' He showed her the small cut on his hairline, caused by him falling over drunk the night before and catching himself on the side of the sink.

'Oh dear,' she said.

'I'm a clumsy oaf,' he told her, laughing.

'You could sue them for ruining your looks,' she said.

And by God, she blushed. She blushed a colour that he had never seen before on an adult, a kind of livid wash that spread up from her neck like lightning. She must have felt it; she put a hand to her face.

Aren't you sweet, he thought. What was she, late twenties? Younger?

But she was really just like a little girl.

'We could play truant all afternoon,' he suggested. 'The Louvre. Have you been in it?' She raised an eyebrow. 'Of course you have,' he said. 'You're probably their adviser for something rare and strange for all I know.'

'Not yet,' she replied, and laughed as she took his arm.

They never got to the Louvre. Instead, they stopped at the Musée Grévin, the waxwork museum. They had looked up at the flamboyant sign over the tiny entrance: *Cabinet Fantastique Palais des Mirages.*

Of all the things.

Apparence trompeuse.

And suddenly the rain came pouring down in a torrent. She let out a small exclamation, and held her bag close to her chest.

'Are *you* a mirage?' he asked her when they were inside.

She bit her lip.

'What does it mean, the sign? *Apparence trompeuse*?' he asked.

'You should learn French if you're here so often.'

He looked at her in the subdued light, and in the multiplying reflections around her, and he looked at himself alongside her, and he thought that they made an attractive couple. They matched. It reminded him of the clockwork dolls that you saw on some timepieces. The ones that came out when the hour or half-hour was struck. They looked well fed and clothed, what people might say were a decent couple. He saw that they had a deceiving air of ordinariness, and until that very second he had had no idea how fortunate that could be. To be ordinary, so that someone might look over you and misjudge you. All his adult life he had tried to outdo others. Now he saw in a flash how that might be achieved in a way that he had never contemplated.

To be just a little invisible and unthreatening. To be quiet, as she was, standing back with that small shy smile on her face, and all that cleverness hidden away. He saw that she had a beautiful gaze when she raised her eyes from the ground. Clear hazel-green eyes with flecks of blue. Unusual.

'Misleading reflections,' she said. 'That's what *apparence trompeuse* means.'

'Is it? Fancy that!' He snorted in delight.

'Have I said something funny?'

'No, no,' he murmured. He pointed at the mirrors. 'But look at that.'

'Look at what, exactly?'

'Your eyes are like the sea,' he said. 'I bet they're the same lovely colour as the sea in Trewarith. They're the colour of the eyes of Renoir women and girls. That same blue.'

He really meant it.

And it surprised him that he did.

The afternoon drew in quickly. The lights of the restaurants shone on the rainy pavements. 'I'm going to buy you dinner before you get the train,' he told her.

They sat in a tourist restaurant in Montmartre and drank a lot of wine.

'You'll sleep all the way home,' he said. 'They'll have to wake you in London.'

'I'll fall off in a heap and disgrace myself. I don't drink really.'

He poured more. 'Don't you go out in London, with your girlfriends?'

'Yes. But not much.'

'Why?'

She shrugged. 'I'm probably a bit anti-social.'

After they had finished eating, he reached out to stroke her hand across the table. 'Tell me your secret,' he said.

'I don't understand.'

'The secret,' he repeated. 'What's the painting?' He nodded towards the bag at her feet that she had guarded all day. 'What is it? Is it valuable?'

She jumped a little, as if guilty. 'No, I don't think so.'

'Ah, you're lying,' he told her reprovingly. 'Can I see it?'

She didn't move.

He considered her. 'You know that dealer is a con artist?'

'Who, Christophe? Why do you say that?'

'Ah, "Christophe" is it?' he teased. 'He's a cheat. He gets worthless sketches and so on, dabs a bit more paint on them, and sticks an old label on the back—'

'There's no label on this one.'

'I heard that he recruits an artist in Provence to paint something in the style of… whatever. Then he takes it out back to the farmyard and sprays it with mud. Then he bakes it in a kiln and puts a tint over the whole canvas—'

'There's no mud and there's no label.'

'Then it's so routinely bad that he hasn't bothered. You've got to be careful, Keira. This business is full of jackals.'

'You think so? I don't know any.'

'Oh, come on. That's naïve.'

She pursed her lips, still looking at him and running a finger round the rim of her wine glass. Then she gave him a slow, tipsy smile. 'We'll see.'

'Are you going to declare it at Customs?'

'Of course I am. But I don't have to. It only cost fifty euros.'

He started to laugh. 'Fifty euros! Daylight robbery! The old devil!'

They went out into the drizzling evening, and he walked her all the way to the railway station. They stopped at the entrance.

'Thank you for keeping me company all day,' he said.

'Thank you for dinner.' Her charming embarrassment was back. The telltale flush of colour over and above the heightened blush from the alcohol. She glanced over her shoulder at the station clock. 'I'll have to run.'

He kept hold of her hand a fraction longer. 'Can I see you sometime?' he asked.

She didn't say yes, but they exchanged numbers.

And he watched her walk all the way through the concourse, until she was out of sight.

5

THOMAS HAD PROMISED ISABELLE CROSBY THAT he'd have some new work to show at the exhibition in the summer, but the preparatory work was interrupted by a phone call the following Saturday morning. It was a bright, windy day. The daffodils were in flower along the lane to the beach. As soon as Thomas got up, he felt that the discomfort he'd experienced, and the dreams, and the peculiar otherness of Ruskin's six o'clock walks, was something he ought to put behind him. Ruskin, with all his broad smiles, his barely hidden irritation, his questions – in fact, the peculiarity of him was actually none of his business.

He arranged his easel to avoid the strong shaft of sunlight in the little sitting room, and began. It had taken him longer than usual because he couldn't find the three smallest brushes. Eventually he'd glimpsed them under a chair, lined up quite neatly as if he'd put them there.

Not half an hour later, his phone began to ring.

'Mr Maitland?' asked a woman's voice. 'Mr Thomas Maitland?'

'Yes.' He could hear echoing noise in the background. Voices, the clattering of dishes.

'This is St George's in Weirport.'

It was the large teaching hospital nearest his own house in Dorset.

'I'm ringing on behalf of Mrs Christine Portman. I believe she's your neighbour.'

'She is, yes.'

'I'm sorry to have to tell you she's had a fall.'

He sat down, staring at the painting he'd begun. He'd made a good start – it was shaping up. He'd planned to work all that week. No pub lunches with Bill. No walks. Just head down and paint.

'I'm not at home. I'm in Cornwall.'

'I see. Well, if you can't come, that's quite understandable.'

Thomas chewed on his lip. 'Is it serious?'

'She's quite distressed. She keeps asking for you. She has a broken hip.'

Christine. He couldn't imagine anything worse for her. Christine who was always up early, stomped about in her wellingtons, kept her vegetable patch, walked in all weathers up to the village. He thought of her forgetfulness last year, and the tears that she'd tried to conceal after he'd told her about the six-month lease.

'What time is visiting?'

'Oh, anytime.'

Perhaps she was worse than the woman was letting on, he thought.

'Has she had other visitors?'

'No. I believe the postman called an ambulance. He found her outside.'

He would do. Christine only sat down inside her house when she was eating. And drinking, of course. *Come inside, I'm cooking you supper.* She never took no for an answer, especially since Fran had died. She would reprimand him for being too alone and for the ready-meal packaging that went out with his recycling. Christine, with the long plait of grey hair loosely tied falling down her back, and her characteristic way of using both hands to sweep back stray strands from her face, and her self-conscious tidying of herself when she saw him, as if her habitual untidiness embarrassed her.

He thought of her coming to the hospital when he was recovering, bringing him newspapers and books, and biscuits she'd made.

'I'll drive up today.'

'Thank you, Mr Maitland.' She gave him the ward details.

It took him nearly three hours to drive back. Back over through Bodmin and Honiton, back to another coast, the south as opposed to north Cornwall. Weirport was busy and the car park was full. He had to go back along the high street and park there. The Saturday market was just clearing up.

He reached the ward at two o'clock.

A young male doctor was at the nurses' station, and introduced himself. 'Let's go to the relatives' room,' he said, and led Thomas along the corridor to a small area with windows looking out over the town, and two rigid sofas facing each other. As he sat down, Thomas couldn't help thinking of all the other conversations that must have taken place in here.

'We've made her comfortable,' the doctor began.

'Will you operate?'

'We tend to observe at first.'

'Even for a broken hip?'

'It does depend on the break. But the odds are that she will go to surgery. She's had a scan. I'm sorry. There's a bit of a bleed in the brain. It may have caused her fall. And her age. Eighty-four.'

'Eighty-four?' Thomas repeated. He shook his head incredulously. 'I'd always assumed she was younger. She never told me her age. And she was found outside?'

'Apparently so. In the driveway between two houses.'

Between *their* houses. What had she been doing, going to check on his?

'Had she been lying there long?'

'We don't know. The paramedics said she was very cold.'

'Oh, Jesus,' Thomas murmured.

The doctor opened the paper file that he was holding. 'She has a heart condition, among other things, of course. Rather a complicating factor.'

'Has she? I didn't know.' He felt foolish having to admit that he knew so little. Foolish and selfish that he'd never been too concerned. She'd always seemed so independent, so capable. Perhaps not so much lately, but then he'd still evidently not paid proper attention. 'What kind of heart condition?'

'Cardiomyopathy.'

'What does that mean?'

'Disease of the heart muscle. She's been…' he consulted his notes again, 'treated for it for the last two years or so.'

'She never said.'

'More accurately, alcohol-induced cardiomyopathy.'

Thomas immediately thought of Christine pouring the last of a bottle into his glass, and getting up to retrieve another from her kitchen cupboard.

'But she was never drunk,' he objected. 'Never once.'

The doctor paused, giving him a sympathetic smile. 'I think her alcohol intake would be quite heavy,' he said kindly. 'Perhaps a bottle or two of wine a day for five or six years, something like that?'

'She's always bright. Capable.' But even as he said, it, he knew it wasn't true. In the past maybe, when he and Fran had first moved there. And even after Fran had died. But not now.

Thomas sat back abruptly in his seat. He ran a hand through his hair. 'That's quite a lot of things,' he muttered. 'I mean, that's a bloody challenge for her.' He still couldn't quite get his head around the fact that Christine was eighty-four. Then the rest. The heart, the bleed, the fall. He suddenly realised that she couldn't go on living at her house.

'She won't be able to be at home, will she?' he said. 'She'll need help.'

The doctor read through the notes again. 'Help was arranged for her last year. It seems she sent them away.'

'She would.'

My God she would, he thought. She'd beat them down the drive and out into the road. The thought made him smile to himself. And then he thought that she must have been afraid for a long time, and he clasped his hands in front of him.

'The alcohol hasn't helped, of course.'

'You mean it's damaged her heart?'

'Not just the heart. It's a cumulative process. Alcoholism will make it very much worse and results in various conditions. Perhaps alcoholic dementia, that kind of thing. Progressively.'

'Is her heart too weakened to operate, is that what you're saying?'

The doctor gave a half-shrug. 'These things can be unpredictable.'

Thomas momentarily put his head in his hands and closed his eyes. 'She's out every day. She gardens. She's always doing something.'

'Perhaps not so much this last year or so.'

Behind his hands, Thomas tried to think. When the studio had caught fire – in the midst of all the other trouble – he remembered Christine standing at his kitchen door, sympathetically offering a bottle of whisky. It seemed a tragic irony now.

'She'll have felt progressively weaker,' the doctor was saying.

'She never told me. I never noticed,' he repeated. He looked up, and away at the view of the town. That was the truth of it. He'd been so preoccupied that he'd rarely registered what Christine was doing, or how she looked.

'Would you like to see her?'

'Yes.' He stood up. 'Will she be able to go home, after surgery?'

'Not if she lives alone.'

'So she'll need to go – where? A nursing home or something?'

'She'll certainly need help. As next of kin—'

Thomas put a hand on his arm. 'Next of kin?'

'She named you next of kin at her GP's.'

'But I don't even have a power of attorney. Don't you need that to make decisions?' Thomas spread his hands helplessly. He realised that he sounded callous, as if he was trying to offload any responsibility as soon as it had been hinted at. He lowered his voice. 'If she stopped drinking, would she get better?'

The doctor closed the file. There was an air of finality about it.

He opened the door. 'Would you like to come with me?'

Christine was in a side ward, lying with her head turned towards the window. Sunlight lay across the bed.

He thought that she was asleep at first, but as he walked around the far side of the bed, he saw that her eyes were open. Her hair had been tied in a ponytail and lay across one shoulder. She was wired up to a monitor. The doctor, having delivered Thomas to the right room, closed the door quietly on them.

'So here you are,' Thomas murmured. He took hold of her hand.

She had a yellowish look and under the covers the body seemed concave, as if all the air had been drawn out of her. The blankets were drawn tight.

'How long did you lie there?' he whispered, not expecting a reaction.

But she suddenly returned the pressure of his hand. Tears filled her eyes and her mouth worked. It contorted into a smile. 'This… shit,' she whispered.

He smiled back. 'It really is.'

'Home,' she said. She grimaced.

'You must rest and get better,' he said. 'Don't cry.'

But cry she did. He looked around for a tissue or a cloth, and in the end was forced to dry her face with a crumpled paper napkin that he'd had with his coffee when he stopped for petrol. 'I'm sorry,' he said. 'I should have brought you something. It was a bit of a rush.'

'Sorry.'

'Don't worry about anything,' he said. 'I'll go to the house and make sure it's locked up and so on.'

He could see she was struggling to form a word. 'It's all right,' he reassured her. But her grip momentarily tightened.

He put his face close to her to see if he could make out what she was saying.

'Her,' she gasped eventually. 'I know.'

When he got back to the car, he sat for a few moments, his hands in his lap, staring ahead.

Her. I know. Know what? It seemed vitally important. Was she even thinking of him, or herself? Who was the 'her'? Was she talking about a memory from her past? He'd read somewhere that people sometimes reverted right back to their earliest memories when they suffered a stroke, or something like it. Like the man who had kept smelling his mother's perfume just before an aneurysm. The actor he'd read about whose newly recovered voice had a Russian accent, the accent of his émigré father. Christine often talked about her parents. Had she gone right back to the childhood she'd once told him about? She was the daughter of a farming couple, working a tenant place in the Vale. Her earliest memories were of a cattle shed, the warm breath of the animals in the winter cold, and of summers when the grass grew higher than her little body and she was lost in a field, wailing until her mother found her and scooped her up in her arms?

He sat wondering if she was not in that bed at all in her mind, but instead was walking back through the tall grass, her hand not in his but in her mother's. She'd told him that her mother's kitchen always smelled of sugar and soil, that strange combination, because the flagstones were laid over raked earth.

She remembered, she said, opening a sticky-topped jar in her father's outhouse and licking the top and screaming because it wasn't the familiar sticky sweetness of the kitchen but an almost-empty jar of turpentine. Turpentine and sugar and soil and the breath of cattle and frost-covered gates. Was she there now?

He started the car and drove back through the Dorset lanes to his own house. It wasn't long since he'd left, but it seemed unfamiliar. Lost-looking down the long drive, the thatch ridge line sagging slightly. Like someone else's home, the curtains drawn. He parked, and looked up at the roses that he had trained and pruned last year, but that this year were going their own way, reaching up towards the thatch. He ought to get a ladder out and see to them, he thought. He stepped back and considered the windows at the front, all locked tight. Keys in hand, he walked around the back instead of to the front door, and opened the gate into the garden. The lawn looked wet, sloping down to flowerbeds filled with leaves. He walked down and put his hand on the fence that divided upper from lower garden.

All that was left of his studio was the concrete base. While he'd been in hospital a few months ago he'd asked Christine if she'd get a contractor to come in and take the waste away: the charred timbers, the remains of his picture-framing machinery, the mess of broken glass and roofing felt and the charred carcase of the old paraffin stove. They'd done a good job. All that signified the fire was the brown grass and muddied soil around the base.

He looked at the opposite field, and went as far as the stream. His dog used to have a fascination with the water because somewhere further out towards the woods there were water voles and they would appear under the road bridge and out into the scrubby marsh that lay beyond. He wondered if they were still alive, still out there. And then the memory of his dog came rushing back, and he turned away.

He glanced at the vegetable patch, a similarly muddy mess that needed attention. On the far side, underneath the oak tree, he noticed a spade wedged upright in the soil. Frowning, he walked over to it. He hadn't dug the garden over at all this spring. The weather had been too wet, and the garden, being on clay, had been a squelching mire. The wet, grey depression of it all had added to the feeling that he must get away.

He pulled the spade out of the ground. A little bit of the patch had been dug, but down rather than across. Someone had been digging a hole. He tried to think if he'd left the spade out instead of locking it away in the garage with everything else. And then, looking at it, he realised it wasn't his. Similar, but not the same. He shook his head. Who could possibly have been in here, digging a hole?

Only Christine.

Over the hedge he could just see the upper-landing window of Christine's house between the trees that lined the drive. He made his way back up the garden and through the gate.

Halfway along the stretch of tarmac, he noticed something. In the verge was a discarded wrapper, the kind that he'd seen often enough in hospital. It would hold a cannula. He stopped and picked it up. A few yards further on was a tyre mark in the grass. The ambulance had parked here.

He got to the road, and took the turning into Christine's yard. The door to the house was closed, but unlocked. He went into her hallway. A couple of waxed jackets and pairs of boots were slung on the floor. He stepped into the kitchen and was momentarily aghast at the chaos. Christine wasn't a tidy person by any stretch, but this was different. Several newspapers were open on the table, a milk carton was on its side and the contents soaked into the newsprint. There was a half-empty wine bottle uncorked. Several dirty plates, the food congealed. In the corner, the fridge door was open. He stepped across then closed it, checking inside but only seeing a tub of margarine and bag of rotting tomatoes.

He tried to imagine what she'd been doing. She'd left in a hurry, it seemed, that same morning. Gone back towards his house, back along the lane. Heard something? Seen something? He thought of the spade, perplexed.

He went on through to the living room, where the coffee table and couch were full of paper. He saw that she had two or three of the kind of scrapbooks that he thought had gone out of fashion years ago – the sugar paper kind, with a picture of a clown or a horse or a fairy on the front. Kids' sticker books. Around them lay a pile of newspapers – more newspapers, and old ones at that. He picked up the nearest. Last year's, cut through at various places. He sat down and looked through the litter of cuttings.

The first thing he saw – the thing that leapt out at him – was an image of Alice Hauser. The headline. A photograph of John Lord. The police cordon on the rocks below, and a coastguard RIB moored close by. And then himself, a picture taken from his service days, ten years younger. *Retired Police Officer Injured.* And further down the page, a photograph of Helen McAllister, the woman who had disappeared and never been found. Alice's partner. The woman that Alice had accused him of murdering. The journalist had adroitly tied the two stories together, though had not been in a position to know of Alice's accusations.

Christine was cataloguing everything. Half the articles were stuck in the scrapbooks, half lay on the table and floor. For the first time he read the pieces from which his stay in hospital had shielded him. The speculation at first. The commendation at last. There was no mention at all of Helen McAllister, until he leafed through the second of the scrapbooks.

Christine had kept these for a long time. Long before last year's attack. She'd begun ten years previously, cutting out articles about Helen McAllister and Alice Hauser. Thomas propped his chin on his hand and chewed on his thumbnail. She'd known from the start – connected him to Helen McAllister's disappearance and his involvement in the case. Maybe Fran had said something. Maybe he had? He couldn't remember. He doubted it, though last year he had explained it all to her. Why had she not told him then that she already knew it had been his case, even that he'd known Helen?

Her. I know. Christine's hand gripping his that afternoon. *I know.*

And then he wondered if it was Christine who had told the journalist of the connection between the deaths at the cliff house and the disappearance of Helen ten years before. Had she rung up the newspaper? Would she? And if so, why? Or perhaps someone had come round trying to get background while he was in hospital. They'd have gone to his house and then perhaps to Christine as the nearest neighbour.

He looked again at the picture of Alice Hauser's down turned head, her handbag clutched close to her body. And at Helen, a snap from the school where she taught. The school where he had met her. He put his fingertip on her face.

'Nobody found you,' he murmured.

Why don't you kill me?

And here was Christine, silently documenting every step of the way. She'd never said a word in all those hospital visits to him afterwards. Never reminded him of their talking about the case. He hadn't really registered that at the time. It would have been natural of her to ask, but perhaps she thought he'd gone through enough. She kept her opinions to herself, it seemed. Suspicions, even. What exactly had been going through her mind? If she had felt this way, he wished that she had taken his hand in the hospital, leaned close to him and said, 'Where is she, Thomas?'

But she never did.

He took his hand away from the papers, resisting the urge

to tidy them. If she ever came back, he didn't want her to know that he'd looked through them. He got up and went back to the kitchen, picking up a carrier bag from under the sink and filling it with the remains in the fridge, the milk carton, the wet newspaper on the table. He scraped the food off the plates and washed them and put them away. Then he took a cloth over the table and floor. He unhooked the key from the panel next to the outside door, took the carrier bag to the bin and wheeled the bin to the gate for collection.

He went down to the henhouse that stood in the shelter of the hedge. He replenished the food and water, but he didn't know what else to do. They probably ought to be let out, and the eggs collected, he thought. As he stood in Christine's garden, he got out his phone and looked up a name that he remembered from the village, a man who owned a ramshackle place, a sort of animal sanctuary. Hearing Christine's news, the man promised to look in on the birds for her sake.

Thomas stood by the hedge looking into the rough pasture between Christine's house and his own. He wondered how many years she had actually lived here. He had never asked her. In fact, there was so much that he hadn't asked her.

I know.

He went back to her house and locked the door.

He stood for a while turning the key over and over in his hand before putting it in his pocket.

6

It had been snowing that morning in St John's Wood when Aiden Ruskin had come back for the kill.

Colonel Kingsbury's place was set back in a little gravelled yard, and the bell was a pull-handle job set in the crumbling texture of a Victorian wall. He waited on the step for a couple of minutes, getting slowly drenched by the rain.

When the door opened finally, Hector Kingsbury greeted him in all his military glory, or the remnants of it: upright posture, obligatory checked shirt, regimental tie, flannel trousers and well-polished brogues. And a walking stick slithering on a wooden hallway floor.

Aiden had extended his hand. 'Sir. Nice to see you again.'

'Come in, come in,' the old man had ordered. 'Don't you own a raincoat?' He shut the door behind them with a crash. 'Take off your shoes. I don't want all the muck of the streets in here.'

They entered the drawing room, where over the fireplace hung a portrait of Kingsbury's wife, who had died just six months before. Angela Kingsbury had been a great beauty once, and even in old age she had retained a hint of glamour. As Aiden glanced up at her again now, Kingsbury caught his glance.

'She wouldn't approve of this today, I don't doubt,' Kingsbury told him. 'They were her paintings. I know that you saw her last year. But she couldn't bring herself to sell.'

'I remember,' Aiden murmured. 'I was sorry about that.'

'Can't be helped now,' Kingsbury replied. 'I want to move abroad.'

He indicated the piano in the corner of the room, which had several canvasses stacked against it. 'I've brought them down.'

On his previous visit, Angela Kingsbury had told him frankly that they were short of money. She hadn't elaborated, but the downturn of her mouth had suggested that her husband had debts – that he was 'fond of frittering away the family silver'. Said with a shrug and a heavy taint of disapproval. Aiden had guessed at gambling, even another woman. Perhaps bad investments in the financial messes these bastards got themselves into. He knew of at least one other dodgy old boy who banged on about colonial glory. There was a flagpole with a Union Jack flying in Kingsbury's back garden. That said it all.

Waved on by the old man, Aiden picked up the paintings now and turned all four of them to the light of the bay window, stacking them side by side. There were two impressionist images of rivers by Taisia Afonina: next to them, an Arkhipov and a Bakst. Just looking at them again now set Aiden's heart beating wildly. The Afoninas had never been seen before, but he had found the others listed in a gallery showing of 1956.

Kingsbury crossed his arms. Standing next to his unsuspecting prey, Aiden could smell neglect. He wondered when the man had last had a bath. He tried to ignore it as he looked at the haul, putting his hand across his nose and mouth with an air of concentration.

In later life had Afonina produced lyrical subjects like these: the river, the still lives, the light playing in darkness. Kingsbury had said that his wife had bought them from a friend who had been briefly seconded to Moscow. 'Exchanged for flesh and bread,' Kingsbury had explained. He had given a brief lascivious smirk.

As for the Arkhipov and the Bakst, they had apparently been a gift to Kingsbury's wife while she had been in New York before they were married. Perhaps he didn't like the idea that his wife had taste – or a generous lover who had taste. He thought then that it wasn't just money that drove Kingsbury, but a brute disdain that was decades old.

When Aiden had been called to this house six months ago, he had expected a routine visit. He made a lot of them. The elderly selling off what they could, usually dull fragments. Occasionally – very, very occasionally – he would come across a beloved prize.

A Constable sketch had passed through his hands about three years ago, found in a small cottage in Norfolk, cast off by a son who had hated his parents. Aiden had been patient, and eventually had taken a hefty slice of the million that it had made purely because the son had been rude to him. The son didn't care about the money or the Constable: he was a hedge-fund manager anxious to be rid of his father's pestilential 'rotten stuff'. Sketches and plaster of Paris mouldings and a house thick with brocade curtains and cretonne couches and with curious wrought-iron gates between each room. 'He was queer,' the son had explained, almost spitting. 'He led my mother a dog's life.'

People gave you secrets like that. They were useful.

'I don't like auctions,' Kingsbury had said within the first few minutes of Aiden meeting him. 'I don't like their charges and I don't like the public nature of them. I want you to find me a buyer privately.'

Aiden had shrugged. 'There's only a narrow market, I'm afraid.'

'Nonsense,' Kingsbury had retorted. 'Russians. They're still buying, aren't they?'

Under all his bluster, Kingsbury was evidently no fool, so Aiden had given up immediately on that tack. 'Yes,' he'd agreed rapidly. 'They are.' But he still thought the paintings should go to auction. He'd persuade him eventually.

He liked the mild courting that his job entailed. The dropping of hints and the loading of the bait. The art of looking away when someone wanted something desperately from you was something that he had polished to perfection over the years. It was a satisfying little game. It gave him hours of quiet pleasure.

He had told Kingsbury that he himself was a middle man, nothing more. Portrayed himself as a minor cog in the machine, a willing slave in the holy transaction. But imagine having the Arkhipov on your wall. Imagine owning that. Nevertheless he had trained himself to let things slip through his fingers in pursuit of a greater prize.

Kingsbury paid rapt attention during the details of their conversation. He sat with a ramrod-straight back, eyes narrowed. Then, 'I want proper secure professional transport.'

Aiden nodded, letting a few seconds pass as if he had to consider it. 'Actually, do you know the best form of security?' he asked. 'No security at all. No advertisement of the fact that you have anything worth the trouble. You run the risk of a burglary down the line, you see? I'll put them in the car under a blanket. I shan't stop anywhere until they go into a secure spot in my father's house.'

'That's the way it's done?' Kingsbury asked, frowning.

'It's the way I do it.'

'You'll give me receipts.'

'Of course.'

He could see doubt battling desperation for the money in Kingsbury's face. Then, 'If you hadn't said that your father was in the Guards, and if you hadn't told me that your wife was the assessor...' the old man murmured. A long pause, then he held out his hand. Job done.

'Give me a minute to wrap them.'

'I can wrap them, if you wish,' Aiden offered.

'No, I don't wish.'

'Then I'll go for a walk,' Aiden said. He knew the process of goodbyes.

He got out of the house and walked down a London street slick with rainwater. *My father and my wife*. Fabrications both.

Lies that Kingsbury wanted to hear. Lies he loved to tell, different every time. Aiden started to walk quickly, something taking hold of him, infuriating him. His talent was nothing to do with the past. He was his own flexible construct. His father had not been in the Guards; he was a grasping, lying shit like himself. As for wives… Aiden made casual profit out of the possessions of others, wives included. He caught the things that people carelessly threw away like a cricketer in midfield.

He stopped by the Tube station and turned his face up to the sky.

He realised that a woman standing on the other side of the road was watching him, her hand wrapped around the leash of a giant dog – some kind of wolfhound – and that she was smiling at him. He pointed to the dog, and she gave a comic shrug as if to say, *well, you know, ridiculous*. He crossed over the road, dodging traffic, and he petted the animal. 'Fab dog.' The owner was at least twenty years older than him, and she blushed. *In your dreams*, he thought, pleased. And walked away while she was replying.

As he turned back to Kingsbury's house, he felt increasingly that the old boy was getting a good deal, that he himself had been accommodating and patient. He unlocked his car and brought it into Kingsbury's street, and manoeuvred it into the narrow drive, and heard a slight crunch as he clipped the stone wall at the front. He turned off the engine and closed his eyes. That settled it.

As he stepped into the hallway and glanced down, smiling, at the canvasses next to the door, he said, 'I must admit to a slight deception.'

Kingsbury paled. You could see the alarm bells ringing loudly in his head. 'Oh?'

Aiden spread his hands. 'I'm terribly drawn to that sweet little watercolour that you have.' And he nodded towards a framed image by the stairs.

Relief telegraphed itself across Kingsbury's features. 'What, that?'

'A print of course, but nice. I've an affection for pastoral scenes.'

'Have you?' Kingsbury said, with a note of disdain. 'Young man like you?'

'Your wife's choice again?'

'Good God, no. It was my mother's.' Another flicker of contempt crossed the old man's face.

Aiden walked across and made a great show of inspecting it. He gestured to ask if he might take it down, and then walked to the hall window with it and looked at it in detail in the better light. 'Yes, a good print.'

'It's got some sort of signature.'

'Has it? Oh yes. Prints do.'

'Indecipherable scrawl. I've never liked it. Amateur.'

'Yes,' Aiden agreed. 'Out of fashion. But I've a soft spot for these.'

'Cheap chocolate box stuff.'

'Quite so.' Aiden smiled. The Arkhipov, Bakst and Afoninas were one thing. But this... 'They are rather ghastly. That's the appeal, I think.' He laughed, and Kingsbury laughed in response, as if sympathising with Aiden for having taken leave of his senses.

'I'd like to have it for myself, at home,' Aiden told him. 'May I make you an offer?'

7

IT TOOK THOMAS LESS TIME TO get back to Cornwall. The roads were clear, and a full moon rose as he crossed Bodmin Moor. He'd spent the remainder of the afternoon pruning the roses just as he'd done last year, trying not to think too hard about his little terrier watching his every move then, following him about. He'd grown to love that dog, and the same day that he'd pruned the roses it had died.

He slowed down as he approached Colliford Lake, now in the darkness of the spring night. There was no urgency to get to Trewarith. No one waiting for him. Except the memory of Fran, and she wasn't there. She was here in the centre of this moor. He took the left-hand turn off the dual carriageway. The road was unlit, meandering for a mile or two until he pulled up past a scattering of houses. He got out of the car and began to walk down through the trees until he saw the church.

Temple Church, dedicated to St Catherine, lay in a fold of the land with the Warleggan River below it. Thomas made his way carefully in the moonlit darkness until he was standing in the graveyard. He and Fran had come here several times but once, memorably, on a night just like this. The Knights Templar had built this chapel nearly a thousand years ago for pilgrims crossing the Cornish peninsula to Fowey on their way to Spain. It stood now with the moon in the sky behind it, sunk in ancient silence.

He remembered Fran linking her arm in his. 'Shall we get married?'

He'd looked at her, puzzled. 'That's funny. I could have sworn that I married you twenty-four years ago.'

'But you didn't run away with me,' she'd told him. 'People used to come here. Couples escaping their families. They called it the Gretna Green of the south.'

'Did they?' he'd replied. 'You know everything don't you?'

'Yes,' she'd said. 'Ask me a question, any question. I'm the fount of all human knowledge.'

'I believe you.'

Arms linked, they'd looked at the silhouette of the tower against the sky. 'Think how happy they must have been to get here,' she'd murmured. 'How passionately in love. And now thousands of others thunder past on the main road every day and don't care at all.'

'Terrified, more like,' he'd replied. 'Afraid of being caught.'

She'd nudged him with her elbow. 'You are the least romantic person I've ever met.'

'No I'm not.'

'Prove it.'

He'd wrapped his arms around her and kissed her. 'Will you marry me?'

He stood in the quiet now. He felt that Fran was close. He could almost feel the whole moor breathing, whispering. Full of secrets. Not far away were Neolithic stone circles – Nine Stones, Trippet, Stripple. Supposed to be girls dancing on a Sunday centuries ago, and turned to rock as a punishment. But, Fran had told him as they had walked back to their car, far more likely to be monuments raised to lunar standstills.

'What do you mean, lunar standstills? The moon doesn't stand still.'

'Every eighteen years,' she'd replied. 'Look it up.'

He thought now of couples running away to be married, and of men and women long before Christ labouring to make the circles, and of Fran who had that unearthly quality of stillness inside. Still even when he had held her hands in those last days. She'd died on another eerily moonlit night at four in the morning long before sunrise, and while he'd been asleep in the chair next to her. Moving away from him soundlessly. He'd seen so much violent death in his lifetime and hers was so different.

He put his hands in his pockets now and stared at the ground. 'Ah, Fran,' he whispered.

Frost was forming. It was going to be a bright, cold day tomorrow.

When he got to the cottage, it was past midnight. He saw a light burning in Ruskin's house as he walked by. As he put his key in the lock, he heard movement. A window opening and closing.

He put the light on in the kitchen and paused, hand still on the door. There was something different inside here, but he couldn't think what. He closed the door slowly and stood with his back to it, looking about. There was a paperback on the table where he had left it, but he thought the chair was at a different angle, sitting now facing the door. He looked to his left-hand side. His breakfast plate was propped on the draining board of the sink just as he had left it. He walked up to it and picked it up and put it back in the cupboard, along with the teaspoon and mug. He pushed the chair back to its usual position tucked under the table.

It was only as he was going up the stairs that he thought of what was missing. He turned and went back to the kitchen, looked again at the table and the sink. Then he opened the drawer underneath. The knife he had used at breakfast, the old one with a bone handle, was in the tray. He knew that he'd used that knife and left it with the plate on the draining board. He couldn't think why he would have put that away but not the other things. But – like the chair – it was such a stupid detail.

I'm getting crazy with all the dreams, he told himself. Forgetful too. He'd end up like Christine if he wasn't careful, immobile in hospital because he'd let anxiety get the better of him. Howling at the moon at Temple too, probably.

'Crazy,' he muttered to himself. 'Idiot.'

He closed the drawer and went slowly upstairs.

It took him a long time to get to sleep. He kept thinking of the church and of stillness, and of the moon standing still in the sky. He thought of Christine and the pile of papers. When he did eventually sleep, he found himself on top of the ridgeway path, looking down on the coast on a summer's day. Fran was alongside him, her hand in his but glancing at him with such an expression of sorrow that it woke him again.

He saw the first light through the window, and got up.

He was ready this time when Aiden Ruskin left his house.

There was, as he'd predicted, a slight fringe of frost on the ground. He watched the other man go through the gate before following him. There was no one else around. The field was bright green with maize and the hedges just coming into leaf. He saw Ruskin go through the gap at the bottom of the field and onto the coast path.

As he grew closer he could hear that slow withdrawing roar of the tide as it retreated gradually over the quartz-striped rock pools. When you got closer, those pools ceased to be as picturesque as they looked from a distance; ancient volcanic shifts had tilted them on their sides like uneven teeth. He knew from past experience that you could fall on the slippery surfaces festooned with weed.

He saw Ruskin up ahead standing looking out to sea. There was a slope just there, a descent to the pool, he remembered. On summer days, the water captured in the man-made basin looked inviting. But it was always breathtakingly cold. He thought of the helicopter landing on the other beach a few days before, and wondered if Greta had died of a heart attack. He stood hesitating, thinking that the autopsy apparently determined it was a drowning. Pascoe had said as much, hadn't he? The drowning of a fit and able woman, whatever her age.

He walked along the path, and saw to his surprise that Ruskin wasn't at the pool, but had stopped just out of sight and was waiting for him. He had that mechanical smile on his face, hands in his pockets.

All his life Thomas had learned to trust his instincts, to read faces and make judgements, but first and foremost to listen to his gut. Your body would always tell you what you couldn't decipher with logic alone. And now, looking down at Ruskin poised halfway between the path and the pool, Thomas felt his stomach curdle. A lazy flip, a downward lurch.

'Mr Maitland,' Ruskin called. 'Are you following me?'

He smiled back, and began to carefully make his way down the slope, feeling his boots slithering where the frost had taken hold. Ruskin didn't move. But he kept smiling.

'Am I intruding?' Thomas asked.

'A question for a question,' Ruskin said.

'Yes, I followed you.'

'Because?'

Might as well be honest. 'Your gate wakes me every morning. Every day at six.'

'Ah.' Ruskin looked at his feet, but didn't answer. He turned and made his way down to the edge of the water. The surface was bright, a mirror of the blue sky. Thomas followed. A hundred yards out, the waves churned on the last of the raw-edged rocks.

'This is where we found Greta,' Ruskin said, his gaze focusing on the breakers. 'Not long before Christmas.'

'At six?'

'Yes,' Ruskin told him.

'And you come down here every day?'

Ruskin didn't reply. He sat down close to the pool edge.

'In all weathers?' Thomas persisted, joining him. 'Rain or shine?'

'I owe her and Keira that much.'

As he watched him, Thomas realised something else that was unusual about the younger man. He kept unnaturally still. Not Fran's relaxed stillness at peace with herself, but a lack of movement that was full of tension. There was no fidgeting, no shifting in position, no movement in his hands or fingers. His hands lay clenched together in his lap and his back was straight.

'You said "we".'

'Yes, Keira and I. Greta hadn't been at home the night before. She'd vanished. We'd come along here, but it was high tide. I thought she might have collapsed while walking. We came back to the cottage and tried to sleep, but couldn't. We got up at first light and came back. Greta was floating in the pool.'

'I'm sorry.'

Ruskin turned his head. 'Don't be. She was old.'

Thomas recoiled at the off-handedness of the comment. 'So she'd been out here all along?'

'The police thought the tide had come into the pool and taken her out to sea and then washed her back to the same place.'

Thomas thought about it. Possible. But not probable, he decided. At some time the previous day, Greta Brodie had gone into the water. Perhaps here, or perhaps even at the next-door beach. Would have depended on the currents. Presumably the local force had checked she hadn't been a passenger on a boat. There would have been an assumption that even though she was a strong swimmer, she'd made a mistake. Gone in at the pool or even further out, where the breakers were, and miscalculated the speed of the tides. But to be washed back to the exact point you'd gone in?

'She might have even done it deliberately,' Ruskin said.

'Done what?'

'Drowned herself.'

Thomas doubted that too. It was bloody difficult to drown yourself. The natural reaction was to breathe, even if you intended to end your life. You couldn't do it alone. You had to weigh yourself down, or go in fully clothed. A thick coat that rapidly filled with water. Even then, it was usually shock of the cold or the strength of the current that killed you. No. If you wanted to die, there were easier ways.

'It must have been devastating for your wife.'

'She went straight in to get her. In that freezing water.'

'She did? Into the water, on her own?'

'Yes. I'm not a very good swimmer. Keira dragged her body to the side. Right here. We tried CPR but it was no use, of course.'

'Was Greta clothed?'

'What difference does that make?' Ruskin stood up abruptly.

Thomas stood up with him and together they negotiated the slope back to the path. He noticed that Ruskin hadn't answered the question. He supposed it was a step too far, too intrusive. But, despite himself, it was the police officer that was asking. And clothed or unclothed? It made a hell of a difference.

They said nothing more as they walked back towards the cottages. Then at the field gate Ruskin paused, his hand resting on the latch. 'I hear you've been invited to see the lady of the manor. Isabelle Crosby.'

'Yes.' Thomas was going to ask him how he knew, but Ruskin was already talking.

'Greta was always up there. She did Isabelle's garden,' he murmured. 'Loved to stir things up between them, those two old bitches. Thieves, the pair of them.' He suddenly held out his hand. 'Have a good day,' he said.

The smile was back.

That same afternoon, Thomas was at Chalfont Edge and considering Isabelle Crosby across a half dozen of the smaller paintings that he had brought back with him from the house.

She was taking her time, finger to her lips. She picked up the canvasses and walked them around the studio space, looking at them in different lights. Wherever she went, the retriever went slavishly after her.

'What do you think?' she asked.

'It's more to the point what you think.'

'I think they're very small, Thomas,' she said. 'I was hoping for something like that.' And she pointed to *Riverside*.

He nodded. 'I'd love to, but I haven't the space, either at home or here.'

'Can't you rent somewhere?'

'I could.'

'But you don't want to.'

'I hadn't considered it.'

She took hold of his hand. 'Let's have a drink,' she said.

This time, it wasn't coffee, but Macallan. He accepted a tiny measure.

'Ever the policeman,' she observed. 'I suppose you'd rather it was tea.' She brought over a tray complete with pot, cup and saucer, sugar and milk. 'There you are,' she told him. 'Enjoy'. And she poured herself another whisky. 'Medicinal,' she said.

'Oh?'

'Hodgkin's.' She waved her hand at his expression of concern. 'Don't worry, I'm not going to fall down dead. Not just yet, anyway. They don't recommend this stuff, of course. But what the hell.'

They sat in the meagre warmth of the kitchen, Max lying next to them. After a while, the dog rolled over and began snoring. Isabelle rolled her eyes at the noise.

'Ever been to Venice?' she asked.

He couldn't see the connection at first. Then it occurred to him. 'Peggy Guggenheim.'

'Ah, full marks.'

'She married Max Ernst.'

'She did indeed. I got Max here when I came back from Venice eight years ago. He was foisted upon me, a rescue. Another old lady who'd shuffled off this mortal coil. I'd been travelling. The Med. Guggenheim and Ernst were on my mind.'

'At least you didn't call him Guggenheim.'

'Yes, imagine calling him on the beach.' Laughing, she paused. 'But you haven't answered the question.'

'No, I haven't been.'

'And you an artist,' she teased, smiling. 'You should go, Thomas. You would love it. The light, the water, the history. Spread your wings.'

'What makes you think that I don't?'

She contemplated him for a few moments. 'You strike me as dutiful. To your past perhaps. Your career. To other people. You should break out a little. Be wild for a change.' She leaned forward. 'For instance, why are you here in Cornwall?'

'To paint.'

'But why here exactly?'

'Because Fran and I came here for years.'

'And would she want you to come back?'

'I have a lot of happy memories here.'

'Make some more.'

They sat in companionable silence for some time. The day hadn't cleared. There was no sunshine, but being in Isabelle's company gave a pleasing end to the day nonetheless. 'I saw Aiden Ruskin this morning,' he said. The last time that he'd mentioned Ruskin's name, she'd merely acknowledged that she knew him. 'He says that Greta was a friend of yours.'

She sat swilling the whisky around in her glass. 'Yes,' she murmured. 'We went to art school together. A little place in

Lancaster, but good.' She nodded towards the window. 'She's the friend who'd be outraged at the state of the garden.'

'You relied on her.'

'Very much. She did Chelsea, you know. Got a silver gilt.'

'She must have been talented.'

'She was. She was one of those people who could just look at some plant or other and it would grow. By contrast, I only have to look at something and it dies.'

He laughed. 'Did she do Chelsea every year?'

'No. Her husband fell ill and she nursed him. In London. He was much older than her. When he died, she came to Cornwall. We did a lot of things together.' She nodded wistfully. 'It was like the old days when we knocked about as students. She was a lot of fun. And she made a good living here as a garden designer.'

He was trying to tie the two opinions of Greta together. The man who said emphatically that she was cold. The friend who adored her. *She was fun.* And Bill Pascoe's *she was a nice person.*

'And he destroyed her garden.' He was thinking aloud, speaking quietly.

She put her glass down on the table. 'Do you like Aiden Ruskin?' she asked. There was a distinctly acid tone in the way she spoke his name. 'Are you friends?'

'No. Just the neighbour.' He did not say that Ruskin was nevertheless interesting to him.

She took a deep breath. 'Does Greta haunt the houses? She should. I hope she haunts *him.*'

'Perhaps she does,' Thomas said.

'We can only hope.'

'You don't like him.'

'I don't.' Her mouth had set in a drawn-down, disapproving line. 'In the beginning, he used to come here sometimes with Keira. She would come to help her grandmother. She said it was good to be outdoors. She called it decompression from London.

At first they seemed happy – he was forever complimenting her in…' She looked about herself as if trying to find the words. 'In a peculiar way. Too much. Too— ' She gave a twirl of her hand. 'Too fussy. Empty. Vacuous. He used to look at Keira and ask me if I thought she was pretty. She was, of course. But it was "isn't she pretty, isn't she clever, aren't I the lucky man?" – you know, over and over. It made my flesh creep.'

'Did Keira mind it?'

'Greta hated it. She told me so. She said he was false. Keira just said he was all talk, and she would roll her eyes and smile. Early on, that is. It was different later.'

'How?'

'She'd say nothing. I once saw him walk up to her and roll her long hair around his wrist and pull, so that she had to raise her head. And she's only a small woman. It was dreadful to see.' She got up from her chair. 'Hang on a minute.'

She went to the other side of the room and took a notebook from the dresser. From it, she extracted a photograph, and handed it to him. 'Greta took this. This is Keira.'

He held the image towards the last light of day coming from the window. He saw a blonde woman of about thirty. Blue eyes. A full mouth.

'That was when they first met,' Isabelle said. 'She lost some weight after only a month or so. She started coming here on her own. She barely spoke. She'd been such a bright girl, you know?'

'And you think this was all Ruskin's doing?'

'She stayed here after Greta died and told me that she was going away.'

'She didn't say where?'

'No.' As soon as she said it, eyes fixed on his, taking a last draught of the whisky, Thomas knew she was lying. 'Then *he* came and asked me where she was. Demanded. Insistent, you know. I told him to leave and not come back.'

Thomas crossed his arms on the table, and leaned on them. 'He goes out of the house at the same precise time every morning. Six. And he goes down to the seawater pool on the beach.'

She put her glass down suddenly. 'Does he indeed? Greta was found there.'

'I know. He told me.'

'And what else?'

'That Keira pulled her grandmother out of the water.'

'And did he tell you the rest?' she demanded. 'That he didn't go in himself? He let her haul poor Greta out alone while he stood and watched. She did CPR alone while he phoned for an ambulance. He walked away, up onto the path. He walked halfway back to the cottages, saying he couldn't get a signal. He left that poor girl with her grandmother's body. Did he tell you that?'

'No.'

She straightened her shoulders. 'He broke Keira, you know. Or tried to.'

'How do you mean?'

'What I say.' She thumped her hand on the table. 'Pretty girl. Successful, too.'

'And they never got married?'

'No, thank God. He asked her all the time apparently.'

So Bill Pascoe was right. Ruskin wasn't married. 'Why didn't she accept?'

'She didn't trust him. Greta thought that was the reason.'

'Over what, though? Other women, money?'

'Why money?'

'He said he didn't have any. Or implied it.'

Isabelle snorted derisively. 'Made a fortune in London cheating people, and he hasn't got any?'

'Did he?'

'He and his father both.'

'Did his father live there? London?'

'House near Harrods.'

He asked about an issue that had bothered him before. 'Did he not inherit the house?'

Isabelle poured herself another drink. 'I try not to think about their escapades, actually.'

'What kind of escapades?' He was thinking of Ruskin saying Greta and Isabelle were 'a pair of thieves'.

She didn't reply. Her mouth set suddenly in a stubborn line.

Thomas sat back, thinking. 'Why was Keira with him in the first place, if he was so unlikeable?'

'You've met him. Very manipulative man.'

'But she was in business with him, I understand. A gallery.'

She put her hand to her forehead and sat back in her chair. 'Nonsense.' Then she pointed at him. 'Listen, Ruskin learned everything at the foot of his father, Archie Ruskin, who was a devious old bastard of the first order.'

'I thought he owned the gallery with Keira? And he lived there. And gave up his share in the gallery in exchange for the cottage he's living in. That's what he said.'

'Hmm,' Isabelle murmured. 'All lies. In the beginning, Keira kept a lot from Greta because she wouldn't want to worry her. Nevertheless, Greta *was* worried about it all. More worried than I'd ever seen her.'

'Keira didn't confide in you?'

'No. Not this time.'

'And you don't know where she is?'

'No.'

There it was again. Thomas hadn't spent much of his working life without being able to tell a lie from the truth. She gave a classic tell – touching her mouth briefly – before she stood up, picked up the tea tray, and said over her shoulder, 'I don't want to think about Ruskin any more. Let's talk about something else.'

8

WHEN HE GOT BACK TO LONDON after his next trip to Syria, Aiden hadn't rung Keira Brodie at all. It wasn't that he didn't like her. He liked her too much. She was almost too good to be true, and he felt uneasy about it. It was dangerous, because it was a trespass into his privacy, as if her very sweetness could bring down the barriers.

He probably would have ignored her completely if it weren't for the painting. It hooked him and Archie both, and made it all worthwhile.

If only they hadn't been so bloody cocksure about it. About her.

It had been about six months later. He and his father had been having dinner. Aiden was grateful to Archie, because when he'd first come to London and got the job at Toynton & Mark – before they fired him – he'd gone through some meagre savings in just a few months.

With his life shattered – nowhere to live and no job – Archie had swept up the pieces and neatly packaged them into his own life. He hadn't been a father to his son in twenty-five years, ever since he had walked out on Aiden's mother. But Aiden nevertheless went to see him, standing on his Kensington doorstep one night like a lost dog. Needs must when the devil drives. Archie hadn't recognised him at first, and when he did he didn't invite him in. Archie had made a fortune as a dealer and had been waiting for this piece of failing humanity to turn up on his doorstep. He'd heard rumours, but he wanted to test the boy for himself. He regarded Aiden objectively, asked if his mother was dead as he hoped, and only when Aiden had told him about her agonising cancer did he let his son over the threshold.

Archie had gone downhill since that night four years ago. He had had a triple bypass and didn't walk along the Embankment any more, nor did he go to auctions. Instead, he received clients in his house like a Renaissance king among all his gaudy possessions. When Aiden had first seen the inside of the house, Archie had watched him closely for signs of his own avarice and, catching Aiden's glance, he had started laughing.

'Something funny?' Aiden had asked.

'The glint of greed,' Archie told him, 'is not a professional attitude.'

'You seem to have done well enough.'

'Naturally.'

Aiden's mother had been a sweet soul, but it was his opinion that sweetness was a weakness. Over the next four years, Aiden worked for Archie like a dog as the old man became ever more breathless and tetchy and demanding. But he liked his father for all that. Admired and copied him. Cultivated glacial charm and the enormously satisfying talent for lies. All life was lies when you came down to it. You just had to lie proficiently. There was no room for adequacy.

Over coffee this night, Archie had slapped a trade paper down on the table. 'Read that.'

Aiden picked it up. Archie sat down opposite him. He looked rattled, and that was something exceptional. Giving him another enquiring glance, Aiden read the paper where Archie indicated.

London Man Arrested on Suspicion of Murder.

As he read, he smiled. 'Fuck me,' he murmured.

'Terrible business,' Archie said.

Aiden read on. Kingsbury had put his house up for sale and left London for Spain where, the paper reported, he had bought a villa. After local police had been called to a disturbance – a fight in the street between two middle-aged women – one had flown back to England and promptly reported him for killing his wife.

Aiden began to laugh. He slammed the paper back onto the table. 'The dirty old bastard,' he said. 'Two women on the go. You wouldn't have thought he had it in him.'

'No doubt his new-found wealth had some appeal,' Archie observed drily.

'Ha! Can't play both ends against the middle. Something's gonna give.' He sniggered to himself for a while, then wiped his eyes. 'That's the best thing I've heard in a long time.'

Archie was watching him closely.

Aiden glanced up. 'What?'

'You'd better expect a visit from His Majesty's constabulary.'

'Why? What have I done?'

'You're the source of the money.'

'I think you'll find that *we're* the source of the money, Archie. All above board.'

'The dinky little sketch?'

Aiden shrugged.

Archie pursed his lips and steepled his fingers in front of him. 'Well, we shall hear soon enough.'

'I can't see why. Kingsbury was clearing out. If he told his woman over here anything at all, it would be that the paintings were worth very little.'

'Yet after he sold them, he went to Spain. They'll get a forensic accountant to go through his bank accounts.'

'So what? He sold them. We paid him. He sold the sketch too. Paid for that just the same. So what if he didn't know its value? More fool him. Business.'

Archie leaned forward and placed a hand on Aiden's arm. 'It's not the paintings per se that I'm worried about,' he said quietly.

Aiden's face was expressionless. 'Kingsbury was pleased she was dead. I'd be happy to tell them that.'

Archie said nothing. He took up the paper, turned to another page, and folded it. Then he passed it back to Aiden.

'Moving on,' he said. 'Take a very deep breath.'

It was an item in the Market section. It concerned a small painting of Queen Mary II when she was a girl of fifteen, a portrait of her before her marriage in 1677. The painting was to be put up for auction. It was deemed to be a find of unparalleled rarity, and one of two that the court painter had completed when he had been in England from the Netherlands in 1675. Both paintings had been known and documented in the eighteenth century, and then both had been lost for nearly three hundred years.

One of them was still missing, but the other had now been restored.

It was said that it had been found in Paris earlier that year.

'Is it the same one, do you suppose?' Archie asked. Aiden had told him the story of Keira Brodie's ridiculous purchase. Now, as Archie looked at him, an icy calm descended. As pleased as he had been about the sketch, Archie did not like acquisitions to slip from his fingers.

'I don't know,' Aiden admitted.

'Rumour has it that it was her find.'

'Really,' Aiden replied tonelessly. He carefully refolded the newspaper and smoothed it down. 'Well, how simply super,' he said sarcastically. 'How too marvellously, marvellously clever.'

He was thinking that he had told her when she was standing in Clignancourt that she must buy what she liked. He had said it with a patronising tone, he knew. And the jibe about her being innocent and too trusting. Jesus Christ.

He put the paper down. 'How much do you think it's worth?' he asked.

Archie shrugged. 'Millions, who knows? And that's not all.'

Archie liked to tease him with what he knew and didn't know. It was one of his more irritating habits. When they'd last spoken about it, Archie had told him to be patient. 'I've told you about this. You must combat it. You telegraph your greed on your face.'

'I do not,' he'd retorted.

Archie, laughing, had patted his hand. 'Don't sulk.' Now, he smiled. 'I was speaking to John Cotter the other day about your girl,' he said.

'She's not my girl.'

Archie raised an eyebrow. 'Another error of judgement,' he commented wryly. 'Miss Brodie had identified a Van der Weyden for a client. Fifteenth century.'

'And?'

'Guess which client.'

'How am I supposed to know?'

'The Earl. Keddington.'

Aiden leaned back in his seat. He raised his arms and let them drop in a gesture of amazement. 'Just lying around, I suppose? Just like that?'

'No, no. Hung in plain sight on a wall in his study. It's said that the dear boy didn't like it.'

'Shit,' Aiden retorted.

Archie looked away and shrugged a little before turning back to Aiden. 'You remember the *Descent from the Cross* in Madrid, of course, when we went three years ago.'

'And she's found something else by him, something unknown?'

'Apparently so, while doing an inventory for the old boy of his Roman and Greek stuff. All those ghastly statues of boys wrestling snakes and the like.' And he laughed. 'I shall never know why he dropped us.'

'Maybe you offended him.'

Archie placed a hand on his chest. 'I offended him? Impossible.'

'You nearly kissed his feet. He hated that.'

'Simply polite.'

'You were fucking obsequious. We were hardly through the door when he threw us out. We never even got to the main house. The rumours are the place is a gold mine.'

'Oh, such a big word. Obsequious,' Archie hissed at him.

They were quiet for a few moments. Aiden tried to read his father's expression. 'You look like you want to do something about it.'

'I wonder if Miss Brodie might be persuaded to go into business with us,' Archie murmured.

Aiden managed to laugh. 'Not a chance.' He remembered Keira politely returning their card to him and walking away down the V&A's stone steps. Nevertheless, he thought about it for a while. 'Why would she go into a partnership anyway?' he said. 'What would be the benefit? She's making a fortune on her own. And so are we.'

'That's not really true,' Archie said. 'I think she's probably out of our league entirely.' He began to stand up, waddled over to the sink and stood for a while gazing out at the darkened garden, faintly visible through his own reflection. Then he turned, crossing his arms over his body. 'She has a world of contacts,' he said. 'Better even than mine. We're small fry by comparison. And she has one prime advantage.'

'Oh, what might that be?'

'She isn't you.'

Aiden stood up. 'Thanks.'

'You lack a certain quality.'

'And what's that?'

Archie pointed, with a tight smile, at the Rolex on Aiden's wrist, and gave a flourish at the rest of his clothes. 'Too much Essex man.' He burst out laughing. 'Pink silk lining in the suit jacket. The Rolex. I mean to say, you need to bin the lot.'

To his own mortification, Aiden felt himself blushing. He

couldn't match Archie's sly superiority nor the expensively down-at-heel look that Archie had mastered. 'Okay,' he muttered. 'Anything else that Keira Brodie has and I haven't?'

'Oh yes. She is trustworthy. She is honest.'

Aiden turned away. He strode over to the couch and slumped down on it.

'Do you want my advice?' Archie asked.

'No. But you'll surely give it, won't you?'

'Marry the girl.'

'Very funny.'

Archie shrugged dismissively. 'With all my worldly goods I thee endow, et cetera?' he asked. 'Ah well. Simply a suggestion, boy. You need to have her in your court. In your possession, if you like. Open with her secrets and money but not privy to our own.'

Aiden smiled. 'Cold-blooded, Father.'

'Profitable, child.'

9

IT WAS POURING WITH RAIN THE next morning.

Over his breakfast, Thomas rang Weirpoint hospital. Christine was due for an operation that day, he was told, and had once again been asking for him.

'I can't get there today,' Thomas told the ward sister. 'Maybe in a couple of days.'

'I see.'

'So it was decided to go ahead?'

'It's a femoral fracture. She'd be immobile without the operation.' The woman paused. 'Have you any idea if you'll be able to care for her at home?'

'I really can't. I'm working away. We're just neighbours.' He heard his own feeble excuses.

'Is there a nursing home nearby?'

'I don't know. You think she should be transferred there, if I can find one?'

'That would be best. She'll need post-operative care for quite some time.'

'Okay.' He didn't really know what he could do with this information. He wasn't family. It wasn't as if he were Christine's son, or brother. Still, he felt a loyalty to her, all alone in the world and clinging on to him as if he had the answers, asking for him. 'I'll ring later to see how it's gone,' he said.

'Please do.'

As he ended the call, he wondered if Christine had any money to pay a nursing home, or if that was covered by the health authority. He had absolutely no idea. There was the house, of course. Christine's house. That could pay the bills if it were sold. But he was damned sure she wouldn't want that. Even if she were in a nursing home, she'd be adamant that she would eventually go home. Did she have savings? He didn't have a right to ask. There was no power of attorney. Perhaps she had a solicitor he could see. Perhaps he or she could release money?

'What a mess,' he muttered to himself, getting up and clearing away the breakfast dishes. As he washed them up, it occurred to him that if he had a similar emergency, there'd be no one to care for him either. He had no siblings, no wife. He hadn't seen a doctor in years, or a solicitor. The last will he'd made was when Fran was alive.

He went out to the car, running along the narrow track of lane through the rain to the parking area near the beach. The tide was in and the bay was deserted under a low grey sky. He drove up to the shop and asked if they had a bottle of Macallan. The answer was no. That evening, he told himself, he'd go into Padstow. He needed to stock up on food anyway. In the meantime, he had a job to do at Chalfont Edge. The bottle was for Isabelle.

The day before, after their conversation about Ruskin, Isabelle had come up with a plan to enable him to work on larger pieces. She would clear a corner of her studio – or he could, she'd added, smiling.

'I'll be up in the morning,' he'd promised.

All the way there he thought of Christine and what a bloody awful neighbour he was turning out to be. He ought to have been driving in the other direction over Bodmin Moor and back to Weirpoint, so that he'd be there when she woke up. He kept thinking of what the doctor had said about her heart condition, and about the way she'd looked in the hospital bed, suddenly fragile and wrestling with her words. It was a God-awful situation. What were the chances she'd even survive the operation?

As he pulled into the drive of Chalfont Edge – waiting at the gate for the Post Office van to turn into the road away from the house – he sat cursing himself for his indecision. Christine had always been in his corner, even while fighting her own doubts. She'd been a rock after Fran died. She'd even hugged him after the road accident that set all last year's horrible events in motion. And he couldn't even be at her bedside when she was afraid.

He looked in the driving mirror. 'You heartless sod,' he told his reflection, and got out of the car. He'd go inside and tell Isabelle.

He ought to be in Weirpoint, not here.

The side door that Isabelle had encouraged him to use was locked. He used the key she'd given him. As he went in, he called out Isabelle's name.

There was no reply.

He went to the kitchen and found it empty. He went out to the hall, and called her name again. His voice echoed up the stairwell. There was no Max either. He quickly went through the downstairs rooms, and noticed letters on the mat by the front door. He picked them up and looked at them. One or two circulars and a white envelope with the franked stamp of Truro hospital. He put them on the side table. Then he stopped and listened. There was a draught coming along the hall from somewhere. He walked past the other rooms and came to the back door. It was open, and its gentle tapping against the door frame was the sound he had heard.

The door to the studio was open too. He looked in and saw only the room as they had left it yesterday, nothing missing. The car installation was an explosion of colour. His own painting, a mass of blue and fractured light. Thomas hesitated, an awful certainty gathering in his mind. He'd heard this kind of stillness before.

The stillness of sudden absence, as if the house was a living thing that had suddenly stopped breathing. It wasn't something you could quantify, but he knew exactly what it was. Years of walking into the houses of the dead had taught him.

He went to the back door and looked out. A path ran directly towards a beech hedge with a gate in the centre. The gate was open, swinging slowly backwards and forwards in the wind. He walked down the path and out into an old herb garden, shielding his eyes from the rain. Beyond the gate, the land sloped downwards onto a lawn with some sort of summerhouse at the far end. Nobody had cut the grass here for years. It was knee high and full of weeds.

Two giant copper beech in the centre of the grass were just coming into leaf. All around the edge were rose beds, wildly overgrown, the soil obscured by rotting beech leaves. He ran to the summerhouse, feeling a sick apprehension, but the door was locked. Inside were stacked garden chairs. Nothing had been touched here since last summer. Then, at the edge of the rose bed, he saw Max. The dog was hunched down, lying among the weeds and leaves, drenched to the skin.

'Hey,' he called. 'Max. What's the matter? What happened? Come here, boy.'

The dog skittered backwards, tangling itself in the rose trailers. Thomas took a couple of steps towards him.

'Come here, Max,' he said quietly.

He turned and looked back towards the house.

Isabelle was lying in the grass, face down, almost under the beech hedge. His heart thudded. Her feet were bare and she was dressed in what seemed to be a thin dressing gown with the hem of a nightdress showing underneath. One arm was underneath her, the other flung to one side. She was soaked through, her short grey hair matted with blood. He stood for more than a minute, looking from her to the gate and the house, wiping the rain out of his eyes. There were no discernible footprints in the grass near him. But that didn't mean they weren't there.

He edged slowly towards her, looking about himself at the ground. When he got closer, he could see that the sole of one foot had been bleeding. He crouched down and felt for a pulse. Nothing at all, and her skin was icy cold. She had run down the path, he thought. By the state of her clothes, perhaps during the night or very much earlier that morning. Out of the house and down the path to the open gate and, turning to her left, run through the long grass for no more than half a dozen paces. If it had been dark she was perhaps trying to hide in the stretch of woodland beyond the garden. But at that point, he guessed, whoever it was who was chasing her had hit her in the back of the head.

'Isabelle,' he murmured, even though it was no use.

He took out his phone.

10

IT DIDN'T TAKE THEM LONG.

Until they arrived Thomas paced in the hall, then went to the front door, undoing the resistant bolts. He had managed to coax Max out of the garden and into the house. Grabbing a tea towel from the kitchen, he had rubbed him down. The dog shook persistently. His lead had been by the back door and Thomas fastened it to his collar and then the handle of the door, in case the dog wanted to be near Isabelle out there in the rain and ran out again. He squatted down and stroked Max's head, and pulled the dog bed close so that Max could lie down. He didn't, however. He stood shivering and looking out towards the back of the house.

'It's okay,' Thomas murmured. 'It's okay.' Even though it wasn't.

Finally he heard the cars, and opened the door. The detective was a woman of about forty or so, white-blond hair tied back, short, and square in the face. She introduced herself as DI Laura Cullen. Her sergeant, James Mills, was the opposite: tall, slim, dark. Thomas let them in and the two shook the rain from an umbrella.

'Uniforms here?' Cullen asked.

'In the garden.'

'You'd better show us.'

They went down the hall and past the kitchen. Max whined pitifully.

The thing Thomas felt most – really, more than anything else, even the shock – was guilt at leaving Isabelle where she was. It made him sick to the stomach. He wanted to pick her up and wrap her in something. Absurd, of course. But the contrast between the uniformed officers who'd secured the scene and her thin body soaked in the grass was awful.

'I've got this overwhelming urge to move her,' he admitted to the detective.

'Thank goodness you knew better,' Cullen replied. She walked to the nearest officers and spoke to them. They seemed to shake their heads at every question. She looked around at the garden. A cordon had been set up to preserve the scene.

'Forensics are here,' said the sergeant. They stepped aside as the team moved forward, then Cullen nodded towards the house. 'Any objection to taking your DNA?'

'None at all. Do you want my clothes?'

'Have you a spare set here?'

'No.'

'Then Mills will follow you home.'

'All right.'

You're in the frame, he thought to himself. It gave him an odd, unaccustomed sensation. Vulnerability. Now he knew what it was like on the other side of the fence.

'Am I a suspect?'

She smiled briefly. 'Routine,' she replied. 'Let's talk.'

They sat in the drawing room, since Thomas had told them that Isabelle never used the room. Max settled by his side. 'Anything look out of place?' Mills asked.

'I don't think so.'

They sat on the edge of the dusty sofas.

'When did you last see Lady Crosby?'

'Yesterday afternoon.'

'How did she seem?'

'Just as usual.' He paused. 'I've only actually met her a handful of times. She invited me here to talk about an exhibition.'

He went through their conversations. He took them to the studio. He said that she had told him that she had Hodgkin's. When prompted further, he told them about Aiden Ruskin, only because it had been part of their conversation. And he told them that Isabelle had given him a key to the house.

Cullen raised her eyebrows. 'When she'd only known you less than a week?'

'I was due to use the studio. She knew my work.' Self-consciously, he pointed out *Riverside*. Cullen and Mills looked at it blankly and without comment. They'd done the same when they saw the whole contents of the room, even the Tate exhibit. They walked back to the drawing room. On the way, Cullen pointed at the back door. 'You came through here?'

'Yes.'

'You let us in through the front. Would Isabelle have opened that door?'

'Never. Or almost never. I knocked and she opened it to me on the first day, but told me to use the side door afterwards. I had a job to budge it to let you in.'

'Why?'

'Why what?'

'Why tamper with the front door? Why not wait for us outside?'

He didn't have an answer for her. He was aware he should have touched as little as possible, but he didn't think that even a complete stranger would try the heavy door. They would reason that there must be easier points of entry. He said so.

Cullen narrowed her eyes. 'Take me through this morning.'

He told her when he'd arrived and what he'd done. And how he'd found Isabelle.

'I checked for a pulse,' he explained. 'It was obvious she was dead.'

'It's not always obvious,' Mills pointed out.

'I know that,' he replied. He was actually at that moment remembering a man lying prone in a children's playground early one morning, absolutely still. It must be twenty years ago now. A very cold December day, and frost on the man's coat. He stank of alcohol. When Thomas had touched him he'd suddenly opened his eyes.

'Is something amusing?' Cullen asked.

'No,' he told her. 'No. Something completely irrelevant. Sorry.' Cullen frowned at him.

'I don't mean to be disrespectful,' he murmured. 'She was a nice person. I liked her. Individual. Interesting.'

'In what way?'

'Because,' he began, 'she'd had a life. Was still living it. She had opinions. Experience.'

'You've some experience yourself,' Cullen observed.

'Thirty odd years.'

'And you retired…?'

He told her. Ten years ago now. She glanced at her phone. 'The case last year. Near Asham Ferry. That's you, isn't it?'

'Yes.'

'It was linked to ten years before that.'

He looked at her, raised an eyebrow.

'I know Richard Ellis from way back,' she said. 'Your name rang a bell. The location at Asham. I've been to that beach myself, doing the coast walk. It stuck in my mind.'

'You've spoken to Richard?' Ellis was his one-time colleague, the man who'd been embroiled in the case last year.

'On the way here. Just doing my job.'

'Nothing personal, right?' He smiled at her. He'd have done it himself.

'Where do you think Helen McAllister went?' she asked.

'We never knew.'

She changed the subject. 'Do you know anyone with a grudge against Lady Crosby?'

'I don't. I don't really know her or her past. I don't even know if she had family.'

'A half-brother in South Africa, apparently.'

'We didn't discuss that.'

'Just art. And this Ruskin man?'

'And her friend Greta Brodie.'

The two officers glanced at each other. 'Greta Brodie, the drowning?'

'That's right. I've rented one of the cottages that Greta Brodie owned. Aiden Ruskin lives next door.'

'I know Mr Ruskin,' Cullen said.

It was the first time she'd mentioned it. She'd given no other reaction when he'd said the name, and she didn't elaborate now.

Thomas carried on. 'She told me that Ruskin came here to ask where his wife was. Or partner, I understand. She went missing after her grandmother's funeral.'

'Why did he think that she knew?'

Thomas shrugged. He couldn't say for sure. It was only a hunch.

'Did she say he was annoyed?'

'Yes.'

'With her specifically?'

'She said that his partner, Keira, had come here a few times to help her grandmother.'

'I see. And why did she tell you all this?'

'We were discussing Mr Ruskin. She asked me if I liked him.'

'And do you?'

'Something doesn't sit right.'

She pursed her lips for a second. 'Copper's nose?'

He shrugged again.

'Could he be aggressive?' Cullen asked.

'I'm not going to guess. I don't know him well enough.'

'But did she say he was aggressive to her when he came here? Threatening?'

'No, she didn't. She just said he "demanded" to know where his wife was.'

'Demanded is stronger than simply asking, would you say?'

'Yes.'

DI Cullen said something in a low voice to her sergeant. He nodded. 'Lady Crosby reported him for coming here after the funeral, so I'd guess he was quite a nuisance.' She paused. 'Have you spoken with him?'

'Briefly.'

'Recently?'

'Yes.'

'How was his mood?'

He tried to frame it correctly. 'He seemed tense. Perhaps bitter.'

'Over what?'

'The subject of his wife – partner.'

'Anything else?'

'He mentioned Greta Brodie by name. He said she was stubborn.'

In the silence, Thomas looked at the stopped clock on the mantelpiece. His eyes ranged over the mirror above it, and the ornaments on a cabinet to the left of the fireplace. They looked antique. And expensive. He reasoned that whoever had been in the house late yesterday evening, or early this morning, was after Isabelle and her alone. There was a fortune sitting in this room, more than enough for your average burglar. And there must be things in the other rooms, the ones she hadn't shown him. The medieval hall. The library. The Georgian portraits too would be worth something. He frowned, and stared down at the carpet.

'Something bothering you?' Cullen asked.

'Only that they weren't after money. Just her.'

'Well,' she murmured. 'Let's not leap to conclusions.'

They got up. He was told to stay in the area and keep away from Isabelle's house. He thought of Christine and the journey he was supposed to be making, but decided not to raise it. He'd ring the hospital. At the door, Cullen asked for the house keys that Isabelle Crosby had given him. He handed them over.

'You'll be all right with the dog?' Cullen asked. 'We can always take him to the pound.'

'Isabelle would hate that. I'll look after him for a while, at least.'

'Fair enough,' Cullen responded, and walked away.

Max was obediently waiting where he'd been put. Thomas adjusted the lead, coiling it around his hand in case the dog refused to budge, but he needn't have worried. Max followed him out of the house, head and tail low.

At the car, however, Max planted both front feet in the gravel of the drive, an unrelenting protest despite them both getting steadily soaked. Eventually Thomas relented and allowed him to jump into the passenger footwell. He laid his hand on his head. 'Let's go home,' he said.

The rain hammered on the car roof.

He drove down the road slower than usual, with Mills in a car following him.

Water was streaming down the hill like a river.

11

THEY HADN'T HAD A DECENT CATCH for months. Archie kept nagging him, in that sly insistent way of his, to get in touch with Keira Brodie.

'She's ready to set up her own business,' he told Aiden one night after dinner. 'Looking at a little gallery off Sloane Street. Word is she's bought it.'

'Christ! How much did that set her back?'

'Eight hundred thousand. Tiny place, and a wreck.'

'She's refurbishing it?'

'Would have to.'

Aiden whistled between his teeth. 'More than a million then.'

'More than, easy.'

'Where's it all coming from?'

'Keddington's dying, they say. She's got the clearance brief.'

'What, the whole house?'

'So the story goes.'

They looked at each other. 'Hence the gallery,' Aiden muttered. 'Branching out. Aren't we the brave little businesswoman?'

'Hence the gallery,' Archie agreed.

'Selling his stuff?'

'Well,' Archie said, steepling his fingers as he regarded him over the dinner table. 'Why don't you find out?'

Aiden rang her mobile the next day, the number she'd given him in Paris. He apologised for the months of delay. 'I've been out of the country.'

She said nothing.

'Greece, Tunisia.'

'Oh,' she replied. He imagined that rosy little face, quite childlike in its way. He remembered her blushing.

'It is all right to ring this number? You gave it to me.' She said nothing. 'I've been working,' he said. He didn't want to come across as an amateur, or someone who had the time to swan about Europe on a breeze.

There was another long silence. At last she murmured, 'Mr Ruskin, I'm about to go into a meeting.'

'It's Aiden, please. Did you have a nice Christmas?' he asked.

'Sorry?'

'A nice Christmas?'

A small exhalation of breath. Whether she was laughing at him, or just exasperated, was hard to tell. 'Yes. I went home.'

'Ah,' he said. '*I must go down to the sea again, the lonely sea and the sky.*'

'I'm sorry, I really must go.'

'What are you doing tonight?' he asked. It was Valentine's Day. He suggested meeting her at South Kensington Tube station after work. 'I won't embarrass you by waiting directly outside the V&A.'

'Whatever for?' she said. 'How do you know I'm there today?'

Because he'd asked around. He didn't tell her that. 'How about dinner?'

'Dinner?'

'Please. A very quick bite to eat.'

In the background, he heard a heavy door open and close, and a trio of muted voices – a woman, and two men. *Clients*, he thought.

'Just a drink, then?'

She hung up.

He left work early and walked down the walkway leading from

the museum that ran parallel to the road. In the winter before Christmas there was always a skating rink nearby; it was bleak now though, in the dreary drizzle of a February night.

He had bought an enormous bouquet of roses. People were parting to let him past. He stood there hoping that she hadn't left early and had long ago made for South Kensington along this path. Then, after twenty minutes, he saw her coming quickly along, her coat collar pulled up. She was wearing expensive-looking knee-length black boots. He liked that. He liked the boots.

He held the bouquet in front of his face. He let her get within a couple of feet – she was stepping to the side to let him pass – when he lowered the bouquet and held it out to her. 'For you.'

But she didn't take it. 'For me,' she echoed, surprised and frowning.

He laughed in what he hoped was a charming, artless way. 'Well, you're supposed to take them.'

'But...'

'What?'

'I haven't seen you in months.'

'I know,' he said. 'There's so much time to make up.'

He didn't allow her to agree with him. Or disagree, for that matter. He took her arm as if they were already a couple, turning her back in the direction he wanted to go. She resisted, stopped. The bouquet kept clipping the bodies of people who passed. It was so ungainly and had such weight that he couldn't grasp it properly in his one free hand. She looked embarrassed by the attention they were getting, but also by the amazing inappropriateness of the gift. She kept glancing at it as if he'd tried to hand her a ticking time bomb. Which it was, of course.

'What's the matter?' he asked. 'We need to hurry. The restaurant booking is at seven, and we've got a way to go.'

'Mr Ruskin,' she said. 'I can't accept these.'

He tried to look astonished. 'Why not?'

'And I don't want to go to dinner.'

He rocked back on his heels as if she'd slapped him. 'Oh, I'm sorry.'

'I'm going home,' she said. 'Excuse me.'

He smiled at her. 'You're quite a stubborn little thing, aren't you?'

She gave him a look of pure ice. 'I'm not stubborn,' she replied. 'And I'm not a thing.'

'No, of course.'

She indicated the flowers. 'What on earth were you thinking? Did someone else stand you up?'

'No! They're for you. We'd arranged to meet.'

'Actually, we hadn't,' she pointed out. 'I thought you might take the hint. I'm afraid you've wasted your time.' She looked again at the bouquet. 'And your money.'

He nodded, thinking, *I never do that. That's the last thing I do.*

'Look,' he said, 'I know I'm no good at this. I thought it might be over the top. I knew that it might be. But I was in the shop. I saw them in the window, and I thought of you. I thought they might persuade you that I was serious. I didn't want to get some poxy bunch from the station.'

'Serious?' she repeated, frowning again, puzzled. 'I don't understand you. I don't want flowers at all, Mr Ruskin. I don't know you.'

'But Paris? You remember? You do remember, I know you do. You just said that you hadn't seen me in months. Please call me Aiden.'

They stepped to the side to let the crowds past them. He leaned against the stone pillar and gazed at her. 'I told you I was clumsy.'

'You were right.'

He gave a gesture of helplessness. 'I've got to start somewhere,' he said suddenly. 'But I don't know how. You frighten me.'

Now, at last, she laughed. 'I doubt that.'

'You do. I've made a mess here. Forgive me. I'll put the flowers in a bin.'

She shook her head at the expression of pitiful pleading on his face. 'This is stupid.'

'It is. It *is* stupid.'

He gripped the bouquet more tightly and turned to the first woman walking along. She was middle-aged, rather glamorous, tapping along in high heels. 'May I foist an unwanted gift on you?' he asked. 'Or else they'll be thrown in the street.'

The woman took the flowers and raised her eyebrows at Keira. 'Are you serious?' she said to her. 'I'll take the flowers *and* him if you want.'

The three of them stood in the freezing walkway, getting in everyone's way. The woman smelled the flowers and over the top of them she smiled at Aiden.

He smiled back, but offered his arm to Keira.

'For God's sake,' Keira muttered. 'Just a drink.'

12

SITTING IN THE COTTAGE LATER, THOMAS had the phone in his hand, staring out of the window. He had rung the hospital. The operation had gone well, but Christine was sleeping. He had explained to the nurse that a friend had been killed – even as he said the word it sounded unreal – and he had listened to the commiserations on the other end of the line. He had promised to ring again in the morning and asked them to pass on his best wishes.

By his side, Isabelle's dog looked at him with patient expectation.

There was so much unknown and waiting to be known, and he had that crippling feeling of last autumn in the lee of the storm, as ignorant as anyone about where Helen McAllister had gone, as horrified too. The newspapers talking about the deaths. Reporters at the door. He'd felt wrapped up, fenced in by killing. His own house had crushed down on him.

He'd spent the most miserable Christmas of his life thinking about his loneliness in a rut of self-pity. He would go out and walk up the road into the village and circle back along a little-used lane, past a farm that had a sign on the wall saying they were poultry suppliers to a supermarket. He stood at that gate a couple of times thinking of the years when he and Fran had got their turkey from here, and it now struck him that it was a bizarre and bloody business. Bloody and murderous. All kinds of twisted conclusions like that came into his mind. Once, walking in an afternoon of chilling sleet along the same muddy lane, he'd thought of burying

Helen McAllister, getting hold of her somehow and putting her under the ground. He was bitter. Helen had vanished. That was all that anyone knew.

Instinctively now, he reached down again to touch the dog.

He was standing in the kitchen making himself tea an hour later when he saw Cullen's car pull up in the lane. He watched her walk to Ruskin's gate, then heard her knocking. It lasted a long time. Then he saw her walk out again and come along to his own cottage. He went to the door and opened it before she had a chance to knock.

'Come in,' he said.

She accepted a mug of tea. When he sat down next to her in the cramped space, she took the tea and drank it in silence, then asked, 'Have you seen him?'

'No.'

'Heard him at all today next door?'

'No.'

'Any ideas where he is?'

'His car has gone.'

'Yes. We're onto it. Did you hear him go out in the night?'

'No.' And he immediately wondered if Ruskin had missed his early morning walk. He'd heard nothing at all and woken late, noticing that Ruskin's car wasn't in the driveway only later when he went out himself. He told Cullen.

She sighed. She seemed apathetic. Or perhaps just tired. 'Did Lady Crosby mention anyone else visiting her?'

'Never. Well – just Greta Brodie and her granddaughter last year.'

'Keira Brodie also seems to be missing. Did Lady Crosby tell you where she is?'

'No. But I'm sure she had nothing to do with this.'

Cullen put her mug of tea firmly back on the table. 'Oh, you know that, do you?'

'No, of course not. Just speculation.'

'Did you used to make a habit of ruling people out on the basis of speculation?' She didn't expect an answer, and didn't get one. She sat back and examined her hands, flexing them as if she were cold.

'I only say that because Isabelle said she didn't know where Keira had gone after she left her house, and it immediately looked like a lie to me.' He paused. 'I think she'd have been quite distressed if Keira was genuinely missing as far as she knew. And she wasn't distressed. She was defensive.'

'Protecting her?'

'I don't know. Perhaps.'

Cullen took a manila A4 envelope from her bag. It had his name written on the front. 'We found this,' she said. 'It doesn't seem to have any relevance except that it's dated yesterday. But maybe you know better, since you know so much.'

He took it. He didn't like her tone. 'You've got a problem with me, have you?' he asked.

She sighed. 'Please have a look and tell me if there's any significance.'

It was a bulky item. Opening it, he found about a dozen photographs, a couple of postcards and a small guidebook. Venice.

It really touched him. He spread the photographs out – evidently her own. The Rialto Bridge crowded with tourists, the Grand Canal. Other places he didn't recognise. He turned each one over. He looked up at Cullen. 'She must have sorted these last night. We only talked about Venice yesterday.'

Cullen picked each one up. 'Any particular meaning to you in these?'

'She had said that I should go.'

'But why these particular places in Venice?'

'I've no idea. Colour? Paintings?' He turned to the two postcards. One of her own house in much better days. One of

Maggi Hambling's *Scallop* sculpture on the beach at Aldeburgh. There was a leaflet too, about a V&A exhibition.

'Aldeburgh?' she asked.

'She told me that I ought to see more places. I suppose she wanted me to see the sculpture rather than the town.'

'And the V&A?'

'I don't know. She liked art. History.' He was glancing at an image from the leaflet. *Henry Willett's Collection of Popular Pottery.*

Cullen pushed all the images back to him. 'If you think of anything, let me know,' she said. She turned, and got to the door before she looked back. 'With anyone else I'd search this house.'

'Be my guest,' he told her.

'I wouldn't expect an ex-detective to keep evidence,' she said.

'I wouldn't, if I'd killed her.'

'Did you?'

He sat with crossed arms staring at her.

She opened the door. 'Thank you for the tea,' she said.

After she'd gone, he went out to his car, taking Max with him.

He drove down the coast all the way to Bedruthan Steps. Max seemed to know the place – he negotiated the steep cliff more confidently than Thomas himself. When they reached the bottom Thomas let him off the lead and the dog ran joyously out across the sand, splashing through tidal pools and barking at the sea. A strong Atlantic wind was blowing and the white rollers were up. The sky was clearing. For a minute or two, walking head down against the wind, eyes screwed against the sudden blast of sun, Thomas lost the dog. He eventually found him lolling in a pool with an expression of delight on his face.

'You daft animal,' Thomas said, laughing. He clipped the lead back on. They walked right along the beach for almost a mile between the huge sea stacks, and eventually sat down on the thinnest fringe of dry sand he could find. The dog slumped against him. It was a long time since he'd felt any living thing so close.

He missed contact like that. The warmth of it. He sometimes stayed downstairs deliberately until past midnight. Not because he was afraid of the sight of an empty bed, but because it lacked the comfort of Fran next to him. He hated himself for being so morose about it, for hanging back every night until weariness drove him upstairs. It was no good crying. What bloody use was it? What could it solve? He came from a generation that had been taunted for showing tears. And yet sitting here now with Max and the sea rolling in front of him, he felt completely choked with sorrow. Not just for Fran but for Isabelle and, less strongly but still poignantly, for John Lord and his brother. He wanted to shut them all out. He wanted to put Fran away somewhere. Somewhere safe where he could look at her and not feel that familiar twist in his gut. He heard the far distant voice of his mother in his head telling him to be a grown-up boy. He put one hand over his face, clutching Max's fur in the other.

'Thomas?' said a voice.

He looked up to see Bill Pascoe bending over him.

'You all right, Thomas?'

He was going to say that he was fine, but he couldn't.

'Hey, old chap.' Pascoe put a hand on his shoulder. Next to him, his own dog was jumping about as if on springs. 'Hush up, Pat. Bloody fool.'

Max had got to his feet. Thomas unsteadily copied him.

'Let them run, eh?' Pascoe said. Thomas let Max off the leash, and they watched the two dogs chasing each other in wild circles.

'Your dog?' Pascoe asked. He was still frowning in concern.

'He belongs to Isabelle Crosby. Belonged.'

'Oh, aye? She given him to you or what?'

'Isabelle Crosby died this morning. The police let me take him.'

Thomas wiped his face. 'I found them both in her garden. She'd been attacked sometime during the night.'

'Christ in heaven!' Pascoe patted his shoulder. 'You did? No wonder you're in a state.'

'It's not that. Not just that. It's...' He paused. 'Been a shit year.'

They walked back towards the steps together. After a while the dogs, panting hard, followed them.

'Listen,' Pascoe said before they began the climb. 'You ever want to talk, come and see me. It's your wife, is it? Never goes away.'

Thomas nodded. 'It's been a long time now. I want to find a place that doesn't...'

'Trip you up every fucking day.'

At the sound of Pascoe swearing, Thomas looked at him in surprise.

'It doesn't go away,' Pascoe said. 'Don't try to make it.'

They went home to Pascoe's house, Thomas following him back to the village in his own car. The older man sat Thomas down, gave him a brandy and made up a fire. He took Max away and fed him along with his own dog. As the room warmed up Thomas felt himself drifting off to sleep. By the time he woke up it was dark and the curtains were drawn. Pascoe came in and smiled. 'Made us something to eat.'

'You didn't have to do that. Sorry for this afternoon.'

'Nonsense. Stay where you are.' He had brought in a plate of stew and roast potatoes and gave Thomas the tray.

'Where did you learn to cook like this?'

'Necessity,' Pascoe told him. 'Did you eat lunch?'

'No.'

'Eat, then. Can't do without decent grub.'

He did as he was told. When they had finished, Thomas asked him if he had internet connection. There was none at the cottage, and only a poor phone signal. Pascoe brought out his own laptop. 'Ruskin not fitted you with a connection?'

'My phone tells me there's one nearby.'

'That'll be him.'

Thomas shrugged. 'Being cut off is a relief in some ways.'

'But now you need to see something?'

'The police gave me an envelope,' Thomas explained. 'Photographs, and a Victoria and Albert museum leaflet. Addressed to me from Isabelle. The photos were of Venice, and we'd been talking about it just a few hours before. I said I didn't know the place. I've been wondering about the significance of the leaflet, though.'

Together, they looked up the V&A exhibition. Henry Willet, it seemed, had been a prolific nineteenth-century collector of objects.

'Why was Lady Crosby interested in this?' Pascoe asked.

'I think she was a Friend, a regular visitor.'

'But why this one exhibition?'

'I don't know.' They clicked on each image that came up on the website.

The only thing that really caught Thomas's interest was a terracotta model of something called the *Tichborne Claimant*. They were no wiser until they searched it and found a man who had claimed to be Lady Tichborne's long-lost son in 1865 after being lost at sea and turning up as a bankrupt butcher in Australia.

'Fraud,' Pascoe murmured. 'Sounds like a chancer. Was that all there was in the envelope?'

'Just a postcard of a sculpture in Aldeburgh.'

'Any significance?'

'That's what the police asked me. None that I can think of.'

'And why did they bring that especially?'

'It was dated yesterday.'

Pascoe stretched out his feet and sighed. 'You're the last person to see a dead woman. Always going to be a suspect. Got an alibi?'

'At home alone.' He gave Pascoe a half-smile. 'I was a suspect last year, too. Briefly.'

'Were you now? That's damn careless of you.'

Thomas told him the whole sorry story.

13

AIDEN MADE SURE THAT THINGS WENT quickly.
He took Keira out. Expensive places. He complimented her. But not too much. Keira wasn't a pushover like some. She'd be hard to take down. That made it all quite the entertainment. He didn't talk about work. That was the last thing, he understood that very well. Never to mention her success, never to talk about his trips or his sales. Never to mention names. He let her think that was something common to both of them – confidentiality in business. Obeying Archie, he toned down his look. Once he even turned up with shoes that let in water and he limped a little. He was delighted that she cooed over him and took pity, but he still noticed that slight percentage of distrust in her face, as if she couldn't quite believe him. Or, he hoped, couldn't quite believe her luck. Then, one evening, it struck him. Oh, she was lonely inside. It was the way that she talked about her grandmother as if she was the only real friend she had in the world. Once he saw it, he couldn't think how he'd missed it. Professional and smart but lonely. It was the one and only defect in her character, and it was the way in.

They went down to see Greta Brodie one summer weekend.

It was hot for June, really too hot. Keira drove with the top down on her second-hand VW Beetle, a pitted old yellow number with one bumper taped up. He couldn't believe his eyes. Here she was, everyone's favourite expert if you listened to the rumours, driving about in a rust bucket. He was ashamed to be seen in it, cringed when he opened the door. He hated the way that the gears made a grinding sound, and she refused to let him take the wheel. 'It takes skill,' she'd told him, laughing.

'What do clients think when you turn up in this?' he asked.

'They can think what they like,' she said. 'They're buying what I know, not the car.'

Learn from her, his father said. *She's got style.*

He would have liked the inside story of how she'd got Keddington's clearance brief, but she didn't give anything away. His enquiry was only a gentle nudge, but she promptly replied that Keddington was a very private person.

Of course, he knew that. Maybe Keddington had already told her that he and his father had been to visit and of how badly it had gone. Keddington, shuffling along in the ruinous place that had belonged to his family for twelve generations, seemed to suddenly decide he didn't like them. Archie had been too boot-licking, too intrusive. Claiming he'd known Keddington's father for one thing, when Keddington probably knew the two had never met. It was a clumsy move. They'd only got halfway along one of the corridors when, between rooms, Keddington had suddenly asked them to leave. He and Archie had argued in a bloody and wounding way on the way back to London, blaming each other.

But Keira… Keira had the key to that door. And she, like Keddington, had locked it against them. She couldn't be budged. Not even for all his careful persuasion. He thought he was particularly good at that. It was one of his skills. Until Keira. She could be goaded and punished in some ways. But not in business.

He didn't want to learn from her, either. He was superior to her in every way and the confines of trying to be modest irked him. He itched to show her what he could do and was dumbfounded when she seemed not to be impressed. He once pointed out a wealthy mid-European customer and she gave him a curious smile. 'Don't burn your fingers,' she told him. 'I know what I'm doing,' he retorted. He was too discomfited to ask what she meant.

Now and again he would spend a whole evening gently prodding her resistance, trying to find a weak spot like a thief trying to find where a security system may be badly designed. At first, he'd succeeded only minimally. Over the dress, for instance. She was only human after all.

They had been meeting Archie for dinner. She'd bought something new. He occupied himself making them purposely late and told her she'd delayed them. As she was locking her door and they stood outside on the steps, he looked her up and down. 'Is that new?'

'Yes,' she said. 'Do you like it?'

'It's too late now,' he told her. 'It'll have to do.'

She never wore it again. That was a disappointment to him, actually. He hoped she'd fight a bit harder and cry. She'd done that once and he'd comforted her. 'Sometimes I don't think you listen,' she'd said. 'I do,' he'd responded, holding her hand. 'I listen to you all the time. I remember what you say. Why would I not listen? You're the most wonderful person I've ever met. You're everything to me.'

He tried it again, several times. She seemed to not care about her looks, but that was just a smokescreen. She cared all right. At a gallery opening for one of her friends, he'd whispered, 'You look delicious in that dress. All wrapped up like a sweetie in a Christmas box.' She'd stared, aghast. 'It's too tight? Too bright?' He'd thrown up his hands in mock despair. 'My God, I can't even compliment you.' And another time she'd shown him her photograph in a trade paper. 'Don't you look cute?' he said. She'd frowned. 'I don't want to look cute exactly.' He'd nodded. 'No. You're right. Professional would be better. But never mind. It doesn't matter.'

He bought her flowers, of course. It was a kind of joke between them after Valentine's Day. Sometimes they'd be expensive and sometimes he might just pick something from the pavement or a park. Weeds, more often than not. And she would say it was romantic, just the single flower. Christ! She was naïve when it came to men. He kept changing his mind as to whether it was an attractive quality. He wanted her to be knowing, steely, worldly, so that he could bend her into his shape. And then he liked her childishness, the childishness and innocence that hid behind her cleverness. It was that which translated into charm for customers, he realised. And it was completely unforced. It wasn't a sales trick. It was an unusual, shifting kind of characteristic. The sharp assessment in her eyes over work. The wide-eyed surprise at other things. Insults, for instance.

'Why do you say those things?'

'What things might they be?'

'Telling jokes about older women.'

'They don't care, do they? They don't know.'

'But I know, Aiden. I hear you.'

'Spending their husbands' money. Rarely any taste at all.'

'Even so.'

Those kind of women were his bread and butter. Either the tarts clinging to a wealthy man, or a wealthy woman who ought to know better clinging to a younger man, or all of them wanting taste, his taste. Or rather Keira's taste. She had begun to advise him. They went to a few auctions together and she had an uncanny ability to know when something wasn't exactly right. It maddened him. He felt his gut screw up inside. It was her job, of course. Only her job. She wasn't trying to get one over on him. And she always pointed it out in a quiet, nice way. It wasn't personal but he took it personally. Lying in bed alone at Archie's he would think about it and he'd have to get up and pace the floor to rid himself of his insane frustration.

He took her away for the weekend. This time they'd taken his car, a new Audi. She'd smiled to herself when she'd seen it, but said nothing. He put the car through its paces, clipping the hedges of country lanes, overtaking at speed. She still said nothing. It suddenly occurred to him that he'd get a noise out of her later. She'd cry then.

They went to Rye. It was early spring. He'd booked a room in a half-timbered hotel on the outskirts. It was a rural fantasy, complete with duck pond and distant oast houses. All the blossom trees were out. If he had got himself a location manager or a scriptwriter it couldn't have been more perfect. They sat outside in the evening, wrapped up against the night chill. He'd put his arm around her. 'Would you like to live somewhere like this?'

'It's a bit far from anywhere.'

'But in the future.'

'I don't know where I'll be in the future.'

He'd turned in his seat to face her. 'But you'll be with me?'

She gave that peculiar warped smile of hers. 'Perhaps.'

'Perhaps? You're not certain?'

She wouldn't meet his gaze. 'Nobody can be that certain, Aiden.'

'But I am.'

'That's nice.'

'Nice!' He dropped his arm.

'Look, please don't get offended.'

'Why not?'

'Because…'

He took the gamble. 'Keira, I love you,' he said. 'Surely you understand.'

She bit her lip.

'You don't feel the same.'

'I would…'

'You would? You would if what?'

'This,' she told him. 'Getting annoyed.'

'Have you ever heard me lose my temper?'

'No.'

'Have I ever hurt you?'

She didn't reply.

'Oh God,' he said. 'If I ever have, I'm sorry. I told you I'm clumsy. I told you that in February. You make me that way. I can't get my head straight around you. But I can't imagine living here or anywhere without you.'

'It's not clumsiness,' she replied slowly. 'I can't put my finger on it. Sometimes you barely speak at all.'

'You think I'm secretive.'

'Yes.'

'I've got a remedy for that,' he said. 'Merge the talent. We'd be one hell of a team.' He kissed her. He took hold of her hands. 'I'll be the junior partner,' he promised. 'I'll do anything you say. I'll change. Do you want me to change? I'll always have your back. I won't even travel. I can be home warming your slippers if that's what you want. Or I'll work like a dog. Tell me what I have to do, Keira. Marry me.'

He surprised himself by how much he meant it.

She shook her head.

It was eight weeks later that they went down to Cornwall to see Greta.

He didn't know what the hell to expect. She hadn't said much about her grandmother, only that she was a gardener. He'd imagined some old woman pottering about in a vegetable patch. Someone ready to be impressed.

Keira parked in a dusty lane and they walked to two cottages set back from the road. Going down the path of the first, Keira took out a key and opened the door. He put their case down in a tiny kitchen and looked about him.

'She's not in,' Keira said. 'But I know where she is.'

They went back towards the village. Going up the main road a little way, they turned into the driveway of a house. He'd noticed it as they passed. Under the massive oak trees were two skips filled with rubble. Keira strode on ahead, calling him over her shoulder. She looked different down here. More relaxed.

'Gramma,' she shouted.

A woman emerged from a knot of people standing at the edge of a lawn. Greta Brodie was taller than her granddaughter, but not by much. She had shoulder-length grey hair and wore jeans and an oversized man's shirt. She held out her arms and the two women embraced.

'Well, here he is,' Keira said. 'This is Aiden.'

He shook Greta's hand. 'Sorry about the dust,' she said. 'We're digging a pond. Hit granite. Waiting for the digger.' She looked him up and down. 'Overdressed, aren't you?'

'I wasn't until I got here,' he said, and smiled.

'Have you got anything old with you?' she said. 'Fancy giving us a hand?'

You can fuck right off, he thought. But like a good boy he went back to the house and changed his clothes. He spent all afternoon following Greta Brodie's orders, sweating. He could feel his neck getting sunburned and longed for a drink but understood this was some sort of gladiatorial contest with a seventy-five-year-old whip carrier in charge. A test of some kind. When he cut his hand at the end of the afternoon she at last took pity on him. 'That's enough,' she said. She turned to Keira. 'Got your swimmies on?'

'Of course.'

'And what about Mr Ruskin?'

'I'll watch,' he told her.

It was when he first saw the seawater pool. It looked brilliant blue in the sunshine with its beautiful dramatic backdrop of rocky shoreline. Greta and her granddaughter peeled off their clothes to reveal the swimming costumes underneath and waded straight in, striking off across the pool with confident strokes. Keira swam back to him. 'You're really not coming in?'

'You might have told me the dress code.'

She laughed. 'You've got underwear on, haven't you?'

Another bloody test. All right, he was up for it. He peeled off the sweat-stained T-shirt and jeans, went to a rock ledge, and jumped in. The cold was shocking. He rose to the surface spluttering, his heart pounding. The two women gave him barely a glance. They were locked in deep conversation at the far edge. 'Jesus H fucking Christ,' he muttered. He floundered about for a minute or more, trying to get his breathing back under control. He lay on his back with his face turned up to the sky and wondered what was next. Lion taming, juggling fire, greased pig wrestling he didn't doubt, or whatever passed for an occupation down here in deepest tourist land, home of the wild and the free. He doubted there was a decent drink within fifty miles. Keira had told him on the way down that her grandmother swam in all weathers, rain or shine, winter or summer. He could believe it. Greta Brodie was a competitor, not an admirer. And so here he was. Come down here for a bit of tea and cake maybe, a walk on the beach perhaps, and found himself in unarmed combat.

He saw Keira dive down under the water. Squinting against the sun and shading his eyes, he glimpsed her swimming close to his feet. She caught hold of his ankle and surfaced. 'You should try it,' she said. 'It's fairyland down there.'

Greta came swimming up at a leisurely pace. 'Cooled off?' she asked.

'Yes thanks.'

'Not a swimmer?'

'Not much.'

'So I see,' she said, and pinched the flesh of his shoulder. 'My father's generation used to call that lilywhite,' she said.

'And what do you call it?'

'The same,' she told him, and got out.

That evening, when Keira went up to bed, Greta held up her hand to stop him following her.

'Can I talk to you a minute?'

'Yes, of course.' He sat down again. Here it came, the interrogation. He was expecting it. *Well come on then*, he thought, *I'm ready for you.*

She didn't beat around the bush. No false politeness.

'Keira tells me that you want to marry her.'

'I do.'

'But that she hasn't given an answer.'

'That's right.'

'Annoy you much?'

'Annoy me? No. She'll come round.'

She sat looking at him. The window was open to the garden – a beautiful garden, all her own work apparently – and he could hear the sea rushing beyond the fields. The fading heat of the day rolled in.

'Keira has her own mind,' Greta murmured. 'You think you can change it?'

'I hope I will.'

'At the risk of sounding like a Victorian father, what can you offer her? She seems to be doing very well without any help from you.'

'I know. Better than my father and I at the moment. But that isn't what marriage is about in the end, is it?'

'Isn't it?' she asked. 'When the rosy glow wears off, it's about compromise and respect and support.'

The full sermon, then.

'I give her those things already.'

She was sitting in the armchair with her legs crossed, and her uppermost foot began tapping the air. She didn't like that, she didn't agree with it. You don't trust me, he decided.

'You can trust me,' he said.

She didn't reply, but she kept her gaze on him. Perhaps that same gaze had unnerved others. But it wasn't going to deter him. The prize was there for the asking, and it wasn't going to slip out of his grasp. *How long can you live, you old witch?* he wondered. Not long with any luck.

'Tell me about your father,' she said.

14

THOMAS WAS ASLEEP IN BED THAT night when his phone rang. He'd put it on the windowsill that night in the hope that it would get a better signal, and the sound pulled him out of sleep, out of the edges of the dream. In it, he'd been on that same chalk ridge but this time with Helen and not Fran. As he came awake, he was aware of a blinding fury as bad as any migraine. He reached for the phone.

'Hello?'

'Hello, Thomas. It's Richard Ellis.'

'Richard? What's the matter? What time is it?'

'It's late. Half eleven. I'm sorry. Did I wake you?'

'Yes,' he said. He got up, the phone still to his ear. 'It's okay.'

'Look, I won't beat about the bush. Are you coming back up to your house any time soon? I need to talk to you.'

'What about?'

There was a pause. 'Can you be there?'

'Not really. I'm supposed to stay in this area. A woman I know—'

'Yes, Laura Cullen rang me.'

'She did? Again?'

'She's okay if you come home for a few days.'

He tried to digest this. The dream was still gnawing away his concentration. 'Why do you need me, Richard?' he asked eventually.

'I'm sorry, Thomas. But I've got a search warrant for your house.'

*

It was a very strange sensation to be interviewed at the same station in Brimham where he'd served so many years. He drove back at first light, stopping only when he got to the abbey town. He had to take Max with him. He'd had no answer when he rang Bill Pascoe, so he got Max in the car again where the dog sat in the footwell as before, too big to curl up and gazing at him all the while in mute sufferance.

It was barely nine o'clock when they reached Brimham and only one café was open, the same one where he'd eaten lunch or had a tea break for so many years. It was a new face at the counter though, a much younger woman than he remembered.

'What a lovely dog,' she said.

'Is he allowed in?'

'Not really. But sit down anyway.'

He took his cup and a bacon sandwich to the window seat. Having been given part of the sandwich, Max slumped to the floor and promptly began to snore. Thomas looked out of the window. He'd always liked this town, the old-fashioned nature of it. The abbey tower rising above the roofs. It was twelve hundred years old, built on an Anglo-Saxon church. There was an abbey green and clergy buildings and a fee-paying school in the grounds beyond. Good pub here too, an old one with a low doorway and open fire and CAMRA ales. The car park behind the shops on the other side of the street had pay machines that worked only with coins and the library alongside it had a noticeboard advertising whist drives and knitting circles. There was a train station here, but almost the end of a line, as if even that had given up on ever getting anywhere busier. The twenty-first century was barred at the traffic lights on the main road.

At half past nine he got up and walked down the road to the station.

Richard Ellis was waiting for him at the door. He raised his eyebrows on seeing Max.

'Isabelle Crosby's dog,' Thomas explained.

'Ah, I see.'

With Max being fussed over at the front desk, they went to the interview room.

'Do I need a solicitor?' Thomas asked, bemused.

'Up to you.'

He'd been joking. He sat back in his chair. 'Tell me what this is about,' he said.

'Your neighbour, Christine.'

'She's in hospital. She had an operation. Do you know how she is?'

'She's been sitting up in bed demanding to see me since yesterday afternoon.'

'You? What for?'

Richard sighed. There was a table between them and a folder that he had kept closed, his hands folded across it. 'This is difficult, Thomas.'

'I guessed it would have to be if you have to drag me up here.'

'She says that you killed Helen McAllister and buried her in your garden.'

He tried to look surprised, but he wasn't surprised at all. He'd half guessed as much but didn't want to believe it of Christine. The papers in her living room had made him think differently over the last few days, though. He gave a short laugh that had no humour in it at all. 'Do you know how crazy that is?'

'I have to listen to what she says. She's very angry, Thomas. She says she's been asking for you and you won't come and see her and you won't do anything about getting her out of hospital.'

'I've been to see her. And now I've been stopped because of Isabelle Crosby's death. I hope you told her that.'

'I did. I know she's elderly, Thomas, and I know she's ill and disorientated. Nevertheless…'

'I expect you've been to her house.'

'She insisted.'

'And saw all the papers, the cuttings.'

'Yes.' Richard sat back in his chair. 'You know about them?'

'I went in there when the hospital first called me. I tidied the kitchen. There was food rotting.' He stopped. 'I thought then that it was unlike her. She's been distracted for some months.'

'Distracted how? Upset with you?'

'No. Forgetful.'

'What are you getting at? That she doesn't know what she's saying now? She seemed pretty much on the ball when I spoke to her. Eloquent, in fact.'

'When I saw the cuttings I thought it looked obsessive. I had no idea she was thinking that. We were friends.'

'And yet she thinks you've committed this crime.'

'Evidently.'

Richard continued to look uncomfortable. 'Will I find anything?' he asked.

'Good God, Richard. Investigate if you must, but don't ask me that.'

'Nothing to tell me?'

'Do you seriously think that all through our investigation I knew where Helen McAllister was? That I'd somehow spirited her back to my house and killed her? And lied to you all?'

Kill me.

Why don't you kill me?

Richard scratched his head, and then tapped his index finger on his lips, a gesture that Thomas remembered. 'Christine says that you were digging in the patch of ground at the bottom of the garden after McAllister disappeared. She's got it in her head about your affair. She asked me how someone could just vanish and why hadn't we suspected you at the time.'

'You did.'

'Not me, Thomas.'

'Plenty of others.'

'There was nothing taken seriously.'

Thomas felt pity for his former sergeant, but not enough to let it go. 'Why not?' he asked.

'Sorry?'

'Why didn't you suspect me, Richard?'

'Because you were incapable of it.'

Thomas shook his head. 'That's bad policing.'

'It's good instinct.'

'I've had a lecture from your friend Cullen about speculation,' Thomas said.

Richard was watching him intently. 'Christine didn't come forward until now,' he pointed out. 'She's presented us with what she insists is evidence. She says you were very secretive.'

'I didn't discuss cases with anyone. Not even Fran.'

'I get the impression from the staff that she was asking for you, and when you didn't come—'

'She accuses me.'

'But it isn't just the accusation now, Thomas,' Richard said. 'The stuff in the house shows she's harboured suspicion for some time. I have to follow this up.'

'Then you think you have grounds.'

'She's telling the staff at the hospital that you got away with it. I had to persuade her not to go to the newspapers.'

'Succumbing to pressure?'

Richard looked affronted. He sat up straighter. 'Yes, all right then,' he said. 'I can't ignore it. I do have grounds.'

15

KEIRA TOOK AIDEN TO SEE THE gallery.
He had asked her – in what he complimented himself as being a perfectly offhand way – if she would show him her new prize.

To be fair she was modest about it. They went there one foggy morning in October. All the leaves on the trees were changing colour. It sat back from the street slightly, a narrow Georgian frontage just the width of a window and a door, but it went back for twice the depth of a normal property. She told him that it used to be a farriers.

'A farrier?' he'd said. 'In central London?'

'There were three hundred thousand horses in London in 1900. They had to get re-shod somewhere.'

'Uh-huh,' he said. He always made that noise when he wanted to smack her. She used a tone of voice he didn't like, a sing-song sound, making fun of him with a smile. Sometimes she would nudge him as if prompting him to stay awake. 'If you think about it there must have been loads.'

'Uh-huh,' he said.

They walked through. The walls were stripped back to bare brick. She told him that someone had tried to renovate and given up.

'Why?'

'Why what?'

'Why did they give up?'

'Money, apparently. But they rewired, put in an office and a loo. See?' She was standing right at the back, pointing out a tiny room. 'Look at that.'

'What am I looking at?'

'This!' She walked over to the far wall and patted the top of an iron box painted a thick, viscous-looking green. 'It's a safe.'

She opened the back door. There was a small cobbled floor, the remnants of a yard. The walls were eight-feet high and backed on to the rear of an anonymous grey block. 'Offices,' she said. 'But I'm not overlooked.'

He looked back into the room with the safe. There was a table and two chairs. 'We should christen it,' he told her.

'I haven't brought anything.'

'Yes you have,' he said. He wrapped an arm around her waist and pulled her to him. 'I think we have everything we need.'

'Aiden,' she said.

'There's a table. And a floor.'

'A dirty floor and a dusty table.'

She was wriggling.

He walked her back forcibly. 'Or there's a wall.'

'What? No. No.' She protested a bit more, but not enough to mean anything. He had her on the floor and she lay quiet. She was so pretty with that crushed-looking mouth and flushed face. It didn't take long. If she was disappointed, she never said anything. She always seemed shocked or thoughtful in her peculiar, vacant way. Afterwards, she sat up with her back to the wall and tidied her clothes and he kneeled over her and stopped her.

'You are a brute,' she told him in a soft voice.

'I can do better.'

'You can be a better brute?'

'Always.'

*

121

'Listen,' he said later, when they were sitting in an Italian restaurant by the river. 'We should go halves on the gallery.'

She stopped what she was doing, turning a glass around in her fingers, and asked him what he meant.

'Exactly what I say. I want to help you. I told you that. Even in the state it's in, it must be costing a fortune.'

'I have enough.'

'How? How could you have the money? You mean a mortgage?'

'I'm giving up my flat. I'm going to live in the gallery. There's a room upstairs. I'll put in a shower.'

'You only rent your flat. Where's the cost of buying the gallery coming from?'

'I have enough,' she repeated. 'But actually, it's none of your business.'

It floored him. The almost casual way that she said it. She was looking away from him.

'Keira,' he said. 'Look at me.' She did, with her chin dipped. Looked at him from under her lashes like Bambi. If she thought it was a way to get around him, she was wrong. He grabbed hold of her hand. 'Listen to me,' he said. 'I know it's your business, but you can't live there alone. You can't run a business alone. Why should you? I told you I want to help. Why won't you let me help? I want us to be together. I want us to run the gallery together.'

'It's my place,' she murmured.

'But you must be stretched handling all that by yourself. I can give you half. Don't you want a partner, someone to support you?'

'I'll manage, Aiden.'

'But that's what I'm saying. You don't have to manage. It must be so lonely by yourself. And it's not safe.'

'Why is it not safe?'

'Oh, come on now,' he told her. 'A woman alone. You'll have builders in and they'll soon see that you're alone and they'll take advantage of you.'

She smiled. 'That's paranoid, Aiden.'

'Am I paranoid in wanting to protect you?'

'Yes.'

He shook his head as if despairing of a small child wanting independence. 'You see, that's how you think. You're too innocent, Keira. You need me.'

'It's kind of you, but I don't need help. I'm hardly innocent.'

He let go of her hand. 'You are so bloody insulting.'

Now, she looked up directly. 'I'm not insulting you.'

'Oh yes,' he said. 'You don't want me.'

'Aiden, please don't start this.'

'I'm not good enough. Tell me why I'm not good enough.'

'Let me do this on my own. It's been my dream. Please, Aiden.'

'You don't think I'll bring anything to the business. You don't like my contacts. You turn your nose up at them. You won't let me come with you to see Keddington. You correct me when I want to bid for something. You're not interested in what I *can* do, the Middle Eastern art.' He knew he was raising his voice and that other customers were looking at him, but he didn't care. He made a fist on the table. 'I've got a couple of paintings, they're good paintings. I could get a lot more for them in the right setting, like the gallery. But I suppose they won't be good enough for you.'

'Aiden, you can put a painting in the gallery if you want. Let me see it.'

'You see? This is what I mean. You want to vet it first because you don't trust my judgement.'

'I appreciate—'

'No,' he said. 'No, you don't appreciate. You don't appreciate at all. I've got experience. Six years of commercial experience since I left Uni. I've got a degree in art history. It might not be a First, it might not be from Oxford—'

'That's unfair.'

'Is it? I'm the same as you. I never had rich parents backing me either. My father doesn't count. He keeps a lot from me. I'm stifled. I want my own way, my own business. I can't set up completely on my own. I can't afford that. But I could afford to help you. If you won't take half, take a third.'

She shook her head slowly.

'Is it your grandmother?'

'Is *what* my grandmother?'

'She doesn't like me. She's told you to avoid me.'

At this, she laughed. 'No, she hasn't.'

'I know she doesn't like me. I don't get the two of you.'

'What do you mean?'

'I mean she's opinionated.'

'You don't like that?'

'She can have her opinions.'

'Oh,' she said, and a high spot of colour came to her face. 'That's gracious of you.'

'You're deliberately misunderstanding me.'

'I think I do understand,' she said. Still in that same calm, soft voice. 'You want people to listen to you, don't you?'

'Doesn't everyone?'

'You want to be in charge.'

'When it comes to you, I think I should be.'

She regarded him steadily. 'Is that so?' she said.

'No, look, not in charge. You're putting words in my mouth.' He could feel the conversation slipping away from him. 'She's warned you against me. You won't marry me, you won't commit. Why?'

'Greta has had nothing to say about you at all. Not a word.'

'If you won't marry me, you could at least do this for me,' he said. 'I love you, Keira, and you treat it like a joke. You treat *me* as a joke. Why would you be cruel like that after all I've done for you? I want to be with you every day. I could live over the shop with you. I'll run the place if you like, as long as it means we can be together.'

She looked steadily at the table. The food was delivered and she didn't touch it. He began to eat fast. It almost choked him, he was so angry. He glared at her, infuriated by her immobility. She still wasn't going to say anything. She was going to sit there all night holding her precious little mysteries, her irritating little skills, to herself. If he could just get his foot over Keddington's threshold again he wouldn't mess it up like his father had done. He'd stand with Keira and let her take the lead. Keddington was a gold mine and she was going to take it all for herself. And then she'd have the key to that fucking gallery and never let him over the doorstep.

It wasn't going to happen.

All that money.

Not happening.

'Aiden,' she said eventually. 'I think we should stop seeing each other for a while.'

'What?' he exclaimed, shocked. He was suddenly jolted out of his own inner narrative. 'What are you talking about? Are you kidding me?'

'I don't like being bullied.'

'Bullied?' he repeated. 'Bullied? I'm trying to help you.'

At last, she looked up at him. 'I'm sorry, Aiden.'

'Keira,' he whispered. 'I can get my hands on two hundred thousand. That would pay for initial stock and the renovations. Start in a small way. I know what you want. You want to be exclusive. I can do exclusive. I can do anything you want. Let me help you. I won't interfere.'

'You're interfering now.'

She began to eat her food. He sat with his heart pounding in his chest. He wanted to upend the table and throw that food at the wall. He sat with his hands in his lap trying to breathe. She was so calm. He watched her finish every scrap and place the knife and fork precisely alongside each other. She reached for her handbag and took out her purse and put fifty pounds next to her plate.

He used his last skill. He began to cry.

'Aiden, stop,' she said.

'I'm so sorry I've made you feel like this,' he whispered.

'And I'm sorry it didn't work out,' she told him.

She stood up and headed for the door. Opening it, she paused and looked back at him. Several of the customers were watching her, and watching him for his reaction.

'Bye then,' he called across the room. 'Take care now. See you soon.'

16

ELLIS HAD SPECIFICALLY TOLD HIM NOT to go to the house, but Thomas couldn't resist driving past.

Things were moving quickly. The long drive was taped off and he could see a contractor's van and a police car parked there. The gates to Christine's had been closed, too. Irritated and uneasy, he drove into the nearest village and went to his local pub. It was a seventeenth-century place that had once been a farmhouse, and was set back from the road in a garden, with a car park to the rear. At weekends it was always busy, but not today.

He walked in with Max.

'Hello, Stan,' he said to the landlord.

The man ignored him, but his wife Jenny behind the bar came over to serve. 'Don't take any notice of him,' she whispered. 'His father knew Christine.'

'I know, but—'

She patted his shoulder. 'Like I say, take no notice. People got nothing better to talk about.'

'I went to see her.'

'I know you did.'

'And all this up at the house—'

'Nonsense, I know.' She smiled at him. 'Having something to eat?'

He ordered the ploughman's and took a packet of crisps too. He saw Stan go out of the bar and heard the back door slam.

'Nice,' Thomas muttered to himself. He opened the packet of crisps. He sat thinking about Aiden Ruskin, wondering where he was. Wondering too where Keira Brodie could be. He leaned his head on his hand and tried to consider Ruskin and Isabelle Crosby as he once would have done, putting himself in Cullen's place. He thought about the postcards and the leaflet that Isabelle had left for him. And he kept coming back to Ruskin's expression when he talked about Greta, and the fact that Keira, who was Isabelle's friend, owned the gallery near Sloane Street. He thought about the way that Isabelle had described Ruskin, about how Keira had changed so much after being with him. He thought about Keira leaving Ruskin after her grandmother's death and how Ruskin had destroyed Greta's gardens. So much rage in one man. So many questions unanswered. He wondered if Ruskin actually did know where Keira had gone, and as that idea crossed his mind, he was suddenly frightened for the woman he had never met. Rage had to go somewhere. It could burrow deep down in a person and change them, like a virus. After last year, he knew that better than anyone. Unconsciously, he touched the scar on the back of his head, feeling the ridge under his hair.

Finally, he wondered if in Cullen's place he would try to find Keira. How long had she been missing, and why couldn't the police find her? In this day and age, that ought to be easy. They would be watching everywhere for Ruskin and for his car's number plate on ANPR, but what about the woman he called his wife?

After a while, Jenny brought his ploughman's, and a bowl of water and a biscuit for the dog.

'Thanks, Jenny.'

'I love goldies, but they're guzzlers, aren't they?' she said amicably. 'I'm glad you've got a new dog after Fish. Poor little chap. That was all so terrible last year, Thomas.'

He didn't have the heart to explain about Max. Jenny sat down on the stool alongside him and leaned forward, lowering her voice. 'Don't think everyone's against you,' she said. 'I don't believe a word of it. You and Fran were always lovely.'

'Thanks,' he said.

'Like you would kill anyone,' she said, and shook her head and widened her eyes as if to show how ridiculous the thought was. 'Christine's not been right, you know. She came along and asked for milk a couple of weeks back, got us mixed up with the garage shop. I said to Stan then, she's going a bit like her mother did. Alzheimer's, she had.'

'I didn't know.'

'Oh, awful. She went about accusing people, too. Even wrote letters. You know, saying bad things.'

'Did she?'

'Oh, take my word,' she said. 'Getting a bit fuddled. Christine's fall on your drive. Things like that shake old people up, Thomas. I think when she gets better she'll regret it. All this'll blow over. Stan and the rest of them know it too. Like I say, they love a bloody gossip.'

He didn't think for a moment that Christine would recant, but he smiled in gratitude. 'Jenny, could you do me a favour?'

'If I can, love.'

'Could you look after Max here for a couple of days? I have to go up to London.'

She looked doubtful. 'I don't know as Stan would like it.'

'I might even get back tonight. But I can't promise.'

She looked down at Max and ruffled the dog's fur. 'You'll let us know when you're coming back? You'll ring us?'

'I will. Tomorrow afternoon at the latest. Can you wrap the food up for me, a bag or something? I'll take it on the train.'

She went away, and came back with the cheese and bread sealed in a Tupperware box. As he stood up, she put her hand on his arm. 'You're coming back, aren't you, Thomas?' she asked. 'You're not disappearing on us?'

'I promise,' he told her. 'See you tomorrow.'

17

IT WAS PAST MIDNIGHT WHEN AIDEN got to his father's house.
He walked all the way from the restaurant along the Embankment, fuming. Keira was out of her mind. She thought she was in charge in this relationship. He would prove to her that she wasn't. Bloody ungrateful bitch.

In vengeance, he followed a woman walking by herself alongside the river from Chelsea Bridge. She picked up her pace and then suddenly turned up Embankment Gardens, a crescent that would bring her out again onto the main road. Silly girl. He had half a mind to wait at the Gardens exit, but by then the fun had gone out of it. He was headed for Tite Street anyway, the next turning along.

He had always promised himself that he'd live there, among the memories of the great and glorious. The rock stars he didn't care about – it was the painters and poets – Wilde, Sargent, Whistler. The statue of Whistler was not far away, looking at the Thames as if he owned it. When Aiden was growing up he told other kids that he was related to the great Victorian art critic Ruskin, just because he'd been famous, but he changed his mind later. He'd gone to the library and found out that Ruskin had said Whistler's paintings were like throwing a pot of paint in the face of the public. He thought that was funny, and got a book on art and leafed through all of Whistler's paintings. Mostly, they were gloomy. He liked that too. It was probably where his fascination with art began.

Whistler had taken Ruskin to court for his insult, and won, but was given only a farthing in damages and was bankrupt soon after. It didn't matter. He did things big. Claimed he was things he was not. Fathered kids all over the place. And he was clever. You had to hand him that. Lost and lost big, and sodded off to another country. Married a woman and left a faithful mistress fuming and broken behind him. That was how you lived a life.

There was a lecturer at Uni who loved Ruskin and would say 'Mr Ruskin' to him with a flourish and a smirk, quoting the old story that Ruskin lost his wife to Millais because he couldn't bring himself to touch her – that he was 'revolted with her person'. When he came into seminars, this clown would say 'Good morning, Mr Ruskin, sir,' or 'We hope Mr Ruskin here' – with a flourish, as if he was taking off his hat – 'hasn't the same problem.' And he'd say, 'Shall we ask Mr Ruskin, who knows so much?' and 'Mr Ruskin has an opinion, I'm sure.' The old fart never got tired of his jokes. But he got his own back. He followed his tutor's fifty-something wife for the whole three years he was on that course and she eventually gave in after a faculty party, up against one of the trees in the chaplaincy garden on campus. Of all places. He took her picture that night and sent it to her husband on the last day of term.

Walking now into Tite Street, Aiden got to where Whistler's house used to be. Something similar had been built in its place. He stopped and looked at the windows and doors, trying to overcome an urge to crawl onto the step and lie there like an animal waiting to be let in. A Mercedes coupé turned the corner and slowed down as it passed him, then drove on. He showed it the sort of flourish that his tutor used to give him, with the difference of the middle finger. *Fuck you, bastards.* Bastards every one of them. He belonged in places like this, famous places, opulent places, places where the prices ran into millions. These were the kind of houses that would have fabulous art hanging on their walls. Keira had wormed her way into this world somehow with that pretty little face, butter wouldn't melt, a childlike face hiding a heart of granite. He stared at the pavement in a renewed fury. Men of Whistler's time wouldn't have stood for it. They didn't consider women equals. Their world was run by men who threw over the rules but who were still in charge, with women under their heel. They owned their wives and children wholesale.

He looked up again at the house while his mood cooled. Whistler had been bankrupted by building it. He'd been forced to sell the house, his own art and his collections and he'd gone off abroad. There was that. You had to be careful even if you thought you were in the driving seat. Ruskin had kept his reputation and his fortune after the court case. There was a lesson there somewhere. Take the long way. Regulate power. Never lose sight of the prize. But if you had a woman like Keira, Christ! She had to be made to understand, and for the life of him he couldn't see the way to do it.

He trudged on towards his father's house, slower now and taking no notice of stray women. He wandered on in the exclusive darkness of well-kept streets. He'd come almost full circle and Keira's gallery was near here, hiding halfway down one of the alleys, with Sloane Square and the Saatchi Gallery and the Royal Brompton all within a couple of miles and thousands of people with money down every road. Red-brick mansions and white-painted stucco townhouses facing nice little parks. The gallery wasn't far either from a row of Georgian houses he'd always liked, only a half dozen of them in an odd bit of road that must have once been right at the edge of London. Fashionable relics. He felt that by deliberately installing herself nearby Keira was putting two fingers up to him and his father. He nursed this thought for the next fifteen minutes, until he got to his father's street and took his door keys out of his pocket.

The house was at the end of a mews. A little road that now

boasted a fancy restaurant where a pub had once been. His father had made a good investment in the sixties just before all the world flocked to the King's Road. This house had then stood empty, once a mechanics workshop, double-sided with metal shutters drawn down at night. Aiden's grandfather had lived on the other side of Chelsea in Cremorne Gardens. Not exactly the flashiest address then but this was the sixties and the whole area was flooded with fashion, art, music and drugs. His grandfather, a tailor, was all the rage for probably no more than eighteen months making multi-coloured velvet suits, until he died of an overdose in 1967.

His grandmother had clung on in a rented flat, dying when her son was twenty. By then Aiden's father had worked the sixties scene, buying up whole containers of Victorian trash, great dressers and mantelpiece mirrors and rocking chairs and God knows what and shipping them in containers to the States. In his mid-twenties he met Aiden's mother. By then he'd had the old workshop for four years, and turned it into a house. It was worth a million now. At least.

Aiden's mother had only been married two years when she walked out. She fled to her own mother in a crappy little village in Hertfordshire, where Aiden grew up. All through his childhood Aiden heard the stories of his father's women and his travels in the Med buying up sackloads of tomb-robbed merchandise. His mother called her husband filthy and immoral. She told her son to work hard and get a proper job, a respectable job. But with the ghost of his hero Whistler rattling around in his head – and all those flashy bohemians who loved themselves so much – and with a weak-willed hippie for a grandfather and a crook for a father, he hadn't stood much of a chance, had he?

Aiden looked up at the city skyline now and the sky beyond it and laughed to himself. *Be fair*, he thought. He was never going to be honest. Where was the fun in that? He had tried, but not for long. His mother died thinking that he still worked for the London auctioneers that had given him a job straight out of university. He never told her that he'd been booted out for thieving a little sketch, failing to sell it and then trying to replace it in the store. They had literally chucked him out into the street. Nice people, huh. He had turned to his father and polished up his act with three simple ambitions: make a quick fortune, tell an expert lie without a flicker of changed expression, and have a woman like one of Whistler's mistresses, clever but obedient. That had been the plan.

He turned the key in the door now, and walked in.

Archie was sitting in the wing armchair, asleep. He'd been reading the newspaper, and it lay in his lap. Even from the doorway Aiden could hear him breathing, wheezing like a broken accordion.

'Archie,' he said.

The old man opened his eyes. He looked his son up and down. 'Well?'

Aiden threw his door keys on the nearest table and sat down. 'She'll come round.'

Archie folded up the newspaper and threw it on the floor. 'Empire builder,' he said sarcastically.

'I can't help it if she's got her own ideas.'

'Another failure with Miss Brodie,' Archie retorted. 'Never going to make it.'

Aiden put his fist to his mouth and chewed on his knuckles. It was an old habit.

Archie sighed. 'I've shown you all I can.'

'Much good it did me.'

'You're lacking stamina. You've got to stick at it months and years. Not have a few profits and then sit on your arse. Why do you think I suggested Keira Brodie? Because you'll never do it alone. You haven't got it in you.'

'Thanks.' *I have,* he thought vengefully to himself. *I'll show you both one day. I'll make a killing.*

'Look at you,' Archie muttered, pointing a finger. 'Case in point. You sulk. You sulk when something goes wrong, you sulk when a woman won't have you. You fester, boy. You bear grudges. If you can't get Keira Brodie, for God's sake move on. Plenty for the picking. Try an old one next. Or maybe not. They'll see through you. There must be dozens of young tarts up from the Shires on Daddy's money. Do your research. Stick at it. Follow through. You've only got to walk out of this house and out onto any street. Bars and clubs reeking with inherited cash.'

'I've worked hard.'

'Fits and starts. And what are you doing now? Fixated on this woman and she's too fuckin' clever for you by half. My mistake. Find another mark.'

Aiden sat smarting from his father's criticism. It wasn't as if he'd followed his own advice. He'd married young and for love, not money.

As if reading his mind, Archie sat forward in his chair. 'You're too like your mother when it comes down to it. You get stuck and then you complain. Drop them! Can't make a deal, move on, stick it to someone else.'

A long silence ensued. Aiden crossed his arms, willing himself not to move. He'd like to punch his father right in that fat slack mouth of his. He was used to Archie goading him, but it was hard to take tonight.

Archie said, 'What did she do? Stand you up?'

'No.'

'Showed you the gallery?'

'Yes.'

'Good place. Good location.'

'It will be. It needs work.'

'And she's got the money to do it all?'

'Apparently.'

Archie considered. 'Maybe the grandmother's helping her.'

Aiden shrugged.

'The old girl didn't like you either, did she?' Archie snorted. 'Got your number.'

Aiden said nothing. Probably his father was right. Maybe Greta was better off than he thought. Maybe she owned more than the two cottages. Maybe she had savings. He hadn't asked Keira and now he regretted it. Archie had said it. Poor research.

'Did you go to dinner?'

'Yes.'

'And said what?'

'Doesn't want help.'

'Not even cash?'

'No.'

Archie began to laugh. 'Can't even get a foot in the door. Can't even buy your way in,' he said. 'I've never had to buy my way in my life. She must hate you.'

Aiden bit his lip. He had plenty to say but he couldn't afford another argument. Archie lost his temper pretty rapidly, and last time he'd threatened to throw Aiden out. He had nowhere to go. Archie had him by the throat and he knew it. He'd started to ridicule him every evening as a form of sport. Aiden put his hands on his knees and rocked slightly in his seat. Archie knew what hold he had, and he loved showing his contempt. He'd done it all his life with customers, buyers and sellers both, women and men alike, shoving deals through with the force of his character, his ability to suddenly turn on charm like a faucet, his way of wrong-footing anyone, making them believe black was white. Mostly he thought he'd learned Archie's lessons well. Then came the crushing criticisms. He realised that he was Archie's toy, something to amuse him. Someone to take his old age and immobility out on.

He wanted badly to leave but he couldn't go. Not when his father was sitting in a million-pound house in central London.

He was Archie's only child. If he could just hang on long enough, take the insults, live on his allowance that Archie grudgingly gave him, he'd be all right. But there was still the issue of Keira.

He thought he'd got her more than once.

Showed him that placid face. Fooled him.

Snake.

He was suddenly aware that Archie was trying to get out of his seat.

'What do you want?' Aiden asked. 'I'll get it.'

Archie said something, but it was unintelligible. His breath rattled in his throat. He began waving his hands. His face turned deep red and his mouth opened and closed like a landed fish.

Aiden stood up. 'What's the matter?' he asked.

Archie slumped backwards, half on and half off the chair. Aiden stepped forward and tried to haul him back into a sitting position, but he made it worse. Archie's body slithered off the chair and he crumpled to the floor.

Aiden knelt down and pulled on his arm.

'Dad. Dad.'

Nothing. He put his hand to Archie's throat and his fingers disappeared into the folds of flesh. He grabbed the hand lying at his side, flaccid now in Aiden's grip. He tried to feel a beat in the wrist. He noticed that his father's lips were turning blue. Archie smelled of whisky, and sweat, and unwashed clothes. Distantly, as if picking up sounds from another world, Aiden heard the clock chime in the kitchen. One o'clock in the morning.

He sat back on his heels, then looked around the room. He saw his phone lying with his keys, and got to his feet. He felt sick himself now, and he opened the door and breathed in the cold night air of the street. He looked back into the room, and then down at his phone.

Then he closed the outside door, and walked around the room a couple of times. He stood in front of a landscape that Archie had always liked, and then a portrait of an Arabian child, and then he carefully looked at everything else that Archie owned. An overstuffed sofa with tapestry cushions. A Kazak rug by Archie's chair and another by the stairs. The Anatolian kilim that had been made into a stair runner. Bits of Dresden porcelain. And the watch on Archie's hand. The gold signet ring.

A house worth a fortune.

Aiden sat down and waited for half an hour.

Then, slowly, he dialled 999.

18

WHEN THOMAS GOT OFF THE TRAIN in London, it was half past five.

It was a long time since he'd been in the city, and he took a moment or two to adjust to the roar of Waterloo Station. Rush hour was in full swing. He got the Northern Line to Leicester Square, and then changed for Knightsbridge, walking slower than most, elbowed in the crush. He'd once had an ambition to work for the Met and was glad he hadn't. He had enjoyed his country patch, the nearness to the sea.

Life in his home town hadn't been without drama, though. Bodies washed up on the shoreline or caught in nets were few, but still had their grim impact. He'd seen his fair share hauled from the ocean: a boy who'd drowned after jumping off a pier, two little girls of seven or eight who'd gone under the waves and been pulled out by the current. Summer accidents in riptides. Summer fights at night. On the beach one night two teenage boys had threatened each other with knives over a girl. Neither of the boys had known what it really meant to cut another person. One died almost immediately from a cut to his femoral artery in the struggle. The second, when Thomas had got to the hospital, lay sobbing in his mother's arms, still covered in the other boy's blood. Life was fragile. Death could be very quick.

He tried not to think of last year. He got on the escalator and at the top he looked at the Underground map to orientate himself. *Why don't you kill me?* He decided to walk just to rid himself of that voice. He ignored the cabs and crossed the road, unconsciously putting a hand to one ear as if it would block out the recurrent sound in his brain. He seemed to have stopped dreaming about Helen lately, but the relief had been short-lived. Instead, in the last eight hours his thoughts had started running back obsessively to the garden where Richard Ellis was organising the dig.

They would find nothing at that end near the stream, nothing in the vegetable patch, and nothing under the trees and hedge. Even if they'd brought in a cadaver dog it might only circle for a while. He imagined Richard Ellis standing with his hands on his hips, watching the soil turning over, a frown on his face. Richard would follow the dog, notice it working. The handler would say that it was distracted by the compost heap, an untended mess where Thomas knew – or guessed, by the way that his own terrier used to stand guard over it – there were rats. It was the country, after all. There were plenty of smells in competition. There'd been a dog otter in the stream once. There were deer and foxes in the field behind. He'd once seen a dog fox sprinting across the field and a few minutes later, the hunt came after him. Poor bloody creature. Although the scent of a dead body – the very thing the dog was trained for – that was something else again. He knew that some dogs were capable of finding a single human bone buried twelve-feet deep.

He bit his lip and walked on.

It was only fifteen minutes to Keira Brodie's gallery, hidden down a narrow mews behind a pedestrianised shopping street. When he'd searched online for the name Ruskin had given him, it didn't give an exact address, only the area, but a question in the first shop had shown him the way.

The sun was out and the city was much warmer than the coast. He was hot inside his wool coat, and felt out of place and slightly grubby in the evident sophistication of the street. He saw the gallery the moment that he turned into the mews. It had a grey-painted frontage and a grey sunblind, and a potted bay tree on either side of the door. Grey blinds were drawn down over the window and the door was like that of a private house. The bell was a brass-handled affair in a recess and that, together with the number of the gallery painted onto the brick, looked original. He rang the bell, but there was no answer.

He stepped back and looked up at the house. To one side was a narrow entry, but a door was bolted across it. He noticed the CCTV camera above, and the casing of an alarm high up on the wall near the roof. He knocked this time and waited. There was no sound from within.

At that moment, the man who'd directed him walked into the mews.

'I meant to tell you there's no one home,' he said. 'There hasn't been for a while.' He had an upper-class accent, the kind that belonged in a country estate in the Cotswolds, more at home with his dogs and horses than in a little bijou interiors store.

'I can see that,' Thomas replied.

'You're a customer?'

'No, no. Just a friend.' He paused. 'Well. Not a friend exactly.'

'Police?'

He used the phrase that Bill Pascoe had given him. 'Of a kind.'

The man put his hands in his pockets and looked him up and down. 'If you were police, you'd know that she isn't here.'

There was no answer to that. The man walked closer.

'I say,' he said quietly. 'Insurance?'

'Yes,' Thomas lied.

'Look old chap,' the man said. 'She's done all the security. You can see that for yourself. And there's nothing of value in there. She cleared it all out. It's empty.'

'I was hoping to talk to her.'

'Were you indeed?' The man took a step back and looked Thomas up and down. 'You'll have her phone number then.'

'Yes,' Thomas lied again. 'I do. Thanks for your time.'

As he walked away he could feel the man's eyes drilling into him. He stopped when he reached the main street and looked back. Sure enough, he was standing where Thomas had left him, outside the gallery, frowning. Thomas wondered if this was Keira's pet guard dog, someone who she had asked to keep an eye on the shop, and – probably more importantly – to report back who came and went. If so, the man was doing his job very well.

Thomas walked on down the main street and at the far end he stopped at the outside tables of a café and ordered a coffee. 'Are you eating tonight?' the waitress asked him.

He glanced at the prices on the menu. 'No thanks,' he said.

He took off his coat and watched the world go by. Most of the shops were closing. The crowds were thinning out. A couple of the restaurants were busy though, getting ready for their evening trade. Belgrave Square was just around the corner, and Harrods a half mile away. Belgravia, Knightsbridge, Sloane Square. He wondered how on earth Keira Brodie had ever afforded a place here. It must have cost a fortune. Several fortunes. What had gone on at the gallery? Had Ruskin come here, looking for Keira, and made some sort of fuss? Why would she leave a lucrative business like this one, and a place – more to the point – at the very heart of the art world that gave her a living?

Thomas sat thinking of Ruskin's face as he described letting the gallery go, giving it to Keira in exchange for the cottages. Or one of the cottages, more precisely. The resentment in his face. Was a part share in a London gallery a fair exchange for a tiny cottage in Cornwall? Thomas didn't think so. The gallery, even empty and not trading, was still a piece of prime real estate. He got out his phone and looked up a property website. After a while he found a beachfront cottage, much restored, in Cornwall for nine hundred thousand. Then he looked up the price of a Belgravia mews house, a shop with living accommodation above. Tiny places were a quarter of a million for a leasehold. However, the gallery here looked quite large, a narrow front but with depth. Greta's cottages were certainly in desirable Cornwall, but they needed repair. He decided that Keira had a good edge over Ruskin in the so-called deal. Keira Brodie must have some very influential clients. Very.

When he'd looked her up online, her website was sparse. It listed her as an art curator and valuer. It gave the address and phone number of the gallery but nothing more personal. A couple of paintings shown online as being in the gallery were very old, sixteenth and seventeenth century. Obviously they weren't there anymore. How did anyone get a job that involved pieces of historical work like that? More importantly, how did anyone sustain such a career? He knew enough about the art universe from his strictly distant experience – revolving on the edge of the art galaxy like an anonymous planet – that it was contacts that mattered in their world. It was who you knew as much as what talent you had. Maybe she'd gone to the right university and picked her contacts up there. Maybe it was from working at the V&A. But how did you get accepted in a prestigious place like that – contacts, or talent? He guessed at the latter. He wished that he'd asked Isabelle more about her.

If this trip had confirmed anything at all, though, it was that he'd been right in his instinct. Keira Brodie was in trouble. Enough to make her leave London. Confirming just that made it worth the trip.

Isabelle hadn't given much away about the backgrounds either of Ruskin or his supposed wife. And although Greta Brodie owned the cottages in Cornwall, she'd lived there a good few years, long before Cornish cottages became fantastically expensive. If the family had money he would have expected them to live somewhere grander than two little places sold as one unit as the old coastguard station but with no heating, no phone line, no parking. Greta Brodie had evidently lived for being outside and didn't care for much else. So how did her granddaughter get here, where the streets were almost literally paved with gold?

He finished his coffee and paid a ransom for the privilege, took up his coat and held it over his arm. He decided that he could do with a walk rather than face the Tube again, and turned down Sloane Street. At Sloane Square he looked down the King's Road, a place of enduring myth to a boy like him who'd been born in 1967. He smiled to himself. When he was 15, he'd wanted to be Mick Jagger living in Tite Street, the place where Singer Sargent had lived and Oscar Wilde. Whistler too. He'd wanted to be in the crowds of King's Road and Carnaby Street on a Saturday morning, going in the shops there and buying a vintage 1960s velvet suit. When he told his father that, the old man had laughed. 'A bloody velvet suit, is it?' he'd said. 'What do you want with a velvet suit?' He'd taken Thomas's news badly that he wanted to study art. 'A man earns a living,' he'd told Thomas. 'A proper living. You can't earn a living painting.' Ten years later, after trying to prove his father wrong, going to a local art college and selling precisely one piece of work – and that to an aunt – he gave up his dreams. He joined the police force and hadn't taken up a drawing pad again until long after he had had to retire early.

He hesitated on the junction of King's Road now. If he stayed up in London he could go to the V&A tomorrow and see Tite Street and the Embankment for himself. Perhaps someone at the V&A could give him more information about Keira's time there. He thought of the exhibition listed on the postcard that Isabelle had given him. And Tam Jefferies, who'd sold his paintings when Fran was ill and had a gallery in London. He might even know Keira Brodie himself and be able to give her a message.

As he stood there trying to decide, his phone rang.

It was Richard Ellis.

'Thomas,' he said. 'Where the hell are you?'

19

H E TOOK THE TRAIN BACK LIKE a good boy. Ellis was there to meet him at the station.

'This is your idea of staying where you're needed?' he said.

'I've come back, haven't I?'

The two men stood on the old Victorian platform and watched the train leave through the darkness, chugging its way with its last four carriages towards the coast.

'Where's your car?'

'Outside.'

Ellis turned to leave, but Thomas caught hold of his arm. 'What did you find?'

'Let's go and get a drink.'

They went to the pub just below the abbey green, the same place where he'd had his leaving do six years ago. It hadn't changed: low doorways, nicotine and smoke-stained beams and a bar that had been makeshift in 1930. Ellis bought him a half, since by then Thomas had already said that he had to get back to his local near the house and pick up Max. He'd phoned the pub and heard relief in Jenny's voice.

Thomas watched Richard come back with their drinks and realised that his once-young protégé was showing his age. He was married now with young children. Perhaps that accounted for his weary look.

'I guess we wouldn't be here if you'd found anything,' he said as Richard sat down.

'We didn't.'

'You sound almost disappointed.'

Richard sighed. 'Expensive business to justify.'

'Ah.' Thomas took a sip of his drink. 'I should go and see Christine.'

'They've moved her to the Oakley.' It was a small hospital on the Brimham road, about five miles away. It was that wonderful thing: a cottage hospital that the mighty centralising machine of the NHS had overlooked.

'Is she the same?'

'You mean, is she still accusing you? Yes. Apparently they're doing some cognitive tests.'

'Jenny Rackham at the Fleece told me that Christine's mother had Alzheimer's. I never knew that. She never told me.'

Richard leaned forward. 'Something's puzzling me,' he said.

'What's that?'

'Why you were so worried. Don't bother to deny it.'

Thomas looked down at his hands. He ought to be in Cornwall, he thought, using white spirit to wipe his fingers clean of paint. Instead he'd done what he always needed to do, chase up a wrong smell. He'd seen terriers let loose in a barn once, grabbing the escaping rats and shaking them until the neck was broken, then tossing each one aside and snatching the next. Two or three seconds work and the assembly-line quickness of it, each dog utterly focused. He knew that he was like that, driven by the odour of something wrong. It was an irritation that the world didn't sit right. He wanted to make the pieces fit, rearrange and smooth them until he had an answer. Unfinished business irritated him, and Helen McAllister irritated the hell out of him, the irregular threads of her disappearance trailing across his life.

'I keep dreaming about her,' he said.

'Who?'

'McAllister.'

Richard sat back, waiting for the explanation.

'I keep hearing her tell me to kill her.'

'What!'

Thomas waved his hand. 'Not when she disappeared,' he said. 'It was in Exeter Airport when we got back from Italy.' He glanced up at Richard. 'If there's one thing in my life I would change, it's that stupid bloody weekend.'

'Why did you go?'

'If I knew that, I'd probably sleep better. Male vanity. Her insistence. Boredom, temptation.'

'Bored with Fran.'

'I haven't even got that excuse. Bored of myself more than anything. I was a happily married man, Richard. You remember what Fran was like before she got ill. Before the cancer.'

'Yes, I do.'

'Life and soul. Kind. Intelligent. Loving. I had all that.'

'Yes.'

'Fran was going away that week to York. A conference.' Thomas shook his head. 'I found myself out there, San Gimignano. The photograph on Helen McAllister's bedside in her house when we went to look at it. You remember? She'd cut me out of it, but it was taken that first night. I look back and I think, why would I be that stupid? Why did I let her dictate to me?'

'Everyone's allowed moments of madness, Thomas.'

'Four days isn't a moment. And it was bloody awful. The first morning I woke up I felt choked, suffocated, guilty. It's that same feeling that I dream about.'

'And this thing she says?'

'*Kill me. Why don't you kill me*? I told her that it couldn't go on. That I didn't want it. I wasn't interested. She laughed and said it then. A joke. You know, "*Oh, why don't you be more merciful and just kill me?*" But a savage kind of joke. She had this venomous side to her.'

'It stayed with you, even though it was a joke?'

'Because when she disappeared I thought, she's said that to someone else. And they did.'

'And you still think that.'

Thomas sighed. 'Got to be, surely.'

Richard seemed deep in thought. If he was disturbed by the confession that Thomas had known the photograph when they first inspected Helen's house, he didn't show it. He looked saddened, though. 'You kept this to yourself all these years.'

'It seemed irrelevant after Alice Hauser told you all that I'd been involved with Helen.'

'We pitied you more than anything.'

This was news to Thomas. He stared at Richard for a second, then looked down. 'Pity,' he murmured. 'Better than disgust, I suppose.'

'Nobody was disgusted, Thomas. Surprised maybe. Shocked, even. It was so out of character.'

'I think McAllister had done it before. She loved taunting people. She liked taking them apart. We all know what a bitch she was to Alice.'

'How did Fran take it all?' This was something that Thomas had never confided in him. 'What did she say?'

'What I deserved to hear. Hated me. Wouldn't speak to me for weeks. Not *really* talk, you know? And then – it was only a few months later – she got the cancer diagnosis.'

'Surely you don't think that's your fault?'

Thomas said nothing.

In the silence, they watched other pub customers come and go. There was a slot machine in the far corner with three or four lads around it. A middle-aged couple came in and sat by the bar. It was almost closing time.

Richard Ellis reached into his pocket and took out Thomas's house keys. 'All yours.'

'Thanks.'

'Are you staying there tonight?'

'Have to. Too far to get back to Cornwall tonight. I'll go and see Christine tomorrow, and then drive back to Trewarith.'

'I'll ring Cullen.'

'She's been on to you?'

Richard smiled. 'You'll have to mend your fences there.'

'Have they found Ruskin?'

'No.'

'Jesus. Another missing person.'

'You've got a talent for it,' Richard observed wryly. Watching Thomas putting the keys in his pocket, he touched his arm briefly. 'You still haven't answered my question,' he said.

'Which question is that?'

'Why you were so worried about us searching the garden.' Thomas opened his mouth to speak, but Richard held up his hand. 'I know you, Thomas. I even know why you'd hare off to London on a wild goose chase. I know when you've got a conviction or a suspicion about something. Cullen thought it was bloody peculiar that you'd go to London. You've got to tell her why you do these things. But you've got to tell *me* why that garden bothers you.'

'I don't know how to say it. It makes so little sense.'

'Try me.'

'It was during Fran's first chemo. She had time off work and it was summer. She used to sit in the garden.'

'And?'

'Things were still different between us. Better, but different. We never got back what we had before. And it turned out there just wasn't time.' He stopped, remembering how Fran had turned in on herself as if in some strange way she was actually nursing the cancer. She wouldn't tell him how it felt. There were only a few things that she liked to eat at that time, and he'd go further afield trying to find them. Organic foods from farms, and a cordial that she preferred which was only stocked in a shop eight miles away. She took a sudden dislike to sourdough bread and fruit and eggs. He'd make her salads and she'd refuse them because it had one particular thing that now turned her stomach. She'd sit in the garden and stare at the fields beyond.

'One night she asked me if I'd done it.'

'Done what?'

'Killed Helen McAllister and buried her in the garden. She asked if Helen had suddenly reappeared and come to the house.'

'She was ill, Thomas.'

'I know. And she knew it was impossible. But, like me, she went over and over it and sometimes she'd ask me a random question. I think maybe even she wished that woman dead. I didn't blame her. I'd felt that myself, Richard. And when you said that Christine had come up with the same idea – these two women who I'd been so close to, two women I liked and loved – when you said you'd have to dig the place up, it flashed into my mind that Helen must be *somewhere*. And if she was dead, someone killed her. It wasn't me. It couldn't be Fran. And so...'

They looked at each other.

'You thought it was Christine,' Richard said. 'Christine who was so obsessed with the case. Christine who was home the day that Helen disappeared. Christine whose mother used to make outrageous accusations because she had dementia. You thought that Christine could easily have been home the day that Helen disappeared.'

Thomas didn't reply, but he spread his hands in a helpless gesture.

'You thought that if Helen had come to your house and found you both out, she'd have gone round to Christine's to ask where you were,' Richard said slowly. 'And if Helen was in a temper, she might have told Christine a few unpalatable truths.'

'It can't be,' Thomas murmured. 'It just can't.'

'But you thought it just the same.' Richard stopped suddenly. 'And it's not really your garden you're concerned about, is it?'

'No,' Thomas admitted. 'Not my garden. But Christine's.'

20

Archie's funeral was in the first week of November, just at the time when the trees were beginning to turn. The wind was bitterly cold. At the gates of the crematorium the dead leaves were so thick Aiden couldn't see the pavement. He stood waiting for the hearse, shuffling his feet in the debris, scuffing the leaves to a pulp.

Keira arrived just after the hearse. He saw her car turn left for the car park, and he kept his eyes on where she'd gone, ignoring his father's coffin as it was taken out of the car. She came hurrying along the path as the doors opened to the chapel and the undertaker ushered him in, whispering to him quietly. The man probably thought that he didn't want to be at the ceremony, but the truth was he was more interested in Keira. Reaching him, she gave him a strained smile.

'I didn't know you were coming,' he told her.

'I couldn't leave you by yourself,' she said.

There were only a half dozen people in the congregation and apart from Keira he knew none of them. Old men with his father's face. Reddish and bloated, or scored with cynicism. Testament to what this business could do to you. You started out liking art, maybe creative yourself, interested in history, knowledgeable about artists. Then a lifetime of trade took hold of you. You concentrated on the value of things and forgot to appreciate anything else about them. Your living, your survival, depended on other people's money. You grew to hate the clients who hesitated in front of a piece, men who jangled small change in their pockets, women with their Amex Gold. If you started with nothing, you were climbing the greasy pole all your life. Only those from a wealthy background really succeeded. That was his opinion, anyway. Keira was the only person he knew who bucked that trend. Keira and just a couple of others.

They all stood up when the service started. The undertaker had asked if he would give a eulogy. He had said no. Instead, he gave a few details to the priest, some guy who looked more like a rugby forward stuffed into a clerical collar, a man he'd never met before and was damned sure his father didn't know. The guy said that his father had been respected and Aiden heard someone behind him laugh.

Keira stood beside him. He was so bloody grateful for that.

He felt nothing but relief when the curtains drew across the coffin. He would never again have to steel himself when he went into the house, never have to see to his father's laundry, all his stinking underwear, or strip and remake the bed or open the windows to get rid of the smell. Old age was a bugger, a curse. There was nothing dignified about it, not if you'd lived like his father lived. Archie used to sometimes talk about his own father's death, the way his mother had found him sitting on the toilet with a needle still in his arm. A fashionable death at the time. A lot of people died that way. Drugs were new and cheap. Archie told Aiden dozens of times the story of his own mother taking a Polaroid picture of her dead husband, and she'd gone into the boutique that sold his suits and said, 'He won't be taking any more orders,' and shoved it into the face of the dealer who'd given him the heroin. She'd said that there was a band in there, a famous band, buying stuff, and nobody said anything.

That was where his father came from, and what Archie had walked away from. Done well as a young man, married a nice girl, worked hard doing all the markets, getting up at four in the morning in the dark. Camden Market, Portobello, antique fairs in Essex when it was pissing down, bigger venues as he got wiser, richer. Then the decay set in. Tempted by easier money he started tarting up so-called Jacobean sideboards with plywood, smelling of linseed oil and white spirit, became mates with forgers, mislabelling stock, tripling prices. The dirty end of the business. In the house was what he called his treasures. Behind a fibreboard false wall he kept little pieces of mosaics – buyers liked animals, faces – and small figurines, jewellery, stonework. He had a safe deposit box in a bank in Wembley, an ordinary-looking place on a busy road surrounded by charity shops, pound shops, bookies, where he put the more valuable stuff. Not in the millions, but tens of thousands. You could sell things online at first with no comeback. Archie never went abroad and his line of supply was long, threading through Beirut or Amsterdam. Then when Aiden joined him he sent his son to small island ports in the Mediterranean. Aiden had picked up stuff in cafés, car parks, hotels. They weren't the biggest business and didn't pretend to be – it was too dangerous – but they scooped off what was left after the major players had had their fill, like crows picking up roadkill. In the house there was still some jewellery: Assyrian, Etruscan. There was a pair of garnet and gold earrings from three centuries before Christ, Nimrud cloisonné bangles, a gold clasp. All his now. All the nice roadkill, all his.

It was what Aiden's mother had tried to keep him away from. She hated it and she hated Archie. She took him away to live with his maternal grandmother and she inherited the house when the old lady died. They tried to make him decent. It was a word he'd heard all his childhood, 'decent'. Far away from filthy overdoses, safely away, she thought, in the leafy countryside. She never even knew about how much Archie made. Even he didn't know exactly. But he would find out now, and he would open that safe deposit box that Archie had toiled to once a month, struggling out of the taxi with his newspaper-wrapped packages under one arm and his walking stick in the other hand. Aiden had always stayed in the taxi and watched him, the greedy git with a seedy business who made himself out to be a connoisseur. Then when he got too fat and too ill to make the journey, Aiden did it for him. Everything was tightly wrapped and Archie timed him, questioning both him and the driver if he took too long. Secretive old bastard. The safe deposit box was packed now, but what exactly was in it he wasn't sure. But he would soon find out.

He glanced at Keira at his side. It was a shame really. Such a shame. The two businesses combined could far exceed what Archie had made in a lifetime of under-the-counter trade. She of the nice clean face, he the grafter, the silent partner. And when he couldn't be bothered to trek out on his journeys to those hotels and car parks and the coffee houses near museums in sweltering cities, he could kick back and guard her gallery in Belgravia while she plied her respectable livelihood. Art curator. Valuer. All above board. She didn't even have to know about the other stuff. He didn't actually have to tell her. It could have been such a sweet little business. He could have had a nicer life.

The eight or nine people who made up the congregation walked outside. The sun was coming out. He saw another hearse waiting at the gates of the crematorium. He shook hands with the undertaker and the other men and Keira came alongside him as they all walked away.

'Do you know that woman?' she asked. With an incline of her head, she pointed out someone standing at the edge of the grass by the few flower wreaths, reading the inscriptions on the cards.

It took him a moment to recognise her. 'She used to know Dad a few years back,' he said. 'Her name's Isabelle Crosby.'

He raised a hand, and the woman walked over. He introduced her to Keira. It was a miracle he remembered her name – old women were just marks, but this was no mark. She'd set him straight once, following him as he came out of a dealer's in Athens and taking his arm suddenly as he waited to cross the street. 'It's Aiden Ruskin, isn't it?' she'd asked. Easy as you like. Friendly, smiling. 'Let's find somewhere quiet.'

They'd ended up in the foyer of a hotel. She'd ordered a cold drink for them both. And then, very politely, she'd told him to fuck right off.

'I don't want to see you in Athens again,' she'd said, swilling the ice around in her glass. 'Or in Venice.'

'I haven't been to Venice,' he protested.

'Then don't,' she said.

'I've a perfect right to be wherever I want to be.'

She had smiled. 'Tell Archie you met me,' she said. And that was it. He had watched her walk out of the hotel.

When he'd got back to London, Archie had flung up his hands. 'What are the odds?' he said.

'You know her?'

'Oh Christ,' Archie said. 'She had – what shall we call it? – an arrangement with a couple of archaeologists.'

'She actually told me to fuck off.'

Archie laughed. 'She would.' He sighed then. 'Do as she says.'

'I don't see why I should!'

Archie had grabbed him by the shoulder seam of his jacket and pulled him close to his face. 'I see, and you don't need to,' he told his son. 'Just go where I say.'

Seeing Isabelle Crosby here now was like a blow to his sternum. She was older, of course. Much older, and she didn't look exactly well. He summoned up what little courtesy he could. 'You should have come in,' he told her.

'I did.' She turned and looked at Keira. 'I hear there's a gallery,' she said.

'There will be, yes.'

'Taking some time?'

'Builders,' Keira replied.

The two women nodded at each other. Isabelle turned away.

He looked at Keira. 'Do you know her?'

'She knows my grandmother.'

'Does she now?' he said. 'Well isn't it a small world?'

'Yes,' she replied. 'It is.'

Keira came back with him to the house. She didn't need much persuading, and it cheered him up. He saw for the first time how being the grieving son might work in his favour.

'Drink?' he asked, when they first got through the door.

'I'll have a cup of tea.'

'Ah, come on Keira. Toast the old man.'

'Just tea. Thanks.'

She was looking at the paintings along the wall just before the stairs. He brought back the tea for her, laid it out, and went back for a large Scotch for himself. She glanced at the whisky, paused just for a second but said nothing. He was carrying the bottle with him, and held it up for her. 'Macallan's,' he said. 'You're sure you won't?'

'I won't.'

'Dad's favourite. He told me one of his women introduced him to it years ago. Would never touch any other brand.'

She didn't comment, though she looked at the bottle again and gave a little nod. She turned back to the paintings. He sat down on the couch and watched her.

'I suppose you're going to tell me they're fakes.'

She looked at him over her shoulder. 'Why would I do that?'

'It's how Archie made his living.'

'That's not true, surely.'

'I wouldn't put it past him.'

'Was he ever caught out?'

'Never.'

'Then how do you know?'

'I don't. But it's the kind of thing he'd do. He knew one or two big forgers, until they got caught out.'

'And then he stopped?'

Aiden shrugged. 'Haven't the faintest. Only guessing.'

'It would be harder to do now.'

'Don't count on it. You know what it's like. The scramble for the masterpiece.'

'Auction houses are more careful.'

He laughed. 'What trust you have.'

She walked away from the paintings and sat down opposite him. 'What will you do now? Will you sell the house?'

'Maybe.'

'Stay in London?'

'Maybe.'

She took a sip of her tea. 'You're being very secretive.'

He slammed his glass down and stared at her. 'My father just died,' he said angrily. 'On the same night you gave me the push. Forgive me if I haven't got my bloody mind straight yet.'

'I'm just making conversation, Aiden.'

He got up and paced backwards and forwards. 'What is it?' he asked. 'What is it that makes you come back here? Casing the joint? Want the house for yourself? Make me an offer.'

'Don't be silly.'

'Ah, silly. I'm silly. You know what I think, Keira? I think you aren't the nice little girl you make yourself out to be. I think I got you wrong. I think you've got a calculator for a brain. I don't even think you like art. I don't think you care much for people, either. In fact, I think you're worse than Archie and his father before him put together. You don't know the value of anything. You only know the price.'

She put her cup on the coffee table and stood up slowly. 'You've just given a good description of yourself, Aiden.'

He took a swig of the whisky. 'Go on and march out,' he said. 'You've had a look at the paintings. Or maybe you want to see the rest of the house.'

She picked up her handbag. 'I've seen the rest of the house,' she said. 'Your father showed me.'

He let her get almost to the door before the realisation of what she'd said caught up with him. He sprang over and grabbed her arm. 'What are you talking about?' he demanded. 'What do you mean?'

'Let go of me, Aiden.'

'Not until you answer the question.'

She stayed silent and eventually he relented, but he leaned his whole bodyweight against the door so that she couldn't open it.

'Archie invited me here several times,' she said quietly.

'What for?'

'To assess what he had. Even those imports. And to pick my brains.'

'About what?'

'The paintings, for one. And get them cleaned.' She regarded him with her head tilted to one side and a small smile on her face. 'You never saw they'd been cleaned, restored?'

Aiden suddenly felt cold. 'The imports are his, not mine. I never had anything to do with it.'

She shook her head. 'I don't care,' she told him.

'It's from years ago. He collected unusual stuff then. He's never sold it. Never traded in it.'

She smiled. 'But you have. And as for fakes – I don't want yours in the gallery. You think I don't know that's what you're trying to foist on me? Like you say, it's a small world, Aiden. People talk, and you more than most. You're careless. At least Archie had a little bit of class about him. But you're just a petty crook.'

He reached out and closed a hand on her neck.

She held his gaze. 'Really?' she said. 'Really?'

For a long time after she'd left, he stayed right by the door.
Seething, weeping.
Sometime during the night, he finished the Macallan.

21

Out of habit, Thomas woke the next morning at six.
    It took him some time to realise that he wasn't in Cornwall and that Ruskin wasn't walking past his door. He got up immediately and nearly stumbled over Max, who at some time during the night had followed him upstairs and lain next to his bed.

'Hello, old boy,' Thomas murmured. Max's tail thumped in greeting. 'Let's go for a walk.'

They went out of the back door of his house and into the long sloping garden, but both stopped halfway down. The digger brought in by Richard Ellis had gouged out tracks across the grass, and left mounds of earth where the vegetable patch had been. Thomas edged slowly down in the predawn half-light, feeling his feet sinking into the mud, and stared at the mess they had left.

'Thanks for nothing,' he muttered.

There was a way out of the garden at the bottom by crossing the stream. The hedge was quite overgrown – on the far side, it belonged to the farmer – but the two of them got through and walked up the long slope. Max trotted happily ahead, nose to ground. At the crest of the hill, Thomas looked back at his house lying in a fold of the land, only faintly visible in the first light of dawn. There were a lot of years tied up in there for him. Happy ones for the most part. But it was peculiar how time had the knack of making years seem opaque. You thought you had something solid, something that would always stay the same, but then in a moment it could slip through your fingers. He had a curious feeling that the house didn't belong to him anymore, or that he'd been cut free from it.

He took another moment to find the roof of Christine's house in the shadows of the trees along the drive. He stood frowning, hands dug deep in his pockets.

They walked on through the woodland and out onto the next field. Here, Thomas sat down on the stump of an oak tree that had come down in storms three or four years previously. He thought about being here one evening with Fish, his terrier, and there had been a herd of cows in the far corner. They'd come barrelling over to investigate the dog and had nearly killed him, chasing him around like bovine teenagers. Fish had eventually escaped by plunging through the hedge and back into the trees, barking wildly all the time. Thomas looked down at Max. He couldn't imagine Max dodging about to avoid heifers – he'd more likely lie down and give up.

The dog was now looking at him expectantly.

'Hungry?' he asked. 'Breakfast?'

They walked out onto the narrow lane that led back down into the valley. The horse chestnut trees were already in leaf. Next month they'd be full of white candles. He thought of the countless number of times that he'd driven along here to go to Brimham, usually very early like this. He wondered where Ruskin was. Surely they must have spotted his car by now. Thomas had few doubts that Isabelle's death was Ruskin's doing, but the reason mystified him. What could Ruskin possibly want with an old lady like her? The only answer he could think of was that Isabelle knew where Keira Brodie was. But what was the sudden urgency to find his supposed wife? The key lay hidden from him, he thought. It was somewhere in that rage connected with Keira's grandmother. It was somewhere in Ruskin's phrase *a pair of thieves*.

Greta was the link between them, and an apparent love of art was the cement that secured the friendship. But this threw up another puzzle. From the scant details on Keira Brodie's website, her speciality was from two, three, even four hundred years beforehand, whereas Isabelle supported the modern stuff. And although Aiden Ruskin was supposed to have been an art dealer – he had said that he worked with his father – he had no website and there was nothing online to give a clue to his life.

Thomas stood still as a realisation struck him. The Wikipedia page about Isabelle. Her support for various charities. The old photograph of her petitioning parliament for women's refuges. Isabelle had said that Keira Brodie had changed after meeting Aiden Ruskin. That she became quiet, even withdrawn. Wherever she was now, had she run to escape him? Was it urgent, life or death? Did she suspect Ruskin of killing her own grandmother? She'd disappeared right after the funeral, not only from Cornwall but London too.

He got back to his house and let Max in the door. He filled the dog's water bowl and gave him a couple of biscuits. The sun was now up and streaming into the kitchen and Thomas sat down at the table

'Why do they say "a dog's life"?' he mused to himself. 'Seems a lot less complicated to me.'

His phone began to ring.

He was back in Trewarith by one o'clock.

Laura Cullen was waiting on his doorstep.

'The traveller returns,' she said, a sarcastic edge to her voice.

He didn't reply. He unlocked the door, put his overnight bag inside, and then closed the door again without inviting her inside. He clipped on Max's lead. 'It's taken us four hours,' he said. 'Accident on the A38. We could do with fresh air.'

'As you like,' she said.

They went down the lane and through the field gate, staying

alongside each other without speaking until they hit the coast path. Thomas turned left, towards the pool. At his side, Laura seemed deep in her own thoughts. They reached a wooden bench that looked out over the rocky beach, and sat down.

'Can we agree on something?' she said eventually. 'Will you speak to me again before disappearing? I asked you to do that. It's called courtesy.'

'I'm sorry.'

'What was so urgent in London?'

He turned in his seat to face her. 'What do you know about Ruskin's relationship with Keira Brodie?'

She gave him a faint smile. 'If I know anything, I'm hardly likely to discuss it with you.'

'And if I know anything?'

'Then you have to tell me.'

It was his turn to smile. 'You surely don't think I killed Isabelle Crosby?'

'As it happens, I don't. Though your presence is all over the ground floor of that house.' She paused. 'But then so is the postman's.'

'And Ruskin's?'

'We don't have Ruskin's prints or DNA, so your guess is as good as mine.'

'Nothing on the body?'

She looked away from him.

'Okay, don't tell me.'

'I don't intend to.' She inhaled deeply once or twice and tilted her head back, closing her eyes. 'You chose a good place to spend the summer.'

'I like it.'

They both listened to the waves for a while. The tide was out, far back beyond the ridges of limestone and quartz, but the line of surf was clearly visible, bright in the sunshine. She opened her eyes again and nodded in the direction of the path. 'Greta Brodie drowned here last December, in the pool.'

'I know. Isabelle told me about it. So did Ruskin.'

'Did he?' she said. 'And what else did he tell you?'

'How much he hated both Greta and Isabelle.'

She sat forward. 'Elaborate.'

'Well, more accurately, he certainly hated Greta. He called her cold. It was Isabelle who seemed to have a thorough dislike for him. She knew Greta very well. They were students together years ago.'

'I think I knew that. She was at Greta's funeral and spoke to me.'

'About Ruskin?'

'Carry on with what she told you.'

He nodded, admitting defeat. 'Isabelle said that Greta told her that Ruskin was false,' he continued. 'She said that Keira Brodie suffered in the relationship – that she'd once seen Ruskin grab Keira by the hair and pull back her head. She lost weight and became closed down, shut in on herself. Isabelle's assessment of Ruskin was that he was very manipulative.'

Laura was listening, biting her lip. 'You must have seen this before. Cases of coercion.'

'You think that's what it was?'

'Don't you?'

He spread his hands and dropped them into his lap. 'When I began my career there was no such thing. Not a word we knew. Domestic disputes, yes. On the whole we kept away from them unless there was actual harm. There was no training.'

'Nobody cared?'

'Of course we cared. It was difficult. Say a man smashed up the house on a Friday night. A neighbour might call us out. Perhaps even the woman herself. Then she wouldn't press charges. There were no refuges then. There was a feeling that we'd get involved in social work, not proper policing.'

'Proper policing,' she echoed, quietly.

'You know the history, Laura. When I started there was deliberate delay. Cases didn't come to court often. We weren't after victims, we were after perpetrators. People we could take to court and get successful prosecutions. Domestics were a really grey area. Victims were somebody else's job. I'm not saying it was right. It wasn't.'

'And that's it, that's all you have to say about it?'

'What else do you want me to say?'

'God,' she muttered. 'Your generation.'

'I'm not that bloody old,' he said. 'I retired early, remember.'

She narrowed her eyes. 'Actually yes, I do remember.'

'What's that supposed to mean?'

She waved her hand as if to dismiss it. He realised with indignation that she knew about his affair with Helen McAllister, probably from Richard Ellis. He burned inside. He'd expected Richard to have more discretion. But maybe it wasn't Richard. The rumours flew back then, evidently as far as here.

'And just a helpful hint for you here,' Laura was saying. 'Women have called themselves survivors, not victims, since the eighties. And a woman who gets out from under a man like Ruskin is just that. A survivor. That's what Keira Brodie will be.'

He took a breath, trying to get his irritation under control. 'Coercion is another universe. To be fair, I don't think anyone understood that in my time. Many still don't.'

'People like me? Are you serious?'

Christ, she was touchy.

'I don't know you, so how can I say?'

'That's right, you don't.'

She looked away from him, pulling her coat around her.

'Did Keira Brodie ever report Ruskin?' he asked.

'Not in this area.'

'You've looked into it, then?'

'Of course we have.'

'Neither here nor in London?'

'Look, I'm concerned for Keira Brodie but I'm more concerned to find Ruskin.'

'You don't think he's gone to her?'

'How can he, if he doesn't know where she is?'

'Maybe he does by now. If you found her, maybe you'd find him.'

'You really think I'm some sort of plod, don't you?'

'No, that's not true.'

'You're telling me my job. I know my job, and I want you to keep out of it.'

He opened his mouth to speak, then thought better of it.

She shifted in her seat. 'As it happens, I know more than I'd like about coercion,' she told him. 'My sister Milly worked as a nurse. Three years ago, she was drafted onto a new scheme within the same hospital and she came up against an NHS manager who seemed to take a dislike to her from the start for no apparent reason. A woman. She was older by about ten years or so, recently divorced and a real stickler.' Laura sighed. 'My sister was easy-going, you know? She gave this person a lot of leeway because she figured the woman had had some kind of bad experience with her marriage. But it didn't seem to matter how nice Milly was – and she did try hard not to ruffle this woman. One day, she called Milly in and said there'd been a complaint about her. It turned out to be nothing – a really minor issue, a misunderstanding – but from then on things got much worse.'

'How so?'

'There would always be some comment about Milly's appearance. Milly had shoulder-length hair and she'd tie it back but apparently that wasn't good enough, it wasn't neat enough. Or she was asked one day about her make-up. Then it was her punctuality. Milly often worked longer hours than her contract but if she was late for a shift—'

'She got spoken to?'

'Nothing outrageous. And it wasn't this woman's role to say anything in the first place, but she did nevertheless. Nothing outright rude. It was more picking away. Milly told me the woman made her nervous. But what really sealed it was when she got engaged.'

'The woman got engaged?'

'No. Milly. We were all so pleased because Mark was a nice guy, a junior doctor. Before you know it, Mark's job has been moved somewhere else. It was a good opportunity and the woman had nothing to do with it – that we know of – but she seemed to really relish the fact that they wouldn't be seeing so much of each other. Made a few snide comments. Milly told me about this and we came to the conclusion that this woman was a sad individual and probably jealous. Milly tried to get on with work but by now she was feeling anxious, so she applied for a job in a private hospital. It wasn't what she wanted, she wanted to stay in the NHS, but the pay was better and she'd be out of this woman's remit.'

'Probably best.'

'Yes, but it was irritating that Milly had to change her life. But that's bullying for you. Insidious. It gets under your skin.'

'What did Mark think?'

'He didn't really take it seriously. I mean, to be fair, none of us did. We had no idea.'

'What happened?'

'Things started to go wrong. Just details at first. She found a scrape on her car one day. Another time she actually found it unlocked, and she was sure she hadn't left it that way. It happened several times and eventually I said we could maybe look at the CCTV in the hospital's car park. We did see a woman walking away from the car a couple of evenings, but it was winter and we couldn't see if it was the same person. And we didn't actually see her next to the vehicle. Christmas came and went and nothing much else happened, and then the letters started.'

'What kind of letters?'

'Really filthy things. One said that Mark was having an affair, another just made taunting comments about Milly looking fat enough to be pregnant. No threats as such. But they were upsetting all the same.'

'And you think they came from this same woman?'

'Milly was sure of it. Then, in the spring, we had the wedding. It was at a nice country hotel. The service went beautifully but when we all went to the dining room the cake was in pieces. Someone had taken a hammer or something to it. The staff had seen no one.'

'Good God…'

'I mean, you can stand so much. Milly had no concrete evidence, nobody had seen this woman, Milly couldn't understand why she should be a target, and Mark had had no trouble at all. We all tried to reassure her and the rest of the day went okay. They went off on honeymoon to New York.'

'Was that the end of it?'

Laura shook her head. 'No,' she told him. 'Three months later Milly told me she was pregnant. It was great news. It was what Milly had always wanted. Sadly, she lost the baby at five months.'

'What was the cause?'

'There's hardly ever a definite reason. The baby had simply died. Milly went for all kinds of tests, but she was very quiet and she stopped coming to see me. Eventually I went round and Mark said she'd sunk into a really deep depression. He said the letters were back. Had been back from the day they returned home from honeymoon.'

'That's outrageous.'

'Yes, it's outrageous. It's cruel and vicious and disgusting. The sister I knew had changed gradually over the couple of years this was happening. She got so that she wouldn't go out alone. She was always looking over her shoulder at work. She didn't like working late. She thought that one day this woman would be waiting for her. In the end I paid the woman a visit. It was unbelievable. She was super nice, very concerned for Milly, pretended that she didn't even know that Milly had got married.'

'Was there anyone else with a grudge against either of them? Could it have been an ex of Mark's?'

'You think I didn't look into it?'

'No, no, I'm sure—'

'They were popular, you know. Nothing like this had ever happened to either of them. I always used to envy Milly in school because she never had an enemy, and you know how cruel girls can get. Or maybe you don't? But they do. Milly was always the happy one, the bright one. She did well, and she was well liked at work.'

'Except for this woman.'

'Except for this woman.'

'When you saw her did she say anything at all negative about your sister?'

'Not a word. Honestly, Thomas, it started to get to me as well. Here was my sister, a shadow of the person she used to be, and that woman was responsible. I couldn't prove it and I realised that I probably never would. That's the nature of bullying, coercion, whatever. It's gradual and insidious and it's so devastating.'

'How is Milly now?'

Laura flinched slightly before she replied. 'She began to say that it must be her fault. That she must have done something to make this woman annoyed. Of course we all told her that was ridiculous. But she wasn't the person I knew any more. She stayed indoors and watched TV all day. She forgot to eat. She lost a ton of weight.'

'What did you do?'

'Everything I could. I could see that this woman was probably a serial abuser, that she was probably a sociopath of some kind. I think maybe she was jealous of Milly for some crazy, twisted reason. But coercers and abusers hide their real selves. How often have you heard that someone was a "pillar of the community" or just "the man next door"? They live in plain sight, and they steadily ruin lives. It's habitual to them, something they can't break. And if they lose one target, they just start on another. Bullying makes their targets sick, you know. Sick at heart, unsure of themselves, desperate. These bastards don't pick on helpless and frightened people. There's no fun in that. They choose successful, confident, pretty people. And then they take them down, piece by piece, day by day. They don't *pick* on suicidal women. They *make* them.'

'Suicidal?' He hardly dared ask.

Laura wasn't looking at him. She was looking down at her feet. 'One evening after Mark left for work – he was on nights then – she got dressed and walked away from the house. She went for four miles across country until she got to a level-crossing gate. It was about ten o'clock, pitch dark. The driver in the car waiting at the same gate thought it was odd that there was a pedestrian so far out in the country. He said he noticed that Milly had ordinary shoes on with a heel, not walking shoes. And she was wearing a nice coat. A "posh coat", he called it.' Laura's voice wavered for a second. 'He was right. She'd dressed in her best things. And then, when the train was coming, Milly dodged under the gate. She was killed instantly.'

'Oh God.'

'I heard about the interview of the car's driver. As soon as he'd seen her make a move, he'd jumped out, but it was too late. He was pretty traumatised.' She bit her lip briefly. 'You see how these things spread out and touch others? It's a virus. It infected us all – our parents, Mark, her workmates, me…'

She wiped her eyes, and sighed. They sat in silence for some minutes.

'I'm so sorry,' he said, at last.

'Yes. Thanks. Everybody's sorry afterwards.'

'What happened to the woman?'

'Nothing at all. About a year later she moved to another part of the country. But not before she came to Milly's funeral.'

They looked at each other. After a moment, Laura seemed to gather herself. She gave a shrug of defeat. 'So... you think that about Ruskin? You see a similarity?'

'Certainly it's possible. Maybe even probable.'

'And the smile,' she said. 'There's an emptiness somewhere. A misfiring connection in their heads. Some synapse or other not joined to the rest.'

'That's the feeling about Ruskin that took me to London.'

'The copper's conviction again,' she said. 'So convinced that you went to find out where Keira Brodie had gone.'

'Are you going to tell me it's none of my business?'

'Would it have any effect?'

'No.'

She gave him a weak smile. 'Anything else you found out in London?'

'The gallery was cleared out completely according to a neighbouring shop.'

She raised her eyebrows. 'Want a job?'

He laughed. It was the first sign of any warmth between them. 'Bit old,' he said. 'Bit knackered.'

'I wouldn't have said so.' She laughed too, but more of a sigh than anything. He liked that she wasn't really joking. 'Were you always like this?' she asked.

'Like what?'

'A loner. Going off on a tangent.'

'No. I always wanted a team. It was a good feeling.'

'Just bloody intrusive lately then? Last year, and now. Lucky Richard. Lucky me.'

He hadn't thought about it in exactly those terms, but she was right. He was a loose cannon rolling around in her territory. A potential liability, primed to derail an investigation or make it harder to get to court. It was surprising that she wasn't more annoyed with him. 'Was anyone at the gallery?' she asked.

'No. It was locked up.'

'She's gone to ground,' Laura murmured.

'You don't think…?' He paused.

'Think what?'

'Could Ruskin have done something to Keira?'

'Of course he could,' she replied tartly. 'That's why I want to find her as well as him.'

She glanced back at the sea. The water was marginally closer. The tide was coming in. 'Do you know when's the most dangerous time for a woman – or a man – being coerced and dominated by their partner?' she asked. 'When they leave.' She stood up, smoothing down her coat and retying the belt. 'I think Keira has gone to ground. None of her contact details work. She's hiding somewhere.'

'I hope you're right.'

'So do I.'

Thomas stood up too. He thought about it from all angles. It could mean that Keira was dead. On the other hand – and much more positively – Isabelle seemed defensive about Keira, not distraught. He concluded that she hadn't been worried. She knew where Keira was. He repeated all this to Laura now.

'Maybe,' was all she would say. She turned as if to go back to her car.

'Hold on a second,' Thomas said. 'There's something about Isabelle Crosby's scene that doesn't make sense,' he said. 'I've been thinking about it.'

'Go on.'

'Well, if Ruskin had come again to the house demanding Keira's address, she'd have stood up to him. I think she'd have stood up to anyone. She wouldn't have run away. I can't see it. I can see her refusing but I don't see her running. I can see him attacking her where she stood – in her bedroom, or the kitchen. And I think she'd have fought him. There would be defensive wounds.'

'Maybe she was already in the garden,' Laura said.

'At night? In the rain? What could have taken her out there?'

Laura pointed at Max. 'You're looking at him,' she said. 'Maybe Ruskin tried to silence him in some way, and Max barked. Maybe Ruskin manhandled him into the garden and that didn't shut him up.'

'Past the gate and the hedge.'

'And that's why Isabelle came downstairs,' Laura continued. 'She wasn't running away from Ruskin. She was running in the rain towards Max, and Ruskin was waiting for her behind that hedge.'

Thomas considered it. 'It's a decent theory,' he murmured.

'Well thank you,' she retorted. 'So pleased you think so.'

He shrugged by way of apology.

'Listen,' she said. 'You know enough not to bugger up this investigation, I hope. If you must chase this – and I'm telling you not to for all the bloody good it does me – but if you must—'

'Tell you.'

'Promise me you'll do that. For my sake.'

She didn't wait for a reply, and she didn't wait for him.

She turned briskly back to the path, and walked back alone.

22

AIDEN WAS PREOCCUPIED THAT AUTUMN.

He had something in mind. It was something so fantastic that it needed money. A scheme in the Med, with one of his old contacts who had avoided prosecution. After Archie's funeral in November, he'd tried ringing Keira but the number came up unavailable. He thought of going round the gallery and teaching her a lesson, and it was tempting. Messing him about. Coming to the house after the funeral and then ignoring him. It was precisely that which made him come up with the scheme. *Petty crook*. He'd show her how wrong she was.

He spent a couple of weeks just sitting in the house. He took everything to pieces. He got the contents of the hiding place out and put it all on the dining table, and then thought that there must be more. He had cleared out Archie's wardrobes and knocked every panel out in case the old man had hidden something behind the walls. There was a patch of plaster in the bathroom that had always looked odd to him, and he pried that away too, only to find damp brick behind. He'd emptied every kitchen cupboard and where one of the units had an obvious gap behind it, he'd pulled that unit out and found nothing but mouse droppings. He spent hours of the night pacing the floors, kicking skirting boards. He got all the paintings down and all the prints and all the etchings. He took some of them to auction.

The Hockney print raised a bit, enough for a holiday or two. The painting of the Arab boy though was returned to him as unlikely to be by Leighton, and the sketch of a child posing on the deck of a Thames barge was definitely not Tuke. He couldn't understand it. It wasn't like his father to have fakes in his own house. Sell them to others, yes. But not have them staring at him on his own wall every night.

In a temper he put all his father's clothes in black plastic sacks and took them to the local tip. He wore the signet ring for a few days until he looked at his hands and had the horrible conviction that he was becoming his father. Sometimes he thought that he even heard Archie in the house, making his way up the stairs at night when Aiden was in his own bed. One night he'd woken in the early hours and heard Archie breathing next to him, making that awful death rattle. The terrible thing was that Archie had taken a huge breath in those last moments, but not breathed out. And Aiden realised that he was obsessed with that breath. It happened a few times, and when it did he got up and started walking the streets. He stopped turning towards the Embankment or Chelsea. He considered moving back to the village where he'd grown up, such was the feeling of claustrophobia. But he'd never go back there. He tried to get the memory of his parents out of his system by walking across Knightsbridge and up Park Lane and right through Mayfair. Berkeley Square and Grosvenor Square and up to Oxford Street and back along Bayswater Road to Lancaster Gate.

At first light as soon as the park gates opened, he would come down the North Ride to the Serpentine and stand by the boathouses and look at the lake. Archie had insisted on being brought here in 2018 to look at Christo's *The Mastaba*, the giant pink floating sculpture on the water, and they'd argued about it. Archie had been in favour. The old man sometimes had surprised him, he'd give him that. Like inviting Keira to the house when his back was turned, for instance. He found that so bloody hard to get over – the idea that they'd conspired at the house together.

He could just imagine Archie being the gracious host – the old toad – but he couldn't figure out why Keira had been there at all and what Archie's endgame was. Had he tried to get Keira to take him to Keddington for another try? Or maybe there was some other sodding duke who Archie fancied for a quick touch? Just how many of them had she got tucked under her belt? He loathed the mystery of her. The fact that she still had that after all he'd done to bring her down was just so bloody intolerable. It irritated him as if she'd got under his skin like one of those burrowing insects that hatch into your bloodstream. She'd made him sick.

He swapped his Audi for a Lotus Elise. He enjoyed a few days swanning about London in it, but the bloody thing was murder to get in and out of. It galled him to feel that he was feeling his age when he was only in his thirties. Just. People he'd been at Uni with were mostly married now with families, but he didn't want that. He saw how having children slowed you up, robbed you of your independence. Nobody he'd known when he was twenty-one went out at night on their own now, or had a thought that wasn't linked to their goddamn family. Family! It was another disease. He saw men of his age walking in the parks at weekends with kids on their shoulders and he pitied them all. He'd sit on the grass and watch them go by and think of how they were wasting their lives. They'd get to fifty-five and then those same kids would leave them and they'd end up walking round a golf course or trying to kill themselves on a squash court and they'd realise that their whole lives had passed them by. No, it wasn't for him. He planned to be something so much better than that.

And he wanted to possess more than a car and more than the profit raked off his father's paintings and steel engravings. It was all small fry. Driving through Edmonton one day he saw a Bentley, old school 1960s model, waiting at the lights opposite him and he had a flash of yearning that it was all taking too long. He started to get a pain in his chest and for a while it worried him so much that he went to get checked over. He lay on a bed in the GP's while they gave him an ECG and told him he was fit, and asked whether he was worried about anything. He could have floored the doctor there and then. *I'm not worried,* he wanted to shout. *I just want what I can't have. And I want it now.*

The same doctor had asked him how he was getting on after his father's death, and had he considered that the chest pain might be the stress of grieving. He'd laughed in his face.

'I'm not grieving,' he'd told him. 'I'm glad.'

It was the end of November when he went into the National Gallery on an overcast day. The sky threatened rain and the air seemed stifling under a grey sky. He got into the gallery with relief and wandered about with no particular aim, but after a while he looked for Parmigianino's *Portrait of a Collector* because he always thought that it looked like a young version of his father. The man had an expression of contempt on his face, as if he possessed every last piece of knowledge about lovely and collectable things, and everyone else was a peasant. The first time he'd seen it he'd smiled because it was so like Archie's habitual expression. But he couldn't find the portrait today. Angry at himself, he walked into Room 41. There was hardly anyone about except for a girl sitting in front of Rousseau's *Surprised!* She had a drawing pad on her knee.

He stopped in front of her.

'I always think the tiger looks horrified more than surprised,' he said. 'Or maybe it's the viewer who's surprised?'

She glanced up at him but said nothing.

'Are you an art student?' he said. 'Your drawing is very good.'

When again he didn't get a reply, he crouched down next to her. 'I'm an art dealer,' he said. 'It's my job to notice talent.'

She stopped drawing. 'I'm trying to work,' she said.

'I see that,' he murmured. He looked her up and down and smiled. She had long dark hair and she'd covered herself up with a long black skirt and a shapeless sweater. Why did girls do that? They were young, they had bodies to show. 'Have you had lunch?' he asked.

'Please leave me alone,' she said.

He thought that was very rude. He stood up, mortally offended. 'I'm not asking you,' he protested.

This time, she did look at him. 'Yes, you are. Why?'

He shrugged. 'There's no need to get offended.'

'And there's no need to keep bugging me,' she retorted. 'So fuck off.'

'Very nice,' he said. 'Very polite.'

She started gathering up her things. 'Are *you* being polite?' she asked. 'I don't think so. I asked you to leave me alone.'

He held up both hands by way of surrender. 'Pardon me for living,' he said. 'I'm just trying to be friendly.'

'I don't want your friendship,' she said.

He watched her walk away. A couple of men standing twenty feet away were watching him. He grinned at them. 'You have to try,' he said.

'No you don't,' one replied.

He deliberately took the opposite direction to the girl, giving the men a look of disdain as he passed. He wandered around for another hour, past *Whistlejacket* and Wright's *An Experiment on a Bird in the Air Pump*. He stared at that for some minutes trying to think of why he liked it so much and why he always came to see it. In the end he decided it was the two little girls in the foreground, looking afraid and hiding their faces from the dying bird while their father tried to persuade them to look at the marvels of science. Poor little girls. Poor bird. He'd like to touch the face of the smaller one, the little blonde staring upwards.

He had lunch in the café, resenting the hordes of others trying to do the same. Then he walked out onto Trafalgar Square and crossed over to Landseer's lions. He contemplated walking up the

Strand to go to the Courtauld Gallery, and while he was looking in that direction he saw the same dark-haired girl going into Charing Cross Tube, carrying her drawing pad under her arm. He ran across the road dodging traffic, ignoring the screeches of brakes and blasting car horns. He went down into the subway and stood hesitating. She was nowhere to be seen among the crowds. Which way had she gone, Northern or Bakerloo? Where did she live? Paddington, Kilburn? Where would an art student live? Camden, Chalk Farm? He took a chance.

Luck was with him. When he got to the Northern Line platform she was standing right at the end, head down, looking at her phone. He watched her put it in her pocket, then look along to the announcements board. *High Barnet 4 minutes*. And then she saw him. She immediately looked away. If she left the platform, she would have to come straight past him. That was the idiocy of standing at the end, away from the exits. He waited. The train came in. He walked towards her. She saw him coming and waited until the last few seconds before getting on. But he was as quick as her. He got into the same compartment.

She sat down next to an older man. He took the seat opposite. He didn't look at her once, but he saw her fidgeting, moving her feet. When the first stop came up she got up and moved down the carriage. He followed, but she didn't get off. She sat down next to a group of boys her own age. He stood holding the bar, deliberately facing away as if reading the adverts above the seats. He stayed there for the next two stops. When Warren Street was coming up she got up and went to the doors at the other end of the carriage. He wondered why she'd said nothing to the group of boys, told them she was being followed, pointed him out. But she didn't. She got off and so did he, and she joined the few passengers going to the escalators for the street.

He guessed that she'd decided against going home. She didn't want to lead him to where she lived. He smiled to himself. This was fun. He watched her on the escalator above him, her distinctive long hair. She didn't turn round. When they got to the top and through the ticket barriers, he saw her run to a guy in a uniform, a guy lounging against the far barrier with an expression on his face as if he was in a little world if his own.

Aiden dodged out of the station. Piles of rubbish bags were on the corner ready to be collected. He ran over the road to McDonald's and stood inside, a few paces back from the window, watching the Tube entrance. It was a good five minutes before she emerged with two men, both her own age. He recognised one of the boys from the train carriage. All three of them looked up and down the street and walked to the edge of Tottenham Court Road, looking in both directions. He watched their mimed conversation as the traffic roared past. A delivery van turned into Warren Street and momentarily obscured his view, and when it was gone he saw that she was standing alone. She looked back at the station, hesitating. Then she turned down Warren Street itself. He waited a while, keeping her in view, then walked out and followed her.

Warren Street was a nice place if you just judged it by the houses. Georgian, Regency? Three and four storeys in varying pale bricks. It had taken a lot of bomb damage during the war. He saw her turn down Whitfield Street, where the Telecoms Tower reared up beyond the roofs. Maybe she lived here after all, or knew someone here. He was about a hundred yards behind her when she turned round suddenly. She was alongside Whitfield Place, where there was a little park and a baseball court. She looked straight at him.

He stopped walking and waved, grinning at her like they had an arrangement to meet just here by the benches. He saw her look around herself, and he began to run. He'd had a client here once. Or somewhere very near. Queer who'd hit on him. Coincidentally enough, in the National too. Poor man wasn't to blame. After he'd told him that he owned some nice eighteenth-century drawings that he wanted to sell, Aiden had offered to assess them. Before long he'd been asked to dinner. He'd gone back and eaten the food and paid him for the drawings and tolerated the hand on his back and arm and the fumbling for his belt. To stop him, he left him with a reminder of his visit, just a little nick under his jaw with the vegetable knife on the counter. He had asked for it, really. It was almost funny, the guy's surprise. Not so much an injury as a goodbye kiss bleeding all over his floor. Flesh wound. Satisfying. He had been offended not so much by the guy but by the smell of gardenias in the flat. Gardenias! What was it, the 1950s? A mother's smell. Disgusting. He got a great profit on the drawings though.

The girl hadn't moved. He had almost caught up with her. Perhaps she thought it was better to confront him on the street. She held her drawing pad in front of her like a shield.

'Where are you going?' he asked in a conversational way. 'You're going back to Tottenham Court Road? Maybe the Tube on Goodge Street?'

'No,' she said.

'I'll walk with you. Do you live round here? I don't think you do, do you? Why don't you come to my house?'

'No,' she repeated.

He was enjoying her stricken expression and tried to take her by the arm. She stepped back. 'Why are you being so awkward?' he asked.

Just then a rubbish collection van came around the corner. Two men in high vis were walking alongside it. She started to scream. They stopped and the van stopped. He turned on his heel and ran back along the street, turning down Grafton Mews, running now, hearing the distant shouts at his back. There was no one much about, only a woman walking a dog and taking her keys out of her pocket. He had a sudden thought to push her into her house and close the door until the drama had passed, and it was interesting to think of what he might do to the woman, at least frighten her – but then she would know him again – and he reached Howland Street and crossed the main road again and kept running.

Only when he got to Russell Square did he stop. He sat down in the gardens for a while getting his breath back. He watched while the world went past. Nobody would know him again, possibly not even the girl. She didn't know his name or where he lived. She might guess he was English from his voice and perhaps say he was fair-haired, but what else? He wasn't that dissimilar to a lot of people in any street. And London didn't actually take much notice. It was a great amorphous mass of humanity, each person anonymous in their skin. He could have gone a hundred different ways away from Warren Street. It was a good job he could run.

After a half hour or so he got up and walked to the British Museum just three minutes away. He went into the Great Court. He stood under Norman Foster's roof and next to the Knidos lion, looking up at it and thinking that thousands of years ago someone had this positioned over their tomb at the edge of the sea, and all his irritation came flooding back. He would bet his own life that whoever had that tomb never ran away from a woman. He smarted with renewed humiliation. What was she worth, anyway? What were any of them worth? He was better than that. He deserved better than the treatment that Keira had given him, too. It was unfair. He ought not to have allowed it. He'd been too kind and too patient. She was an unbending and ungrateful bitch. He started to tremble with the injustice of it and the stone lion looked down on him with pity.

It seemed to him that all his life had come to this. He was at a starting point now if he just took the chance. The plan that he'd been carrying about with him was like a friend tugging at his elbow. All it would take was courage. You never got anywhere just standing on the sidelines. You had to take that leap, place the bet. He closed his eyes and thought of all the other things in here.

The treasures that had just been taken. Life was short. You had to grasp what you could. In one of the upper galleries in here was the bronze head of Augustus that had been torn from his statue and buried under a temple raised by Sudanese tribesmen and then the British came in and Kitchener rode off with the lot – the head, the horse armour, the taxes. Life was bloody *and* short. Civilisations destroyed each other, what was he doing but picking up the pieces? That wasn't his fault either. Roadkill. All he was doing was cleaning up after the blood was spread all over the road. He could do better than that. Much better. On his phone was the number of a man in Slovenia and another in Rome. He only had to make the call. And, of course, find the money.

He would put the house on the market.

23

THOMAS COULDN'T HAVE ASKED FOR A better day. The weather was perfect.

He and Max had walked along the coast all the way past Stepper Point until he got to Padstow, and then they had taken the ferry to rejoin the path at Rock. All the way, the sun shone in a cloudless sky. Max kept a steady pace alongside him and jumped onto the ferry as if he'd done it many times, lolling his head against the rail with a stupidly happy expression on his face.

Thomas had been painting for the last four days and when the forecast was so good he'd decided to walk to Daymer Bay and St Enodoc's. He carried his sketch pad in his bag and as he walked he thought about *Riverside* and if he'd have to go and bid for his own painting at auction. Eventually his dark thoughts about Isabelle and the rain-soaked morning at Chalfont Edge receded. He came down through the lanes and into the town by what he always thought of as the back route. The hedges were in new leaf.

It was the Friday of the first May Bank Holiday weekend. The crowds were out and the car parks at Padstow full; when he joined the ferry it was crammed with people all trying to get to lunch at Rock or join the coast path like him. On the other side, he walked up for his first sight of Daymer, and stopped in the sun to look at the beach. Max slumped down on the sandy turf. Thomas's head hurt a little from the exertion of walking. For the hundredth time, he wondered where Keira Brodie was and he thought about the eerie stillness of the house next door. For more than half an hour he considered the postcards that Isabelle had left for him, the V&A exhibition and the sculpture on an East Anglian beach and felt an old anxiety picking at him, the anxiety of someone missing.

By the time he and Max reached St Enodoc's, coming down to the churchyard through the sand dunes, they'd walked over ten miles. Thomas sat down in the porch, grateful for the shade, taking off his sunglasses and the old cotton hat that Fran had always hated. 'It makes you look a hundred and five,' she'd told him once. He closed his eyes and thought of his own house and the walks in woods nearby that were full of wild garlic at this time of year.

From inside the church, he could hear the murmur of voices. When the door opened, a crowd of women came out. To his surprise, Laura Cullen was among them. She stopped in her tracks.

'Were you listening to the music?' she asked.

'I didn't realise there was any.'

A friend was waiting alongside her. 'It's okay,' she told the woman. 'I'll see you tomorrow.'

She turned back to him. 'We're singing at a wedding. We had a practice this morning. Not an obligation to easily get out of.'

'Lovely place to get married,' he said.

'Yes.' She sat down alongside him.

'You're in the church choir?'

'Oh no,' she said. 'A singing group.'

'And you give concerts?'

'Not very many,' she admitted. 'We're all a bit terrified of the wedding. But it's one of our group that's getting married.' She smiled at him. 'Have you been here before?'

'A few times,' he told her. 'My wife was a Betjeman fan.'

They'd always come to pay their respects at Betjeman's beautiful gravestone here. Fran would usually repeat the same stories about the poet laureate failing Oxford and his loathing of one of the tutors and the fact that he had a teddy bear called Archibald Ormsby-Gore. For a while it had been Thomas's own nickname. If he started quoting the law over some subject or other, out would come the name. It wasn't Jobsworths for them, it was Ormsby-Gores. 'That's enough, Ormsby-Gore,' Fran would tell him. 'You love a bloody regulation, don't you?'

'Long surf breaking in the midday sun,' Laura said.

He smiled at her. '*Cornish Cliffs.*'

'Yes,' she said. 'My dad had a copy of the Collins Guide, the one about churches. We never went anywhere without that bloody thing. I can't tell you how often I've been dragged round something that Betjeman liked.'

'Your dad was Cornish?'

'No. London. He retired down here. When he got ill, I got a transfer.'

'From London?'

'That's right.'

'You haven't got an accent.'

'We're not all characters in EastEnders.'

He smiled. 'Quite a change for you all the same.'

'Well,' she said. 'There was more than one personal reason.' They sat in silence for a while. 'Look,' she said finally, 'it's against my instinct to tell you anything. I suspect you'd go after it like a dog chasing a Frisbee. I reckon you can't help it.'

He raised an eyebrow. 'But you're going to?'

She fussed with the music folder she was holding for a moment or two, then shut it with a sigh. 'We found his car.'

'Where was it?'

'Somerset. Close to Castle Cary railway station. There's a minor road going to Somerton off the railway bridge, and further down there it was parked in a field entrance. The farmer reported it.'

'When was it left there?'

'They couldn't say.'

'So no CCTV, obviously?'

'No.'

He knew the station vaguely – had passed it a few times visiting Bath or Bristol, going north through the rolling green countryside. Old Roman roads with innumerable branches off to tiny villages. Farming country with the occasional line of low hills. You came upon the station with a kind of surprise, seemingly in the middle of nowhere, north of the town.

'Do you think he caught a train?'

'We've trawled through a week of station recordings. It's a busy station on a weekday. Direct line to London. Hard to make out faces in the crowd. But I don't think he was among them.'

'But what was he doing there in the first place? It must be over a hundred miles from Trewarith.'

'A hundred and fifty,' she said. She glanced at him. 'The car was out of petrol.'

He thought about it. 'He'd avoided garages, then.'

'Yes. Cameras.'

'So not caught anywhere by ANPR?'

She shrugged. 'There's not exactly a wealth of ANPRs on country lanes. And the number plates front and rear were filthy.'

'Deliberately?'

'I would say so.'

'How did he avoid the motorway and A roads?' he wondered aloud.

'Not easy. There'd be a lot of doubling back on himself.'

'Where was he heading?'

'Could be anywhere, couldn't it?' she said. 'But it seems away from the coast. London? He used to live there.'

Thomas put a hand to his head. 'God, I'm slow,' he murmured. 'Did you already know Aiden Ruskin? Has he come up in some investigation or other while he lived in London?'

'Not in any of my cases.'

'But in someone else's?'

'His father did.'

'For what?'

'I knew someone in the Art and Antiques Unit.'

'Some kind of fraud?' Suddenly, Isabelle's postcard – the fraud of the Tichborne Claimant – sprang into his mind.

'Nothing proven. But Ruskin Senior had a murky reputation. Nothing major. Then his son joined him.'

'And inherited that reputation?'

'He was borderline implicated in a death.'

Thomas sat back in surprise and stared at her. 'What kind of death?'

'A man called Kingsbury was arrested for murdering his wife. It took a long time to get him back from Spain. But once here he said that his wife had died after Aiden Ruskin had visited her.'

'Good God.'

'Aiden was interviewed. He protested his innocence. Kingsbury claimed that he'd been out when Aiden visited, and he'd come back to find her very distressed. She didn't want to sell the paintings, but her husband did. He was convinced that Aiden had gone back again afterwards because he went out one morning, and came back to find her dead. He said he thought he'd seen Aiden's car parked nearby. But nothing came of it all. The post-mortem said it was natural causes, heart failure. She was very frail. In his defence, Aiden said he'd sold some paintings for Kingsbury and the old man bore a grudge for the percentage he'd charged.'

'Which was?'

'A lot. I don't know the exact details. In the end there wasn't enough to charge Kingsbury and certainly not Aiden. Kingsbury died six months later.'

'Anything to do with Aiden?'

'No. A glioblastoma – brain tumour.'

Thomas had been watching her intently. He saw some flicker, some unhappiness, when she talked about hearing of the case. 'Did you know the person who investigated him? Did they tell you all this?'

'Yes,' she said. 'We were married at the time.'

He had already guessed as much. 'You must have been shocked last year when Greta Brodie died, finding Aiden Ruskin here.'

She nodded. 'Putting it mildly. Shocked. Suspicious. Yes.'

He considered it. 'Following you about like a bad smell.'

This time, she looked directly at him. 'He *is* a bad smell,' she said. 'When I saw Isabelle's body I felt exhausted. I knew what this man was. I knew it in my bones.'

Thomas studied her face for a few moments. He liked this woman. She wasn't going to let Ruskin go. They had that same gut feeling.

'I want to help you, Laura,' he said.

'I know.'

He returned to the issue of the car. 'What about his credit cards, phone?'

'Hasn't used them.'

'Where the hell is he then?'

She stood up, gathering her things together. She gazed down at him. 'Your professional opinion?'

He considered it. 'Someone picked him up at Castle Cary.'

She nodded. 'That's what I'm thinking, too.'

They walked together back out into the sunlight.

'Well,' Thomas said. 'It could be anybody. He could have thumbed a lift. Or several.'

Laura looked up at the sky and sighed. 'Needles and haystacks,' she murmured. Then she looked back at him. 'Are you walking back?'

'Maybe not. Twenty miles could be too much for both of us.' And he patted Max's head. 'I'll get the bus in Padstow.'

'Want a lift?'

'That would be great, thanks. If you don't mind Max in the car.'

'I'm hardly going to make him run behind.'

It was still a decent walk into the village, and most of the way Thomas wondered if he should ask her to lunch. He was hungry. Fortunately, when they were almost back to Trewarith in the car, Laura took a turning for a farm shop. 'Do you know this place?' she asked.

'Duck pâté?' he said.

She laughed. 'Bacon roll.'

'Bit common.'

'Wow,' she said, laughing. 'Thanks.'

They sat in the car park with their food. The breeze that had been blowing gently in from the coast suddenly dropped and it felt like summer.

'I've got a question,' he said when they'd finished. 'Or rather, a hypothesis to put to you.'

She wiped her fingers on a paper napkin. 'Let's hear it.'

'Suppose,' he said, 'that Greta Brodie went down to swim in the seawater pool late in the evening. She'd done it a thousand times. But she wasn't exactly young. Suppose this time she gets into difficulties and she drowns. The tide takes her out and – unlikely as it sounds – it brings her back again within a few hours. Ruskin and Keira find her the next morning. And suppose you don't believe a word of it.'

'And why would that be?'

'Because she's clothed.'

'Who told you she was clothed?' she asked.

'You did, just now.'

'Very clever.'

'Was she?'

'Yes.'

'And the explanation?'

'That she must have fallen in while walking.' She paused, with a tone of disbelief in her voice. 'At night, in winter.'

'Ruskin wouldn't answer that question when I asked.'

She raised her shoulders and spread her hands. 'No defence injury. Of course, it was difficult. The sea had pummelled the body. Aiden Ruskin appeared as distraught as Keira. He never wavered from his account. More importantly, Keira never contradicted him.'

'Did that bother you?'

She narrowed her eyes in what Thomas had come to recognise as an astute, calculating expression. 'Why should it?'

He crossed his arms, looking our through the windscreen but seeing only the cottages in Trewarith in his mind's eye. 'Keira loved her grandmother. They were more like mother and daughter. Bill Pascoe in the village tells me that Greta disliked Ruskin, and I'm sure if Greta told Bill, she certainly told Keira. Also...' He paused. 'I think you already know something more about Ruskin, and I think you found it out soon after Greta died.'

'We looked into him.'

'And found out a lot more than I know.'

'Yes, some. Circumstantial.'

'But enough to set alarm bells ringing.'

She looked at him steadily.

'And I think you're one hundred per cent sure he murdered Isabelle and you're as worried for Keira as I am. You think Keira was too afraid to contradict him over Greta's death because she'd finally realised what a danger he was and she had zero confidence that you could protect her. Or the police in general, in fact. She disappeared soon after. She went back to London and she closed up that gallery. She did it all so quickly that she slipped through your fingers. Slipped through Ruskin's fingers too. I'm guessing that's why he tore out the gardens. Vengeance.'

She was listening, head on one side, but said nothing.

'And ever since you've felt frustrated because you might have nailed Ruskin if Keira hadn't fled.' He gave her a sympathetic smile. 'But you more than anyone know why she went away. And I think you're paddling away like crazy, as if your life depended on it. Because Keira's life depends on you getting to her before Ruskin does.'

She studied him for a few seconds. 'And why do I think all that?' she asked quietly.

'Because you know this area and you know the village and no doubt talked to enough people to get a picture of Ruskin. And the more you find out, the more everything about this case is similar to what happened to your sister.'

Laura said nothing at all. She looked at the yard and the scatter of buildings beyond it, and then she very precisely folded up the paper bag that her bacon roll had been served in. 'I'm going to get a bottle of water,' she said.

He gripped her hand. 'And something else,' he insisted. 'You can't let me go racketing about the country finding out what you already know.'

'You went off on your own accord. I specifically told you not to go.'

'I'm guessing you knew already that Keira closed the gallery straight after Greta's funeral. Let me go back to London and see if I can find out more.'

'Thomas,' she said. 'You're not a police officer. You're a member of the public and if I let you do whatever, you'll compromise the investigation.'

He sighed. 'I'll make sure I don't do that.'

'It's not a great idea though, is it?'

'Look,' he said. 'I think Ruskin killed Isabelle, but I don't know the reason. Maybe you do. You'll have looked into the victimology. I think Isabelle and Ruskin had a deeper connection than just Keira. There was real rage in that attack. A feeling he's probably had all his life. Rage and narcissism. He wanted something she wasn't going to give. Maybe it was Keira's location, though I do think – given she was Greta's lifelong friend – that she'd gladly have died rather than tell Ruskin where Keira was.' He stopped to see if there was a flicker of agreement in Laura's face, but found none.

'But I also think there must have been something else between them. Art... something in her past and his. Perhaps even his father's. Did she buy from him, or did he buy from her maybe?'

'I don't know. I'm waiting on the bank accounts.'

'He felt cheated over something,' Thomas said. 'Not just Keira. Has he got a criminal record?'

She sighed. 'No.'

'Ruskin told me he worked for an auction house in London before working with his father. Anything there?'

'Look, Thomas—'

'Find his problem, and I think you'll find the link to Isabelle and the reason she died.'

'Isabelle was an absolutely reputable person. Please stop telling me how to do my work. I have a few years on this job as well as you. I don't need you mansplaining cause and effect to me.'

'That's not my intention.'

'All right. Just...' She paused. 'Never mind.'

'Keira,' he said. 'One more hypothesis.'

'Easy to concoct, harder to prove. Am I right?'

'Yes, you're right. But not impossible. He has to have left clues somewhere.'

'Okay then. Tell me.'

'If I had to make a guess – and act on that bad smell – I'd lay money on Aiden Ruskin killing routinely. He can't tolerate anyone opposing him, especially a woman. Plus, he's obsessive. He went to that saltwater pool every morning at exactly the same time. He fixates, and I think he particularly fixates on women. I think if

194

you went back through all his dealings, even before Kingsbury, you'd find more. More women, more deaths. But this is the first time he hasn't felt able to face it out. He's let himself be implicated. He feels weak. And that's where the connection to Keira comes in. She's the reason he's finally lost control.'

Laura crossed her arms.

'More women,' she murmured. 'I wonder how many.'

24

AIDEN WENT TO THE AUCTION WHERE the last of his father's paintings were sold. He hadn't expected much – his father's tastes were out of fashion – and true enough, he didn't get much. Just over twelve thousand. It wasn't enough.

He sat sulking in his seat until a woman came and tapped him on the shoulder. He looked up and saw a thin blonde with a sallow face.

'Aiden Ruskin! As I live and breathe.'

'Hello,' he said.

She laughed. 'You don't recognise me.'

Trying to be polite, he stood up. 'I'm sorry.'

'Well, aren't you the bastard?' she replied good-naturedly, though her mouth gave a little twitch of disappointment.

He looked her up and down. 'I'm sure I'm guilty as charged,' he said. He held out his hand. 'So you'll have to remind me.'

She took it and held on just a little too long. He leaned slightly closer and caught a whiff of alcohol.

'Celia Cavell.'

Now he remembered. Her father owned a Cotswold house. There had been a party when he first joined the auctioneers, the one from which he'd got fired. Before his disgrace there, a lot of them had gone to Gloucestershire for a weekend.

'How could I forget?' he murmured. 'The pub in Slad.'

'The Wooly.'

'Laurie Lee's place.'

'You *do* remember.'

He remembered it was August and very hot. He remembered that Celia had got very drunk very quickly and they had sat out until it got dark and then he'd helped her home. Her and two other girls, her friends from boarding school who all now worked – if you could call it work – in estate agents or solicitors offices or in hotel management in Gloucestershire and seemed to hold Celia in some kind of awe. Hangers-on, the lot of them.

No one worth knowing was still in London that month, or so he'd been told. Probably by none other than Celia Cavell. They were two juniors left in London to man the fort over August, so he'd seen a lot of her flitting about the corridors, both of them trying to look busy. He couldn't remember them being lovers. Maybe they were. Or not. It didn't matter now. She wasn't the memorable type.

He had to listen all year to other bastards telling him they were going to their parents' villas that summer or were going to Scotland for the grouse or whatever. It hadn't taken him long to hate them all. He'd only got the job because they'd been desperate. Somebody had left them for pastures new. Those were the words exactly. 'We've been thrown over for pastures new.' His interviewer was an older man, great suit, an entitled air. Some ponce's son. There was one there who was a Viscount. Like it mattered. It was all very condescending. They'd sniffed at his 2:1 red-brick degree. They asked how long he'd spent in Florence. He lied and said a year when it was only a month staying in a hostel. He hinted he knew someone at the British Library. Looking down his CV, they'd questioned the village he grew up in. And then a piece of luck. The heavens opened and the light shone down. The interviewer had an aunt living in the same village. It was the woman who lived next to the school, a batty old witch who shouted at kids in the playground. 'I knew her very well,' Aiden said.

The man pulled a face. 'Died last month.'

'Oh how sad,' he replied, and tried to look suitably grieved. He got the job.

Celia Cavell was one of the girls who hadn't had to labour through an interview. Daddy knew another Daddy and all that. She wasn't pretty but she was – he tried to recall what she'd told him – *'Father says I'm...'* well, what was it? *'Father says I'm loquacious.'* That was it. Bloody loquacious Celia Cavell.

As it turned out, Celia wasn't so much loquacious as desperate. He knew that she'd had some sort of thing going with one of the partners, a married man, and been dumped. Or so the rumour went. Not so much desperate maybe as always being told that she was second best. She had an older sister who was a lawyer – company law, very lucrative. Older sister had married a hedge-fund manager that spring and they lived in tacky splendour in Holland Park. The husband treated Aiden as if he were some sort of spiv, and had known his father. The first and only time they met – Celia showing him off as if he were the world's biggest prize in the autumn after Slad – the husband cut him down in the first sentence. 'Your father sold me a forgery,' he said, lounging back on the faux marble of the kitchen island with a glass of Scotch in his fist. 'I don't think so,' Aiden had replied. 'Oh yes,' the husband said. 'I've had that confirmed only this last week. I think I'll sue you both. I paid forty thousand for that daub.' And he pointed to a little watercolour on the wall, looking like Monet but possibly not Monet at all.

Aiden realised that this man had been waiting for Celia to bring her conquest to his house so he could deliver this body blow. 'My father's business dealings have nothing to do with me,' Aiden retaliated.

'That so?'

'That's so.'

The husband had turned to his lawyer wife. 'What do you think, darling?'

This woman. Bony shoulders. Face like a horse. 'Worth looking into,' she said, smiling.

Celia had lost her temper. 'How dare you!' she cried. 'Aiden is perfectly honest.'

'Oh, I doubt that,' the husband replied.

'Didn't you get it verified?' Aiden asked. 'Always check before you buy.' He returned the husband's stare, knowing that this man had grabbed one of Archie's baits. He'd probably gone to bid on something, lost out, and Archie had sidled up to him in his friendly slimy way and suggested that he might like to buy something of his which hadn't been on the market for years. Husband probably knew it was dodgy – stolen, maybe. These gits recognised a fellow liar when they met them. Archie had a talent for making men like him think they had stumbled into an exclusive private club where art theft was legitimised. The husband had probably congratulated himself for buying under the radar, cheating somebody else out of their possession. And Archie could be very charming, God knows. The old goat. He couldn't help smiling.

Husband advanced on him, slamming down the Scotch glass on the worktop. 'Kindly piss off out of my house,' he said.

I'm right, he thought. *Cheater got cheated*. All the same, he left.

Celia came running after him.

'I didn't know,' she pleaded.

'It doesn't matter.'

'It does, Aiden. I'm sorry. I'll make it up to you.'

He had dumped her soon after the brother-in-law incident, bored with her drinking and clinging ways. But he considered Celia with renewed interest now, all these years later. 'Can you possibly do me a favour?' he asked.

The next day was Friday. From his house, they walked down to Keira's gallery. He felt awake, alert. Celia less so from whatever she'd snorted last night. He'd never taken drugs. They made you weak, dependent. Celia was a case in point. He now realised why she fidgeted all the time. 'I've got a friend restoring a place down here,' he told her. 'I want to play a little trick. Just for fun. Want to help me?'

She clung on to him, glad to be part of his world. 'Sure,' she said. 'What do you want me to do?'

They'd reached the corner by the time he finished telling her. The gallery was down a little mews alley. He could see scaffolding outside it. 'Distract the builders,' he said. 'Think you could do that?'

She could. They walked up to the entrance. The facade was being painted and a man on the first-floor level looked down at them.

'Hello,' Celia said brightly. 'This is my friend's place. I came here yesterday, remember?'

'I wasn't here yesterday,' he said.

'I left my keys. My car keys. Can I go inside and look?'

'I don't know about that. The boss is on lunch break.'

'I won't be long, honestly.'

He shrugged. 'Go on then.'

Celia dodged inside. She was gone for no more than thirty seconds. She held up a bunch of keys triumphantly to the painter. 'Thanks!'

'No worries,' he replied.

Back in the main shopping street again, Aiden inspected them. The gods were smiling on him. They were the door keys.

'Was that what you wanted?' she asked.

'Perfect,' he said. 'Now could you get me a coffee? There's a place just here, look. I'll be back in five minutes.'

He took the keys from her and sprinted along the street and turned the corner. He ran back up to the station and crossed the road to the narrow little shop on the opposite side. Once he got the duplicate keys cut he ran back, avoiding the street where Celia

200

was waiting and going behind it until he came out at the opposite end. He trotted back to the gallery, waving the bunch of keys in his hand. He called up to the painter. 'Wrong keys!' he shouted. He dodged back into the house and put the keys where Celia said she'd found them, on the table next to the safe.

Going out, he shouted up to the painter again. 'Bloody women!'

Celia was waiting for him. He could see her fidgeting with her hair, her back to him, sitting outside in the cold sunshine surrounded by little Christmas trees with red ribbons threaded through them. For a second he thought of leaving her there. She was really tedious. But then, all her cries of appreciation last night had been entertaining. And she would do anything he asked. Crawl on the floor on her hands and knees. Lie still and shut up when he told her.

It was a pity.

She could have made someone a good dog one day.

25

THE WEATHER WAS STILL WARM WHEN Thomas went back to London. Bill Pascoe was away, so he drove back home and left his car at the pub after dropping Max off with Jenny. Both seemed delighted, but he was sure that Max's love was for Jenny's kitchen rather than Jenny herself.

Tam Jeffries, Thomas's dealer for his last and only exhibition, continued to operate out of his place in Bayswater, an arts venue that didn't quite know what it was: gallery, studio or shop. The front was painted a shade of luminous pink that had infuriated the owners of two flats across the road and, bizarrely, a dry cleaner's two doors down. They said that Tam was bringing down the neighbourhood, but he didn't care. Tam Jeffries had lived on the floor above for forty years. His shambolic apartment on two floors was bare of everything but the essentials. No carpet, no blinds. But a mess of books, art catalogues and display easels. A leather lounger chair and a footstool and a well-stocked fridge and a giant bed overlooking an overgrown garden at the back. At this time of year, the magnolia tree there was in full flower.

Tam greeted him like a long-lost brother, though had something to say about his appearance. 'You've lost weight,' he said. 'And you look like shit, love.'

Thomas laughed, because Tam was right. He knew that his jeans, sweatshirt and jacket hung on him.

'Why does that jacket smell of petrol, for God's sake? And

you need a haircut,' Tam added. 'Don't they cut their hair in the deepest south-west?'

'I got it cut a month ago.'

'What, by a sheep shearer?' Tam tutted. By contrast Tam looked his usual resplendent self in a three-piece suit with a lavender check.

'You like?' Tam said, seeing Thomas's gaze. 'Vintage. Old Spitalfields Market.'

'Very nice. Very you.'

Tam smiled, and shook his head. 'Stay there,' he said. He went out and came back five minutes later with coffee and pastries, picking his way through his ground-floor exhibition. 'Get this down you,' he said. 'There's an apricot Danish there with your name on it.'

They sat down, clearing a space among the mass of paperwork on the desk and chairs in the small office at the back.

'So,' Tam said. 'Tell all. Are you working? Painting?'

'A bit.'

'Will you let me see?'

'There's nothing really to see at the moment.'

'So, what's this about? I thought you might be bringing me something.'

It took a while – he tried not to dwell on last year – but when he got to more recent history and mentioned Aiden Ruskin's name, he saw Tam's expression darken.

'You know him.'

'I did,' Tam said.

'Not now?'

'Thank God, no.'

'I take it you didn't like him?'

'Like him?' Tam repeated. 'I threw him out of here once. He was mauling my Clara. She tried to punch him and missed, unfortunately.'

'When was this?'

'Last summer. Late August. '

'Did he speak to you at all?'

'Oh yes,' Tam confirmed. 'I told him to bugger off. He's a nasty little sod. Bore grudges, you know?' Tam frowned. 'It's a bit of bad luck you've had to run into all this, and him particularly.'

'You could say that.' Thomas sipped whatever the concoction was that Tam had brought him. Turmeric latte, he guessed. It was disgusting. 'Ruskin says that Keira Brodie was his wife.'

This time, Tam stopped eating. 'That's a lie.'

'I'm sure it is.'

'She didn't want to marry him. Never. From the moment they met. They had a thing for a while. I warned her against him. I told her he wasn't right. She laughed it off at first. Then she changed.'

'How "changed"?'

'Went very quiet about him. I saw her often at functions. Quite a little sweetheart she is, Thomas. Very personable. Very knowledgeable. But after a while she never came with him. It was like she knew she'd made a mistake. Like she was embarrassed about it. Perhaps even worried, you know?'

'Frightened?'

'Not then.'

'Did Keira know the father?'

'Oh yes,' he said. 'Everyone knew Archie.'

'Did she ever work with him?'

'Why would she? She's got better clients than him, you know.'

'Yes, I know. Isabelle Crosby hinted at it. What kind of clients?'

'All over England. Particularly favoured by aristocracy selling off the family jewels to pay the utilities.' Tam sighed. 'I can't get over Isabelle.' He leaned forward and tapped Thomas on the knee. 'It's him, isn't it?' he said. 'Bloody Ruskin.'

'Probably, Tam.'

Tam gave a weak smile. 'Ever the policeman.'

'It follows me around.'

'But any idea why?'

'I was hoping you'd make a guess at it. What was their connection, Isabelle and Ruskin? Do you know?'

'Well…' Tam fussed with the nearest pieces of paper. 'Only the ancient history.'

'What ancient history?'

'Isabelle and Archie. Years ago. They had an arrangement I hear.'

'An affair, you mean?'

Tam shrugged. 'Some say so. But I mean, literally years. Maybe twenty.'

'But what was their connection?'

'Art, my dear. Art. And worse.'

'Worse?'

'Mmm.' Tam took a sip of his coffee. 'I didn't know them at the time. How could I, just a slip of a lad blown in from the bad lands of Aberdeen?' He smiled. 'Heady days. Archie was quite the man then. Travelled all over. He was pointed out to me as a somebody. Of course, he was a bit of a looker then, not the gargantuan monster he became. Trendy fellow. Ran a Jaguar Mark II. Traded in antiquities. Bit dodgy. He was just a little cog in the wheels really. Not big-time stuff. But enough to make a good living, and enough to keep him out of the line of sight, as it were.'

'Police? Customs?'

'Not a mark on him.' Tam leaned forward and patted Thomas on the knee. 'He used to deal in all kinds of things. Paintings and ceramics were the "legal" face of the business, though he supposedly cheated his customers right, left and centre. His favourite thing was visiting someone in their home and then telling them that one or two things were good and he'd act as their agent because "you can't trust these big auction houses you know" – that was one of his lines – and then at the last minute he'd pretend he'd just noticed something minor hanging on the wall, say it was almost worthless, get them to sell it to him, and then take it straight to those very same "untrustworthy auction houses" where it'd be verified for a bloody fortune. Provenance obscure, of course. In time the big boys wouldn't deal with him, but he'd go out to the provinces and sell it on there. This was before the internet, of course. He'd go to the back of beyond sometimes. And word is, he taught his son the same tricks.'

Thomas thought about it. 'There must be a lot of people out there hating father and son.'

'Oh, I doubt they ever twigged. Mostly elderly you know, or family wanting quick probate. They would tend to focus on the good price they'd been given for the other stuff he took, especially Archie giving them hard cash for the others that he'd said were practically worthless.' Tam finished the pastry and wiped his mouth. 'That was his genius,' he mused. 'Never too ambitious, never too mainstream. Buckets of duplicity.'

'And he trained his son the same way?'

'Yes. Although Aiden never had Archie's subtlety. He made my flesh creep, to be honest.'

'Yes,' Thomas agreed. 'I know.'

They sat quietly considering Aiden Ruskin.

'Isabelle told me that her interest used to be in archaeology,' Thomas said. 'And that she'd been to the Med about eight years ago.'

'Did she?' Tam said. 'I wouldn't know. She dropped Archie, left the scene and went to Cornwall once she married that Sir Whatshisname.'

'She told me that she still travelled without him.'

Tam simply raised his eyebrows. 'Jaunty woman.'

'She said she had some pieces in her house.'

'What kind of pieces?'

'Something with an archaeological connection.'

Tam nodded slowly. 'Well, well. Is that so?'

'Was she trading in them, do you think? Is that how she knew Aiden Ruskin?'

'Your guess is as good as mine. But like I say, she certainly knew the father back in the day.'

'Do you think she and Archie imported these things?'

'Illegally, you mean?'

'Yes.'

Tam looked at Thomas for some time. 'Bottom line?' he murmured, finally. 'We all did.'

'Where from?'

'Well... I used to buy from a guy who travelled in India. Little shrines and statues, that kind of thing. All above board. At least, he told me so.' Tam had the grace to blush.

'Would Isabelle have got these things herself, from archaeological digs?'

'Oh now, that's making quite a leap there, old boy. There's more than one scandal involved in that.'

'But do you think so? Guess so?'

'I wouldn't guess at that, no. Quite an accusation.'

Thomas stayed silent. If Isabelle had been close to Archie, she may well have known his methods. He thought it likely that Aiden too guessed that she had something valuable in the house – perhaps something she wouldn't give up. Or perhaps there was something even more valuable to him. A contact. A source.

'When you were talking about Keira just now, you said "not then",' Thomas said. 'What happened later? Last year?'

'After she'd known him a while, Keira altered. Looked a bit haunted to my eye. But I can't say anything more, Thomas. She came here... I wanted to kill Ruskin there and then. If you knew...' He stopped. 'No, it's a private thing. I can't say.'

'She came here before she left?'

'Yes. A few months before.'

They heard the doorbell go in the shop. Tam glanced up at the CCTV above his head. 'Post,' he murmured. 'Hold on a minute.'

When he came back, his whole demeanour had changed. Thomas realised he'd firmed his decision not to discuss Keira. 'Listen,' he said, 'how well do you know Keira?'

'I don't know her at all. I've never met her.'

'Then I shouldn't be discussing her. Sorry, mate.'

It was Thomas's turn to frown. Tam was the biggest gossip in the business. 'I think she's in danger, Tam.'

'Yes,' he said quietly, looking down at the desk. His quiet acceptance of that raised all kinds of red flags in Thomas's mind, more urgent now than ever.

'After Isabelle Crosby's death, Ruskin's disappeared. I think he's trying to find Keira.'

'Then it's to be hoped to God he doesn't succeed.'

Thomas looked at his friend. 'Do you know where she is?'

'No, I don't.'

'But you knew she was missing. You knew the gallery was empty, closed up.'

'Yes, I knew that.'

'Is she abroad?'

'Thomas,' he said. 'With the best will in the world, I can't tell you what I don't know.'

When Thomas left the shop, he walked down to Marble Arch and into Oxford Street. He was due to meet Laura Cullen at one o'clock in Covent Garden, but still had time to spare. He turned off Oxford Street towards Manchester Square, thinking that he could go and see the Wallace Collection.

It was then, in these quiet streets, that he saw her.

He recognised the way she walked: that confident swing. It was what he first noticed. A woman dressed in a bright green jacket and a pair of cream-coloured jeans crossing the road at Spanish Place. She was diagonally opposite to him as he came up the east side of the square. She paused for traffic to pass her, and she turned her head towards him. He was probably a hundred yards away, but he knew her at once.

Helen McAllister had hardly changed in eleven years. Her hair was cut the same way. She looked relaxed and she was holding a mobile phone. He saw its chrome and the pink flash of its cover as she answered a call. She began to laugh and gesture with her free hand, waiting at the kerb. She looked directly at him, but there was no reaction from her. The thought crossed his mind in an instant that she wouldn't care.

He began to run.

Without thinking, he stepped into the road and a cab squealed to a stop. The driver shook a fist at him, cursing. Thomas held up his hand by way of apology and crossed the road, but Helen McAllister had gone. He ran to the corner where she had been. The cream-and-pink building of the Wallace Collection was to his left. He could see the length of Spanish Place and the main road beyond. She wasn't walking there, nor in front of the Wallace, nor was she in sight in the square itself under the trees. He ran to the streets on the west side, but she could have gone anywhere. He looked about himself in panic. Had she noticed him? She could have gone into any building – any of the eighteenth-century houses on the square. Or the Wallace itself.

He ran back to the museum, gasping for breath now.

A man was standing on the steps.

'Did you see a woman come in here?' Thomas asked. 'A blonde woman in her thirties, early forties? She had a green jacket, lime green…'

The man shook his head.

'Did you see her go past? Did she walk into the square? Did she go towards Selfridges? Oxford Street?'

The man leaned towards him and took him by the elbow. 'I haven't seen anyone like that. Are you all right?' he asked. 'You don't look very well.'

26

SHE HAD A LAUNCH EVENING IN late November.

Aiden didn't get an invitation. He only knew because he walked past the gallery every morning and he saw the flowers being delivered. Through the window he could see her inside speaking to someone he didn't recognise. They were hanging paintings. She seemed happy, smiling. He had to admit that the gallery looked perfect: muted, sophisticated. There was no name on the outside, only the old Georgian number of the house. Admittance by appointment, he guessed, judging by the CCTV and the alarm.

He'd missed his opportunity. He'd made the mistake of going to Italy with Celia. She had spoiled Florence for him with her endless talking. On the third day, he'd lost his wallet with all his credit cards and she had to pay for everything for the next three days, including the hotel bill. He told her he'd reported it to the police and she kept asking for details, which he couldn't give her considering that his wallet was still firmly in his jacket pocket. He'd asked her for peace. She just wouldn't listen.

He walked in circles the day of the flowers. Mid-afternoon, he went home and showered and changed. He had a few drinks, finishing his father's last bottle. He arrived at the gallery at six and the door was open and he could hear music playing. He walked in.

Keira was standing in the centre of the room. There were thirty or so guests and he didn't even notice the man standing to one side of the door. He went straight up to her and smiled. 'Congratulations,' he said.

He was astounded at the pieces on display. Really so astounded that he couldn't say anything else. She'd decided to follow her area of expertise. He stood gaping at a Madonna and child, tiny, beautifully lit. It looked like Masaccio, but it couldn't be. Then he realised the significance of the man by the door and another at the door of the office. Security. She'd hired bloody security. He started to laugh.

'Will you give me a tour?' he said.

She didn't reply. Instead, she looked at the man by the door. Out of the corner of his eye, Aiden saw him move forward, and he felt his arm being grabbed. He didn't even get a drink. He didn't get a drink and he didn't get a reply. Surely he was entitled to a reply. Courtesy. Didn't that matter anymore? It was the least she could do after all he'd done for her. All the attention, all the guidance, all the benefit of his experience. It was worth something. It was worth a damned sight more than being flatly ignored. A couple of the other people turned and looked at him. He didn't know them, but they looked rich. They had that self-satisfied air, the perfect relaxation of knowing that no effort at all was needed. The man at his shoulder leaned down and whispered in his ear. 'This way, sir,' he said.

He found himself out on the pavement. Worse still, he was manhandled right into the main street and was then pushed in the small of his back. 'Go home,' the man said.

He stood exactly where he'd been placed, unable to move. He couldn't believe what had just happened. In fact, for a few seconds, he couldn't *remember* exactly what had just happened. Humiliation coursed through him. He felt the same peculiar twisting sensation in his left shoulder that he'd had after his father died. Fucking hell, he was going to have a heart attack for sure this time. He was going to die like his father. He clenched his fists and tried to breathe. He *heard* the blood pounding in his brain. But the feeling passed.

He looked down the mews and saw that the security man was standing outside on the steps, watching him. *It wasn't a Masaccio*, he thought. She'd engineered some kind of forgery. *Petty crook.* The gall of it, when she was no better than him. And the rest of the pieces – all the same era, he guessed. Couldn't anyone see what she was? An imposter.

For the life of him, he couldn't see what he'd done that was so wrong. He was attentive and forgiving. He was educated, clever, persuasive. He tolerated far more than even Keira appreciated – her grandmother for one. He'd never said a word out of place, kept his feelings shuttered inside himself. Even with the gallery he'd offered to help and she'd refused him. She'd ended the relationship in the cruellest way possible and now she'd banned him from even seeing what she was doing. It was too late to use the keys now – he'd be seen on CCTV and he didn't know the code for the alarm. And that was Celia's fault, wanting to go to Florence. If she hadn't insisted on a holiday together, he would have been able to get in the gallery while the builders were still there and at least get access to the safe. His mind ground down through the various memories of Celia trying to look winsome and appealing. She was unutterably stupid. Vacant, needy. He had thought he might make a few more contacts in Italy but she purposely distracted him. At that moment he hated both Celia and Keira with a kind of religious fervour. How could anyone be kind towards those who betrayed you?

He felt suddenly violently sick. He ran across the street and found himself in Belgrave Square and he tried to get to the trees and made it only to the railings and vomited over them. A passing car blew their horn and he gave them two fingers without letting go of the rails. She'd done this. She'd done it. He fumbled in his jacket for his phone and saw with fury that the vomit had splattered his trousers and shoes. He dialled her mobile. Once, twice. Hearing the tone, he stared at the screen.

She'd changed her number.

He went home and had another shower, changed his clothes.

At eight, he drove over to Celia's flat. She shared it with another wide-eyed daddy's girl, another vacuous moron. When he rang the bell the other girl answered.

'Celia in?' he asked.

The girl seemed doubtful. She looked over her shoulder. 'It's Aiden,' she called.

Celia came out. She looked as if she'd been crying. Or perhaps it was whatever she was on.

'Not ready?' he said.

She wiped her face hastily.

'Don't tell me you've forgotten?' he said. He smiled at the other girl and rolled his eyes. 'Cee, you've got to do something about that memory of yours.'

Celia stepped forward, but the other girl put out her hand to stop her and stared at Aiden. 'You told her it was over.'

'Over?' he repeated. 'I did no such thing.' He smiled at Celia. 'Aren't you well?'

'Yes,' she said, and she glanced at her friend. 'Yes, I'm fine. Give me a minute,' and she disappeared into her bedroom.

He let the car keys swing in his fingers, and held them up. 'I'm going to let Celia drive,' he said. 'I've had a drink.'

'I can smell it.'

'Celebration tonight. My friend opened a gallery.'

'Yes, Celia said. She thought you were there.'

'Just popped in. Bit dismal really. Shame.'

At that moment, Celia emerged. She'd put on some make-up and a dress. She touched her friend on the shoulder by way of goodbye.

'Be careful,' the girl said.

Despite what he'd said, he drove out of London. Celia began one of her monotonous lectures about life, about the auction house, about art. He only listened when she mentioned Keira and told him in her naïve way how successful she was.

'She was in yesterday,' she murmured.

'Is that right?' He put his foot on the accelerator.

'She spent over a million.'

He nearly spun the car off the road, corrected it, and increased his speed. He finally took the M11.

'Where are we going?' she asked. 'Is it far?'

'Cambridge,' he said, randomly picking a destination. He had no idea if he was going there or not.

'I can't go to Cambridge,' she protested. 'I've got work tomorrow.'

'Ah yes,' he said quietly. 'At the place where they let crooks bid for their anonymous bloody clients.'

'Who's a crook?' she said, mystified.

He didn't answer. He was disgusted with her ferociously menial little job, her admiration for Keira. 'Have a drink,' he told her. 'Look in the glove. I brought you brandy.'

'But I don't like brandy,' she said, and she actually pouted like the child she was. 'And I don't want to go to Cambridge, Aiden.' He saw that she was gripping the edge of her seat. He slowed right down and took the junction.

'Have you ever been to the Blackwater Estuary?' he asked. 'Don't you like places on the coast, forgotten ones, empty spaces? Like the world's end. There was a place near my mother's called World's End. When I was a kid I thought it was real, that you dropped off the edge of the world when you got there and spun into space.'

'Aiden,' Celia said. 'Please take me home.'

'You want some adventure, don't you?' he said. 'You don't want to sit in that flat and go to Toynton's tomorrow. That's no fun.'

'Aiden, please.'

He carried on driving. He was thinking of a village called Tolleshunt D'Arcy. It was along this road. There'd been a mass murder there a few years back. A man had slaughtered his whole family and blamed it on someone else. He thought he might show Celia the house.

Celia began to cry. 'Slow down,' she pleaded. 'Slow down.'

27

Thomas had recovered by the time he met Laura. He'd walked to Covent Garden, gathering his wits, reasoning with himself that it was impossible that Helen McAllister could be alive. There'd been absolutely no trace of her in eleven years.

He thought for a long time about ringing Richard Ellis, who even now might be considering investigating Christine's garden. But he hesitated. He couldn't be sure what or who he had seen. He hadn't caught a close-up of her face. It was only the way that the woman had walked, that familiar self-confident swing of her hips. It was said people could change most things about their appearance but it was hard to change the way you walked. And even if she had found some sort of relationship that allowed her to vanish, it was hard to maintain your anonymity these days. While he waited for Laura, he considered the ways in which he was known online and in the contracts he signed. Mobile phone, address, insurances. All those times he'd randomly clicked the 'accept cookies' boxes that gave data brokers a way into his life. Helen's whole new identity would probably have to be created illegally. And why would she bother? She'd not committed a crime, unless her abandonment of her partner was criminal.

It was, in one sense. It had led Alice to descend into paranoia, into wholly wrong assumptions. It had caused his own resignation, not to mention the pain he lived with now.

By habit, he explored the site of the injury on his scalp. He'd been told it might fade, just as the headaches would fade. Or, then again, they might never end. This piece of news had been delivered to him by the neurologist the last time he'd been for an appointment. He wished more than anything else in his life to erase that mark. He grimaced to himself. No, that wasn't quite true. The number one thing he wished for was to have Fran back. She was fading a little every day and he knew that one day he wouldn't be able to remember even the exact way she looked or what her voice sounded like. But perhaps that would be a blessing, a letting go.

He saw Laura come into the Piazza and watched her walk into the sunlight, shielding her eyes. After a moment, he waved to her.

She was smiling as she approached him and stood a little way apart, looking him up and down. 'You've changed your clothes.'

'Only the jacket. Tam said it stank of petrol and smoke.'

She nodded approvingly. 'Thank God. I didn't like to say.'

He grinned at her. 'Good to know I've been wandering about smelling like a health hazard.'

'Maybe not *quite* as bad as that, but lingering enough,' she said. 'Was Tam any help?'

'Some,' he said. 'Are we going to Toynton & Mark?'

She glanced at her watch. 'In an hour and a half.'

'Lunch?'

'Not here. I'm not paying tourist prices. I know somewhere much better.'

They walked down to the river and to a sandwich bar with a couple of tables. 'Italian,' Laura explained. 'They make their own bread. You might think you're in Tuscany.'

They sat down and ordered. 'You've been to Italy?' Thomas asked.

'A couple of times. The last was Le Marche. The east, facing the Adriatic. I had the best meal of my life there once. A farm in the hills, run by two women. Six courses. When they opened the doors to the garden, all the chickens came wandering in. God, the food was special.'

He smiled watching her. 'Just on your own?'

'On my honeymoon. Fifteen years ago.'

'But you're not married now?'

'No,' she said. 'The honeymoon was great. Everything else was absolute shite. Never look at your partner's phone. Never.'

'Oh.'

'Yes, oh,' she said.

'I guess you know my history from Richard.'

'Some. Not all. The part about McAllister.'

He sighed. 'I thought I saw her this morning.'

She looked shocked. 'McAllister?'

'Yes.' He told her what he'd seen. Or thought he'd seen.

She frowned. 'It's not possible, Thomas.' She spread her hands in a shrugging gesture. 'Maybe if you'd glimpsed her on a Pacific island somewhere living in a hut. But not even then, frankly. It's very hard these days for someone not to leave a digital trace. A lot's changed even in ten years. To really disappear she'd have to be in witness protection, and she certainly isn't, unless she'd got herself involved in some criminal almighty fuck-up and had to run to the police. But then we'd know, wouldn't we? And we don't. Richard would have checked it again, I'm sure, cold case. As for walking about in broad daylight in London…'

'I know,' he agreed. 'It was not a good experience, though. It was a shock.'

'I bet.' She frowned, looking closely at him. 'You're okay?'

He quickly changed the subject, telling her all that Tam Jeffries had said about Keira. 'The oddest thing,' he concluded, 'was this comment about wanting to kill Ruskin after Keira had come to see him one night. Tam is the least aggressive person I know. But he wouldn't be drawn on what made him so angry. It was obviously something to do with Ruskin and Keira, but it was, in his words, "private".'

'Personal, private,' Laura mused, drinking the last of her coffee and folding the paper napkin over the crumbs of panini on her plate. 'What would fit that description?'

'Could be anything.'

They got up and walked along the Embankment for a while, looking at the comings and goings on the river.

'What did your colleague say about Keira?' Thomas asked.

'Maybe the answer to the question of Tam's reticence,' Laura said, stopping to lean on the wall and gaze out over the water. 'Keira Brodie reported a rape a couple of months before her gallery opened. She named Aiden Ruskin. And then she withdrew the allegation the same night, just an hour or so later, before she even got to the rape suite. She apologised for wasting police time.'

'That's disturbing.'

'Isn't it?' Laura agreed.

'Was Ruskin interviewed?'

'No.'

'Why would she withdraw it?'

'It's a horrible process, Thomas. But my guess is that she was afraid of what he might do.' She paused, then turned to him. 'Ruskin was interviewed over an assault. A man who'd sold some pieces to Ruskin. Ruskin took a knife to him. Nearly severed an artery. The man admitted himself to A&E and said he'd been attacked because he'd made a move on Ruskin.'

'What happened?'

Laura raised an eyebrow in a sardonic expression. 'Ruskin is a kind of escape artist, you know? He was brought in for questioning and raised all kinds of hell, saying he'd given the client the brush-off – no hard feelings and all that, it didn't bother him – but the guy had been hyped up and hysterical and threatened to cut his own throat if Ruskin wouldn't sleep with him, and he'd left. He told the interviewing officer that he thought all through dinner that the guy was unstable, so he made his excuses. Paid him a good fee for the paintings he was selling and made a quick exit.'

'What was the guy's story?'

'That Ruskin had very calmly picked up the knife and cut him, and equally calmly left.'

Thomas was paying close attention to her. 'You knew all this already. You knew it after Greta's death last year.'

'Well… yes.'

'And this morning was just a refresher course?'

'Kind of. But I didn't know about Keira's accusation until this morning.'

Thomas smiled, looking at his feet momentarily and then back at her. 'Well, I guess you must trust me a bit more.'

'It's not all.'

'And you're going to tell me?'

'It's my ex-husband who's in the Art & Antiques department,' she said. 'Ruskin Senior and Junior have a rotten reputation. But they're both as slippery as eels. Ruskin's been under surveillance for the last year. He has some very dodgy contacts in Europe and he'd been over there twice.'

'What's the suspicion?'

'Smuggling. ISIS pushed a lot of irreplaceable artefacts onto the market, but even more were sold privately. Ruskin met more than one person. They suspect some very lucrative deal is about to go down. It's unusual for Aiden Ruskin, because he's been pretty small fry until now. But he sold his father's house in London just a few days before Christmas. Cash buyer.'

Thomas huffed. 'And there he is telling me he's not got a penny to his name,' he said. 'Well, well. What do the team say?'

'They're as frustrated as we are that Ruskin's disappeared, but their take on that is interesting. They think he was trying to fund a massive deal. An illegal deal, and it's all gone wrong. They think Isabelle Crosby might have formed a link in the chain.'

For a few moments, Thomas couldn't speak. Then, 'Jesus,' he muttered.

'A perfect cover,' Laura said.

'You really think that?'

'It's possible, isn't it?'

'But why? She had more than enough money.'

'She didn't though, did she?' Laura replied. 'You saw the house. All her assets were tied up in it. She was in debt, Thomas. She could well have been tempted to go in with Ruskin. She owed everyone. Even the utilities were about to be turned off.'

'She didn't like Ruskin, though.' He paused. 'Even if she was tempted, she wouldn't have the ready cash. All of that market is incredibly expensive.'

'It *was* expensive,' she corrected him. 'You probably know as well as anyone that a fresh painting or whatever – what we'd call modern art – can sell for thousands one day and be practically worthless the next. From what I can understand, it's all hype and rumour, investment and so on. It's not much to do with the actual art.'

He nodded. 'Yes, Keira's market – old masters and so on – is much more reliable for investment.' He smiled. 'You catch on quick.'

'No I don't,' she replied. 'I've heard this stuff non-stop from my ex when we were together.'

Thomas wondered if that explained her reaction to Isabelle's studio when she first saw it. It wasn't a surprise.

'Did you already know that Isabelle had been a dealer when I first met you, the day she died?'

'I rang my ex on the way. He told me she was old news in the dealing market but hot on buying modern stuff in the past seven or eight years.'

'Interesting,' he said.

'Why so?'

'She told me that she came back from a Mediterranean trip eight years ago. It was when she inherited Max. I wonder if something on that trip made her change her interests. Her "investments".'

'What kind of thing?'

'I don't know – did she run into Ruskin then? Did she have a moment when she realised exactly where the artefacts were coming from?'

'Eight years,' Laura murmured. 'The rise of ISIS.'

They were both silent for some time.

'Possibly a very dangerous link,' Thomas said eventually.

'Those postcards she left you,' Laura said. 'What's the significance? Is it Venice?'

'I don't know.' But he had been thinking about them. The V&A card about a centuries-old fraud. The Venetian pictures.

'There must be something,' Laura prompted. 'She put those together hastily just before she died, and she meant them for you.' She paused. 'Did she know you'd been an inspector?'

'She knew I'd been in the police, yes. But she didn't dwell on it. We talked more about art.'

'So she put together a puzzle for you.'

'You think that's what it is?'

Laura raised her hands in a gesture of helplessness.

'Maybe there's no real significance in the cards,' Thomas said.

'I think there must be. I think she knew that Ruskin was coming, and she was trying to tell you something. I thought when I first gave them to you, you'd immediately see some point or other.'

'Sorry,' he murmured. 'I don't have a clue really. Just places in Venice, islands. Burano's popular, Mazzorbo less so I think.'

'A hideaway?'

'God. I've no idea. You're the one looking into her affairs.'

'Williams is on it.'

'You mean she might own a place there? Somewhere usually overlooked by tourists?'

'And then there's this fraud case, the V&A card. Someone who claimed to be something he wasn't?'

'She must mean Ruskin.'

'Or Keira.'

'What have you got against Keira all of a sudden? We're trying to protect her aren't we?'

'Well, you are,' Laura said. 'I prefer to keep a more open mind.'

He felt reprimanded.

'To get back to Isabelle,' Laura continued calmly, 'it's possible that Ruskin was still smarting over some long-ago deal that she had with his father, or a scheme that went wrong. It's possible her death was nothing to do with Keira. Collectors are crazy, you know. Whether it's art or archaeological pieces or watches or wine... whatever it is, they'd sell their soul – including breaking the law – to get that rare, exclusive item.'

Below them, a passenger ferry docked, churning the water against the Embankment wall. People began to stream from the boat and onto the street.

'However, we are talking about her distant past by considering that,' Laura continued. 'All appearances seem to be she was a genuine art lover in recent years and not someone like Ruskin trying to make fortunes out of it. Maybe she'd completely changed her mind because she knew her life expectancy wasn't great. But I think she'd been a collector of antiquities for years, and I still don't know how much Ruskin might have taken from the house the night he killed her.'

'Perhaps if nothing else Ruskin wanted some valuable piece that she owned,' Thomas observed. 'Something she wouldn't either give or sell to him.'

Laura pushed herself away from the wall and glanced again at her watch. 'Toynton & Mark can tell us more about that hopefully,' she said. 'Not only did they used to employ Ruskin, they're doing Isabelle's inventory and sale.'

28

AIDEN GREW SICK OF THE REMAINING presence of Archie in the house.

He got decorators in, clearing the Augean stables that had been Archie's room. He nearly killed himself hauling an armchair down the narrow stairs, and it stank of smoke. He got a house clearance around, shysters who tried to con him out of a few pounds and kept looking past doorways to see if they could spot anything more valuable. They complained that nothing had any worth, but eventually they gave him £50 and took away the chair, a couple of sideboards and a nest of tables. Aiden knew very well they were Ercol and would raise a nice sum, but he didn't care. He ripped out all the carpets and the underlay and got a man with a van to take them to the rubbish tip. He discovered the floor downstairs was parquet and he got it polished and cleaned. When he finished there was only a bed and a cabinet in his bedroom and a single sofa downstairs with a fold-up table in one corner. He felt better after it all. But he still didn't feel good.

It was then that he decided to put the whole place on the market. The estate agent told him that nothing would happen three weeks before Christmas, but he was wrong. Even before it went up on the website there were four offers. He knew it was a gamble, but with cash in hand he could get in quickly and seal the deal for the pieces – over four hundred of them – sitting in a warehouse in Marseilles. The sellers wanted shot of them. To have a buyer in the dead of winter was more than a temptation.

One morning, hyped at the prospect, irritated at one buyer for the house who was being particularly pedantic, he decided to walk to Celia's. He hadn't seen her in three weeks or so. He rounded the corner and came face to face with her flatmate, the tall moon-faced girl who had tried to stop Celia going out with him on that last evening. When she realised who it was, her expression changed.

'You,' she said.

'Good morning,' he replied. It was brisk and bright and cold, frosty underfoot. His breath hung between them in a pale cloud. 'How are you?'

She pushed him. It bloody hurt. It wasn't a weak effort. It was more like a punch.

'Hey,' he protested.

'What the fuck are you doing here?' she said. 'You dare to show your face!'

'What are you talking about? I've come for Cee.'

The colour had risen in her face. A couple of people passing by glanced in their direction.

'That will be fucking difficult!' she cried. 'Where've you been? She died ten days ago.'

He thought that the state of this girl was interesting. She looked wild. He wondered how she could get so worked up about someone like Celia, a vacant waste of space in anyone's world, of minimal use and no interest.

'I'm sorry to hear that,' he said.

'Are you?' she demanded. 'The funeral was this week. Her parents have been here.'

'I didn't know,' he told her. 'How did it happen?'

The girl suddenly began to cry. He felt mortified for her. She became even uglier, wiping her nose on the back of her hand. 'She took an overdose.'

'Oh dear,' he murmured.

Her eyes widened. 'Oh dear?' she mimicked. '*Oh dear?*'

He shuffled a little, hoping to get past her.

'Don't you care?' she said. 'I found her.'

'As I say—'

'Aren't you ashamed?'

'Of what?'

'Oh Christ,' she said. 'She left a note. It was about you. She loved you. Didn't you know that? Didn't you realise?'

'No,' he said, truthfully.

She grabbed him by the collar of his jacket. 'Have you got any feelings?' she said. 'Any feelings at all? You crucified her. She was already down and then you appeared and two months later she's dead. What did you do to her? She used to cry all the time.'

'It wasn't my fault if she'd been mistreated before I met her. I tried to make her happy.'

'Happy!' she exclaimed, and started to laugh. 'You absolute bastard.' She dropped the hold on his jacket and stepped away from him, looking him up and down. 'I hope you burn in hell.'

She brushed past him and began to run. He watched her go and gave a shrug. Amazing. Women were lunatics. Lunatics like Celia and this woman, or predatory scheming bitches like Keira. Nobody understood him, no one ever gave him the benefit of the doubt, no one. He was sorry about Celia, of course. But it wasn't as if he'd handed her the dose. He'd never encouraged her to take drugs. In fact, he'd tried to tell her how wrong she was. He'd said more than once that it made her less attractive. He always hated the way she would slobber over him when she was high, like a bitch in heat. He'd done his best. But she just never listened.

He stepped out into the road, brushing down his clothes, shaking his head at the absurdity of it all.

It was the last thing he remembered.

*

When he opened his eyes, he was in a shadowy space.

He'd been dreaming that he was in the garden of his mother's house, and that she'd been walking towards him with both hands outstretched, the way she used to. She was saying something in that sing-song way of hers, the voice that she used to calm him down. He was rooted to the ground, wanting to run, but his body wouldn't obey him. He saw lights behind her briefly, as if she was floating just above the ground. Flashing lights. Blue. His mother smiled. She came close and kneeled down at his side. 'You must try not to get angry,' she said. She brushed his brow with her fingertips. 'Bad things happen when you're angry,' she murmured.

She tipped her head on one side with that vaguely disappointed way she always had, and someone else got hold of his arm. 'I want you to hold still,' they said. He *was* still. He was doing just as he was told. He opened his eyes once and saw a man he didn't know a couple of inches from his face, and a light was shone into his eyes. He closed them tightly and went away, away from his mother. He felt very calm, almost sleepy. He had the sensation of being rocked roughly from side to side.

When he next opened his eyes, Keira was standing next to him.

He tried to move his head to look at her, but she put her hand on his shoulder. 'Don't move your head,' she said quietly. 'You have a neck brace on.' She leaned down so that she was very close to him. He could feel her breath on his face. 'You're in hospital,' she said. 'You walked out into the road and a car hit you.'

'Why?' he asked.

She smiled broadly. 'Because he couldn't avoid you. What were you thinking?'

'I don't remember,' he said.

'You've had a CT scan,' she told him. 'Do you remember that?'

'No.'

'They're checking the results. You've got a fracture in your leg.'

He tried to make sense of it. 'How?'

'You walked into the road, Aiden.'

'And what happened?'

'You walked straight into traffic.'

The curtains of the cubicle opened and a doctor walked in. 'He keeps repeating himself,' Keira told the man.

They spoke for a minute or so. He watched Keira's face without taking in the sense of what she was saying. The doctor was explaining something to her. She looked back at him and gave him a sympathetic smile. All this time he had been trying to get back to her and now she was here. He had no memory at all of how he had managed that. He had magicked her out of thin air, brought her here, wherever he was. Eventually a nurse came in. He stared down the length of his body at the tubes attached to his arms while behind him the monitor beeped at regular intervals. The nurse busied herself at his side and the blue of her uniform flooded his vision. She put something into his vein. Then others came in and another machine was positioned over his bed. The people moved back and they called out. X-ray. More business across his body. More whispers. The doctor standing by his feet looked like Millais, all sideburns and domed forehead. Aiden laughed to himself. He felt hazy and unconcerned, although there was pain somewhere in the centre of him, under his ribs and around his back.

Time thinned and lengthened. Another doctor. Noises from other bays. Images that floated past. Keira came back to the bedside.

'They're taking you up to a ward for observation,' she said. 'And I'll go back to your house and get a change of clothes and some night things. Is there anything else you want?'

You, he thought. But the words wouldn't come out.

'She's dead,' he muttered.

'Who's dead?' she replied. 'There was no one but you, Aiden.'

'Dead,' he whispered.

'No one's died,' she told him briskly. 'Listen. I have your house keys. They were in your coat pocket, along with a card for my gallery.' And she held them up so that he could see. 'All right?'

He felt that it wasn't all right, but he couldn't think of a reason why.

'I'll be back later on,' she said.

And she leaned down, and kissed him.

29

Toynton & Mark was a place of sepulchral stillness. It was hard to believe that any business at all was transacted in it. It felt more like a church. Thomas waited to one side as Laura gave their details at reception – a reception desk that looked like an altar. Columns rose either side of it.

Laura beckoned him.

'We've got a pass to the underworld,' she said, with a wry smile. 'Or human resources as us mere mortals call it.'

They got into a lift.

'I feel I ought to take off my shoes,' Thomas said.

She laughed. 'Despite how it looks, I'm told that they're considered nouveau riche, grafters. You know, *tradesmen*.'

'As opposed to what?'

'Old money. The ones that started in the eighteenth century. This lot have only been going since 1890.'

The lift doors opened and they were met by a perfectly turned out woman in a black suit and high heels. She introduced herself as Imelda Yates. They followed her to an office where she motioned them to sit down.

'We're here about Aiden Ruskin,' Laura began.

'Yes,' the woman responded. 'He worked here seven years ago.'

'I believe there was some sort of problem and he was asked to leave.'

'Can I ask why you need to know?'

'Can I ask why you question the need?' Laura responded.

231

'Will what I tell you be completely confidential?'

'If I can do that, yes.'

Imelda gave her a frosty smile. 'We do have a rather antiquated way of doing things here,' she said. 'We like to keep our business close. We don't generally broadcast either our success or our...' she paused. 'Less favourable outcomes.'

'Was Aiden Ruskin a less favourable outcome?'

'He was asked to leave, yes.'

'And why was that?'

'He stole a piece of stock.'

'A valuable piece?'

'We consider all our stock valuable,' Imelda replied. 'It was a small Impressionist sketch.'

'When did you realise it was Aiden Ruskin's fault?'

Imelda sat back a little. Thomas noticed a small spot of colour in her face. 'Did you know him personally?' he asked.

'I knew him, yes.'

'How would you describe him? Was the theft a surprise?'

Imelda looked away from him. She fiddled with a thin gold bracelet on her wrist. 'He was a very convincing person,' she said. 'And, as it turned out, quite the storyteller.'

'In what way?' Laura asked.

'He would... embellish. He would elaborate, rather guessing at things than actually having the facts to hand.'

'Defraud?' Thomas said.

'Not quite. Not in any obvious way. He was rather good with clients. Seemingly warm, welcoming. He was very industrious. Always there if needed.'

'*Seemingly* warm?'

'He had quite a low opinion of people. I noticed it more than once. Not in public. But in unguarded moments. He would gossip. I caught him out in an outright lie more than once, I'm afraid.'

'About what?'

232

She shrugged. 'Oh, claiming that he knew people. Several older ladies. He had a way with them. Very deferential with some clients, uncomfortably so. When he was spoken to about it – we don't invade anyone's privacy, you understand? – then he would say that he'd been to their homes. Not for valuations. But before and after sales, for instance. As social calls. And then he would come out with something quite cruel, said in a very blasé fashion. He could be unkind.'

'But that's not what got him fired?' Laura asked.

Imelda shook her head. 'I'd spoken to Mr Sanderley – our senior partner – a couple of times about him,' she said. 'It was more of a feeling, you know? There was a kind of dishonesty about him, saying one thing and doing another. Then we had a complaint.'

'What sort of complaint?' Thomas asked.

This time, Imelda took a few moments to reply. 'We had a gentleman come in here, the son of a client. We'd acted for his mother. We had sold some Asian bronzes on her behalf. Qing dynasty. Quite valuable. And some rather lovely vases. Not large, but rare. After the auction, her son came in to complain about Aiden Ruskin's relationship with her.'

Laura frowned. 'What kind of relationship?'

'Not a professional one,' Imelda said. 'Not professional at all. But it reflected badly on us here.'

'What had he done?'

'It was difficult,' she replied. 'Aiden had begun to call on her at weekends and after working hours. She'd become very fond of him by all accounts. Recently, it had been necessary to move her into a nursing home and she complained that Aiden wouldn't visit her there.' She paused. 'But it was more than that. There was a fifty-year age gap between them, but it seems that this lady believed that she and Aiden were romantically involved. So involved that she was heartbroken at his absence. Her son had thought it was just foolishness on her part, and he and the family tried their best to distract her from it. That was when she told him how often Aiden had visited. And he said that items were missing from the house.'

Laura and Thomas looked at each other.

'Items?' Laura prompted.

'Three little pieces, the kind of thing that you could easily put in your pocket or case. His mother said that Aiden had told her that he'd get a better price for her privately and that she wouldn't have to pay him a penny.'

'Why not?'

Imelda blushed. 'Because he loved her very much. Those were the son's actual words, quoted from his mother. Aiden "loved her very much".'

At his side, Thomas noticed Laura put her hand briefly to her face.

'This lady even claimed that we had defrauded her, putting a low estimate on her belongings and then selling them too cheaply.'

'What was "cheaply"?' Laura asked.

'Between five and six hundred thousand pounds.'

'And the missing pieces?'

'Were worth about the same. We had assured her that we would get the very best price for her, but after the first sale she changed her mind. We think that was probably Aiden's influence.'

Laura leaned forward. 'Do you think he stole those last three pieces?' she asked. 'Did your valuer see them in the lady's home?'

Imelda sighed. 'He thought so, but there had been a considerable amount. Nothing could be proven. There was no inventory of the pieces in the apartment. The lady had inherited a great deal from her grandfather, who had lived in China and Japan, and so there were no receipts. Nothing to say they had ever been in her possession.'

'How was everything resolved?' Laura asked.

'I'm afraid it wasn't,' Imelda told her. 'Aiden was asked about the whole thing, said that he had never taken anything from the house. He was really incandescent with rage. He said that the son was overbearing and heartless towards his mother and that only her money was important to him. He even implied that the son had taken the pieces and was trying to blame the loss of them on him. It was impossible to prove what had actually gone on.'

'But you must have had some deep misgivings about Ruskin after that,' Thomas said.

'Of course. Although things like this do sometimes happen. Families get very worked up about inheritance. It's always a difficult, even tragic time.'

They let that sink in. Thomas was feeling queasy. Art was a commodity here, a balance sheet. It was all very nice and polite and refined, but he had the increasingly uneasy feeling that Ruskin had learned all he knew from working in places like this.

As if she'd read his thoughts, Imelda looked directly at him. 'We are very respectful in what we do,' she said. 'We have a spotless reputation.'

'Of course,' Laura murmured. 'But it changed over this Impressionist sketch? Who had that belonged to?'

'Does it matter?'

'It might,' she said. When no name was forthcoming, she continued. 'What happened?'

Imelda gave a little shrug. 'It was a very small watercolour, just a landscape. Not much detail.'

'How much was it worth?'

'We had an estimate of forty thousand. It was part of a group. Five sketches in all.'

'When did you realise that it was missing?'

'On the morning of the sale, first thing.'

'Had Aiden Ruskin been involved in the preparation?'

'Not directly. He'd accompanied one of our senior staff to the home of the owner, however. On the way back, he'd made some sort of passing remark that it was all inconsequential stuff.'

'And was it?'

'Of course not. This was Cezanne.'

'Top stuff,' Thomas murmured.

Imelda gave him an icy stare. 'As you say, "top stuff",' she remarked sarcastically.

'So you found the sketch missing,' Laura prompted.

'Before the sale opened, of course,' Imelda said. 'We were all frantic. An hour or so passed, Aiden Ruskin was seen in the stores, and soon after another of our staff discovered the piece where the others had been kept.'

'An oversight then?'

'We don't make oversights like that,' Imelda said. 'It was decided that Ruskin had something to do with it.'

'Don't you have cameras down there, security?'

'Of course we do. We saw Ruskin clearly on the CCTV, but we couldn't see what he did.'

'If anything.'

'Well. That was his line of course.'

'He must have had clearance to be in the stores, in the safes?'

'Well… yes. In retrospect, that was a mistake.'

'But he was fired after this.'

'We had a meeting the same day, it was felt by senior management that he was untrustworthy, and we let him go.'

'Did he object?'

'Yes.'

'But no one accepted his version?'

'No.'

There was a silence for some moments.

'Why would he do that though?' Thomas mused. 'He couldn't have believed he could get away with it. Was he trying to test your security?'

Imelda shrugged. 'He didn't even bother to make that case, flimsy as that would be,' she replied. 'He just sat there smiling and denying it.'

That sociopathic smile, thought Thomas.

'What's the purpose, actually, of this visit?' Imelda asked.

Laura answered. 'Do you know a woman called Isabelle Crosby?'

'Yes,' Imelda replied. 'We knew her.'

'So you know that she's been killed?'

'Yes. Awfully sad. This is about her?'

'Was she involved with the business here?'

'It's some years since she was on the scene, you might say. A long time since she bought anything. Or sold anything, for that matter. I believe she bought modern art elsewhere sometimes.'

'So you know that she was a dealer?'

'Of a minor kind. Years ago.'

'What kind of thing did she deal in?'

'Oh, I couldn't tell you off the top of my head. Is it important?'

'If you could find out, it might help us.'

Thomas realised that 'minor' might mean something very different in this place, where pieces were sold for hundreds of thousands of pounds, or more. On the way over, Laura had said that her ex-husband had looked up the latest auction prices, and a hefty percentage were sold in the millions. So 'minor' could mean a paltry fifty or a hundred thousand – small fry, in other words. In that way at least, Ruskin's 'inconsequential' had been right. Nothing changed hands under ten thousand, at least. It was company policy, in line with many other auction houses like this one.

Imelda made a move as if she was preparing to leave, but stopped.

'Is there a relevance to you asking about Ruskin, and referring to Isabelle Crosby? Am I to infer that there's a connection?'

'Thank you for helping us,' Laura said.

Imelda stood up, but Laura stayed where she was. 'Do you know Keira Brodie?' she asked.

'Yes, of course.' Imelda's expression relaxed. She even smiled.

'Do you know that she had a relationship with Aiden Ruskin?'

The smile vanished. 'No.'

'Do you have a contact number for her?'

Imelda hesitated. She looked from Thomas to Laura, and back again. 'I'll have to look into it.'

'Please do,' Laura said. 'As soon as you can.'

They all walked to the door, and back out into the corridor. As they waited for the lift, Imelda murmured, 'I'm not sure if it's relevant. But if you want to paint a further picture of Aiden Ruskin, there was another death.'

'Oh?' Laura said.

'Perhaps it's a coincidence.'

'Whose death?'

The lift arrived, but none of them moved, and the doors closed again after a moment.

'We had a young woman who worked here,' Imelda said quietly. Thomas noticed that her fingers strayed again to the thin gold bracelet on her arm, as if for reassurance. 'Celia Cavell. She'd been here when Ruskin was employed. I believe they had a friendship then, or so I'm told. Late last year she committed suicide. Overdose. She left a note saying something rather garbled about Ruskin. They had been in a more serious relationship lately. She had been in love with him.'

'Was he implicated? Was he there when she took the overdose?' Laura asked.

'No. Her flatmate found her.'

'Was he questioned?'

'I don't know, I'm afraid. This is… this is something that I've heard, you understand. I don't know any details.'

Again, the fingers on the bracelet, and this time there was a stricken look on Imelda's face.

You've been there yourself, Thomas thought.

Evidently, Laura had come to the same conclusion. She put a hand gently on Imelda's arm. 'Were you and Ruskin close?' she asked.

Imelda straightened up, and pressed the lift bell again. 'A very long time ago,' she said. 'And nothing I care to remember.'

When Thomas and Laura got back outside in the street, Laura stood staring at the passing traffic. When she turned back to Thomas, she whispered, 'So many women.'

He put his arms around her.

30

Christmas is coming, the goose is getting fat
Please put a penny in the old man's hat

AIDEN HAD TAKEN TO WALKING AGAIN. He was slow. But it soothed him.

The goose is getting fat
Please put a million in my account.

It was the tenth of December. Things were certainly moving fast. He liked it. Appreciated it. He needed the money. It had to be somewhere else by the second week of January. He wasn't sleeping that well because of the bloody ache of his leg. He kept thinking that he was taking a horrible chance because these people screwed you over, or could do. He'd taken them at their word and they were polite. They were forthcoming. They were brisk. They'd set a timescale and when he'd talked to their London man at a bus stop in Westminster – *Westminster*, right by the Boudicca statue – her looming over the pair of them with her stupid spear, he'd noticed two other men on the opposite side of the bridge, the pair of them looking like a cartoon version of villains, all black leather jackets. They were farcical. He stopped as he was walking.

He was outside Liberty's in Regent Street, hobbling along with his hospital crutch.

He stared up at the windows, at the colour. There was no colour at all in his house. Almost everything he owned was in packing cases.

He loved this place. Of course, it had changed in the time he'd been in London. He'd been so impressed with it when he first came to the city and he'd lived in horrible digs in Camden. He'd still had his Victorian fantasies then, his obsession with Whistler and his namesake and Wilde, and then he'd been converted to Art Nouveau and Art Deco and he loved this building and walking around inside it.

He looked up at it now and felt nothing.

All he could feel was the gnawing anxiety that all his money was going to be handed over to someone he didn't really know, someone that Archie and Isabelle had known a very long time ago, the same family but now the flint-faced grandsons. He'd tried to appeal to that 'all the same family' vibe and got rebuffed for it. They still wanted his money though. Talking to the man that day last month, he'd got the sensation that he was missing something. That something had gone down that he didn't know about. It was as if a piece of information, vital information, was shifting in and out of focus and just beyond his grasp. They'd smiled at each other, and he knew – it was funny really – that they were alike. The smile of the rat baring its teeth to another rat in the sewer.

He shook his head. He was imagining things. That was what happened when you couldn't sleep. And his leg hurt him. Sometimes he thought he could actually feel the metal in his thigh.

Keira had been good to him, he'd give her that.

She'd come in after he was discharged from hospital, stocking up his fridge with ready meals. Sometimes even cooking. He'd had to sleep downstairs and she got two guys in to bring his bed down. It took up most of the living area. He thanked God there was a toilet downstairs, or he'd have been fucked, or filling up a bottle and taking it to the sink. Thank God the break seemed to heal quicker than expected.

He'd been disgusted with himself. Keira thought it was funny. He found her laughing once or twice. He told her it was unfair, and she told him he'd lost his sense of humour.

'I've never had a sense of humour,' he'd replied.

'That's true,' she'd told him. Still smiling.

'I don't know what you're so pleased about,' he'd said.

'Don't you?' she'd replied. 'That's a pity.'

In hospital, he'd dreamed about Celia. A couple of times he thought Keira was Celia. He'd got it all mixed up in his head.

'Celia?' she'd asked him.

'Nobody,' he'd told her, but then one day she'd come in – still using her key, but he hesitated to ask for it back – and she'd said that she knew who Celia was.

'I don't know any Celia,' he'd told her.

'You kept talking about her in hospital.'

'I don't think so. You must be mixing me up with someone else.'

'Don't tell me I'm mixing things up,' she said sweetly. 'Celia Cavell. She was the one who died.'

He didn't reply. Full marks for finding out. What did she want, a prize?

She was quiet after that. He preferred it. She would sit in the last remaining chair and listen to him. She never asked about Archie, but she was interested in his grandfather and his mother.

'I wish I'd met them,' she said.

'Why?'

'Just to see where you get it all from.'

'What, exactly?'

'I don't think it's your mother, is it?'

'She was weak.'

Keira had put her head on one side, considering him.

'Archie was the hard-working one. He had the sense to buy this house and convert it. He saw the way the market would go.

He worked the streets. Leather Lane in the early eighties. Like an episode of *Only Fools and Horses*.'

'He didn't exactly sell out of a suitcase, Aiden.'

She was right. She was always right. Archie had got the inside track on plundered grave goods long before the war in Syria. He'd gone out to Iran before the Revolution. He had a kind of nose for the dirty stuff.

'What about your great-grandfather?'

'How the bloody hell should I know? What does it matter?'

But she looked it up. She went online and she showed him. 'The Census of 1911,' she said one day, turning her laptop towards him. 'Here they are. He worked on the lighters. The boats on the Thames that ferried goods back and forth between the boats and the wharves.'

'So?'

She turned the laptop back towards her, and closed it. 'You ought to be proud of people like that,' she said. 'Hard-working. Not thieves.'

It was said so calmly, in such a matter-of-fact voice.

'Who's a thief?' he demanded.

She didn't answer. She got up and took his dinner plate from him and went into the kitchen. He heard her washing it up. When she came back, she was carrying a cup of tea, and put it on the table beside him.

'I think you can manage all right now, can't you?' she asked. 'I don't think you need me anymore.'

He stood up, grabbing the crutch from the side of the chair. 'Why did you do all this?' he demanded. 'Why did you come here?'

She was putting a few things into the portfolio case that she always brought with her. 'I have a long journey tomorrow,' she said. 'Good luck, Aiden.'

He manoeuvred himself to stand in front of her. 'You haven't answered the question.'

She took a long time to answer. 'I thought it might change you,' she said eventually. 'I wanted to see if you'd choose a better life.'

'What do you mean, a better life? Who are you, a fucking priest?'

'You're still in touch with Archie's agent.'

It took the wind out of his sails.

'It's none of your business,' he told her.

'No,' she said. 'You're right. It isn't. Not now.'

She put her hand on his shoulder. She looked as if she was going to say something else. Then she took out his keys from her bag and laid them on the table. 'Be good,' she told him.

He hadn't seen her since and she changed her mobile number for the second time. She blocked him on social media. She went out of his life all over again and he thought about it constantly. Her and Celia. They were like two ghosts: one that had ended her life and implicated him in it, and another who kept her real life secret from him. She'd once confided in him and now he knew nothing. When she'd first cared for him after the accident he thought he'd got her again, hoped for it, hoped for that sly rosebud face underneath him. But she had just come to see his humiliation, to get pleasure out of his injuries. Playing nurse while she hated him.

Through the first days of December, he sat at home wondering about her, thinking she'd always been elusive, perhaps she'd led him on to think so. He'd assumed she was uncomplicated and she was anything but. Archie had been right when he said at the very beginning that it was best to get her under his control. But he'd never managed it. The failure of that ate into him.

On the last night in the house, before the removers came to take his few possessions into storage, he made a promise to himself. He sat with both feet propped up on the coffee table, watching a light snow fall. He would make a fortune out of his investment. He had a guy in the Borders lined up, him and two others. These people were gluttonous, stuffing their multi-million-pound homes with objects that they kept locked behind walls. Lust, avarice. He loved them for it. He was going to spend a million to get another two. His profit didn't matter to them, and would move him up, way beyond Archie's old orbit.

I thought it might change you.

Watch me.

31

ON THE WAY HOME, THOMAS THOUGHT about last Christmas. He'd known at the time that Christine was alone in her house just as he was. He hadn't invited her around for a meal. That was bad enough after all she'd done while he was in hospital, but it struck him now that he hadn't got an invitation from her, either. When they'd met in the lane after New Year, she'd said something about going to a cousin's, but she didn't meet his eye. She'd a scarf over her head and a coat pulled around her in the rain and he hadn't suggested so much as a cup of coffee. As he drew into the car park of the nursing home, it weighed with a new significance.

Shady Oaks was next to a bottling factory and a railway line. As he went in the door, he was met with a framed certificate saying they had some sort of registration for 'end of life care'. The first thing that a family or patient would read as they came in the door. He hid his frown and smiled at the receptionist.

'I'm here to see Christine Portman,' he said. 'I understand she's been transferred from the cottage hospital.'

'Yes, she has. Just yesterday,' the woman told him. 'You're her first visitor, Mr… ?'

'Maitland.'

She paused and glanced at him again from behind the barrier of her laptop. Behind her, he could see the rota for the staff wedged between two faded prints of Constable country, and a cheery banner, *Love Makes the World Go Round!*

'Maitland?' she repeated.

'Yes.'

She got up. 'You'd better come with me.' She led him upstairs and along a corridor. She knocked on the last door, where a window gave a view of the bottling company yard.

'Christine,' she said as they went in, 'you have a visitor.'

Christine looked up. She was propped in a bed with the sheets pulled tightly around her, and her hands clasped on the flowery duvet. She looked peculiarly puffed up, her face like a little pink balloon. What shocked him more than anything was that someone had cut her hair and it fell about her face in crimped grey curls. It was and it wasn't Christine. She gazed at him as he sat down.

'How are you?' he asked. 'How are you feeling?'

'I'm all right,' she said.

'I've been living in Cornwall,' he said. 'And I had to go to London.'

She gave him a look of such poignant affection that it wrung his heart.

'How is your hip?' he asked.

'Oh,' she said. 'They do wonders now, you know.'

'Have you been able to walk?'

'Oh yes. They get me up to walk. You have to be mobile. And when I'm properly recovered, I can go home.'

He didn't know what to say. He was rescued by one of the staff bringing in a tea tray, but mortified to see that they'd provided a tippy cup for Christine as if she were a child. He wanted to knock it out of the carer's hands and give Christine a slug of Merlot instead, but she didn't seem to care. She took the cup with a docile smile.

She talked for a while about the cottage hospital, about a woman who had been in the next bed. 'She got married,' she said.

'Who did?'

'The woman next to me.'

'When?'

'When she was there. While they were taking the oxygen pictures.'

He put down his cup of tea.

'Did you go into my house?' she asked.

'Yes. I tidied up.'

'Thank you,' she murmured. 'I had a neighbour,' she said. 'But I don't think he lives there anymore.' She was shaking her head. 'Can you put on the television?'

There was a tiny set in the corner of the room. He got up and switched it on.

'I want to watch the racing.'

He picked up the remote and went through the channels. 'There doesn't seem to be any.'

'There's always racing.'

'Perhaps it'll come on later.'

When he turned back, her mouth was dropped open in shock, and the pinkness had gone from her face. 'Thomas!' she exclaimed.

He smiled and came back to the bed. 'Yes, it's Thomas.'

'Where have you been?'

'Away for a little while.'

She started pushing at the covers. 'You mustn't be here,' she said. 'You can get out. There's a fire escape. You have to go. Don't let them see you.'

He held her hand. 'It's okay,' he told her. 'Everybody knows I'm here.'

She clutched at him. 'I told them a story.'

'What story?'

'I told them something wrong,' she said, and began to cry. 'It was because of Fran, you see? She said things about Fran, and I liked Fran.'

'Who?' he asked. 'Who said things about Fran?' She was pulling at her clothes now. He reached over and pressed the alarm call for the nurse.

'I couldn't let her say things. I told her to go. I did, Thomas!' The tears were pouring down her face. 'I'm sorry,' she said. 'I'm sorry.'

The attendant came back. Thomas stood up and away from the bed, while the nurse hushed Christine. She looked up at him and made a motion of her head. 'Perhaps she ought to rest,' she suggested.

He went out down the corridor and back to the woman on reception.

He could still hear Christine crying that she was sorry, sorry, sorry.

'Everything okay?' the receptionist asked brightly.

'Not really,' he told her. 'Can I speak to the manager?'

He was back at his own house with Max by the evening.

He'd collected the dog from the pub and endured another obstructive silence from Stan, though he had a long conversation with Jenny. He told her about Christine.

'What is she so sorry for?' Jenny wondered as he finished his story.

'I don't know,' he said, although he thought he did. At least, he guessed it. That conviction was a dull ache in the pit of his stomach.

'What's the place like?' Jenny asked. 'We haven't been able to get there yet.'

'Not great,' he told her.

'Well, the family think the house ought to be sold,' Jenny said. 'To pay for somewhere nice at least. It's a good size. It would make a family home.'

She wouldn't take payment for looking after Max again, so he gave into temptation and ordered one of her curries. The evenings were getting longer and he went outside with Max to savour the last of the light.

'I'll take you on a proper walk tomorrow,' he promised Max. 'We'll go out to Lambert's Castle and you can chase the rabbits before we go back to Trewarith.'

The dog put his head on his knee in an eloquent plea for the last of the naan bread on his plate.

'Want to live with me?' Thomas asked. He knew he couldn't put Max into a rescue kennel. Isabelle Crosby would haunt him for the rest of his life, as if she wouldn't already.

He drove back to his own house and let the two of them in, thinking that he ought to buy Max a proper bed and toys. He went to a cupboard where he'd kept all the things that had been associated with Fish. Opening the door brought it all back: a harness and lead that Fish had never liked, a roll of doggy bags, and several toys. He took one down: a lurid orange elephant that had been nearly new when Fish died.

He put it in front of Max and the dog sniffed it with suspicion.

'Please yourself,' he muttered.

He looked around the kitchen. He ought to move, he thought. Like Christine's, this house was too big for one person. Even now he couldn't bring himself to go along the upstairs landing and look at the spare bedroom that Fran had insisted on using when she got ill. Sometimes he had heard her moving about but if he got up she'd tell him, more often than not, to go back to his own bed and get some sleep. Towards the end, of course, he ignored the rebuff. He would go in and sit at her side. When she was eventually transferred to the hospice, he would get up on the bed and hold her in his arms. She never objected.

He slumped down on a kitchen chair.

He knew she wasn't here, and she wasn't in the churchyard nearby, although he would go and tidy the grave sometimes. He could almost hear her saying what a waste of time that was. 'Go out and live,' she had whispered to him a couple of days before she died.

He had tried. Grief was a bloody awful companion, though. It was like dragging a rock around. People wanted you to be happy, to recover, and so after a while he found himself manufacturing smiles. He had started volunteering at a local National Trust place, first in the house and then in the grounds. He'd done his damnedest to be sociable and he never discussed Fran with a soul. It was a kind of performance. He went out on the stage and he acted a life. And Fran became a breath, a shadow that passed by him sometimes. But strangely enough, never in this house that had been their home.

He wondered what Fran would make of Laura Cullen. He guessed that they might like each other. Neither were sentimental, although both had a soft heart that they rarely showed the world. He had come back from London in Laura's car and although they hadn't done much talking he'd listened to her singing along with the radio for a couple of songs. She had a nice voice, light. A soprano. He watched the lights of London disappear while she turned off the radio and sang *There but for Fortune*.

He had smiled. 'That's an old song.'

'Shall I stop?'

'No, no.'

'Sorry. It's a habit.'

'Really, carry on. It's fine.' But she didn't, suddenly self-conscious. She carried on driving for a while, then told him, 'I often think about those lyrics. Just a twist of fate separates someone from a crime, or being a victim of a crime.'

'That's true enough.'

'There's a connection between Isabelle and Ruskin.'

'Yes, I think so.' He wondered where she'd go with it. She'd said so before.

'And that's why she died.'

She announced it with certainty. He knew that she'd probably seen the bank records. It was perhaps the subject of the phone call she'd taken before they had got in the car.

'A trade?' he asked. 'Recently?'

'Nothing recently,' she told him. 'She actually didn't spend much. And only a couple of things in the last two years in London. One was for a purchase at a gallery. Your painting.'

'And the other?'

'A hugely expensive bill at a London florist last year. It was for a funeral wreath. Archie Ruskin.'

She'd dropped him off at his own house a couple of hours ago, but refused his offer of an overnight bed. It had been a bit of an awkward moment.

'I mean, there's three spare rooms, it's a four-bedroomed house,' he'd heard himself gabble. 'I can easily make up a bed. It's a long way back to Cornwall, two or three hours. I can make you up a bed no problem…'

She'd burst out laughing. The she'd kissed him on the cheek. 'No thanks. But it's great to see a man blushing such a colour.' And she'd got back into the car, still laughing. He'd watched her car go off up the drive and turn onto the road.

He sat in the encroaching dark of the house now, Max at his feet.

He kept tying both Keira Brodie and Ruskin together in his head, trying to weigh up their relationship. By his own admission, Ruskin had lived alone in Trewarith for a few months. Why? Didn't he have a place in London? Did Archie Ruskin own a house, and wouldn't his son have inherited it? Surely Archie Ruskin had left him something. Where had that money gone? From Tam Jefferies' account of him, it seemed that the son didn't have the father's touch in business. He was, if Imelda Yates was to be believed, fond of the sound of his own voice. And controlling with women. He guessed that Ruskin had a track record that he might regard as a string of successes, but anyone else would think of as disasters. Crimes, even.

He considered Christine, comparing the situation to Ruskin's older female client who had believed that Ruskin was in love with her, and from whom he was suspected of stealing a great deal of money. He imagined that poor woman incarcerated in some nursing home as bewildered as Christine seemed to be, and felt absolute pity for her. Dementia was an awful diagnosis – he'd seen it once or twice, the last case of his career being an older couple where the husband was ill and the wife had been trying to cope when a couple of bastards came to the door and told her that they were roofers and they'd noticed a problem with her house. As she came out to look, the second man rifled through the property, taking her own mother's jewellery. Listening to her account afterwards, trying to console her, he'd felt boiling rage about those two men. He sat now feeling a similar helplessness. What was it that Ruskin had stolen from Keira, or Greta, or Isabelle? *Had* he taken anything at all? And why had he been there at Greta's death, with Keira? How had that unfolded? Why hadn't he been in London?

Thomas sat gnawing on his thumbnail, irritated that he had no real answers. He thought that Imelda was right about Ruskin, and that Laura was right when she said that Ruskin also knew Isabelle before Keira ever came into his life. The connection to Archie – the flowers at the funeral – confirmed it. The floral tribute said a great deal without words. Ruskin would surely have seen it. What was she saying to him, if anything? Did it upset him? Was it a message that Isabelle still had her fingers in Archie's business? Thomas sighed heavily. Max pricked up his ears and sat up. Absent-mindedly, he stroked the dog's head.

'Who was she really?' he asked Max. 'Who came to the house? I wish you could tell me.'

He got up, opened the back door, and went out into the garden.

Everything was still. There were no street lights here, and only a couple in the village a mile away. All around him the fields rolled away in the darkness. He breathed in the silence, glad of it, trying to clear his head.

On the day that he and Fran had moved into this house all those years ago, it had been Christine who had come walking cheerfully up the drive, holding out her hand to shake theirs, offering them a cup of tea. They'd gratefully taken up her offer and afterwards sat in the chaos of the removal boxes in the kitchen, savouring the home-made cake that she'd brought and 'a little something to keep you going', which turned out to be a quarter bottle of brandy. Fran had laughed, holding up her cup saying, 'I think we're going to like it here!'

Poor Fran. She hadn't deserved the last few years of her life, first trying to come to terms with his short-lived affair with Helen, and then with her own illness. The church had been filled to overflowing on the day she was buried. She'd been so loved. He remembered Christine sitting two rows back from him, weeping silently. He'd turned to look at her and she'd given him the same sort of wavering smile of affection that she'd given him today.

Both Fran and Christine were far better people than Helen. Helen had been a selfish narcissist. By all accounts no one at her school had liked her. Although she'd inspired devotion in the two women who loved her, each of them had been used and betrayed. Not for the first time he relished the idea of putting his hands around Helen's neck. She'd ruined him, but he had allowed her to do it by being what Fran had called 'the cliché of the middle-aged male'. She had been right. His own words for it were summed up in the reality – a dismal, dirty four-day aberration ending in Helen mocking him and his marriage.

Kill me. Why don't you kill me?

What had Christine meant today with all her apologies, and

her frantic sense of guilt? Was that for him, or for her? Was it her who was terrified of being found, or found out?

He'd tentatively asked at the nursing home if Christine had said much at all in the last twenty-four hours. The manager had replied that they heard a huge number of things in every dementia patient which they had to dismiss. 'We've had people saying their husband or wife is dead, or that they never had children,' she'd explained kindly. 'And the family come to visit every day. Then we have people who say their son or whoever comes to see them all the time and brings them presents, when we ourselves know they've never had a visitor.' She'd smiled at him. 'She mentioned your name,' she told him, 'in the first few minutes she was here. She was upset. But we take everything with a large pinch of salt, Mr Maitland. For instance, a month ago one of our gentlemen said he was sorry that he'd been – well, familiar – with one of the staff. Catherine, who's eighteen. And informed us that they'd bring up the baby together.'

'I see,' Thomas had murmured. He wondered if it was inappropriate to smile.

'Sometimes it's a reflection of what's actually happened in their lives. Perhaps in that instance it was a relived conversation of years ago – who can tell? But we don't pry, it's not our business – but we listen, we console, we distract.'

'Hard work,' he said.

'Oh yes,' she told him. 'We had a lady who got out of her bed every night and hid in the corner because she said her husband was coming home. A member of staff would sit with her, sometimes putting her back to bed after she fell asleep where she sat.' She shrugged. 'It's best not to dwell on what we hear, or make judgements.'

'My God,' he murmured.

She'd leaned forward and patted him on the arm. 'So whatever Christine says – and I know what happened in the hospital, the accusations – I understand it was followed up, so that's a closed book as far as I'm concerned.'

He'd thanked her and left, saying that he'd come in again tomorrow before he left for Cornwall.

Thomas wandered down to the end of the garden now. The stream made a soft murmur just a few feet away. He looked back at what had been his vegetable patch, now churned over by the investigation. He thought of the spade that he'd found that he was sure Christine had taken there before her collapse. She must have said that she suspected Helen was buried there. But in her current state, had she meant her own patch? Richard Ellis had baulked at investigating Christine's garden after the excavation of Thomas's had drawn a blank, but they'd both been thinking along similar lines.

He looked out through the trees to the dark shadow of Christine's house. He thought of the many times he'd sat at that table in her kitchen eating her food, talking for hours after Fran's death. She'd never hinted at anything wrong. Even when he'd briefly mentioned Helen McAllister, he didn't recall that her expression or her body language had changed, and he thought he would have noticed something if it had. After all, he was a police officer, trained to do so. But maybe he'd overlooked something that was staring him in the face because he'd never for one moment had any suspicion that the answer lay so close to home. Literally.

Kill me. Why don't you kill me?

Had Helen said the same thing to Christine?

It was a question that had waited for an answer for far too long. The answer that Fran had never been given, nor anyone else – not himself, not Alice Hauser, not Helen's employers, not any of the officers who had worked the case. Helen had joined the two thousand or so people every year who disappeared and we never heard from or seen again – those lasting, frustrating, agonising mysteries. The gaps, the questions, the emptiness where a life should be. Or a death, a funeral, an epitaph.

He put Max back in the house and walked along the lane to Christine's gates.

He didn't have the house keys anymore, but he didn't need them.

He went around the back of the house and looked at Christine's land. It too sloped down to the stream.

When they had first moved here, Christine kept a couple of goats in a little enclosure. That lasted a few years, until both animals had died. Then she had bought the chickens. He thought, sadly, that she had needed something to love and look after. That had become him after Fran died. Christine had moved the hens' enclosure about from time to time. It was all very make-do-and-mend. And then suddenly, she'd bought a henhouse. There was a company four or five miles away that made fancy little houses on wheels, all painted up to appeal to the hobbyist. He stood now and tried to remember when that had been. He thought it was about a year after Helen had disappeared, and just at the time when Fran fell ill.

Unsurprisingly, he'd been distracted then. He walked over to it now. The paint had faded and peeled, but it was still in the same position close to the hedge. Such a strange purchase for Christine, who never seemed to buy anything new. She'd once told him that everything she wore came from charity shops. It was a point of righteous observance for her, like a religion. So why had it been important to buy something this substantial?

It was inside a small enclosure made of chicken wire, and the shutters of the henhouse itself were closed. Evidently the guy in the village had kept his word to look after them and they were shut away for the night, safe against the foxes. Thomas got out his phone and shone a light at the ground. It was paddled pretty solidly flat and dotted with bits of feed and straw. In those few minutes of considering it, his liking of Christine and all their history, and her love for Fran, battled in his mind with the newspaper cuttings in her living room and her wailing protests of late. One voice in his mind told him that what he was thinking was impossible. The other, much stronger, told him that Helen McAllister had disappeared one summer afternoon, an afternoon when both he and Fran were working away, and that there was a possibility she had come here looking for him, a possibility that Christine's apologies today could confirm.

He put the phone in his pocket, and hesitated. Then he walked back to Christine's house to a lean-to at the back, an old outside toilet where he knew that she kept gardening tools. He took out a spade and walked back to the chicken pen. The flimsy gate to it wasn't locked. He began to dig. Not near the gate, but in the narrow space between the back of the henhouse and the chicken wire, reasoning that if something were hidden it would be in the most inaccessible part. The ground was just as compacted here, and he was going down into clay. He kept at it for a good twenty minutes, digging through three or four feet and hitting nothing but stone and soil.

He straightened up and looked at his watch. Nearly one o'clock in the morning. He rested his hand on the side of the henhouse and wiped the sweat from his face. He felt the structure shift slightly. He bent down and put his hand underneath it. The soil was slightly looser. He walked to the other end of the structure and took up the two handles that were lying – and had always been lying – on the ground. The thing had been made to look like an old-fashioned wagon that had been pulled by a horse, or a miniature shepherd's hut – all fantasy, of course, but the kind of thing that people liked to have. The two struts resisted for a second, and he felt the wood joints shift. There was a wheel lock on both sides, and he released them. Immediately the house rolled back slightly, but not far. He pushed it, holding the struts. Eventually he managed to move it back six or seven feet, until it rested against the fence behind it. He retrieved the spade.

Sure enough the soil was much looser once he went down a foot or so. He dug solidly.

It was half an hour later that he heard the spade scrape against something. He stopped, reaching down. At first his hand touched stones, and he picked them out. But there was something else down there. He took out his phone again and aimed the light towards the ground.

After a moment, he got up and walked straight out of the enclosure and stood outside Christine's house, looking up at the old cat-slide roof and the darkened windows. Above it, the sky was cloudy, and beyond it was the lane and the line of trees. Everything was absolutely still.

He dialled a number, and waited until a sleepy voice answered. 'Richard,' he said quietly. 'You need to come and see this.'

32

THERE WAS NO MONEY.

Holy Christ, there was no money.

No money!

Aiden was in a hotel room. The house was sold. He had woken after a long sleep and pulled the blinds up and looked out onto a freezing cold London. There was sleet in the wind. Today was the day.

He opened his laptop and there was the amount. Yesterday.

And today it was gone.

He dragged on his clothes and went running out into the street. He hailed a cab and got to the nearest branch of his bank and demanded to see the manager. It was a woman. Christ, as if he needed to see another woman. She was very cool, very polite. She smiled at him.

'I want to know where's it's gone and I want to know who took it out,' he told her.

'You did, Mr Ruskin.'

He slammed his hands, palms down, on her desk. 'How many times?' he demanded. 'I did not take this money out. They've cleared my account. Don't you understand? Nearly a million!'

'Nine hundred and three thousand,' she corrected him. 'Agent's fees.'

'I see that, I see that,' he shouted. 'Do you think I'm blind for Chrissake? All right, nine hundred thousand. That's my money. I didn't take it out.'

She looked at her laptop again. 'You have twenty-two pounds in your account,' she said evenly. 'Do you wish to extend your overdraft limit?'

'No, I want my bloody money back!'

'Please don't raise your voice, Mr Ruskin.'

'Shit! Somebody just stole nine hundred thousand from my fucking account! What am I supposed to do, laugh about it?'

'You took it out yourself from this bank.'

He was gasping for breath.

'It was transferred to another account,' she explained.

'What account!'

'A number in the Turks and Caicos.'

'Turks... Turks...'

'And Caicos. In the Caribbean.'

'I know where Turks and Caicos is!' he shouted. 'I didn't transfer it.'

'It was authorised on your account, Mr Ruskin.'

'Who by?'

She leaned forward with a sympathetic smile on her face. 'By yourself, Mr Ruskin. Online. Would you like me to pass this to our fraud department?'

The room was spinning. Yesterday, he'd walked out of the empty house with a single suitcase and his laptop. He'd had lunch at the Green Bar at the Café Royal. Fucking *spectacular* lunch, it was. He'd deserved it after all he'd been through. Bloody Mary, rock oysters and a bottle of Rathfinny Estate, and another bottle shared with the two girls next to him who said they were from some place in Scotland. He got a whiff of the fine aroma of grouse moor and money, and then they moved to his table and they all shared food, and they all had Laphroaig and the one closest – the blonde – said something about her brother. She looked vaguely familiar, though he couldn't place her. Maybe she used to be at auctions. Had Keira introduced her once, or Cee? He tried, unsuccessfully, to fumble his way through the memories of clients or Keira's clients or friends of Cee. This woman had told him that her brother was an estate manager and she asked if he knew the Loch of Stenness. He remembered that much, and he remembered her arm linked in his and her hand on his thigh. 'You must come and visit,' she said. 'The fishing is good.' And she seemed to find that funny.

No. No. He wasn't that fucking stupid.

They were there two hours. She kissed him.

Somewhere in his jacket he had her card.

Still staring at the manager, he fumbled his way through the jacket now until he found the card in an inside pocket.

There was just a kiss.

A kiss imprinted in lipstick on an empty piece of white cardboard.

He gritted his teeth so hard that his jaw ached. 'Yes,' he said. 'Investigate it. This is fraud.' He stood up, lost his balance, and quickly righted himself. 'I didn't authorise that transfer,' he said. 'I want my money back.'

33

I T WAS JUST MIDDAY WHEN AIDEN got in the car.
Traffic was heavy. He fought his way out to Hammersmith and the start of the M4, cursing everyone that got in his way and every red light. He put his foot down as he passed Heston, oblivious to the speed limit. Let them ticket him if that's what they wanted. It made no difference.

A picture kept springing up in his mind of Keira coming into the hospital ward after the operation to fix his leg. She'd been smiling, a pile of magazines in one arm and his laptop on top of them. She'd been in his house. She'd had days to do it. He had a notebook of all his passwords in his desk, hidden under plenty of other papers. How was he to know what she'd done? Nothing went out of either his credit card or his bank account then. She'd just kept turning up both in the hospital and at the house with her usual sweet expression. He'd checked his desk, too, when he got home. Not that he'd really suspected her. It had just been a passing routine thought. Nothing looked like it had been moved.

How long was it before he'd been discharged? Three days? Four? And it hadn't bothered him at the time. He thought she'd come round to him at last. Pitied him maybe, but that was better than nothing. That it was the way in, the way back to her. She must have known what he was thinking, and she'd let him believe it. She'd stroked his hand and asked if there was anything else he wanted. He remembered that. Conniving bitch.

She'd been such a comforting presence, and he'd been so grateful. There'd been nobody else he could have called – nobody else at all who cared. He'd cried about it in a fog of morphine at the time and he cried about it now, self-pitying and angry as he negotiated his way past other vehicles in the fast lane, flashing his lights at those that didn't get out of the way fast enough. A slight rain was falling and the carriageways ahead looked foggy. How many fucking miles to Trewarith? How many miles to the one person he was sure knew where Keira was? Or maybe where Keira herself was? Three hundred. Four hours or so. Three if only the bastards ahead of him would get out of the way.

God damn her and everyone who supported her. Keddington, for one – that queer bastard in his bloody Palladian mansion who'd given her carte blanche and who'd basically run him and Archie off his land, shutting the park gates after them. Aiden still remembered those huge concrete pilasters supporting the arch decorated with his coat of arms and the complicated patterns of the wrought iron in the mechanically operated gates as they clanged shut after them. Keddington, Keira's slave, and who knew how many other queer friends of his and jumped-up land-grabbers. Them, and every dealer and auction house he'd ever encountered. She'd crawled into that world somehow and pulled the drawbridge up after her, shutting him out just as Keddington had.

He wiped more tears from his face with one hand. He thought back to the first time they'd really talked to each other, in Paris. That rainy day he'd been so seduced by the innocent look on her face. She'd let him make a fool of himself then and she'd done the same over the gallery, promoting herself to some sort of pedestal of good taste and leaving him literally in the street. She'd evidently thought that she was going places where he ought not to follow, as if he was a stain on her image. And as for that find in Paris, she'd duped the French dealer, hadn't she? She knew what she had and she'd only paid him fifty euros. That was theft, surely! She did exactly the same as everybody else and then she had the gall to call him a crook. He'd tried to help her and she'd kicked him for it, and this – this theft, this money, *his* money – well, what was it if not pure unadulterated malevolence? Undeserved, out of proportion. His hands tightened on the steering wheel. Wherever she was, he'd get an answer from the grandmother.

At Bristol, he had to stop for petrol. He paid in cash with his last couple of notes. He sat on a dirty grass verge with a bottle of water for five minutes. The rain had stopped, but the clouds were still black. Half past two. Only another hour and a half of light, and already cars were driving with full beam headlights on. He felt empty and sick to his stomach, which cramped as he drank the water. He knew that he ought to get something to eat, but he couldn't face it. He got up with the cold water sloshing about in his stomach, his hands folded over his gut. He opened the car door and got in, grimacing.

By the time he got to the stretch of road over Bodmin Moor, it was pitch black. There wasn't much traffic around, and the weather had closed in, ice on top of rain. He felt the wheels lose traction once or twice, and passed a maintenance crew with their yellow lights flashing. The car was immediately showered with grit, and he slowed down to fifty. The blackness of the day and the surrounding moors was disorientating – he felt suspended in some kind of alternate reality, one where the road would go on forever and he would find himself on a circular route, seeing the same bridges, the same distant grey shadows of houses. On and on and on in a nightmare from which he would never wake.

When he first saw the blue lights ahead – a line of them right across the road – he had the surreal conviction that the road had suddenly come to an end and there was no way forward. He turned out to be right. The lights belonged to several police cars and an ambulance. In his driving mirror, he saw a fire engine speeding up on his right-hand side. There were half a dozen cars ahead of him with their hazards flashing. And then he saw the other car on its roof, and a second and third slewed across the carriageway. Somebody was lying on the ground with their arm inside the car and they seemed to be talking to someone inside. The police were trying to prise them away as the paramedics kneeled down beside them.

It could have only just happened. A minute earlier and he could have been involved. He braked hard and sat with the engine running, his hazard lights on. A police officer came running up. He wound down the window.

'Get your car off to the left-hand side, mate, on the hard shoulder.'

'I've got to get to Wadebridge.'

The officer looked at him as if he were insane. He did as he was told.

Minutes passed. He closed his eyes to block out the image of the upturned car. After a while he got out. There were other cars backed up behind him now. A fire officer jogged past him and he caught the man's arm. 'Is there any way to turn around?' he asked. 'There was a junction a mile back.'

'Ask the police.'

'I've got to get to Wadebridge. It's an emergency.'

The fire officer shook him off. '*This* is an emergency,' he shouted.

Time passed. He sat in his car slowly freezing to death. With dull fascination he watched the fire crew cut the side panel from the upturned car. The driver of the car behind him, a hugely overweight guy, walked up to him and knocked on his window.

'How long do you reckon?' the man asked.

'Who the hell knows?' he said.

The man leaned down. 'Listen, they've got that fast lane left open for the emergency guys. What's to stop us using it? I've got things to do, know what I mean?'

He knew what he meant. Before the other man could get back in his car he'd turned on his engine and reversed, then looped over to the empty lane. He saw the second car follow. Ahead in the gloom, there was a police officer standing in the carriageway, keeping other vehicles to one side. Beyond him, Aiden could plainly make out the slip road. Cars just joining the accident queue were manoeuvring to turn up it, and there were two constables further back. As he and the other guy speeded up to take the slip road, they met others who were trying to do a three-point turn. Aiden leaned on the horn. A driver halfway across gestured that he had to wait for someone doing the exact same manoeuvre behind him. Out of the corner of his eye, Aiden saw the last policeman running towards him, shouting something. He blew the horn again. In the middle of the snarled-up mess was a middle-aged woman, car stalled, hands to her face. There was a six-foot gap between her and the next car. He accelerated through it, missing her but colliding with a car on the inside lane that had mounted the verge and was making for the exit.

He had no option but to stop.

34

THE WEATHER BECAME WARMER.

Despite the coldness of the sea, the crowds started arriving. The surf shop and the café opened up again. Thomas worked on in the cottage. He had cleared every piece of furniture out of the downstairs sitting room, and had spent the last fortnight working on two large canvasses. It was an act of forgetting. He let Classic FM play loud, filling his head and emptying it of anything else. He worked long into each evening. Once or twice Bill Pascoe came to rescue him, taking him up to The Sailmakers, and once or twice they went on longer walks together. He was grateful that Bill took the hint.

He didn't want to talk.

Christine had died four days after he left her. Richard Ellis had been to see her and said that she was quiet. He had told her that a body had been found on her land and asked her if she knew the identity. She hadn't replied, but she'd held onto Richard's hand so tightly that he had to prise her fingers away. The next morning the staff found her lying on her side on the floor in a foetal position, still warm and her hands tucked under her chin. It was eerily the same position in which they'd found the body.

Thomas had stayed in his own house and waited for Richard to come to him. It didn't take long.

'It's a child, Thomas. About three years old.'

He had guessed it. He had only seen the edge of the skull and the top of the spinal column, but it was far too small to be an adult.

'How long ago?' he asked.

'Difficult. Maybe thirty or forty years? A first guess.'

'Was Christine living in the house then?'

'Yes.'

'Anyone else with her?'

Richard sighed, stretching out his long legs and cradling a cup of coffee in his hands. 'She used to have a lodger in the seventies apparently,' he said. 'Somebody called Palmer. He came and went, but the family say Christine was besotted with him. It wasn't a great relationship. Not the kind of relationship anyone would want. He'd been homeless, working the fairs, he had a record of assault. He was a big man, apparently. Drunk more often than not. The whole family warned her against him, but she wouldn't listen. He died in prison in 1990.'

'Prison? What crime?'

'Road rage. He dragged another driver out of his car and beat him senseless.'

Thomas took a moment to take it in. 'But this burial is what, ten years before that?'

'Maybe. We'll know better in a day or so.'

Thomas had his head in his hands. 'Palmer... I don't remember the name.'

'He was working and living in Shropshire when he was arrested.'

'What happened to the other driver?'

'Permanent brain injury.'

'Jesus. And was Christine still his partner?'

'No,' Richard said.

Thomas considered. 'Christine would have been, what? Fifty or so when Palmer went to prison. In her thirties and forties when he lived with her?'

'Seems so,' Richard replied. 'She inherited her house from her father, you know. Never married. The family said that Palmer just saw her as a meal ticket. Hopeful of taking it from her, maybe. Dangerous relationship. Very dangerous.'

'And she never had anyone else?'

'The family say not.'

Thomas sat thinking with a heavy heart about Christine's loneliness. How deep it ran and for how long.

'Who is the child?' he asked at last.

'We're still running DNA. It's a girl though.'

'Do you think it was Christine's?

'Nobody ever saw her with one, and never saw her pregnant. But we'll soon know. We'll have both sets of DNA.'

'Then it was a victim of Palmer's maybe? His daughter?'

'Could be.'

'Method of death?'

'Blunt force trauma to the skull, and a broken neck.'

'Oh God. How terrible.' Thomas sighed. 'Abuse?'

'Evidence of healed fractures. So, yes.'

'Someone must know who she is.'

'If it was Palmer's daughter, then the mother could have died. There are all sorts of possibilities. We'll chase them up as far as we can.'

'I was working in this area in the mid-eighties,' Thomas mused. 'I don't remember any child abductions.'

'I could find no record, though we're working on it.'

'*Could* Christine have concealed a pregnancy, despite what her family say?'

'A pregnancy, perhaps. But a toddler? Hard to believe.' Richard put his cup down, and stood up. 'Are you going to stay living here?' he asked. Thomas had already given his statement and been interviewed. The case was open.

'What do you want me to do?' Thomas asked.

'I guess you'll be wanting to go back to Cornwall.'

'I'll do whatever you say.'

'I can't stop you.'

They walked out of the house and into the pale sunshine. Richard had parked his car at the entrance of the lane, and Thomas walked along with him. The trees were coming into leaf, and Thomas couldn't help thinking that it was exactly this time of year last year when Alice Hauser had reappeared in his life. He thought how he'd driven out down this same lane not knowing the devastation that was about to unfold.

'I think I'll sell this house when this is all over,' he said, as they got to the car.

'Where will you go?'

'I don't know.'

When Richard was in the car, Thomas held open his door. 'What do you suppose Christine was apologising for on the last morning I saw her? She was talking about a woman saying things about Fran, and she kept saying that she was sorry.'

Richard shrugged.

'I suppose it's possible that Helen McAllister came here, spoke to Christine – had an argument even – and then left. Christine was an alcoholic, Thomas. And the dementia… perhaps even guilt over the child… all mixed up together in her mind. Just by the token of the spade, and accusing you – a man she knew well and had feelings for – of burying someone…? It kind of fits together in its own garbled way.'

Thomas stood and watched as Richard drove away, raising his hand goodbye as the other man's car disappeared over the long slope of the hill.

Then he went into Christine's yard and looked again at the house and land, wondering what the hell had happened here.

It was Saturday.

Thomas hadn't registered the significance of the day – not even that it was the weekend – when he walked out along the same route that Aiden Ruskin had always taken. He tried to keep the man out of his mind as he walked down through the field and onto the coast path, but it was impossible. He reached the bench that overlooked the seawater pool and sat down, Max at his side.

The tide was up. The rocks and concrete wall that surrounded the pool were invisible under a white-capped sea. The sun glittered on the water. He couldn't get either Christine or Isabelle out of his head. He wished that he could. Christine, Isabelle, Helen, Alice, Fran. They seemed to be standing around him willing him to make connections. He saw the clear link between Aiden and Isabelle and Archie. But Ruskin's dealings were shadier, less transparent. He'd been a partner to Keira – at least for a while – but how deeply were *they* linked, really? Greta, who had died here, hadn't liked Ruskin. Neither had Isabelle. Had Keira confided in her grandmother about the rape? If Aiden had come to the house, would Greta have accused him of that, been furious, pushed him away? Had there been a fight?

And why did Ruskin call both Greta and Isabelle 'thieves'? Just petulance? A theft from his father, from him, or someone else?

Thomas sat back and sighed. He watched the sea for a long time, seeing how the hills just beyond the bay broke the rollers to one side. There was an area up there on the headland that overlooked a seemingly placid bit of ocean. He got up and walked along the path, Max trotting ahead of him. Every now and then Thomas threw a stick for him, but Max was barely interested. Now and again he chased it, picked it up and then dropped it apathetically as if it was beneath his dignity.

As the ground rose, Thomas took a side route that led him up the hill. He'd come up here once or twice trying to get perspective on the village, thinking of it in terms of painting it, but he'd never really looked down. He did so now, seeing how the water skirted a series of massive boulders. He sat down on the grass and saw how rapidly the tide seemed to leave the bay, churning and rolling as it did so over the serrated lines of quartz. He had no idea really how the sea currents worked but perhaps the bay acted like a funnel when the tide came roaring back in, dragging a vast weight of water with it. Surely anything that went into the sea here – whether it was into the pool or flung from the headland – would be cut to pieces on those sharp-edged rocks. They stretched right across the expanse until the next headland, which sheltered a sandy beach. He could see the roof of his own cottage from here. Surely Greta's body would have been more than merely bruised? It would have torn her clothes, cut her flesh, rolling around on the rocky foreshore like laundry tumbling around in a machine. Unless… He shaded his eyes with his hand. Unless Greta went into the pool as the tide was withdrawing, and got caught there. It was deep. About ten feet deep or so. Her body might never have been out to sea, but caught behind the man-made concrete wall that formed one edge to trap the seawater. By the time the tide was fully out first thing in the morning, she'd simply be floating in the pool.

He shuddered involuntarily, and walked back towards the house, meaning to go back inside and continue work. But before he got there, he rang Laura's number. He hadn't seen her since she dropped him back at his own house on the night that he discovered the body in Christine's garden. He wondered if she was in work today, a bank holiday weekend.

She answered immediately. 'Thomas,' she said. 'How are you?'

'I'm back in Trewarith,' he told her. 'I've been back a couple of weeks. Sorry I haven't rung.'

'I hear you've been a bit preoccupied.'

He smiled. 'Just a bit.'

'I'm sorry, Thomas,' she commiserated. 'What a shitload you've had lately.'

'How are things going?'

She paused. He could hear people coming and going in the background. 'Are you at home?' she asked.

'I'm at the cottage, yes.'

'Want a visitor?'

'I'd be glad of it.'

He realised that he'd be glad to see her in particular, not just anyone.

'I'll be there in an hour or so.'

When she turned up, she was carrying a bag of groceries. 'Hello, Max,' she said, as she came into the kitchen. Max followed in her footsteps, looking at her adoringly.

'What's this?' Thomas asked.

She put the bag on the kitchen table. 'Lunch. I made a guess that you wouldn't have much in.'

'You were right,' he admitted.

She started unpacking. 'Nothing glamorous. Ham, salad, bread. A bottle of cider. A lemon tart.'

'Let me pay you.'

'Don't be an idiot,' she told him briskly.

She saw to the food and he sat watching her. He was glad of someone else in the house at last. She put the plate in front of him. 'Eat,' she instructed him.

They worked through the food in silence. Finally, she sat back with her glass of cider and considered him. 'I hear it was a child,' she said, finally.

'Yes. Terrible.'

'You expected Helen McAllister.'

'I didn't want to think it of Christine, but… yes.'

She paused, then, quietly, 'You may never know the answer, Thomas.'

'I realise that.'

'Can you let it go?'

Hr glanced up at her. 'Can you let Keira Brodie go? Or Aiden Ruskin?'

'No,' she said. 'I'll find them.'

'And if ten or eleven years go by and you still haven't, what then?'

They looked at each other. Then she shrugged.

'What's the latest?' he asked. 'Can you tell me?'

She nodded slowly. 'Aiden Ruskin, no. He hasn't pinged on any system. Keira... her card was used once in Suffolk and once in Norfolk after Greta's funeral. The gallery remains closed. Her car hasn't come up on any system either. It was due for MOT in February and the registration number shows the MOT's expired.'

'East Anglia?' Thomas said. 'That's random.'

'Well, yes and no. The person she was working for, Keddington, has his main residence in Suffolk. We've visited. He hasn't seen her and he can't explain her card being used. He professes to be worried about her.'

'Who is Keddington?'

'He inherited his estate in 1965. It seems it's falling into ruin. You should see it, Thomas – he's a hoarder and there's crap everywhere, and there's these paintings on the walls and bronzes and statues, all covered in dust. Wreaths of cobwebs. It's a mausoleum. Huge padlocked iron gates. We waited nearly an hour and then he shuffled out in his slippers. I've never seen anything quite like it.'

'How strange.'

'He's very elderly – early nineties, I think. He looks about three hundred though.' She was laughing a little to herself and shaking her head. 'Holes in his sweater. Grimy gilet over the top. Looked as if he was a stranger to a bath.'

'But he did speak to you?'

'He said Keira was employed to provide an inventory of the house furnishings, all his art works and so on. He says the inventory is unfinished. He's a real old curmudgeon. Hated us being there. Kept looking at the door. Fretful, you know?'

Thomas smiled. He liked anyone who used the word 'curmudgeon'. It was one of those you hardly heard any more. He wondered if she thought that he too fitted the category.

'What's your guess?' he asked. 'About Keira?'

'She could be there.'

'Search warrant?'

'On what grounds?'

'There are none.'

'Quite.' Laura had got up to make tea. She paused, gazing out of the window. 'It's a huge estate,' she mused. 'You could hide an army in there.' She put the two mugs on the table. 'The house is enormous too. Cellars, outbuildings. Thirty bedrooms. Eighteenth-century heap, basically. You should see the gardens. Massive kitchen garden, huge walls. Big fountain full of rubbish. Everything overgrown.'

Thomas suddenly thought of one of the postcards that Isabelle had given him. The sculpture on the coast at Aldeburgh in Suffolk. 'She's there. I'd bet money on it.'

'Maybe. But why?'

'Hiding from Ruskin? Because…'

She gave him a taut, frustrated smile. 'Because she thinks he killed her grandmother. He sold his father's house in December and straight afterwards he came down here. The very next day, in fact.'

'How do you know?'

'He was given a ticket for careless driving. He had an accident on the Bodmin road trying to get out from the queue after an accident, and he ploughed into another car on a slip road. Nobody hurt, just a scrape. He got points on his licence.'

'Was he coming to see Keira?'

'She was in London, in the flat above the gallery, late that night. A neighbour saw her. Until just after midnight. Then the same neighbour saw her go out into the street – the mews – and get into her car. She hasn't been back since. That night, even though it was snowing a little, she drove to Trewarith. She drove to this house.'

'The same night that Ruskin was caught by the police?'

'That was three hours earlier.'

'And he came here?'

'I think he came deliberately to find out where Keira was, counting on Greta telling him. Hardly likely, eh? He must have been desperate.'

'But why was he looking for her? Why didn't he know where she was?'

'Ah,' Laura said. 'This is where it gets really interesting.'

'Did no one here see them arrive?'

'No one. It was four days before Christmas, and a bitterly cold night. And, as you know, once you turn down this lane it's a dead end. There's only these two cottages at the end of it. There'd be no reason for anyone to see either of them.'

'CCTV on the shop?'

'No. Doesn't catch the lane. Aimed at the shop itself.'

'Video doorbells?'

'Most houses are set back from the road. Two bungalows that aren't don't have such a thing.'

Thomas tried to think. 'So Ruskin comes down here. In a hurry by the sound of it. He'd just got the money from the house sale. Why isn't he on a night flight to the Maldives? Why's he so desperate to see Keira suddenly?'

Laura smiled. 'That's the interesting part I just told you about. It confirmed the suspicions of the investigating team in London. They've got access now to his accounts. The money was transferred offshore.' She waited a second so the next information could sink in. 'Not his account.'

'Oh my God,' Thomas said, realising. 'She stole his money.'

'No proof.' But she nodded.

'He came down here to threaten Greta and force Keira to come and see him.'

'He may have even thought she was here. But yes, that all would make sense. Perhaps he reasoned that before Keira vanished completely she'd want to say goodbye to her grandmother. Or perhaps he thought the offshore account was Greta's, who knows? He was definitely in a hurry, probably a fury.'

'Keira came here to defend her grandmother.'

'And was too late.'

Thomas sipped the tea she had made. 'You've always thought that Greta was killed.'

'And I thought he did it.' Laura paused. 'After midnight, he went to a neighbour's house and told them Greta was missing. He said that when he got there the door was open and she was gone. Half the village came out to look for her. Horrible weather. Heavy sleet, pitch black. But no sign of her. The neighbour rang the police but – well, she'd only been gone an hour or so at that point. A local PC was sent down. Ruskin said he would stay in her house in case she came back. By that time people had been looking along the coast path and around their own houses for nearly two hours. It was decided to begin a search proper at daylight.'

'You saw Keira at the time.'

'That same morning. By the pool, with Greta's body. She and Ruskin had gone out at six, while it was still dark. I don't know what happened between them. I don't know what time she arrived exactly, or what Ruskin had told her.'

'How was she acting around Ruskin?'

'Shell-shocked. I noticed she kept away from him. She went in the ambulance with Greta's body. She was very cold herself, of course.'

'Did Ruskin go with them?'

'No. But he was keen to give his side of the story. He certainly acted the role of the distraught relative – though he wasn't, as we now know, related at all. There was something about his behaviour – I couldn't quite put my finger on it. As always with Ruskin, he didn't ring true.'

Thomas considered what an apt phrase this was in describing him. To not ring true – like a church bell with a fault, a crack, repeating a wrong note.

'Isabelle went to the hospital to collect Keira,' Laura continued. 'As far as I know, Keira and Ruskin didn't meet again until the funeral.'

'But you spoke to her in the hospital? You asked about Ruskin?'

'She was in shock, I think. Withdrawn. She confirmed when she had arrived. She said that Greta had left a voicemail for her, simply asking her to come. She said that Greta had sounded stressed. But when I asked specifically about Ruskin she clammed up. Went into herself. Wouldn't be drawn.'

'Did you think she was frightened?'

'Probably. It was hard to tell. She'd got very cold and was in a hospital bed herself. And she'd asked that Ruskin not be allowed in.'

Thomas frowned. 'And Ruskin stayed here over that Christmas?'

'Alone in Greta's house, yes.'

'He must have gone up to Isabelle's to try and speak to them.'

'He did,' Laura confirmed. 'He couldn't get in. They wouldn't answer the door. Isabelle reported him as a nuisance caller and he was, as they say, escorted off the premises.'

Thomas nodded. 'This must have been going through your mind on the morning of Isabelle's death.'

'Of course. Your being there made it a tad more complicated for a while, of course.'

'Sorry about that.'

'I guess you're forgiven.'

'When did Keira leave?'

'After the funeral. But I'm guessing that Isabelle strung Ruskin along until Keira was well clear. Then, after that, she probably barred him still. And then there was another complaint. The uniforms couldn't find him that time, but she claimed he'd been in the grounds.'

'He must have known Keira had got away from him by then.'

'Yes.'

Thomas finished his tea and pushed away the mug. 'So he squatted in the house. He tore up the gardens.'

'She left him to it. A small price for her freedom.'

'And she had his money.'

'Well, that's a guess, of course.'

'Hmm. Isabelle told me that Ruskin was crazy lately. Now we know why. What did the London house sell for?'

'Just under a million. Bit of a state apparently, and not very big. But still valuable.'

Thomas whistled between his teeth. 'Did Greta and Isabelle have something to do with it?' he wondered.

'He may have suspected it, but no money went into their accounts.'

He raised his eyebrows. 'You've been busy.'

'We have. We finally got Greta's phone records too. She made a call to Keira at just gone midnight. Keira tried calling her back, no reply, fifteen minutes later.'

'Have you got Keira's phone records now?'

'No. She's not really a suspect in Greta's death, nor Isabelle's. So there's only shaky grounds for demanding them. Still trying. However, the number is out of service. Even if you call the gallery it shows the number as unobtainable, so it seems she's abandoned the gallery at least for the time being. I suspect when and if we do get them, the last recorded site for it would be in Suffolk. But maybe she threw it away long before that.'

She began packing her bag with the empty food containers.

'Please leave them,' he said. 'I'll put them in the recycling.'

'It's no trouble.'

He got up, and gently took the bag away from her. 'Please,' he said, taking her hand in his. 'Don't bother with it. And please don't go.'

35

PITCH BLACK. SLEET FALLING.

As Aiden came slowly down the hill to the village he could barely make out the horizon where the sea met the sky. He rolled down the car windows and let the icy wind blow in his face. It was almost midnight.

He rounded the last corner and saw a few scattered Christmas decorations lit in gardens. His face set in an unconscious grimace. He'd never had time for Christmas. It reminded him of his mother carefully folding and smoothing out paper as he opened his presents as a child. Coming down on Christmas morning and being crushed in his grandmother's arms. She always smelled of cooking fat and she always insisted on kissing him. Later in the day she'd start on the sherry and they all sat around watching the tiny television, the Queen's broadcast, the big film. The gas fire popping in the hearth, a tray set for tea, a small almond-topped Dundee cake. The nativity scene garishly lit in the window. Seven years old, he'd broken the heads off Mary and Jesus and buried the baby in the vegetable peelings. He'd thought it was hilarious. His mother had cried. There was church, too. All the maudlin, creepy good wishes, the hand shaking, the clamminess of the hymn book pages, the routine cup of coffee and a bag of Jelly Tots for the children. His grandmother gave him annuals – *Look and Learn*, old *Valiant* magazines. The taint of a respectable Christmas made his gorge rise.

The lights were on in Greta's house.

He knocked on the door.

She took a long time to answer, and when she did she looked shocked.

'Aiden,' she said, finally. 'What are you doing here?'

He pushed her out of the way. The kitchen was hot. She'd been cooking. The smell of summer filled the air. Strawberries. The kitchen table was a mess of flour, and there was sugar and butter in a big glass basin. He looked at the stove.

'Strawberry cake,' she said. 'Frozen strawberries.' She turned off the ring and got behind a chair. Her eyes strayed from the hot pan to him, and back again.

'Where is she?' he said.

'Who?'

'For Chrissake,' he shouted. 'Keira.'

'Keira isn't here,' she said.

He went into the living room, and up the stairs. He looked around himself at Greta's spartan room with its appliqué bedspread and the dreamcatcher in the window. On the wall was a framed photograph of her at Chelsea. He narrowed his eyes, squinting at it. She was a looker when she was young.

She had followed him and was standing behind him.

'What happened to your husband?' he asked.

'What do you mean?'

He pointed at the photograph. 'This him here?'

'Yes.'

'Is he dead?'

She flinched slightly. 'Yes. A long time ago. Bowel cancer. Keira was born after he'd died. Her mother was only eighteen.'

'And *her* husband?'

'She had no husband. She was a single mother.'

'Your daughter, single mother. You, widow. All living here.'

'For a while, yes. Keira's mother got a degree in earth sciences. She's lived in Canada for the last ten years. She got married out there. I encouraged her. Just as I encouraged Keira.' She was frowning. 'What do you want, Aiden?'

He sat down on her bed. 'See, what I'm trying to do, I'm trying to draw a picture,' he said. 'Because Keira never did. A picture of why she does what she does to people like me.'

'What do you mean, "what she does"?'

'Uses. Discards. Steals.'

He noticed that she didn't dispute it. But she suddenly straightened up as if an idea had occurred to her. 'Keira's gone to see her mother for Christmas.'

It was such a transparent lie that he laughed out loud. 'Without you?' he said sarcastically. 'Leaving you here, her beloved grandmother, who's cooking into the early hours, making stuff for Christmas. Why are you doing that?'

'I couldn't sleep.'

He shook his head. 'Either she's here or she's on her way.' He looked around again at the room. Greta shifted her stance a little. She put a hand to her mouth. 'Bit of a hippie, were you?' he asked. 'My grandfather liked that shit too. King's Road. Fancy psychedelic suits. Drug overdose. Sad, sad life. Nonce.'

She looked shocked. 'Was he?'

'Wouldn't doubt it. Free love.' His head was spinning a little. 'But nothing's free,' he murmured. He kept seeing the overturned car and the person that had been lying flat on the ground and reaching inside to the driver. That, and the disorientating drive with the snow blowing towards him. It was still flickering at the corner of his vision.

'Aiden,' Greta said quietly. 'Why don't we sit down for a while?'

He couldn't figure out why she thought it was appropriate. Why she didn't get the urgency of his being here. He put a clenched fist to his forehead. 'She stole my money. You know that. She stole it.'

'I don't know it at all,' she responded.

He stood up. 'My money! People are waiting for it. I've got a deal going,' he shouted. 'Where is she!' A thought occurred to him. 'She's next door.'

'She is not,' Greta said. 'No one lives there.'

He was facing her, both fists clenched now. 'Give me the keys.'

'There's no one there, Aiden. I use it for storage. You know that.' She'd recovered from her surprise now. 'Sometimes Keira used to bring friends down in the summer. You and she stayed there once. You can have the keys if you want. Take them. They're hanging from a hook near the back door. Be my guest. But there's no one there now.'

He pushed past her and took a couple of paces across the narrow landing. There was a small shower room here, and another bedroom. He opened the door. A single bed was made up there, the covers turned back. There was the smell of freshly laundered sheets and towels. A little jar of early narcissi on the dressing table. Another photograph, this time of Keira arm-in-arm with Greta, taken by the seawater pool, the water a brilliant turquoise blue behind them.

When he turned back to Greta, there were tears in her eyes.

'We'll just sit downstairs and wait for her,' he said.

'She won't be here till Christmas Eve,' she protested.

'Then we'll wait downstairs until Christmas Eve,' he told her. 'But I'm checking that fucking place next door first.' He got to the door and turned back. He walked up to her and put both hands gently around her throat, pressing in very slightly with both thumbs. Her eyes widened. 'Ring her,' he said. 'Maybe she'll get here quicker.'

The cottage next door was more untidy than he remembered it. On the ground floor Greta had stacked all her gardening tools, even a strimmer. Maybe she thought the electrical stuff would be safer in the house than her shed. It crowded out the space where there ought to be a living room. There were packs of seed and plastic trays, secateurs, tree loppers, a pile of straw bags and wet-weather gear: waterproof trousers, boots. Greta must have made a real effort the time that he and Keira had visited. He didn't remember all this dross in here then.

He walked up the stairs and stared at the double bed. All the bedding was folded on the top. The curtains were drawn and the room smelled damp. He hissed between his teeth. You could never tell with women. They could be docile and obedient, they could seem easy, and then they did outrageous things. They slipped away like Celia, vanished like Keira, going where he couldn't follow. The feeling of powerlessness was unbearable. Somebody had once told him that resentment was a lack of power and he was completely made of it now, white hot fury running through his veins.

He went back down the stairs and out of the cottage. It was almost pitch black along here – he tripped as he went out of the gate and had to feel his way back. Then he saw Greta's door was open, spilling a pool of light on the threshold. He ran in. She was gone. All the cooking things were just as she'd left them. He called her name, looking in the sitting room and shouting up the stairs.

He ran back out onto the path. Which way had she gone? He guessed the village – someone to help her. He jogged along the lane, repeatedly stumbling and cursing, to where a giant shoulder of rock separated the two beaches. It was high tide, the water glimmering in the darkness. He stared impotently at the few houses and the shuttered café. Apart from a few Christmas decorations, he could see no lights in the windows.

'You bitch,' he muttered. 'What are you doing? Where are you?'

Then he thought about the position of the cottages and the houses in the village. There was barely a signal, it was intermittent, and here in the lowest point of the village before the sea, the reception was hardly better. You had to get up on the cliff path to really be able to make a call. Greta was usually out all day, Keira

had once told him, and lived by her mobile. She'd let the landli.
lapse long ago.

He ran back down the lane to the cottages. He looked out acros.
the fields. He could hear the roar of high tide on the rocks. Her
favourite place, that pool. He sprinted through the field gate and
down the line of the hedge, cursing at the rutted soil. Jesus Christ,
it was cold. He'd left his jacket in the kitchen. What did she have
on? A thick skirt, a sweater. Had there been a coat hanging on
the pegs near the door? At the coast path, he stumbled. It was
nearly impossible to see in the dark. The sound of the ocean was
unnerving. He turned left and saw her standing by the bench
overlooking the pool. She had her phone to her ear. He couldn't
make out what she was saying, but her voice was raised.

He ran up to her. She couldn't hear him above the waves. He
snatched the phone from her. She edged around the wooden
bench, keeping it between them.

'Greta,' he said. 'Come back to the house.'

She looked around herself. He looked down at the slippery
stones that led to the pool. There was nothing to see of it now, and
the water was slamming against the boulders just a few feet down.

'Come with me,' he said. 'You'll catch cold, Greta.'

'Stay away from me,' she said. 'I know what you are.'

'You know?' he repeated. 'What is it that you know?'

'The way you treat people...' She took a step backwards.

'Careful,' he said. He smiled.

'And a rapist,' she said.

The word was carried away in the wind. It shredded in the air
above them.

'I've never raped anyone,' he said.

'You don't know what you are, do you?' she said.

He could see that she was crying. He looked objectively at her
weeping, hesitating with the vast ocean behind her. She really was
a small woman, an inconsequential woman.

angry now. He felt suddenly calm. He was proud of that. He knew where the accusations had come from. Only Keira. Her opinion. More lies.

'Where is my money?' he asked quietly.

She frowned. She was shivering.

'Your granddaughter has stolen close to a million pounds from me,' he said. 'Taken out of my account today. The people I've got lined up don't like to be kept waiting. They don't like anyone going back on an arrangement, do you understand? Where is it? Where is she?'

'I don't know,' she said. She was still frowning.' She wouldn't steal.'

He smiled. He took a step forward. She edged away. 'Mind your step,' he said.

'Keep away,' she repeated.

'Where is it?' he demanded. 'Where is she?' He looked down at the phone in his hand. 'Did she answer?' he asked. 'Keira? Is she coming here?'

'No.'

'Oh, Greta,' he murmured. 'What a pair of liars you both are.'

Behind Greta the sea made an almost human sound. A groan as the waves heaved upwards. Greta glanced behind her. He saw her feet slither for purchase.

He meant to grab her hand but instead only caught her wrist.

She pulled her arm away. He let go.

He watched her fall. It was remarkable how quickly she was gone, instantly invisible. It was as if she'd been taken seamlessly down into the water without a sound, a protest.

He waited for five minutes.

Ten.

Then he threw the phone into the water after her.

*

He ran back past the cottages and into the village.

Sleet was beginning to fall again, whipped up by the wind and blowing horizontally across the road. It stung his face. He didn't look behind him all the way. Which was the house where Greta had been working when he and Keira had visited? He ran up the main street looking for it, his breath scorching in his chest. She had pulled back. If she hadn't done that they could be sitting in the cottage right now. She'd stepped away and stumbled. She'd manufactured her own fall just to get out of his grasp. He had been trying to help her. Her own stubbornness had taken her down.

He suddenly recognised the entrance of the right house.

He sprinted along the drive and hammered on the front door.

A bleary-eyed man in his fifties eventually answered.

'Is Greta Brodie here?' Aiden asked.

The man rubbed his hands over his face. 'Greta?' he repeated. 'No, of course not. What's the trouble?'

Aiden found himself rocking backwards and forwards on his heels, and tried to stop himself. 'She's not at her house,' he said. 'She's missing.' Seeing the man's confused expression, he added, 'I'm Keira's partner. I was working here with Greta in your garden once. When you remodelled it.'

A woman came down the stairs behind the man.

'Greta Brodie is missing,' her husband told her. 'This is…'

'Aiden.'

'Aiden. Yes, of course.'

The woman put a hand to her throat. 'What's happened, exactly?'

'I turned up at the house tonight and the door is open and she's not there,' Aiden said. 'It looks like she'd been cooking. I can't find her.'

The couple looked at each other.

The man reached into a cupboard and pulled out a heavy raincoat and a torch. 'I'll come with you,' he said.

'Why would she be out in this weather?' the woman called.

But they were already halfway down the drive.

36

A WEEK LATER THOMAS MADE A trip to London.

He took a hire van, with Max secured in a harness on the flat seat next to him. The dog hadn't liked it much, but just the sight of the van and the presence of Max had almost made Thomas give up the journey before he even began. Not surprising. The last time he'd been in a van like this one it had been his own, and the unsecured dog on the seat next to him hadn't survived the accident. No way to explain it to Max, though. Thomas leaned against the van for a while that morning, telling himself that it wouldn't happen again. 'Jesus,' he murmured to himself. 'Come on, now.' A crawling pain inched its way across his scalp. Eventually he'd got in, put on his seat belt, and looked at Max's confused expression. 'Believe me, it's for the best,' he said.

He drove up the hill and out of the village in bright sunshine. It was early May, his favourite month. All the horse chestnut trees on the top road were in bloom. Pink and white flowers alternating. He kept thinking of Laura in his narrow bed, and the warmth of her. He was grateful. Too grateful and overwhelmed to put it into words. He was afraid she would think him sentimental. But most of all he had a horror of embarrassing her. Or himself.

He reached Tam Jeffries by one o'clock.

Tam was waiting for him outside the shop, leaning in the fluorescent pink doorway with a cup of coffee in his hand. A man of about thirty or so was standing next to him.

'Joe here will help you,' Tam said. He came to the back of the van and looked in, but said nothing. Joe and Thomas manhandled the three big paintings into the gallery and stacked them, while Max plodded dutifully after. Tam brought in the six smaller canvasses.

'You've been busy,' Tam commented, standing in the centre of the paintings arranged in a circle around him.

Thomas knew better than to hurry him up. He put a hand on Tam's shoulder. 'I've got an appointment,' he said. 'I'll be an hour or two. No longer. Can the van go round the back?'

'Be my guest,' Tam said. He was walking around the biggest paintings, looking at them from all angles.

'And can you look after Max?'

Tam pointed at Joe. Thomas handed Joe the lead.

Max whined as Thomas walked away.

Imelda Yates was waiting for him in a café close to Keira's gallery. Ironically, it was the same one that he had stopped briefly in when he'd visited London on his own a month or two back. Their prices still made him wince.

She'd taken a corner seat.

'Thank you for meeting me,' he said.

'My lunch hour,' she told him. 'So this is still about Aiden Ruskin?'

'Yes,' he said. 'Still trying to fill in the blanks and work out where he might be.' She sipped her green tea, watching him. 'You recognised both Archie Ruskin and Isabelle Crosby's names,' he continued. 'Did you know them personally?'

'No,' she said. 'Just through the business. Isabelle Crosby was long before my time.'

'They were dealers.'

'According to our records, only Lady Crosby bought and sold with us.'

'Not Archie?'

'Too minor,' she said. 'Not his style.'

'Did she come to sales with him?'

'I've no idea.'

'What kind of thing did Lady Crosby buy and sell?'

'She seems to have stopped dealing about twenty years ago. We weren't happy with the provenance of some items.'

'Provenance? What do you mean?'

'Literally, where it came from. I believe there was some hesitation over archaeological items.'

'She travelled in the Middle East, I think.'

'Yes.'

'And she told me that she'd been in Italy. Do you think she sold things there? Perhaps privately?' It was an idea that had occurred to him a day or two ago. That with her association with Archie ended, and her inability to sell in auction, she might have retraced her footsteps to the Mediterranean to contacts she'd made years ago on archaeological trips. Although how she would have got the pieces through customs, he couldn't guess.

'I really don't know,' Imelda replied.

'Were her items illegally imported somehow?'

'Hard to prove.'

'Toynton & Mark just didn't want to be associated with them?'

'That's correct. Attitudes change. Laws change.'

Thomas thought for a second. 'So she would have had things that she couldn't now sell?' It would confirm his guess.

'Possibly. Unless she had some remaining illegal contacts.'

He put his head on one side, looking at her with a small grimace that was nearly a smile. 'But you must know. Your company is doing the inventory of her house.'

'We haven't made a visit yet.'

'Why is that?'

'We're still considering it. She asked us to do it in her will I understand, but we may just handle the art work.'

Thomas now understood. They didn't want to touch whatever it was that she had elsewhere – looted goods, perhaps.

'Do you think that Aiden Ruskin knew what she had at the house?'

'I wouldn't put it past him to find out somehow.' She gave an elegant shrug.

Thomas tried another tack. 'When Aiden was first employed here, was it known that Archie Ruskin was his father?'

'It seems that we didn't join the dots.'

'But Ruskin is such an unusual name.'

'Nevertheless.'

'Someone made a mistake, then. Would he have been employed if the person interviewing him had realised he was Archie Ruskin's son?'

'That person has retired, so I can't say.'

'Did *you* know he was Archie's son?'

'I didn't even know his father or anything about him until after Aiden left. Then it was only because of rumour, not from having any business with him.' She sipped her tea slowly, and then put down her cup. 'Someone told me that Aiden was working with his father after he left here. But Aiden had never once mentioned his family.'

'So you didn't know the connection until very much later.'

She leaned forward. 'You have to understand what a very personable character Aiden was,' she said in a low voice. 'He was just out of university, he was enthusiastic, he was helpful, and he was knowledgeable. Very good looking, and always smiling.'

The smile. Something that had never altered, thought Thomas.

'Did he fit in?' he asked.

'How do you mean?'

Thomas smiled. 'Well, in London. In the old boys' club.'

'He seemed to. He was very good at pretending to be something he wasn't.'

They were both silent for a while, watching the world go by beyond the café windows.

'Did you see a newspaper article a few years back about a man called Kingsbury?' Imelda suddenly asked.

'In what context?'

'He was accused of murdering his wife.'

'Yes,' Thomas said. 'I've heard of the case. What did you make of it?'

'When Aiden had first left us, I followed what was happening to him for a while. He had a few successes. He'd introduced a client to a collector in London and sold a small collection of paintings – Russian – on behalf of this man. It was Kingsbury.'

'So Aiden had – what – been to their house?'

'Acted as a go-between, so, yes. Took a little percentage for his trouble no doubt. Kingsbury claimed that his wife had died after Aiden's visit. Aiden denied it all, of course. He said that Kingsbury would hardly have had him back at the house if he really believed that he'd killed his wife, and if he did believe it, why hadn't he said so at the time? He claimed apparently that it was more likely that the unpleasant Mr Kingsbury had in fact murdered his wife and was now trying to blame it on him. The body was exhumed. Inconclusive. Aiden maintained that at his first visit, the wife had refused to sell the paintings, and he'd accepted it, and left. There was no evidence either way for either of them in the end.'

Thomas thought about it in comparison to what Laura had told him. 'What did she die of?'

'Respiratory problem of some kind. She was an invalid.'

Innocent he might be, Thomas thought. Although his familiar gut feeling told him not. Ruskin had such a taint to him. Thomas could almost taste it.

'The thing was,' Imelda continued, 'Aiden himself sold a watercolour, a sketch, the following year.'

Thomas shook his head to show that he didn't see the relevance.

'Apparently Kingsbury maintained that Aiden had bought that same sketch from him and had told him that it was practically worthless. Aiden had given him twenty pounds for it.'

'And?'

'Minor French artist, but very pretty. Forty-three thousand pounds.'

'But Kingsbury had sold it to him.'

'Oh yes. He was given a receipt.'

'So... business.'

'Quite.' Imelda smiled. 'But I've no doubt that Aiden knew exactly what it was when he gave Kingsbury twenty pounds.'

They both sat back, looking at each other. 'Aiden Ruskin must have made a lot of enemies,' Thomas said.

'They were thieves, Mr Maitland.'

'And yet he became involved with Keira Brodie.'

She raised her eyebrows and shrugged. 'He can be very persuasive.'

'Have you ever had any cause to doubt Keira's business practices?'

'Never.'

'Did they act together, have a business name together?'

'No.'

'We asked if you knew Keira's mobile number?'

'Yes,' she said. 'But I'm afraid it's disconnected. We haven't seen her in a long time. There is no alternative number.'

'And Aiden Ruskin? Any other thoughts?'

She looked him in the eye. 'I think Aiden Ruskin is a monster,' she said.

The sudden vehemence in her voice took Thomas aback.

'He seems very charming. That's his way in,' she said, in a voice full of bitterness. 'Do you know what charming actually means? A dictionary will tell you it means pleasant or attractive. But it's quite the opposite in my opinion. It's a way of keeping people at arm's length. It's a defence mechanism, a device to hide behind. Aiden Ruskin is like that. And the most dangerous thing about him is that he believes he's done nothing wrong.' She paused, her colour heightened. 'No, more than that. He believes he's *incapable* of doing wrong. He will tell you that you've misunderstood him when he's literally standing in front of you with all his casual cruelties.'

Imelda put a hand briefly to her mouth. She finally drew breath.

'Not to put too fine a point on it, Mr Maitland,' she added, picking up her bag with one hand and smoothing her hair with the other, 'I do hope that the bastard is lying dead in a ditch.'

37

RAIN. HEAVY.

Aiden didn't remember leaving Chalfont Edge.

But he knew why he had gone. Even though he'd been there for a different purpose tonight, at the back of his mind he'd hoped that Keira would be there. She'd gone to Isabelle Crosby after leaving hospital, and she went back there after the funeral. But it was weeks ago.

He had stayed. Stayed in Greta's house. He had waited, waited. That ought to count for something. The endless patience. Stayed to support her. He still couldn't get over that she wouldn't even speak to him, and he kept his temper and kept her on a loose rein and *said nothing at all* right through. Didn't bother her and she never acknowledged it. If you can credit that. *Never.* Right through the whole messy business, and she wouldn't tell him even when the funeral was. He had to find that out from other people.

A man he'd never met. Pascoe. He'd knocked on his door one morning. Or rather, Greta's door. And he'd said that he was sorry about Greta and that he'd known her and this same man had had the fucking brazen cheek to ask if he could collect some of Greta's clothes. Keira had asked him. *Keira!* And he was going to take them up to Chalfont Edge, and he'd told this man why would she ask *him*? And there was a stand-off on the doorstep with this guy trying to put his foot in the door and see into the kitchen. He hadn't touched anything. He'd slept in the spare room. He *wouldn't* touch anything. Keira would come and see him. He'd believed that and instead *she'd sent this man*. He'd told him to wait there, shut the door in his face, and then got two suitcases out of the lean-to at the back of the house and he'd filled them with the contents of the wardrobe and drawers and he'd shoved the picture of Greta with her dead husband on the top, and he'd gone back and opened the door and pushed both cases at Pascoe's feet and asked when the funeral was. Pascoe hadn't replied but he reached down to take the cases and he'd grabbed Pascoe's wrist and asked again, and this time Pascoe told him.

He had been at the church when Keira arrived with Isabelle. He didn't sit at the front because he showed some respect, he was *quiet*, he never said *anything* then or later and he let her pass and he stood back from the grave and he watched her and Isabelle's firm grip on Keira's shoulder. And when they walked away from the grave, Keira came to within a few inches of him and she *still* didn't look at him, and he *still* stayed silent because the whole village seemed to be there and they were looking. And nobody at all invited him to the wake but he followed up the main street to the little memorial hall and he walked in and he took a plate of food and sat down with it. And *still* nobody talked to him and Isabelle took Keira home. You couldn't make it up. You literally could not make it up, the treatment he got.

He stopped the car.

He was at a junction.

It was ten to three in the morning.

The rain poured down the windscreen.

He could hear it hammering on the roof of the car.

Where was he? There was no road sign. Small junction joining a bigger road. Still not a big road, not a main road. The lights of the car lit up the verge opposite. There were no houses near. He tried to think.

He couldn't go through Wadebridge. There had to be another way. He scrabbled about in the passenger footwell and hauled out a dog-eared road atlas. Behind him in the car was his own suitcase, his laptop and an empty holdall. Isabelle was supposed to have given him whatever he could carry. He'd waited months. Months. And he'd had enough. He'd even had to get someone to rent the next-door cottage, he was so strapped for cash. His credit cards were maxed out. Isabelle was a brutal, obstinate old bitch. He'd told her that he wasn't leaving until she gave him the equivalent of the money he'd lost and he told her she could get it all back from Keira, because that was where it had gone.

And she'd laughed in his face.

'Keira doesn't need your money,' she said. 'I don't know who's stolen it, but it wouldn't be her. She wouldn't soil herself.'

He felt himself swaying. The memory of the women in the restaurant had momentarily clouded his vision, a cloud passing in front of his eyes, a hazy jumbled image, hand on his thigh and all the smiles. *Where had he seen that girl before? In the street?* He'd turned his back on Isabelle and made for the stairs. She came running after him, and Max started barking.

'Don't you go up there,' Isabelle had said.

He ignored her and took the steps two at a time, his holdall in his hand. When he got to the landing he turned to her. 'Where is it all?'

She clamped her mouth shut, the picture of obstinacy. He smiled at her.

'I got a buyer for all the stuff in the house,' he told her. 'Did Archie fence it for you?'

She didn't reply.

'How much did you make?' he asked her. 'In it together. How long for? Until you got tired of him? Until he wouldn't sell some of it and just hoarded it? I found it. Don't you want to know what it all was? What was in the safety deposit box, too? I found a buyer for it all. London is expensive. Living is expensive. I suppose that was your money, really,' he added in a conversational way.

'Grave robbers,' she whispered.

He looked at her in astonishment. '*I'm* the grave robber?' he said. 'I am the grave robber. Huh. That's rich coming from you.'

She'd clasped her hands in front of her. 'I paid for them,' she whispered. 'It was all above board.'

'Until it wasn't,' he said. 'Until it was illegal. Maybe had been illegal all along. Paid a pittance I suppose to some dirt poor farmer while your friends dug up his land?' He took a step closer to her. 'Or you've been in league with much worse, have you?'

'I haven't traded in a long time,' she protested.

The bloody dog was still barking.

He went into the first room he saw. An empty unmade bed, a ceiling with a vast bloom of damp in one corner. He came out and took the next room and saw that it was hers. She had run along behind him and was catching at his jacket.

'Where are they? Show me,' he shouted. 'I know you must have jewellery. Archie got jewellery from you, didn't he? The stuff he didn't give back or sell. And other stuff. Little things. Portable. You know what I mean. There's got to be a hell of a lot more. Show me!'

The dog was snapping at his heels. He grabbed it by the collar, dropping the holdall, and he pulled it out of the bedroom and down the stairs, and all the way it yelped, and he dragged it along the hall and into the kitchen and out of the back door into the rain and he booted it down the path and it ran away. She came running, screaming something. She followed the dog and ran through a gate in a hedge calling its name and he ran after her and he tripped over the stone edge to a lawn and he picked up the stone.

That was all.

He picked up the stone.

In the rain.

The stone.

He couldn't make head or tail of the map now. It was like looking at a page of hieroglyphics. He noticed a rim of blood under the fingernails of his right hand. He had washed them when he'd got back to his car. Stopped halfway down the hill and doused them out of the open door with a bottle of water. He'd gone upstairs to get his holdall and realised that if he searched her rooms he was going to leave finger marks over anything he touched. When he had got there that night, he hadn't even needed to break open a window or a door – the door to the hall at the back of the house had been open a little way, half on the latch. He'd shoved it with his hip. Careless. She'd come down the stairs in her nightgown, scrawny body showing through it. If she hadn't raised her voice then and sworn at him things might have gone well. They could have come to an arrangement.

He drove on, taking every tiny lane. After one narrow hill he realised that mud had splashed up onto the wing mirror. He wound down the window and the rain felt cold. It was only then that he realised how drenched he was. When a white sign came up in the hedgerow for a farm entrance his hands gripped the steering wheel hard. Isabelle face down, the nightgown saturated. The dog whimpering under the dripping hedge. Water running down his neck. The decaying garden and the wind blowing across it. He'd peered at the stone lying where he'd dropped it. It was already running with water. He'd kneeled down briefly and looked at Isabelle's face. She stared back at him and he had reeled away before realising that her gaze was fixed.

Four in the morning.

It was like the end of the world out here, a country sunk in the dark.

He'd never been afraid of it, even as a child, though his mother always left a light burning. Bedtime ritual. Sit on the bed and say your prayers. *Gentle Jesus meek and mild look on me a little child.* Spoon-fed. But there were no gods. That was the joke. Nobody was watching him. You could do whatever you liked. He'd found that out. Most people were too believing, they gulped it down, not wanting to know that they could be fooled, clutching at compliments, carrying their gullibility about like a prize.

He stopped the car on another high point.

He was thirsty, but the water was all gone.

How long since he'd eaten? He couldn't remember.

Isabelle's eyes with the rain running into them.

It was barely daylight when he reached Somerset.

The car was out of fuel and his phone was out of charge. How long had he been driving?

He was cold to the bone.

He got out, folding the empty holdall and putting it in the suitcase. He had his passport. Isabelle had been going to give him money. That had been his plan. Money and everything else. How had he forgotten that? She lay on the grass. The bony wrist and jaw, the hair matted to her head. Long ago. Other faces, other hands clinging. Celia white-faced with a bruise along her jaw. Keira slumped on the floor in the gallery, immobile.

There was some loose change in his pockets.

He left the car and locked it.

His mind was full of endings. It felt heavy.

When he saw the houses ahead of him he took a footpath. The soil was red here. Red clay mired everywhere. The rain had stopped and the sky was clearing. He walked for a good half hour with the sun warming his back, but eventually his way was barred by a dump of rusted machinery and the hedges began running horizontally across his way. There was no choice but to clamber over a ditch and he found himself on another lane. A hundred yards along was a delivery van parked in a passing place, the driver on his phone. The firm's name on the side of the van was a Birmingham address. He knocked on the window. 'My car's broken down and I've got no signal,' he said. 'Can I borrow your phone to make a call?'

The man frowned, but handed it out.

He leaned on the side of the van, exhausted.

He phoned the number that was etched in his mind, the place he had been headed for.

The last chance at sanctuary.

38

THE ACRES OF KEDDINGTON PARK LAY empty in the afternoon sun.

The house was visible beyond the woodland, but even from a distance it looked as abandoned as the acres unrolling in front of it, the blinds on the windows all drawn down. As soon as he had left Tam Jeffries, he had made for Keddington. Now he was actually here, however, it was a question of getting in.

Thomas had looked for a while at the main gates, passing them twice in the van. They were a sight to behold, a massive stone arch and a gatehouse on either side. Where the wings of the wall joined the gatehouses were the arms of the Keddington family, a royal-looking badge that was a lie. The Keddingtons had never been given their coat of arms, had never had royal favour. They'd been drummed out of society by the scandal that had engulfed them halfway through the nineteenth century when the sole son and heir had been named in a court case as a client of a gay brothel. Society disowned him. No matter that half their aristocratic sons were clients of the same places. The boy fled home. The house died quietly, the chapel tower falling, the glasshouses closed up, and gardens left untended. Keddington was a monument to hypocrisy.

Tam had told him the story before Thomas had left London at midday. Some of it he'd heard before, some he had not.

'Nobody ever took it over?' he'd asked.

'Nobody. Huge bloody mausoleum, falling apart. It passed to various distant parts of the family who didn't want it. Keddington inherited the title because he was the sixteenth half-cousin twenty times removed, or something. In the sixties I think he sold all the tenant farms. No money, see? Poor bastard.'

'Why didn't he sell the house?'

'God knows. And rumour has it that the place is full of art.'

'Hence Keira Brodie's involvement.'

Tam shrugged. 'Keddington didn't like anybody. Famous for it. But apparently he liked Keira.' He looked at Thomas shrewdly. 'Is she there?'

'No idea,' Thomas said.

'Ah well,' Tam replied, frowning at him as if he didn't believe him. 'She'll have to get out now, if she is.'

'Why's that?'

Tam smiled at him. 'You need to read the papers every now and then,' he said. 'Keddington died yesterday.'

After driving round the entire estate – eleven miles completely enclosed by a wall – Thomas drove to a village two miles away. He sat in the afternoon sunshine outside a pub and ate a sandwich, looking at an Ordnance Survey map while Max dozed at his feet. When he'd finished, Thomas went inside to pay.

'Do you mind if I leave the van in the car park?' he asked the woman behind the bar. 'I want to walk the dog.'

'Be my guest,' she told him. As he left, she picked up her phone.

Going through the village he found the footpath marker that took him across the fields. It was pleasant going, the path clearly worn down at the field edges. The sun was very warm on his back. After a while he came to the footbridge and stream marked on the map. The Keddington estate's wall rose up beyond it. Thomas struck out here away from the footpath, walking along the wall. He and Max continued for more than half an hour on field edges and rutted paths until they came to what he'd been hoping for. The wall had half-collapsed, pushed out by a tree behind it. It took only seconds to clamber up, Max following in his footsteps.

A dense woodland stretched away. The incline wasn't easy to follow. Several times Thomas had to pick Max up to get through tangled stretches of briar and dead wood.

'No more pies for you,' Thomas told him. 'You weigh a ton, boy.'

They came out at the edge of the wood. Centuries before, the park had been laid out in the latest Capability Brown style. Thomas had no doubt that a village or two had been razed to provide the main house with a picturesque view. The grass was knee high, but as they walked down closer to a small lake it gave way to a space where it looked as if rhododendrons had been scrubbed out and an attempt made at planting more trees. Most of them were dying.

'What a place,' Thomas muttered. All this land and no one cared about it. Hands on hips, he wondered how much longer it would take to get to the main house that he'd glimpsed from the van. In mid-afternoon, the sun was now hot. He hadn't come prepared for such good weather. He took off his fleece and tied it around his waist. He let Max off the lead and the dog walked into the shallows of the lake.

It was then that he saw an ATV with a small trailer on the back coming across the grassland. It seemed to be heading purposely for him. He shaded his eyes, expecting to see a gamekeeper or some such. As the vehicle got closer, he realised a woman was driving.

He had only ever seen one photo of Keira Brodie and didn't know if this was her. He hesitated as she got closer, but Max had no such reservations. He let out a bark and rushed towards her, leaping up and bouncing around the ATV, tail furiously wagging. Laughing, Keira Brodie got down and tried to push him away as she walked. She stopped in front of Thomas.

'Mr Maitland, I presume,' she said.

*

A quarter of an hour later, they were in the coolness of a sitting room.

'My house,' Keira had murmured when they'd arrived. 'It used to belong to the gardener. When Keddington had a gardener.' It was set well back and close to the estate wall, a small cottage in faded red brick. 'We only have contractors in now and again to deal with the heavy stuff,' she added. He noted the word 'we'. He could hear traffic passing along the lane beyond the wall. A track led away under the trees.

Following his gaze, she explained, 'Main gate that way.' She gave him a wry smile. 'You came the long way round.'

'I didn't think I'd be let in. And even if I was, I didn't think I'd see you.'

'You might have been nicely surprised,' she said over her shoulder. 'Still, you had a good walk. Amy at The Bull says you're welcome to keep the van where it is today.'

He might have expected it. She had people watching over her.

He laughed to himself, outsmarted.

The house was small and simply furnished. He noticed the artwork on every wall. 'Prints,' she said, and smiled. 'Not enough security here for anything else.'

She indicated a chair. They both sat down. Max went to her side rather than his. 'Isabelle's dog,' Keira said softly.

'He recognised you before I did. You've cut your hair.'

'Isabelle told me that if I ever saw Max without her, it would probably be you with him.'

So Isabelle had told her about him. And recently. Had Isabelle planned to give him her dog if her illness became serious, or had she foreseen something much worse?

'You spoke to her within the last few weeks?' he asked.

'Yes, of course,' she told him. 'You're the artist. The ex-policeman.'

He considered this, touched at how strenuously Isabelle must have kept Keira's confidences and how careful she'd been not to reveal them to him.

Keira stroked the dog's head, and then looked up at Thomas. 'I expect you want to ask me a lot of questions,' she said.

He hardly knew where to begin. She'd been in his head for so long. He had imagined asking her for answers ever since hearing that she'd pulled her grandmother's body from a freezing sea. He'd lain awake sometimes thinking of Isabelle's account of Ruskin. And driving here he'd been thinking about Imelda's bitterness. All he could think of now, however, was that this slight figure of a woman sitting in front of him had come close to Celia's fate. Or so he supposed.

'The local police came here not long ago. Asking for me.'

'Yes, we thought that you might be here. Why didn't you tell them?'

'I wasn't ready. Edward answered the door to them.'

'Edward?'

'Keddington.'

He let that go for the time being.

'I'm so sorry about Isabelle. I liked her very much,' he said.

'Most people did.'

'Did you just know her through your grandmother?'

'Oh no,' she said. 'I knew Isabelle when she used to come to the V&A. She liked the faerie painters. Richard Dadd, Fitzgerald, Simmons. I'd only just graduated. She found painters, found modern art after that.'

'She found me.' He wondered if Keddington had known Isabelle too, long ago. Thomas stopped short now of mentioning Ruskin. Instead, he turned back to the subject of Keira's early contacts in London. There were a lot of gaps that he wanted to fill in.

'After the V&A, you set up your own business?'

'I did. I met some good people.'

'Archie Ruskin, Aiden's father?'

'Not then,' she said. 'And I wouldn't call Archie a good person.'

'Did Isabelle know Archie?'

'Yes.'

'Did she buy and sell?'

He already knew the answer from Imelda, but he was trying to feel his way around the subject, watching her reactions. She seemed extraordinarily relaxed. She didn't reply. 'Would you like some tea?' she asked.

'Yes. Thank you.'

He heard her moving about in the kitchen, and sat back in his chair. There was a wonderful view of the parkland. It was, except for the noise of the occasional passing car beyond the wall, very peaceful. He could see exactly why Keira had run to this place weeks ago.

When she came back, he asked her how she and Ruskin had met.

'In Paris,' she said. 'He almost lost me a deal.'

'What kind of deal?'

'He tried to persuade me out of buying something very valuable. He said it was worthless.'

'He must have regretted that.'

She didn't comment. 'He pursued me,' she said quietly. 'It was flattering for a while. I didn't see what was coming. People warned me. But I still didn't see it. Even Isabelle warned me. She knew his father, and that was enough.'

'How long were you and Aiden together?'

'Not long. He wanted me to marry him.' She took a long, slow breath. 'For the money I could make,' she continued. 'I don't think he liked women at all. He had an actual loathing of them.' She smoothed a hand over her face as if to wash the memories away. 'He was forever picking away at what I knew. He resented my degree. Sometimes I think his sole aim when he woke up every morning was to belittle me. With a smile on his face, of course.'

Thomas nodded.

'You know that smile?' she asked.

'I know that smile.'

'Disturbing, isn't it?' she said. 'You know, I never really noticed it until my grandmother pointed it out. She said the way he smiled at her made her feel ill.'

'What did Isabelle say?'

'The same,' she replied. 'It was after the weekend that he first met Greta that I began to see him differently. Small things. He would always take me by the wrist, not the hand. I saw an expression of disgust once. He wiped his mouth on the back of his hand when he'd kissed me. He denied it. He began to tell me often that I was imagining things. That he only had my best interests at heart. When I resisted him, he told me I needed help, therapy. He started to pointedly say that he hadn't a penny to his name. Greta hated him from the moment she met him. I trusted her judgement. She was right.'

Thomas waited. Her voice had lowered, and she frowned.

'The day I took the keys to my gallery, he raped me. He was quite matter of fact about it.'

Thomas frowned, sat forward, but said nothing.

'I told him it was over between us that same night. I went to the police, but lost my nerve at the station. I told them I'd made a mistake.'

'Did you tell anyone at all?'

'One friend, who ran a gallery. The next day. I blurted it out. He promised to keep it to himself.'

He did, thought Thomas. It was as he'd suspected. *Tam Jeffries.*

'You don't get over a thing like that, Mr Maitland,' she continued slowly. 'You get round it. You adjust to it being in your landscape, however ugly. You might eventually move on, but it stays in the rear-view mirror. I never intended just to let it go. I found another way to get – well – justice, if you like.'

'I don't understand.'

311

'I made a friend of his father,' she said. She was relaxed now, sitting back in her chair with her hands laced across her stomach. But her voice had altered. There was a coldness in it. 'Aiden likes control,' she said, 'and Archie wouldn't give it to him. He had all kinds of things hidden about the house, and some in safe deposit.' She sighed, looking out of the window at the endless vista of yellowing grass. 'I thought there was a better way to hurt Aiden.'

He felt the hairs prickle at the back of his neck. 'Revenge.'

'If you like.' He saw the steeliness in her expression. He realised that Aiden had picked the wrong woman to try to dominate.

'Once Archie was drunk, he was invariably maudlin,' Keira continued. 'He was disappointed in Aiden. He said he was weak. He would go on and on about it. Then later, he told me he was dangerous. He told me that Aiden had killed two women. Older women.'

'Did you believe him?'

'I didn't know whether to believe him or not. I thought he was making a fantasy of his dislike. They had an odd relationship. A kind of war.'

'Did Aiden know you saw Archie?'

'No. He didn't know that I stole two paintings from them, either. Put forgeries in their place. Archie trusted me more than he despised his son. He never checked.' She took up her cup and sipped her tea, glancing at him. 'I'm not especially proud of what I did,' she said. 'I felt very bitter at the time. I made a few thousand and donated it to a charity.'

Thomas took a guess. 'A women's refuge.'

'Yes.'

'The same as Isabelle.'

'Yes.' She nodded. 'Aiden had an accident after Archie died. He walked out into traffic for some reason. He needed an operation on his leg. Did he tell you?'

'No.'

'The hospital found my card in his pocket and contacted me. I told them I was next of kin. They gave me his house keys.'

'Did Aiden realise?'

'Oh yes,' she said. 'He's a child when he's hurt. He was grateful. I retrieved his laptop and took it to him at the hospital. He was pretty out of it.' She laughed to herself. 'He thanked me.'

'And you had free rein over the house.'

'I did,' she said. 'Plenty of time to assess what he had in there. And I helped him once he was discharged.'

'Why?'

She shrugged. 'I've asked myself that. Perhaps it was just a game. Watching him suffer and curse. Seeing him incapacitated. But I stopped after a while. I didn't like the person I'd become.'

Watching him suffer. A talent she'd gleaned from Aiden himself. But listening to her now, Thomas couldn't decide if she'd always been that way, a character fault waiting to be ignited lying deep in her personality. He couldn't decide.

'Did you tell Greta what you'd done?'

'No,' she said. 'I felt ashamed, I suppose. Greta always had very high standards. She worked hard and never took anything from anyone. She would have been horrified that I'd become so petty.'

'Perhaps she would have understood, considering the cause.'

'Yes, she understood,' she agreed. 'I told her what he'd done and she supported me in vowing not to see him and to cut him out of anything to do with my business, especially the gallery. But she wanted me to report him. She'd have been very disappointed in the different route I chose. I didn't tell her about that.'

'How about Isabelle?'

She didn't reply for a while. 'Isabelle used to take a hell of a beating from her husband, did you know that?'

How could he? He shook his head.

'Generational thing, I think,' she mused. 'Boss man of the house and so on. Harder to get divorced then. She used to travel abroad to get away from him. Can you imagine that? Years and years.' She sighed. 'I stole quite a lot from Aiden, actually,' she told him in the same calm, measured voice. 'I'd stowed a canvas in Archie's armchair. Something Archie had secreted under the floorboards in his bedroom, believe it or not. Curious man. Quite a hoarder in his own specific way. It wasn't large. About twelve by seven. Corot. Aiden sold the chair to a house clearance after Archie died. I had a hell of a job chasing that chair all over London,' she said, and smiled.

Thomas whistled softly, shaking his head at her stone-cold deception. 'And he never knew?' he asked.

'He never knew.' She gave a little shrug. 'I didn't take *everything*. But I did take the oldest pieces from the safe deposit. Things that ought to be returned to the countries they were stolen from. That's my job now.'

He sat thinking of how hard that might be, and admired her for even trying. And it suddenly occurred to him – thinking of invasions of someone else's space – that Ruskin had probably come into his cottage when he was out. He'd dismissed it at the time – thought he was imagining things – but now he felt convinced doing that might be part of Ruskin's well-honed strategy. To show who was really in charge.

He had another question for Keira. 'Did you know a woman called Imelda Yates, or Celia Cavell?'

'Imelda is at Toynton & Mark, I think. Why?'

'So was Celia.'

'Yes, I heard about Celia. I asked Aiden about her.'

'What did he tell you?'

She avoided the question. 'What did he do to Imelda?'

He leaned his elbows on his knees and looked at the floor. Outside in the kitchen, he could hear an old-fashioned clock chime softly. Four o'clock. Time was moving on, and he still hadn't asked her what he came here for.

'Keira,' he asked, 'where is Aiden?'

Keddington House gave up its wonders one by one.

They left Max in Keira's house and walked through another small copse until they reached the back of the enormous building and to what must once have been the stable-yard, a three-sided enclosure. Thomas was still waiting for the answer to his question. But he was patient.

'Servants' entrance,' Keira said, and smiled. She knocked on a door. It was opened by a tall man in a black and grey uniform. Keira introduced him.

'Security,' she explained to Thomas as they walked deeper into the building. 'Edward didn't care to look after his things,' Keira said. 'So I did.' She stopped outside a pair of double doors, and took out a key.

Thomas noticed the cobwebs on the stairs and statues around them. He thought that this was probably the place where Keddington had met Laura. No wonder the old man was shuffling about, Thomas thought. He was within days of dying.

'He wanted to die here,' Keira murmured, as if reading Thomas's mind. 'But it was impossible at the end. I think he probably hated me for it.'

'A friend told me it was yesterday.'

'No,' she replied. 'It was a week ago. I only told people yesterday. He was in the local hospice.' She opened the doors. 'There was a lot to do,' she said. 'I had to think.'

The room beyond was very dim. She walked over to one of the windows, drew the curtains and let up the blind. 'They have to be protected,' she said.

He saw then what *they* were.

'This is about a tenth of the collection,' she told him.

The first thing he could see was the furniture. Two sofas that might have once been pink. A huge mirror propped against one wall. Two marble-topped *pietra dura* tables at each end of the room. As Keira had pulled back the curtains a fine cloud of dust settled on the figured carpet.

'Edward sold a lot of things about thirty years ago,' she said. 'He lived upstairs and never came to these rooms except to see his pictures. And the truly astonishing thing – terrifying – *none* of them are insured.'

'His pictures,' Thomas whispered. He walked to the nearest wall and looked in disbelief at the first of the framed canvasses hanging there.

'Turner,' she said. 'Four Turners, in fact.'

'My God.' He wanted to touch them, but daren't.

'Do you recognise the Venetian sketches?'

'Ruskin,' he said. He turned. 'Is it?'

'Yes, Ruskin.' She gave a strange little smile, and looked at her feet.

'And this…'

'Velasquez.'

He couldn't speak. He carried on walking. Some he didn't recognise. All left him speechless. He got to the far door and had to rest his hand on the frame. He felt light-headed. 'And there's more?'

'Yes, a lot more,' she said. 'The second earl took the Grand Tour. His son and grandson too. Eighteenth, nineteenth centuries. They all came back with their treasures. Probably because it was the thing to do, not because they really valued them. The house had to be dressed to show off their money. In the next room are Canaletto, Boucher, Tiepolo.'

She walked past him and opened another door. And on they went, one room after another. A couple were completely empty with nothing but sketches or paintings on the walls. Thomas stopped walking after a while. It was almost impossible to take in. 'Does anyone really know what's in here?'

'Not yet.'

'And you… you've kept this secret all the time you've been here?'

'This house is full of secrets,' she said. They were in an elaborate hallway now with a vast entrance door. 'Original door,' Keira said. 'No one's used it for years. In the war, this was a hospital and all the artwork was stored in the attics. Edward's father didn't know the value of his ancestors' art. His only joy in life was either killing some poor animal on the estate, or drinking. Your average cliché. Edward brought all the paintings down in the 1960s after his father died. Some of it was ruined. Warped, damp. Some still is, if you look carefully.'

'But he wasn't a direct descendant, was he?'

'Yes, he was,' she said. 'Who told you that? He was the only son of an only son of an only child back six generations, and they all despised each other. His father hated Edward particularly because he never married. The wives led awful lives. Edward's mother was sent to what was politely called a sanatorium. She literally went out of her mind out here.'

'Did you tell Edward about Aiden?'

'Yes,' she said. 'I told him everything. He was like a father to me. Or grandfather, I suppose. He was a very sweet person, afraid of the world.'

Two lonely people, Thomas thought.

He looked around himself in the echoing space that a very long time ago used to be a home. 'What are you going to do with it all?' he asked.

'It isn't up to me,' she replied. 'There's an army of lawyers waiting to descend on it. I've drawn up histories and valuations, but others might well revise the estimates. The art world loves to bicker.' She paused. 'Oh, and just in case you think differently, I might have cheated Aiden but I haven't cheated Edward. Every single thing is catalogued and accounted for. He might not have cared much for himself, but he cared for his art. He had a record of every purchase and every sale – and I've charged nothing for my work. He allowed me to stay here and protected me recently, and he was a friend.'

What a temptation it must have been though, Thomas thought. One absolute hell of a temptation. There were millions of pounds hanging on these walls.

'If you're thinking what I guess you're thinking,' she added, 'it was another reason not to let Aiden in here. Some time ago he and Archie tried their luck, and Edward threw them out when they hadn't even gone ten paces. He said he didn't like the smell of them.'

'Interesting judgement.'

'Accurate.'

'And the house itself? What's going to happen to that?'

'Edward left it to the country, but I don't know if the country wants it. It's huge, but not especially lovely. And as you can see, falling to pieces. Damp, woodworm. The roof is in an awful state.'

With a pang, Thomas remembered Isabelle talking in the same way about her own house, and how she too liked art over the dreary duty of maintenance.

Keira smiled a little then. 'He left the cottage that you saw this afternoon to me. It was quite a shock in the will, but I'm very grateful.'

'Very nice,' Thomas said. 'Will you stay there?'

'Yes, I think so. And reopen the gallery. But not yet. Perhaps next year.'

'You won't go back to Trewarith?'

She bit her lip. 'I can't.' Her hands were clasped tightly.

He waited.

'You know about Greta's death, of course,' she said.

'Yes.'

'She phoned me at midnight. She was out of breath. Running.

She said that Aiden was there and raging about money. Saying that I knew where his money was.'

'And that's why he came to Trewarith? He thought that you had his money? Did you think that he'd realised you'd stolen the paintings?'

She looked away from him when he mentioned them. 'He owed me that much and more,' she said softly. 'But yes, of course. I thought he'd somehow found out what I'd done. Because I'd cut myself off from him, he had no way of contacting me, so he went to the one person who would know. Perhaps he thought I was with Greta, too. It would have seemed the most obvious answer to him maybe. So I drove straight down, to protect Greta.'

He kept quiet. Keira didn't show any of Imelda's rage, but she had it all the same, buried deep.

'I'd seen him angry before, and it took a lot to shake my grandmother. So I told her to go to someone in the village. Then the phone cut off.'

'Did you hear anyone else? Aiden?'

'No. But I could hear the sea. I got in my car and drove straight there. I got there about four o'clock in the morning. There were people around the house. Including Aiden. Everyone very concerned, of course. But no sign at all of Greta. Eventually it was decided to look again at dawn. The weather was terrible; everyone was soaked.'

'So you were left alone with Aiden? What did he say?'

'He asked me why I'd cleared his bank account. And I told him that I'd done no such thing.'

'Did he believe you?'

'No. He was acting very strangely. He wouldn't sit down. He wouldn't close the door, and it was freezing. But that wasn't the worst of it. After a while he calmed down a little. I cleared up the kitchen – Greta had been cooking – and he eventually sat down and he started saying the most bizarre things. He said that if I'd taken the money he would forgive me, and that we could go and live abroad somewhere. He sat there painting this wonderful picture. He was sitting quite still, hardly blinking. It was a monologue. He seemed quite insane.'

She stood up and began walking about the echoing space, touching the faded wallpaper, wiping her hands through the dust on a side table. 'I listened to him for an hour. Then I went out. I was so desperately worried about Greta. She was a practical person, and strong. He must have frightened her a great deal. I couldn't just stay in there with him not knowing where she was.'

'You must have been frightened too.'

'I'd seen him in a temper before, and I'd seen his storms blow over and then hear him claim he had never raised his voice. I watched him go up and down that night. Just to be sure, I took a vegetable knife from the table and put it in my pocket. Outside, it was still dark. About six o'clock.'

'Did he come with you?'

'He followed me. I heard him behind me running across the fields. I waited for him with my hand on the knife, but when he got up to me he was just sobbing and incoherent.'

'What happened then?'

'I was trying to look for Greta in the fields, on the paths. I thought maybe she'd had a heart attack, something like that? But I couldn't see her. I got as far as the bench by the pool – the tide was going out – and he kept talking and talking, saying that we ought to turn back. And then I saw her.'

'I've heard that you got into the pool.'

'Yes.'

Thomas got up. He walked over to her. 'Did Aiden do it?' he asked.

'I don't know,' she said slowly. 'She might have slipped. It's possible. Aiden could have been with her. Or not. But he certainly didn't help me. He ran back towards the village. The next thing I know is the emergency services...' She stopped. He saw that her eyes were full of tears.

'Did you see Aiden after that?' he asked gently.

'No. I went to Isabelle. I stayed with her until the funeral. We organised it together.' She paused. 'Aiden came to that. He stood in the family pew and he cried. Some people consoled him, those that didn't know better. Most didn't. He stayed there not six feet from us, making a bloody exhibition of himself. He came to the wake, too. He sat there eating his food and bloody well smiling. *Smiling!*'

She breathed deeply and continued. 'I went back to London one night a week or so later. Isabelle kept Aiden at bay. She let him believe that I was still in her house. She told me that he'd moved into one of Greta's cottages. And then after a month or so, she told me that Aiden had the gardens destroyed. She made me promise never to come back to Trewarith.'

'You must have been furious when you heard about the gardens. Why did you let him stay there?'

She sighed. A long pause. 'I let him stay there because at least then I knew where he was. And he stayed because he thought I was at Isabelle's.'

'But then you left and went to London.'

'I came straight here.'

He sat for a few moments digesting this information.

'He kept pestering Isabelle. He wrote to her, too. Saying he needed money,' she continued slowly. 'I thought it was a lie, a ruse to let him in. Then he asked for the second cottage to be let out and to keep the rent for himself.' She gave a short, ironic laugh.

'But you allowed it.'

She leaned her head back against the chair. 'I wasn't really fit to make a decision at all,' she murmured. 'Isabelle suggested placating him. It was really her decision rather than mine. I think she supposed she could keep him in sight somehow. And, as I say, at least we knew where he was. I used to have nightmares about him suddenly turning up, you know. Isabelle kept me up to date. And someone in the village called Bill Pascoe.'

'Ah,' Thomas said. 'Your rearguards. Your defenders.'

She smiled briefly and looked up at him. 'Did Isabelle tell you where I was?'

'No. But she gave me these.'

He took Isabelle's postcards out of his pocket and gave them to her.

She smiled as she looked at each one. 'The V&A exhibition. The fraudster. She means Aiden,' she murmured. 'The beach at Aldeburgh. Not far away from here. Mazzorbo in Venice. She has a little house there. I wonder what's happened to it now.' She glanced at him. 'Do you know?'

'No.' He looked at the picture of Mazzorbo with interest. 'You could have fled there,' he said.

'Keddington was safer.'

'You thought he'd pursue you?'

'Even when he came to Isabelle's house when I was staying with her, he was shouting about money.' She shook her head. 'Why didn't he have any? He'd sold his house. Archie's house.'

'The money from it was taken out the same day and transferred to an offshore account.'

'Offshore?' she repeated.

'You really don't know?'

'No, Mr Maitland, I really don't know.' He saw the colour rise at her throat. 'He dealt with some pretty shady characters. Perhaps someone was getting their own back, who knows? Maybe there's a woman who had access to his laptop.'

'Like you did.'

She shrugged. 'Yes, like I did. But the difference is, I didn't steal the house sale money. They did, whoever they are. Maybe Celia's friends? Maybe any number of others.' She stopped, considering.

'So that was it. He really *didn't* have any money. Good luck to them, whoever they are,' she added, under her breath. She put her head on one side, considering him. She was clutching the house keys. 'What did you actually come here for?'

'To make sure that you're alive.'

'Not just that, is it?' she retorted. 'You've come for Aiden, because of Isabelle. And the police can't find him, can they?'

'Not yet.'

'And you're, what? Helping them, unofficially?'

'You could say so.'

'With their blessing?'

'Probably not.' He hadn't told Laura what he was doing today.

'You just take it on yourself, then? Like, a caped crusader? Mr Maverick? I bet they love you doing that.'

'I have some experience.'

'And you can't let it go. You don't like retirement?'

She was half right. One day his dogged determination might be the death of him. Nevertheless, he carried on with his questions. 'Aiden's car was found in Somerset. He vanished the same day that Isabelle died. Are you absolutely sure he didn't contact you?'

She crossed her arms. 'Let's walk back. I can show you a much quicker way to get to the pub.'

He didn't move. 'Did he contact you?' he repeated. 'That morning?'

'No.'

He scrutinised her face. 'The next day?'

She said nothing.

'Keira,' he said. 'Please tell me if you know where Aiden is. He's wanted for murder.'

She hesitated for a long time. 'He rang the house, here. He didn't have my number. He said where he was. Edward has a very

323

old answerphone in the office, but it works. I didn't pick up the message until late that evening. By then a friend of Edward's had phoned me to say that Isabelle was dead. Killed.'

'Did you ring Aiden back?'

'No. I sat in the office waiting. I sat thinking about the options I had.' She paused for some time, then continued. 'Most of all, I sat thinking of Isabelle and Greta. How much I loved them both. How much I owed them. And who the most likely person was to have killed them. Aiden rang again late in the evening. He asked me to come and get him. He said he'd found Isabelle dead and was afraid he'd be blamed for it. He begged me to help him.'

'So you did.'

She turned to the massive French doors and tried to open them, but they wouldn't budge. 'I need air,' she said.

He guided her to a seat. Gradually, the high colour dropped from her face.

'Yes, I went to get him,' she said. 'He was in one of those open-sided barns you sometimes see, out in the country not far from Glastonbury. He said a van driver had given him a lift. He'd walked for miles and made the last call from a pub.'

'What time was it when you picked him up?'

'Five in the morning. He was wet through and spattered with mud. He fell asleep until we were almost here.'

'Tell me where he is now, Keira.'

She stood straight up. This time he followed her back through the rooms, taking a last longing glance at the art that he was sure he'd have to pay a fortune to see again, if ever. A different security man let them both out. She pointed up at the house as they went back through the stable-yard and overgrown gardens. 'As soon as Edward went into the hospice, I got CCTV and alarms installed. It makes my blood run cold to think of how many years there was no security at all. Once he was gone from the house, I had to preserve it. I'm glad they're all coming to handle it. It's been quite a burden.'

They were back into the parkland now. Thomas had been listening to the restored calm in her voice. Whatever had happened after Aiden got here, she was at peace with it. They reached the little lake and the cottage came into view. She stood looking at it for a couple of minutes, while a warm wind blew over the grass and rippled the water.

'Aiden took away the two people I loved most,' she said. 'Would you be able to forgive that?'

'No,' he said. 'But I'd let the law handle it for me.'

She nodded, without taking her eyes away from the water. 'Well, feel free to tell the law where I am, and that I'm safe.' She finally glanced back at him. 'You can even tell them that Aiden came here. And that he left my house the next day and that I don't know where he went.'

'Is that what happened?'

'You only have my word on that,' she said.

'Did he tell you what he'd really done?'

'Oh,' she said. 'He told me a lot of things.' She paused. 'Perhaps he shouldn't have. Perhaps I shouldn't have listened to it all. Women he'd cheated and abandoned. Women who'd died.' She gave a little grunt of disgust. 'And none of it was his fault, you know? Nothing was *ever* Aiden's fault. One of the last things he said was to try and persuade me of that.'

Thomas put his hands in his pockets, feeling the edges of the postcards, the clues that Isabelle had given him. She wanted him to find Keira. She wanted to warn him that Aiden was a fraud. But what else did she want? Did she know that Aiden Ruskin wouldn't give up coming to her house and that she'd be in danger? Would she want her death avenged?

'Would you like some more tea?' Keira asked.

'I ought to get back.'

325

'To tell the police what you know?'

'Yes. You can expect a visit from someone called Laura Cullen. She's the DI pursuing Isabelle's death.'

'I'll be happy to see her.'

She turned back towards her house. He watched her go, this small slight woman that Aiden Ruskin had underestimated. That Aiden had thought – right to the last – he could manipulate.

Thomas caught up with Keira at her front door.

'How soon after you got him here?'

'What do you mean?'

'Did you kill him in here or the Hall?'

She laughed a little. 'Oh, good luck with forensics if someone were killed in one of the thirty bedrooms, or endless cellars, or the stable-yard, or any of the rooms downstairs. Who would have those sort of resources, even if you had evidence that someone had died? Which you haven't.'

'A body isn't necessarily needed in a murder case if the circumstantial evidence is strong enough. You've admitted yourself that you brought him here, and nothing more has been heard of him. And you had motive.'

There was a lot to do... I had to think.

This house is full of secrets.

She gave a little smile. He had no doubt she'd gone over it all in her mind, the pros and cons, the possibilities, while she had been sitting in that office in the Hall waiting for Aiden Ruskin to ring a second time.

'Where is he, Keira?'

'I've no idea where he went after he left here.'

'But he didn't leave at all, did he?' Thomas insisted.

She looked at him levelly, calmly.

'It must have taken some strength,' Thomas said, 'to drag a man's body onto that ATV. Did you drive far?'

She waved a casual hand at the vastness of the park behind

her. 'It's a very big estate, Mr Maitland,' she said. 'I should think if anyone hoisted a dead body into the ATV, they'd be a fool. It would leave a forensic trace, wouldn't it?'

She gave another little smile. 'You could look forever,' she observed coolly. 'And, like the house, where on earth would you start?'

39

Thomas stood on the Fondamente Nuove waiting for the ferry. He watched it coming across the water, Venice shrouded in a fine fog behind him.

It was April, and he had been travelling since before Christmas. He'd taken the train to Florence. Not much luggage. Not much of a plan. He watched Europe go by more like a dream than reality. On his first night in Florence he'd slept eleven hours. He'd walked all that day and the day after, trying not to think at all. Now and again Bill Pascoe would send him photos of Max on the beach. Bill's last message was *take your time*.

Thomas's head hurt him more than usual and he would sit in cafés, sometimes sketching but more often than not letting the world pass him by. He had a delighted email from Tam telling him that his latest paintings had sold on a preview night that he hadn't attended. Soon after, a ridiculous amount of money showed up in his bank account. In answer to his thanks, Tam said that he hoped he was painting in Italy.

After a week in Florence, he'd at last stirred himself and gone to the Uffizi, only to be stopped short by a portrait of a woman who might have been Keira Brodie. He'd looked closely at the inscription. *Portrait of a Woman, attrib Piero del Pollaiolo, 1475*. She had the same peacefully self-possessed expression that he'd last seen at Keddington almost a year ago.

Laura hadn't been pleased by his visit to see Keira. At all. He had found himself in an interview room making an official statement. He told the truth: that he had been shown Keddington itself, questioned Keira more than once about where Ruskin could be, and left without knowing the answer. He'd given every detail he could but he hadn't expressed his own mind. That came later.

'Personal opinion. Is he there somewhere?' Laura had asked.

'I'm sure he is.'

'And she didn't give any kind of clue?'

'Only that the house was too big to search, and so were the grounds. She maintained that she'd picked him up and that he left Keddington of his own accord.'

Laura had hissed through her teeth. 'And you believed her.'

'I did not believe her, Laura. I think she killed him and he's there. But I don't know how you'd prove it.'

Laura tried. She had Keira in for questioning. She kept her as long as the law allowed. And from what she told Thomas afterwards, there was no shifting her. Keira stayed perfectly calm, and assured Laura that she was trying to be helpful. Laura was determined to charge her with assisting an offender but it hadn't been proven yet that Ruskin was guilty of murder. There were no forensics. They only had circumstantial evidence, and Keira, represented by her solicitor, had actually sympathised with the problem.

'She looked me straight in the eye and said she hoped someone would be found for murdering Isabelle Crosby,' Laura had fumed to him. 'Fucking cheek.'

He had sighed in sympathy.

'You like her, don't you?' she demanded. 'You actually admire her.'

'I think she's very unusual,' he replied. 'You know what she's been through.'

'She's a killer, and I'm going to get her,' Laura said. 'You're playing judge and jury.'

'If she had admitted to it, if she had told me where he was, I would have told you. I'm keeping nothing from you.'

'And yet you sit here smiling about it.'

'I'm not smiling.'

'You're smirking, which is worse.'

'I'm sorry. I don't mean to.'

Her eyes narrowed. 'She told you she'd killed him, and you're protecting her.'

'I am not. Anybody could infer it, but she didn't admit it. And I don't think she ever will.' He was offended, and disappointed that Laura thought him capable of lying to her.

She relaxed, and looked away temporarily. 'I'm sorry,' she muttered. 'But you of all people ought to understand what I'm faced with. For a start, you wouldn't believe how many influential contacts she has. Some people supporting her have real power.'

'I do understand,' he told her. 'Of course I do. But that doesn't mean I don't sympathise with Keira Brodie. And you've got to admit – Jesus, it must have taken some courage.'

'Courage! You're talking about her cold-bloodedly taking a life.'

'I know that, of course.'

'You've lost sight of what we do here,' Laura said. 'And you went there on your own. Without telling me. Again.'

'Yes, I—'

'Why do you do that? Why do you try to undermine me?'

'That wasn't the idea.'

'What was the idea, Thomas? You were going to solve the mystery all by yourself and you know – you *know* for God's sake – how selfish that is. How dangerous to a case. And yet you do it. You get yourself involved because you can't leave it alone and you don't care.'

'I wasn't trying to jeopardise a case.'

'Well God help me if you ever try to!' she exclaimed. 'I'm going to bloody well charge you too.'

She didn't. At least not yet.

He asked her to come to Venice and she had refused him.

'I ought to put a stop on you leaving the country,' she'd said. 'What are you going for, exactly?'

'To get out from under this, Laura,' he'd told her. She'd crossed her arms, sitting across from him. 'And my lease is out in September.'

She'd looked away from him. He told her where he was going.

'Art,' she'd murmured. 'Dead artists. Dead pictures. Like that expanse of conspicuous consumption at Keddington. A memorial to money and entitlement and waste.'

And that was all.

That was the end.

He'd tried ringing her several times. In reply she had sent him only one text, that he should keep his same mobile number and that she'd get back to him when she needed to.

But evidently she didn't need to.

He sat on the ferry to Burano thinking of Isabelle and Christine and the woman he had never met, Greta. How each of them had fought their own battles. He wondered about Christine's lover, the man who still lingered in her mind at the very end. Someone somewhere ought to know where that buried child had come from, and who she was, he thought. Poor kid. He found that his hand had clenched on the rail, and laid it in his lap, taking a deep breath and watching the colours of the Burano houses reflecting in the water.

There was a footbridge from Burano to Mazzorbo. He took it and spent an hour wandering. At a trattoria he had an espresso, sitting outside and wondering which house had belonged to Isabelle. He didn't ask outright. He had no idea what reputation she might have had here. But he felt her longing to escape, and understood. *You're an artist and you ought to go to Venice,* she had said. It was the reason he was here. He walked back over the bridge and down Burano's streets.

He was bone-deep tired. He had no inclination to go home. He wanted what he had gone to Trewarith to find – peace. He watched the boats for a while and he sat down by the water. The ferry back to Venice came and went. The fog lifted.

It was then, as he glanced back at the colours of the walls behind him, that he noticed a handwritten advertisement pasted to the window of one of the nearest houses.

Stanze in affitto, it said.

Rooms for rent.

About the Author

Photo credit © Kate McGregor

Under the names Elizabeth McGregor and Elizabeth Cooke, E.M. Scott has been writing for 30 years and has some 15 novels and one non-fiction work to her name, as well as over a hundred published short stories. Although having worked in various genres, crime is her first love. She lives in Dorset.